Praise for *A Quiet Hero*

"Just when you think you've heard every World War II story, think again. In *A Quiet Hero*, Dwight Harshbarger offers a thoughtful and engaging approach to the untold story of a courageous French general who went against the tide and saved thousands of lives in the process."

–Benyamin Cohen, author of *My Jesus Year: A Rabbi's Son Wanders the Bible Belt in Search of His Own Faith*

"Supported by impressive research and a fidelity to historical fact, *A Quiet Hero* tells a story that might otherwise be forgotten: French hero René Carmille leads a hidden resistance to the Nazi death machine, sabotages the Nazi census, and prevents the death of thousands of Jews."

–Geoffrey Fuller, author of *Full Bone Moon and Pretty Little Killers: The Truth Behind the Savage Murder of Skylar Neese*; editor and podcast host of *Mared and Karen: The WVU Coed Murders*

"A compelling account of an unsung battle against Nazi horrors, *A Quiet Hero* interweaves the intense lives of fictional characters with the true story of General René Carmille, a hidden hero of the French Resistance. This riveting narrative explores the Nazis use of IBM technology in the census of Jews and automation of the Holocaust—and tells us how Carmille sabotaged the Nazi census, saving the lives of thousands of Jews. A story of resistance and grace."

–Kathleen Cash, Ed.D., author of *Sex, Shame and Violence: A Revolutionary Practice of Public Storytelling in Poor Communities*

"This exciting new account of René Carmille's daring campaign of sabotage tells a story that's more important now than ever before. In *A Quiet Hero* we have not only an account of individual heroism, but a compelling look at the dangerous intersection of statistical knowledge and political power."

–Nick Fox-Gieg, animator; developer and producer of *Interregnum*

A QUIET HERO

A Novel of Resistance
in WWII France

Dwight Harshbarger

A Quiet Hero is historical fiction based on the true story of General René Carmille in Vichy France during WWII. Carmille prevented the Gestapo's identification and roundups of tens of thousands of Jews in France. The novel draws on records of WWII and accounts of Carmille's work at Vichy France's National Statistical Service. I have made every effort to remain true to the facts of Carmille's life as well as what is known about persons and events identified in historical records. Fictional characters and events in this novel are products of my imagination.

-Dwight Harshbarger, Morgantown,
West Virginia, July 30, 2018

To General Léon François René Carmille,
the thousands of Jews whose lives he saved,
and their descendants.

www.mascotbooks.com

A Quiet Hero: A Novel of Resistance in WWII France

For more information, please contact:
Mascot Books
620 Herndon Parkway #320
Herndon, VA 20170
info@mascotbooks.com

Library of Congress Control Number: 2018909885

CPSIA Code: PRFRE0419A
ISBN-13: 978-1-64307-276-0

Printed in Canada

France 1940-1944

German Occupied Zone

Paris

Vichy

Lyon

Free Zone

Acknowledgements

Edwin Black's carefully documented *IBM and the Holocaust: The Strategic Alliance Between Germany and America's Most Powerful Corporation* (Dialog Press, 2001, 2002, 2009, 2012) first alerted me to the contributions of Gen. René Carmille and prompted me to initiate research that evolved into *A Quiet Hero*. The evidence supports Black's assertion: without the Third Reich's alliance with IBM, the Holocaust as we have come to know it might not have happened.

Nick Fox-Gieg's animated video, *Interregnum*, engaged my imagination. *Interregnum* tells the dramatic story of Gen. René Carmille's sabotage of the codes of the Nazi census of French Jews. Fox-Gieg cites Carmille as the world's first ethical hacker.

Thanks to René Carmille's grandchildren, Marie-France, René, Michèle and André who talked with me about their grandfather's life and times and provided valuable documents on the WWII experiences of their grandfather, including his speech to the 1943 graduating class of École Polytechnique. They also caught and corrected many errors in my use of the French language and citing of events in France during WWII. I take full responsibility for all remaining errors.

Thanks to readers of the manuscript's early versions: Laura Blanciforti, Cynthia Corbett, Eric Harshbarger, John Kline, Jon Krapfl, Nancy Lane, Andy Lattal, Michael Mays, and Joe Panepinto. Thanks also to Patsy Baudoin, Kathleen Cash, and Bill and Jan Reger-Nash for their repeated readings, in-depth observations, and manuscript edits. Special thanks to Geoff Fuller—his many critiques and creative suggestions led to significant improvements in the manuscript. I am indebted to Betsy Pyle for sharing my commitment to the telling of René Carmille's heroic story and her warm personal support.

Thanks to Elizabeth Rosner for her thoughtful edits and suggestions. Thanks to her father, Karl Rosner, for our discussion about his experiences as a teenage prisoner at Buchenwald. A framed copy of his Buchenwald carte d'identité sits on my desk.

I am grateful for the support of writers and faculty at the Green Mountain Writers' Conference. Yvonne Dailey, conference director, has been an ever-renewable source of encouragement. Thanks, Yvonne and friends.

Christian Bernadac's *The Death Train*, often referred to as 'the last train to Dachau,' documented hour by hour the grisly horrors experienced by the two thousand prisoners locked in the sweltering heat of the boxcars of the Nazi's slow-moving train from Compiègne to Dachau. His descriptions are indelibly etched in my memory.

Readers may find, as I did, the following works as helpful guides to major events of WWII—Martin Gilbert's *The Holocaust: A History of the Jews of Europe during the Second World War* and his *History of the Twentieth Century*; William L. Shirer's *The Rise and Fall of the Third Reich: A History of Nazi Germany*; Robert O. Paxton's *Vichy France: Old Guard and New Order 1940 — 1944.*

Thanks to the following museums for valuable and heart-wrenching documentation and stories of the lives of Jews under Nazis regimes.

Centre d'Histoire de la Resistance et de la Deportation, Lyon, France
Mémorial de la Shoah, Paris
Musées Gadagne, Lyon
Musée de l'Homme, Paris
United States Memorial Holocaust Museum, Washington, D.C.

Special thanks to Kathleen Harner Hall for her continuing gift of a secluded and quiet writing environment.

Prologue

The development of Germany's WWII mobilization, armaments, supplies, and economic recovery relied heavily on automated systems of information processing, principally those of IBM and its German subsidiary, Dehomag. In pursuit of the Final Solution, the Third Reich achieved never-before-known efficiencies of operations.

In the wake of the German Occupation of Europe, the Reich ordered each country to conduct a census and record names, addresses, and other personal information. Census data, including religion, were coded and keypunched on millions of 3x7 IBM cards. IBM machines processed the cards and transmitted the information to printers. The printers produced census-based lists of the names and addresses of Jews. The Nazis used these lists to round up and arrest the Jews of Europe. After arrival at concentration camps, able-bodied Jews became slave labor. Near-starvation food allocations for laborers created life expectancies of seven months. Those who could not work, the elderly, disabled, and children, were soon murdered.

Throughout WWII, IBM and its subsidiaries maintained an uninterrupted and prosperous business with the Third Reich. The Third Reich's economic success and the success of the Reich's Final Solution rested on a foundation of slave labor and IBM technology.

Miriam

Lyon, 3 February 1944

My name is Miriam Meijer. I am twenty-seven years old. This morning I killed a man. A Gestapo agent put a Luger to my face—screamed he would kill me. I stabbed him. He died immediately. I fled to escape arrest. I killed the agent in self-defense. But it weighs heavily on me.

I am a Jew from Rotterdam. I can't go home—in 1940 Luftwaffe bombs created a firestorm in the city, killed my family. Now, four years later, along with thousands of Europe's Jews, my main purpose in life is to flee and hide from the Nazis.

I am known as Miriam Dupré, a name my friend Charles and the French Resistance gave me. They also found me a job. I work for Gen. René Carmille, director of the National Statistical Service, SNS, in Lyon. Well, I used to.

After killing the Gestapo agent, I fled across Lyon. I jogged to an old glass-paneled greenhouse in Vieux Lyon, an emergency rendezvous point Charles and I had selected many weeks ago. "Just in case," he had said. I pushed open the greenhouse's weathered door. I inhaled the building's moist aroma, a bouquet of the scents from blossoming flowers and fresh plant fertilizer.

I retrieved a blanket from a shelf in a far corner of the building. Charles had put it there. "Our just-in-case blanket," he said. I sat on a pile of straw concealed behind tall shelves filled with clay pots. I shivered and clutched the blanket tightly around me.

I remembered Charles's story of a greenhouse in a Deuxieme Bureau, French Intelligence Service, operation. In the spring of 1940, anticipating a German invasion of Europe, Charles had been on an undercover assignment for the Deuxieme Bureau. Near Berlin, he and three fellow agents had planted explosives in a Krupp munitions warehouse. A guard discovered them and called the Gestapo. They chased Charles and the agents. In their haste, the Gestapo neglected to thoroughly search the warehouse. They did not detect the explosives. Charles and his colleagues hid in a greenhouse. They waited until all of that day's incoming shipments of explosives had arrived. Then they triggered the explosion. In the confusion that followed, Charles and the agents escaped. They returned to Paris.

My eyes on the greenhouse door, I wait and watch for Charles. My thoughts return to my struggle with the Gestapo agent, to his death. Cramps twist my stomach.

I put my hand in my shoulder bag. My fingers clasp the bone-handled knife, my weapon. It had belonged to a man in Rotterdam. During my final visit to the School of Economics the man attacked me with the knife. That now seems a lifetime ago.

· · ·

9 May 1940, Rotterdam, Holland

At seven o'clock on a grey and misty spring morning, I jumped off a trolley and walked beneath the brick arch of the main gate of Netherlands School of Economics. Later that morning I planned to board a train to Paris to visit cousin Aimée and celebrate graduation from my training program.

I crossed the school's empty courtyard. My final semester of study had ended the previous week. In my Amsterdam field placement at the Central Statistics Bureau, I had immersed myself in the mechanics and electronics of machine-based information processing, mechanography. I studied hard and worked long hours to develop and hone my skills using the equipment of Dehomag, the German IBM subsidiary. "You've had a glimpse into the future," my supervisor said. I would later appreciate the significance of his words.

But I'm getting ahead of myself. I was angry that I had to take the time to return to campus, but I could only blame myself. The previous day, I had received an unexpected invitation from the dean to be interviewed by a reporter from *The Times of London*. The dean introduced me to M. Charles Delmand. "He is writing an article about the future of electronic technology in data management systems." The dean beamed a smile at me and then turned to M. Delmand. "Miriam is one of our best students, at the top of her class."

During Delmand's interview, I was fascinated by his small tic. When he took notes, his lips pursed and relaxed, as if he was reflecting on what I said. Each time I completed what I felt was an answer to his question, his dark deep-set eyes suggested I say more. In an odd way, I found Delmand handsome, engaging. I wanted to tell him more. I began to think of him more intimately. I forced myself to stop, to pay attention to his questions. At the end of the interview I left my book bag in the dean's office—the reason for my return to campus.

I jogged upstairs to the tabulation room. I glanced at the clock. My train would leave in two hours. I found my book bag. Was my notebook inside, intact? It was. A few weeks earlier a fellow student's purse had been pilfered and pages ripped from her notebook.

I ran down the steps, my long legs taking them two at a time. Crossing the courtyard, I gave little notice to the bright pink clematis in full bloom. I looked beyond the campus's main gate at an approaching trolley.

Just before I exited the campus beneath the arch of the main gate, a large man grabbed me from behind. His hand clasped over my mouth. A sharp point pressed against my back.

"*Gehoorzamen!* Obey—a knife is at your back!"

My judo and self-defense training flashed through my thoughts. Mama had insisted I learn to protect myself. Now, a test! A sudden haze of rage clouded my vision. My heart rate must have doubled. I tensed, felt my body prime for action. I yielded as the man pulled me backwards toward the shrubbery alongside the administration building.

A powerful thrust of my hips forced the man backwards. He loosened his grip on my mouth slightly, and I sank my teeth deep into his fingers. I tasted his blood. My hand clenched the man's wrist. I gave it a violent twist. I jerked his arm, yanking him sideways. Then I whirled around, stepped forward, and drove my right knee into his groin. He fell to his knees with a loud moan. A kick in the gut left him doubled over, gasping for air.

I picked up my book bag and my attacker's bone-handled knife. I shut its six-inch blade and dropped the weapon into my book bag. I ran out the gate, stopped, and leaned against the brick wall that surrounded the campus. I caught my breath and then sprinted down the street. Thankful that I enjoyed footraces as part of my training for skating competition, I closed the distance between myself and the departing trolley.

On board I shut my eyes and began to count each inhale and exhale. One, in, two, out, three, in . . . until my anger and upset settled and my breathing returned to normal.

The streetcar arrived at my stop. I jumped off and jogged home.

Rotterdam to Paris

I returned to my family's apartment to get my suitcase. Not another argument with Mama, I hoped. During my trip preparations Mama had asked, over and over, "Why go to Paris? Why now? Cousin Aimée is not going anywhere."

"Mama, please." I felt the frustration of repeated appeals to her, "I want to go to Paris, to visit Aimée, to celebrate."

"Celebrate here with Margot. Wait until things are more settled. I worry. Anything can happen."

I turned away. I wondered, wished, Mama could accept my growth. I was no longer a student, I was an adult. "Yes, Mama, I know. Life in Europe is unsettled. But I feel confident about a safe visit to Paris. I've visited Aimée many times. Last year I was there for the mechanography seminar. I know the city well. We'll be fine."

Mama stepped in front of me, as if her small angular body would stop my trip. She looked me in the eye. "War, Miriam. It can happen."

"And perhaps it won't. I'll be all right."

"Your father and I were married in Brussels. At the start of the Great War. I thought then as you do now—everything will be fine. He was called to active duty in the army. Sent into combat. He fought to stop the Germans. Then that awful telegram. I was pregnant with you and Margot. At the hospital they'd given him up for dead." Mama poured a glass of water and gulped half of it.

"What did you do?"

"Don't you remember? I told you about it. More than once. I sat in that hospital. I waited. I prayed. All around me, the stench. Do you know what death smells like?"

"No, Mama."

"May you never, I hope you never, see what I've seen." Her voice trailed off. "The blood. Young men."

"Did Papa know you were there?"

"Not at first, but soon."

I hugged her. "You gave him hope."

"Hope. Belief in the future. Ha! Now we're in that future we imagined. Yesterday I had coffee with friends. We talked about Hitler, about Germany. The new laws. You remember the Cohens?"

I nodded.

"They're so scared they're going to America. You want to go to Paris? Into harm's way?"

I kissed the top of her head. In what I hoped was a soft and understanding voice, I said, "I'll be okay. In Paris, like here in Rotterdam, there are no anti-Semitic laws." I turned to my twin sister Margot, across the room. She was sprawled on Papa's large easy chair, her favorite. "Right, Margot?"

"I suppose so. At least for now."

Mama continued, "It's not just the laws. There may be an attack. An invasion."

"Many of my professors believe that war may come. But few of them believe it will break out tomorrow. Or next week. Or next month."

Mama pulled away and stared at me. "Everything ends, Miriam, everything. Including peace. The only question is when."

"I understand that."

We were silent. Conversation over, I thought. I turned, looked into the kitchen mirror, and brushed my hair. Light brown, curly, hard to manage. I looked at my green eyes, one of them crossed, on occasion a source of embarrassment. Over my shoulder I watched Mama gazing at me. The conversation wasn't over.

I straightened my glasses. In a mixture of frustration and excitement, I returned to our Paris discussion. "Mama, please try to understand. My studies have ended. I haven't been to Paris, haven't seen Aimée, for almost a year. I need a break." Then, in a more forceful voice, "I deserve a break. And a celebration."

"You deserve a break? Will you say that to the Germans?" Mama looked toward the window. "Remember my warning." She turned to Margot, who'd been present for the entire conversation. "Aren't I right, Margot?"

In a dismissive voice Margot said, "Well, I wouldn't go."

I cupped my right hand to one ear. "I didn't hear anyone ask you to go."

If Margot replied I didn't hear her. My thoughts had jumped to last year's advanced information processing, mechanography, seminar in Paris. Aimée was in the seminar, too. In a class discussion I said, "In the Netherlands we have hundreds of what we call Holleriths, IBM Dehomag machines, in the government. Also, a card printing plant."

Then Aimée said, "Don't overlook France." She worked in information processing at the Musée de l'Homme. Her work kept her abreast of the status of mechanography throughout the country. "This year we'll use over two-hundred million punch cards. Only people who know the card punch codes can understand what's on the cards."

I said, "Like a secret society."

Aimée laughed. "Yes, a secret society!"

Ninety minutes later I threaded my way through Rotterdam's crowded Delftsche Poort Railway Station. I boarded the train to Amsterdam, the first leg of my trip to Paris. I settled into my seat in the first-class car, my gift to myself for completing my final semester. With my suitcase and book bag secured in the overhead, *All Quiet on the Western Front* in my lap, I relaxed and began to read. Why had the Nazis banned the novel in Germany? Suddenly apprehensive, I looked around to see if anyone was watching me. They weren't. But I was afraid—was fear to be a permanent condition for me as the Nazi presence spread through Europe? Life in Nazi-land, Aimée called it.

Do I have my rail ticket for the Amsterdam-to-Paris leg of my trip? Yes, I answered, it's there—in your book bag, where you put it.

Where you found it the last time you checked, thirty minutes ago. I
shook my head in self-admonishment. Why did I waste time and energy
unnecessarily double-checking everything?

I walked to the club car, bought a cup of coffee, and returned to my
compartment. The train jerked forward. I rocked back and forth in my
seat. The trip had begun.

Traveling from Amsterdam to Paris I thought ahead to my visit
with Aimée. She was in final preparation for her Paris Ballet audition. I
had vivid memories of Aimée's rehearsals during my visit last year—the
graceful moves of her lithe body across the studio, her hair flowing like the
silken mist of a blonde Valkyrie.

During that visit, one evening after returning from a late bistro dinner
we sat on the oriental rug in her living room and drank red wine. Aimée
said, "I know you. You know me. No secrets, right?"

"Right."

"None?"

"None."

"Even about dating?"

I felt my face redden.

"Come on, tell me."

I walked to the kitchen and refilled our wine glasses. I returned
and sat beside Aimée. "Well, Lars, you remember, Lars with the wide
shoulders—tall blonde guy? You met him once in Rotterdam."

Aimée said, "I remember. Wire-rimmed glasses. Blue eyes. You said
they sparkled!"

I laughed. "They did! I've known Lars since we were children on
Botersloot Straat. We studied together for exams. Competed in winter
races, judo classes. Do you remember how Mama told me, over and over,
'Learn to protect yourself'?"

"I remember."

"Lars is nearly twice my weight. In Judo class, I learned to throw him
to the mat. At the Rotterdam games, I raced him on the ice. I won."

In silence, I stretched out on the rug.

Aimée said, "You look deep in thought." She stretched out alongside me.

"Last year, at the start of fall semester, twice Lars invited me out for a movie and coffee. During the second movie we held hands. I liked him a lot. I held his hand so tight my hand ached! Then for two months I didn't hear from him. I asked Mama, half joking, did I injure his hand?"

"She said, 'If Lars wants to see you, he will call.' Then she said to Papa, sitting at the kitchen table. 'Moishe, put down your newspaper. Put down your pipe. Tell your daughter about the bad manners of boys.'"

"Papa said, 'Maybe he had a problem dating a girl who skated faster than him.'"

I said to Aimée, "One night a few weeks later I was in the stacks of the university library wrapping up a research project. I walked to a nearby shelf to get one last book, Keynes's *Treatise on Money*. Reaching for it, I bumped shoulders with Lars. He was reaching for the same book! My hand landed on top of his hand, already on the book. My hand stayed there. So did his.

"My heart pounded. I don't know if I was scared or what. Then Lars's left hand surprised me. I've wondered if it surprised him, too? He touched my cheek and turned my face toward his. I leaned into him. We kissed. Soon our tongues played across each other's lips. I'd never done that!"

Aimée laughed. I joined her.

"Our tongues were like lost children searching for their homes." I laughed and spoke faster, louder. "His tongue probed inside my lips. I did the same to him. I wondered how deep either of us might go. I felt so, well, so aroused."

Aimée giggled. "Keynes probably thought his book was just about economics. Little did he know what it would lead to. We'll have to try that sometime."

"And you? What's happening with you and boys?"

"I have no secrets from you. Well, there is one." Aimée snuggled against my back, gave me a hug. "Something I'm involved in at the museum." Her arms slowly wrapped around me. "It's about mechanography."

"Kind of dull?"

"No, it's not dull. I just don't know how, or if I should, tell you about it."

"Tell me about what?"

"I'm involved with something . . . you remember that seminar? With what was his name?"

"Carmille."

"Yes, Carmille. You always took that mechanography more seriously than me. But the thing I'm doing, we're doing, at the museum involves that."

"I thought you were just cataloguing."

"Yes, that's true. But I hear talk. It's part of something bigger, some kind of network. It involves Carmille, too, as a consultant. At least I think it does. I'm just guessing."

"You're working with Carmille?"

Aimée laughed. "In my mind maybe. I don't know. Forget I said anything."

We lay silent for a moment. Sleep drifted over me. I thought about turning toward Aimée, holding her, stroking her, the way we did when we were children. But I said, "I need to get some sleep."

"Sleep? I don't know if I can."

"We can talk more in the morning."

"But it won't be the same."

I dozed, awakened, and then slept. During the night I awakened and wondered why I had ended the conversation with Aimée. Was I afraid to tell her about my night in Lars's apartment? Did I fear intimacy with her?

After I awakened I drifted into sleep with the sweet memory of Lars shutting his apartment door behind us. He embraced me with a kiss, one that seemed not to end until the following morning. Before I roused myself from Lars's bed, I again ran my hands over his body. "One last touch," I whispered. His was the first male body I had known. "One last touch for me, too," Lars said.

Our touches excited us. We again made love. This time I mounted him. Afterward, I reluctantly left his bed.

Charles
9 May 1940

On the morning Miriam travelled to Paris, Charles sat in an under-heated second-class car of the train from Lyon to Paris. He stretched his long legs under the seat in front of him. Charles wore a tan raincoat and grey suit. He had turned up the collar of his coat. He sat next to a window smoking and reading the latest edition of *The Times*, his briefcase on the empty seat next to him. His carte d'identité, along with the press card in his wallet, identified him as Charles Delmand, forty, a Paris-based reporter for London's influential newspaper, *The Times*.

The paper's editors had urged him to travel first class. When he was working on a story Charles declined. "People in second class are my informants, my teachers." That morning, however, there were few travelers in his railcar. He had the luxury of uninterrupted time to think about a story on the end of the phoney war—England's 1939 declaration of war against Germany but followed by no combat. The story was making its way from his thoughts to the notepad on his lap. He thought about a title for the story, "From Phoney War to Real War?" Charles reflected on the angle of the story. He thought about the dilemma faced by officials and policy-makers—how good they feel when they make a joint decision, declare action. Those declarations of action bring uncertainties. With those uncertainties comes fear. Second guesses. Backpedaling and inaction.

Charles's name, not his face, was well known among readers of *The Times*. His editors had respected, though not understood, Charles's request that the paper not print photos or any other likeness of him. Had they done that, readers would have noted that Charles's face was elongated, his eyes deep set, a handsome yet unremarkable face.

Charles's otherwise ordinary face, when seen in person, had a dynamic feature that people who met him remembered: his lips. As if they had lives of their own, his lips would widen, stretching his mouth to a thin ribbon, then narrow, becoming full and rounded. When he smoked a Gauloise or laughed or scowled, like dutiful servants his lips ceased their repetitive movement.

On the evenings Charles spent with his mistress in Paris, she always asked, "Shave? Please, for me, will you do that?" He always did. Although as he shaved and remembered the joys of nights with her, he wondered about their relationship. The sparks that once lit their passion had dimmed. Dinner at a favorite restaurant, once a prelude to an exquisite evening in bed, had become an end in itself.

That May morning, as the train rolled towards Paris, Charles watched the sun break through rain clouds. Intermittent rays of sunlight brightened the undulating expanse of fields. Some fields had been plowed and readied for planting. Others, plowed and seeded in late autumn, were covered with a mix of winter brown and the bright green of spring's new growth. His thoughts were riveted to questions about what Europe faced in the non-combative state of war declared by France and Great Britain on Germany after the previous September's invasion of Poland. He wondered what it would take to bring the Phoney War to an end. Were Great Britain and France, was Germany, prepared to do battle? And if there were attacks in either direction, what then?

In his briefcase Charles carried a second French carte d'identité. Charles Secœur, the card said, a museum consultant. When asked, Charles replied that his clients remained confidential, though he could have listed the names of well-known clients in Paris, including the Musée du Louvre and the Musée de l'Homme. On the rare occasion when someone made inquiries to Paris museums in order to vet Charles and his work, he was quickly authenticated.

As a museum consultant, Charles worked as an investigative specialist who documented and authenticated works of art and antiquities, specializing in statuary though willing to investigate paintings. He recently began a report to a museum board, "Starting over two-thousand years ago, when the Roman demand for Greek statues far exceeded supply, forgeries have generated a continuous stream of challenges to museums, collectors, and historians." He worried that the same pattern of forgeries could grow with senior Nazi officials seizing rare and valuable art throughout Europe. For the art world, a successful German invasion of France would . . . He didn't want to think about Hitler and senior Nazis claiming ownership of the treasures of the Louvre. But Charles knew that, God forbid, it could happen.

Sometimes a private collector or a museum asked Charles to assess a pending acquisition. On occasion, a client asked that he authenticate a purchased work that had become part of a collection. The antiquities market was lucrative to forgers. The stream of reproductions and newly created "antiquities" by skilled artisans seemed never to end. Museums and individual collectors, often eager to distinguish themselves, were vulnerable to deception. Museums that worried they might've purchased a forgery would engage Charles to perform a meticulous and delicate investigation. Collectors rarely did that. Charles had long ago concluded that collectors preferred to believe a fiction rather than receive bad news. The upheavals of war had already worsened these problems.

Should a forgery be discovered and confirmed, Charles entered into complex legal and financial negotiations and political maneuvering. His fluency in English, French, German, and Spanish served him well. The monies involved in purchase transactions were substantial, often over a million francs, and involved the egos and reputations of powerful donors, purchasers, sellers, and institutions. Charles's work brought him into contact with the rich and powerful art collectors of Europe. This group had an active new member, chief of the Luftwaffe, the German Air Force, and Hitler's most powerful deputy, Hermann Göring.

When engaged in an investigation, Charles's work required long periods of travel throughout Europe and on one occasion to Japan. Senior management at *The Times* had been accommodating in giving him story assignments that blended well with his museum-consulting travel. Charles's fees to museums were substantial and never questioned. *"Toujours aussi vigilant!"* museums' board members and executives often said.

There was an invisible feature of Charles's life that his two cartes d'identité did not reveal. One year after graduation from the École Libre des Sciences Politiques, often called Sciences Po, Charles became a member of the French Intelligence Service, the Deuxieme Bureau. Discreet calls from the Bureau ensured that his photo would never appear in *The Times* or any other newspaper. Also that Charles's museum consulting business would continue in robust financial health.

After arriving in Paris, Charles joined the stream of disembarking passengers. As he had been trained to do, Charles adjusted his gait to the pace of those around him. He became one of a thousand other people walking through the station's main exit. Soon on the street, he relaxed as he became indistinguishable in the crowds of pedestrians.

Streets and crowds, Charles thought, places where he had spent a lifetime blending in. He sometimes felt like a farmer working among fruit trees or tall crops of grain or corn, places where his identity was secondary to tillage and plant growth. Gardens. Orchards. Places where people paid him, the near-invisible gardener, no mind while they often revealed much about themselves.

Ripping the Fabric of Europe
14 May 1940

The day dawned unseasonably warm. Since 10 May, other than early morning exercise Aimée and I had done little more than sit beside the tabletop radio in her apartment and listen to news. We rotated the dial from station to station, to news, news, and more news—all bad. For me, for all of Europe, in four days everything had changed.

News on the radio described a sudden tactical move that surprised the British and French high commands. The Wehrmacht, with Luftwaffe air support, had bypassed the Maginot Line. Invaded France and the Low Countries of Belgium, Luxembourg, and the Netherlands. A news announcer said the attack ripped the fabric of European lives and nations. For certain, it ripped mine.

On the fourth day after the invasion one newsman's broadcast got my undivided attention. He spoke over the roar of exploding bombs. "Yesterday Holland signed an armistice with Germany. Today, unexpected bombings of the country. A firestorm in Rotterdam. Buildings are falling. Flames are searing the city, moving towards us. We will soon have to move to another loca—"

The broadcast ended.

I felt as if I had plummeted into a dark abyss. Aimée, the radio, the room disappeared. I collapsed.

When I awakened Aimée lay beside me, her arms around me.

I sat up. "Something, I must go, do something. But what?"

"Stay in Paris. You're foolish to leave," Aimée said.

"No."

The morning after the Rotterdam bombing, Aimée and her neighbors advised me to stay in Paris. But I repacked my bag. "I'll find my family. I can. I will. Rotterdam is a large city. The Germans couldn't have destroyed all of it."

I returned to the rail station. After standing in a queue for an hour I bought a ticket to Rotterdam by way of Amsterdam. I wore the gray blouse and skirt Margot had given me on my birthday. Maybe they would bring me luck.

Each car on the train had standing room only. In one car, I found a place to stand where I could half-sit on a luggage rack. Even with the windows open, the car reeked with a pungent mix of cigarette smoke, sweat, infant vomit, and the putrid odor of fear.

To make space for a woman who held a crying infant, I pressed against a stooped old man standing next to me. When the train rounded, a sharp curve the old man lurched into me. Knocked me off balance. The old man and I toppled into the laps of a seated middle-aged couple. Their backs stiffened, and their faces reddened. "Ach!" the husband yelled. "Your father stepped on my bunion! Get him off me!"

We righted ourselves. The old man leaned toward me and repeatedly apologized, "*C'est ma faute, mademoiselle, pardon, je suis désolé.*" Each apology pumped a wave of undigested garlic into my face. I said, "*C'est bon, c'est OK, c'est bon.*" My turning away from him brought more apologies, more garlic.

A hundred kilometers from Paris, after entering a small town the train slowed. Then jerked to an unscheduled stop at the railway station. On tree-lined streets, canopies of pink blossoms shaded horse-drawn wagons and a few autos.

Conductors moved through the passenger cars announcing, "*Tout le monde debarque!* All passengers must disembark. All must disembark! *Prenez tout ce que vous avez apporté dans le train avec vous.* Take all that you brought aboard the train with you."

On the station's crowded platform, a uniformed railway employee handed a sheet of paper to each of the train's three conductors. I watched them read the dispatches. Color drained from their faces. They stood motionless. What words could do that? I was afraid to learn.

Children raced back and forth, dodging through the crowd and racing around the platform's perimeter. Parents yelled, *"Reviens.* Come back. *Sois tranquille.* Be still."

The pear-shaped elderly conductor from my car shuffled into the midst of the platform's dense crowd of passengers. He raised his arms and waved, signaling for quiet. Parents shushed their children, rested outstretched arms on their shoulders, and pulled them close.

All eyes turned to the conductor. Like an actor suddenly thrust center-stage, he straightened his cap and rose to his full height. As if with a heightened awareness that we were looking to him for something, he began to speak. His voice was loud though halting. His jowls trembled as if he had to shake words out of his mouth.

"This train can go no further. It is my sad duty . . ." He stopped, took a deep breath. "I must inform you that Luftwaffe bombs . . ." Another deep breath. Then he rapidly exhaled the remainder of the sentence. "The bomb damage to Rotterdam is far worse than first believed." A pause. He closed his eyes for a moment. When he again spoke, his words burst out with the strength of freed prisoners. *"Rotterdam a été détruit!* Rotterdam has been destroyed!"

I muttered to the woman beside me, "It can't be. No! Rotterdam is huge . . ." I clutched her arm. In a voice louder than necessary, for the conductor stood only a few steps away, I said to him, "Sir, Botersloot Straat? What about Botersloot Straat?" I wiped away tears.

The conductor turned to me. He too was in tears. In a soft voice he said, "At the center of the firestorm, mademoiselle."

"No—that can't be . . . "

The conductor placed a hand on my shoulder. "Mademoiselle, my family also was . . ." He paused. His voice quavered. "Was on Botersloot Straat. Reports say no survivors." The conductor dropped to his knees. He put his hands to his face and sobbed, shoulders heaving. He lowered his hands and looked up at me.

I said, "Sir, reports could be wrong. Couldn't they?"

He didn't answer.

Weeping parents hugged children. Mournful cries passed through the crowd. A boy about four years old stood alone. Tears rolled down his cheeks. He extended his arms and screamed, *"Maman! Maman!"* A lady too old to be his mother pushed through the crowd and put her arms around him.

Suddenly unhinged, no home, nowhere to go, I struggled against waves of nausea. My heart pounded. I scanned the station platform then rushed to the door, *"Dames."*

Why hadn't I listened to Aimée? An hour later I began a return to Paris. Scheduled travel had been nearly eliminated. Trains were scheduled and rerouted to bypass troops and combat. I boarded a train to Paris only to have it stop after ten kilometers and disembark passengers. I boarded another, traveled a short distance until it too stopped. Conductors again required us to disembark. My disjointed travel, one crowded train after another, all moving in the direction of Paris, continued.

On my fourth train we passed the tents of an army field hospital. A kilometer from the railroad tracks a bomb exploded. Then a second, closer, explosion rocked my railcar. Passengers screamed. Some dove to the floor. Children cried and crawled under seats. The train stopped. Blood-spattered nurses boarded.

We continued. I wound my way to a rail station on the outskirts of Paris. In hot stagnant air I waited in a telephone queue for twenty minutes only to learn that all phone service in Paris had been shut down.

Children, mothers with infants, and elderly folks packed the station's benches. Hundreds of sweating, disheveled travelers stood, shuffled around—displaced persons searching for paths to Paris, to Marseille, to *somewhere*. In the station's strange silence, few people chatted. Many wept. I found an area behind pillars in the rear of the station. A small, quiet place. I sat on the floor and leaned against a pillar. My once-gray blouse and skirt were blackened with sweat and grime. I inhaled the acidic odor of my body.

After a few minutes of rest, I urged myself to do something. Anything. I walked out of the station. On the sidewalk I stopped a man. "Please, sir, where can I board a bus? Or the Metro?"

"Mademoiselle, the Metro and buses, all public transit—everything, has, well, look . . ." He waved an arm toward streets jammed with vehicles, vehicles jammed with people. In bumper-to-bumper traffic the horns of stalled cars and trucks blared. "Beneath us, even the Metro is not moving."

Hot and sweaty, I walked a few blocks away from the station and discovered moving traffic—all of it going in one direction, south. Out of Paris. Taxis crammed with riders joined caravans of autos and trucks overloaded with people, pet dogs and cats, luggage, and belongings. Bedding and chairs were strapped to fenders and roofs, piled in the beds of trucks.

The man said, "All Paris is in motion. On its way, Mademoiselle."

"On its way where?"

The man shrugged. "Who knows? Wherever the Germans aren't."

My thoughts returned to Rotterdam. Did my family find shelter in the basement of our apartment building? I thought about the days before the bombing, the long months of "*la drôle de guerre*," the Phoney War— what the British called "the Great Bore War." Oh how I had wanted that strange so-called war to last, to become a peaceful order in Europe.

After my professors at the School of Economics warned of Hitler's growing menace, I read *Mein Kampf*. How could anyone take Hitler's rants seriously? But they did. I followed news reports out of Berlin, researched newspapers and magazine articles back to the period when Hitler and the Nazis first gained control of the government. I studied Germany's new anti-Semitic laws and actions toward Jews.

I remembered a cold winter evening in 1938. I had braved the biting wind of a North Sea storm to attend a lecture by a Jacob Ronk, a colleague of Johan Huizinga, the Dutch historian, "The Night of Long Knives, Today."

Huizinga introduced Ronk. Over the past four years Ronk had studied the events of the night of 30 July 1934—Night of Long Knives. That night Hitler ordered the sudden execution of men in the Nazi party. Hitler feared they would oppose him. Many had been Nazi supporters, some of them Hitler's friends since before the Munich Beer Hall Putsch, comrades on his journey to political power.

After the executions, Hitler announced he had acted to stop a plot to overthrow the government. I still have trouble believing he got by with those premeditated killings. But days later, rather than being arrested for murder, Germany's President Hindenburg congratulated Hitler.

Ronk's voice rose as he said, "The Night of Long Knives, now four years ago, is present. Now. Here. Tonight. We must understand—the party activists of Germany's National Socialism, the Nazis, will devour us." He paused. His gaze moved from face to face through the audience. He made eye contact wherever possible then he yelled, "Unless we and our allies confront the German menace. Do we have the courage, the will to do that?"

A man yelled, "Yes!" Others, including me, joined him. "Yes, yes!"

"How much time do we have?" Ronk asked.

How could I, how could anyone answer that?

The man in the next seat turned to me and said, "Less than we think."

Rescue

Late afternoon I arrived at Gare de Lyon station in Paris. I wanted to return to Aimée's apartment. I elbowed my way through dense crowds and streets made near impassible by cars and trucks and horse-drawn wagons loaded with farm families and household goods. People from the countryside and surrounding towns had converged on Paris—a brief stop on the trip to somewhere. Anywhere.

I was too tired to keep walking. No taxis or buses or subway trains were running. When I came to a hotel, I walked in. La Petite Maison was old and shabby. But to my surprise, the hotel had an available room—one I could afford.

After registering, I went to the lobby's small telephone booth to call Aimée. She was my connection in a city suddenly turned on its head. The line was dead.

The elevator was temporarily out of service, so said a sign in the lobby. My room was on the second floor. Mon dieu, had all of Paris stopped working? I started up the stairs. After climbing only two steps I stopped, turned, and listened to loud voices at the reception desk. An irate man leaned over the counter and yelled at the registration clerk. "*Une chambre! Une chambre!*" The clerk, a gnome-like man with a squeaky voice, replied in a controlled manner, "*Monsieur, s'il vous plaît, on a pas de chambres.*"

Lady Luck had smiled on me. I had booked the hotel's last available room. I said a small prayer of thanks. More people streamed through the hotel's entrance, crowded into the lobby. All of them wanted rooms. They yelled and waved at the desk clerk, as if large gestures accentuated with loud voices would secure a room. A short fat man yelled across the lobby. "Gaston, all Paris is leaving. One jump ahead of the Boche." He turned to the man standing next to him. "*Quel dommage*. Paris, the jewel of France. No?"

At a table in the hotel's crowded coffee shop, I found an unoccupied small table and ordered coffee. I attempted to read the train schedules. My hands shook. I braced them against the table. Even if I could find a seat on a train leaving Paris, where would I go? How long would my money last?

A middle-aged woman sat down at my table. "*Je m'appelle Ruth*." She extended her hand. She had thinning grey hair chopped in a straight line at the level of her earlobes. Aimée would call it a rough-cut bob. Ruth's fingers moved to, then away from, her mouth in small choppy and repeated movements. Her nails had been chewed to the quick and bore traces of her thick red lipstick.

For 30 minutes we talked of our lives with an intimacy that occurs among travelers thrust together. People who knew they would soon depart and never see each other again. Ruth was 54. Her husband died three years earlier, run over by a Berlin trolley. "Since I was a little girl, I've wanted to have a child, be a mother. Perhaps it will never happen."

I told her about Aimée and my family in Rotterdam, speaking at first as if they were awaiting my return. I wept as I acknowledged the truth. My family most likely had died in the Luftwaffe bombing.

Ruth patted my hand and gave me a hug. Then she asked about my studies.

"Economics and mechanography—electronic information processing, tabulation."

Then came a flurry of questions. "How long have you been in Paris? Why? Where is your cousin Aimée?"

I tired of her inquisition. But I knew she needed to talk to someone, anyone. And I needed companionship. I revealed more about myself than felt comfortable, but what was the risk? We would soon part, forever.

Ruth continued, "Am I correct? You can't go home, you're afraid to stay here, afraid of the Nazis, afraid of being discovered as a foreign Jew?"

I nodded yes.

"Well, listen to this. I was working in an office in Berlin. After work one evening, two men came to my apartment. Identified themselves as Gestapo agents. I should've known. They wore fedoras, brims turned down, and long black overcoats. They searched in cabinets, closets, under cushions. In every room. For what? They wouldn't tell me. I still don't know. On the other side of Berlin, they arrested my sister. Took her from her home. Why? We're Parisians, is that a crime? I've tried to contact her. And failed." Tears flooded Ruth's eyes. "What've they done to her?"

"I'm sorry."

Ruth wiped her eyes. "Like you, we're Jewish, too. In Berlin the new laws say Jews cannot walk on the sidewalks. We have to walk in the streets, step around horseshit. In the markets, Jews have to be last in line. I went to my favorite restaurant, where I've dined for years. The owner, Hans, who I thought was a friend, said, 'Sorry, no tables for Jews.'" Ruth toyed with her coffee cup. "And now the Nazis are coming to Paris! Will the French go along with all this?" She stared at me for a moment then added, "Will they have a choice?"

Over a second cup of coffee, a tall older man in a dark suit joined us. "Miriam," Ruth said, "this my friend Charles Delmand."

He looked familiar. "Haven't we met?"

Charles smiled. "Ah, *Miriam*. Yes, I remember. Rotterdam, wasn't it? Netherlands School of Economics. Am I correct?" His deep voice and dark eyes commanded my attention. Then as if speaking more to himself than to me, he said, "I was doing an article on technology and information management." He looked me in the eye. "Your professors spoke highly of you."

"Thank you. Nice to see you again, Monsieur Delmand."

"A lot has changed in the short time since we met."

I returned his gaze. I imagined describing Charles to Aimée. Dark eyes. Intense, nearly hypnotic, gaze. He kept alternately widening then narrowing his lips. Not quite grimaces, but close.

"Charles is an old friend," Ruth said, placing one hand on his arm. "He works at the Louvre and the *Musée de l'Homme*."

"Only a consultant, Ruth."

I leaned forward and said enthusiastically, "My cousin Aimée works at the *Musée de l'Homme.*" I was desperate for a human connection.

Charles raised his eyebrows. "Aimée Connaix, the dancer?"

"Yes! Just last week I attended her audition rehearsal." As fast as it had arrived, the excitement left me. "That was before the . . . the invasion." In a near whisper, I added, "And the Rotterdam bombing."

Ruth said, "Miriam is from Rotterdam. She's afraid her family died in the firebombing of the city."

"I'm very sorry, Mademoiselle. All of us, like you, are struggling with the invasion. But on a happier note, you should know that Aimée is doing important work to document the *Musée de l'Homme's* collections. I'm helping her group, the Polar Department, organize their records. Aimée's skills in mechanography are impressive."

He didn't mention Carmille's connection to the Polar Department, to Aimée. Does he know? Is information being secretly coded? Is Aimée part of a secret society within the Musée de l'Homme? Is she in jeopardy? "Please, M. Delmand, I need to talk to Aimée. There is no phone service. Can you help me?"

"I spoke with her earlier today. She was then leaving for Marseille. Some work for the Polar Department."

"She is gone?"

"Yes. But she will return."

"When?"

"I'm uncertain. But I'm confident she'll come back. She has much to do at the museum."

"Do you know where she's going in Marseille?"

"Sorry, I don't." Charles's expression brightened. "Tomorrow I will ask Boris Vildé. He heads Aimée's department. If Boris can tell me Aimée's whereabouts, I'll contact you."

Charles gave a brief nod of recognition to a man across the lobby. "Miriam, will you and Ruth join me at a nearby bistro *pour un dîner simple et nourrissant?*"

Without hesitation I eagerly replied, "*Oui!*" My face reddened. I hadn't eaten that day. My last food? A stale sandwich.

For a moment after my enthusiastic acceptance of Charles's invitation,

Ruth and Charles stared at me. Then they smiled, more at each other than at me. Each of them put a hand on one of my arms. We stood, locked arms. Our trio walked through the lobby's wide oak and glass doors.

In a voice filled with gratitude, I said, "*Merci*, M. Delmand."

"Miriam, please call me Charles."

"Charles."

Allez. Vis ta Vie!
Go. Live Your Life!

We walked a half-block to Bistro de l'Etoile. The owner recognized Charles and quickly seated us at the last open table. Patrons, two deep, lined the bar. The bistro's air was laden with thick smoke and the aroma of garlic. Fragments of conversations rose above the din of animated patrons. They talked about the German army, rail schedules, taxis, trucks, drivers, and about how to get out of Paris along with thousands of Parisians going south.

A photographer moved from table to table. Flashbulbs sent bursts of light through the dimly lit bistro. After each burst he paused and stared at the photographed patrons, awaiting his payment. Only sometimes did he receive it. He came to our table. He spoke to Charles, *"Pour votre dernière soirée à Paris?"* Without waiting for an answer, he raised his camera. The shutter snapped. A flash of light illuminated the three of us. Charles waved him away. No sale.

During dinner Ruth told Charles that I had completed my studies at the Netherlands School of Economics. She reiterated what I'd said earlier, that I had skills in mechanography, and added in a voice of self-deprecation, "Whatever that is."

Charles listened, gazing alternately at Ruth and me. He said, "Yes, I remember. Mechanography—you know, Miriam, there are opportunities in

Lyon." By the end of dinner, he became emphatic. "You *must* go to Lyon! The Military Recruitment Service of the French army needs people with your skills. From Paris, Aimée has been a help to the Recruitment Office."

Aimée spoke of some kind of connection between her group at the museum and Carmille. Could that have been what she was talking about? She mentioned mechanography and codes. Maybe Charles does know about her secret work.

"But Lyon is over 400 kilometers from Paris."

"You cannot stay here *sans travail*, without work," Charles said.

Ruth leaned across the table and waved her arms toward the bistro's front door. "Remember what's happening outside. Soon the Nazis will arrive."

Charles said, "You can't go home to a devastated Rotterdam. I don't recommend that you put yourself at risk in an unprotected Paris. Go to Lyon. Live in the shelter of employment. One day the war will end." He put a hand on my arm. "*Allez. Vis ta vie!* Live your life." Charles sipped his wine. "The Military Recruitment Service may undergo changes, *mais il a besoin de gens.*"

Ruth said, "That's right, the place, like everything else today, may change. But they'll need skilled people."

After a furtive look around the bistro, as if to ensure he would not be overheard, Charles said, "Skilled people like you *who can be trusted.*"

How did Charles know I could be trusted? And by whom? A larger question weighed on me. I said to Charles, "If I go to Lyon, what will you and your friends expect in return?"

Charles ignored my question. "First, I will need to make certain arrangements. Then you must go to Lyon."

"Arrangements?"

Charles inhaled his Gauloise. "Arrangements that will help smooth your travel. And help, too, in finding lodging and employment." He lowered his voice. "To make you French. To make you not Jewish." He looked into my eyes. "Your green eyes are a good start."

"From my father's family, including my crossed eye." I felt anger rising. "I have little money. I am not a French citizen. Maybe I don't want to give up my Jewish heritage. Even if I did, I can do little about it."

"I can." Charles scanned the room then looked at me. "I will take care of everything."

The tone of my voice carried skepticism and near disbelief, but signaled a grudging acceptance of Charles's proposition. "*If* you can do all that, yes, I will go to Lyon." In truth, I had little choice. France and Paris were falling to the Germans.

Ruth and Charles beamed wide smiles.

I returned to a question that nagged at me. "Assuming you can deliver what you've promised, what do you expect from me?"

Charles lit another cigarette. Drawing on it deeply, he sat up straight, then leaned forward and slowly exhaled. Smoke drifted from his nostrils to the tabletop. His lips moved as if he chewed on words of smoke. "*C'est très simple. Nous vous demandons seulement* . . . we ask only that you support us. If asked, that you supply us information."

"Us? Information? What information might I supply? And to whom?"

"About life in Lyon and at the Recruitment Service."

"Always in French?"

"Usually."

I held his gaze. "I was born in Belgium. My father and his family spoke French. I spent my early years there. Then we moved to Holland. Papa often laughed that I spoke French with a Belgian accent. You should remember that I am Dutch. The accent is often present in my speech."

Charles again put his hand on my forearm. I welcomed his touch. Most likely I would welcome any touch.

"Your training in mechanography is uncommon, and very valuable. Our country is falling to the Germans. We need your expertise. We need your assessments of French and German mechanography.

"All around us the people of Paris are packing and leaving. There will be, perhaps tomorrow, a mass exodus. Soon the enemy will occupy Paris. Please, do not wait. *Carpe diem.* Lyon is not yet in the path of the Wehrmacht. Go there. Join us. Wait and you may miss your opportunity."

I needed only one second to assess my bleak options in German-occupied Paris. "*Bien sûr*, if you keep your promises, I will go to Lyon." I stood. "I must go buy a train ticket."

"*Non. S'il vous plaît, asseyez-vous.* Please, sit. Enjoy your dinner. Then go to your room and rest. Sleep, if you can. *Gare de Lyon* rail station is nearby. I will take care of your ticket." Charles signaled the proprietor. "*Encore une bouteille de vin rouge, s'il vous plaît.*"

At six o'clock the next morning, up and dressed, I answered a knock on my door. I found Charles standing tall. He wore the same dark suit as the night before with a freshly starched white shirt. With a wide smile and a flourish, Charles bowed and presented me with a train ticket to Lyon. "*Et, Mademoiselle, votre nouvelle carte d'identité.*"

A new identity card! Eyes wide, I examined the card, complete with my photo. In the photo I wore last evening's blouse—the bistro photographer! The card gave me a Paris address and a new name, Miriam Dupré.

"How—where did you..."

Charles laughed. "I have my ways."

I wondered how such a worn and slightly stained document could be produced so quickly. "I will be Miriam Dupré?"

"There are lots of Duprés in Paris. In Lyon, too. You will blend in. There's more you must do."

"More?"

"You must create the character of Miriam Dupré. Beyond her address, who is she? What does she like? Where did she go to school? Anchor your new identity in the real world: communities, people, and schools. When you may least expect it, you will be asked. Prepare yourself."

I smiled. "As if I'm creating a character in a drama, is that it?"

"Yes. But this is not a dramatic production—don't kid yourself. We're in a game with lives at stake. Someday the German authorities, perhaps the Gestapo, may ask you about yourself."

"I understand. I can and will do what you're asking. *Merci.*"

"The train for Lyon leaves at 8 o'clock."

I picked up my shoulder bag. "I will pay you for the ticket."

Charles raised one hand. "It has been taken care of."

"*Merci, encore.*"

"When you arrive in Lyon, go to the Military Recruitment Service." He handed me a slip of paper with a handwritten address, 10 rue des Archers. "Ask for an employment application. Say this: 'I have come to apply for special employment.'" He went on to give me verbatim instructions. They were straightforward and simple. I quickly rehearsed them, easily committed them to memory.

Charles placed one hand on each of my shoulders, gave me a light kiss on each cheek. He whispered, "*Vite! Allez-y!*" He turned, and after a cursory inspection of the hallway, walked rapidly to the stairs.

I stared at the closed door and took a deep breath. Life had just changed. Again.

Lyon

My train arrived late morning at Gare de Lyon-Perrache, near the southernmost tip of Lyon and the confluence of the Saône and Rhône rivers. Suitcase in hand, I walked along the crowded arrival platform. In the station's cavernous lobby, I paused to get my bearings. Ahead of me, travelers streamed through wide doors beneath the lobby's arched windows, three stories tall. In the center of the arrival and departure hall, a kiosk displayed postcards and maps. I purchased a transit map of Lyon.

I exited the station. With my map as a guide, I boarded a trolley going toward the city's center.

Half an hour later, sweaty in the mid-day summer heat, I walked along Lyon's downtown streets. I crossed La Place des Jacobins. A sign said that in medieval times it was the site of a Jacobin convent. In the sixteenth century the square became a place of political executions. I cooled my hands in a small pool of flowing water beneath the square's large statue.

A few blocks farther I rested in the shade of Place Bellecour's massive equestrian statue of Louis XIV. Soon I arrived at the nearby large stone building, 10 rue des Archers. Next to the main entrance a small brass sign with black letters: Service de Recrutement Militaire.

I pushed open the heavy front door, oak, three, perhaps four, meters tall. Apprehensive, I entered the building. For a moment I felt like a child, empty and alone, on my first day of school.

The reception lobby was warm and stuffy. In the center of the room, the slow rotation of a ceiling fan's wide blades produced an undulating hum but moved very little air. Walking to the reception counter, I quietly recited Charles's instructions. "*Je suis venue postuler pour un emploi spécial . . . I* have come to apply for special employment with the Service. I am trained in mechanography."

Behind the counter, a thin woman with gray hair pulled into a tight knot at the back of her head sorted mail. Beneath her arms, long ovals of perspiration darkened her red blouse. The woman placed envelopes of varying sizes into mailboxes nested in a single large wooden cube. Under each small mailbox was a person's name. Under larger mailboxes, the name of a department.

She glanced at me and raised one hand. "*Un moment, s'il vous plaît.*" Soon she walked to the counter where I stood and then smiled. "Yes?"

In a matter-of-fact tone of voice, I said, "I am Miriam Dupré," and then spoke as Charles had instructed me.

The clerk gave a somber nod. "*Compris. Emploi spécial.*" She turned and walked through a doorway beyond the mailboxes. A moment later she returned and handed me an application for employment. At its top, handwritten, "Charles." She nodded toward a corner table at the end of the counter. I sat at the table and completed the form. I returned to the counter and handed the form to the clerk. After a cursory glance at my entries, the woman smiled. "*Merci.* Please return in two hours."

I walked to a café on the other side of rue des Archers. I sat at a small table next to the café's large front window. For two hours I sipped espresso and nibbled on a croissant. After the first hour the waiter gave no hints, either in words or body language, that I should vacate the table. I remembered Aimée once saying, "In cafés, the French are endowed with a special right, to sit, relax, and enjoy."

On the street side of the window, pedestrians walked in brilliant sunshine. Many carried suitcases. Even in the mounting afternoon heat they walked rapidly. Their shadows resembled agitated phantoms flitting along rue des Archers. Fragments of conversations from the shadows bounced into the coffee shop.

"We leave tomorrow."

"No, we stay."

"Trains have stopped. Roads are blocked."

"No, some are open."

I wondered, was I safe here? Safe anywhere? I thought about life in my family's apartment—about the day Papa thought safety had been negotiated. 30 September 1938. Mama. Papa. Margot. Me. We sat in our living room listening to the BBC news—the long-awaited Munich Conference announcement. We stared at the glowing round dial of our mahogany radio, as if our concentration could produce an announcement of good news. The BBC correspondent's voice rose above the crackle of radio static and the ever-nearer roar of airplane engines. "The British Airways twin engine passenger plane has taxied to the hangar and braked to a stop."

The roar diminished and ended as the engines sputtered and shut down. "We are located a few miles west of London. I am standing on the concrete apron in front of the central hangar of the Heston Aerodrome. BBC has learned that at 1:30 this morning in Munich, England's Neville Chamberlain, France's Édouard Daladier, Italy's Benito Mussolini, and Germany's Adolf Hitler signed an agreement ceding Czechoslovakia's Sudetenland to Germany."

I imagined those men seated around a table bearing a map of Europe—men with the power to redraw that map, the power to reshape Europe. A chill passed through me. How do men gain such power?

"The propellers of the aircraft's powerful engines are now still. The passenger door on the side of the aircraft is opening. Prime Minister Chamberlain, his height accented by his long formal coat and starched collar, bends at the waist and steps out to the top of the aircraft's stair. Now standing fully erect, he smiles and waves to the crowd. He walks down the stairs. On the tarmac, he approaches a brace of radio microphones, stands before them. The prime minister raises one hand. He waits for the crowd, mostly reporters along with some members of parliament, to become silent."

Then came the nasal voice of Neville Chamberlain. It resembled the high-pitched whine of a spool of wire unwinding at a high speed. "My good friends, for the second time in our history, a British Prime Minister has returned from Germany bringing peace with honor. I believe it is peace for our time. We thank you from the bottom of our hearts. Go home and get a nice quiet sleep."

Papa and Mama beamed bright grins and joined hands. Margot yelled, "Hooray!" She jumped up and hugged me. I thought about the first six words of Chamberlain's statement. "A British prime minister has returned." Why do politicians refer to themselves in the third person?

"Papa, Professor Janik warned the Nazi threat is real. Unless we take action."

"Action, Miriam?" he said. "Our leaders just took action. Signed an agreement in Munich. You heard it. Peace for our time."

I took a deep breath. "I'd put it differently. Unless we take action to stop them, the Nazis will devour us. Particularly us, Papa. Jews. Have you read Hitler's *Mein Kampf*?"

The tone of Papa's voice implied a mild reprimand. "You worry too much. You just heard—statesmen are meeting the German challenge. Things are working out."

"My God, you sound like Chamberlain. Chamberlain and Daladier are fools. Churchill knows the truth of appeasement. So does Hitler."

That night my family, along with millions of others throughout Europe, slept well. I did not.

And now in Lyon, I sat alone in an empty café. My family dead, my home and the little places I treasured in Rotterdam destroyed. My eyes filled with tears.

I imagined Papa in the coffee shop, sitting at my table. I again heard him say, "Things are working out, Miriam." I replied, "Yes, Papa, in the worst possible way."

The Military
Recruitment Service

Two hours later I returned to 10 rue des Archers. A young French army officer, tall, trim, his mustache a shade darker than his light brown hair, introduced himself to me. Lieutenant Marcel Lacroix. "Please come this way." He ushered me through a door behind the counter. We entered a small room bounded by glass partitions. We sat on either side of a conference table.

Lt. Lacroix asked me perfunctory questions about myself. "I'm twenty-three," then, testing myself in the use of my newly constructed identity, I lied, "I grew up in the Marais District of Paris. We lived on a small street between the third and fourth arrondissements, rue du Temple. In the exodus, I was separated from my family. I believe they went south, toward Marseille. I jumped at an opportunity get out of the path of the German army. I just arrived in Lyon. I hope to find a place to live this afternoon."

"I see you went to a lycée in Paris. Your advanced education, Mlle Dupré?"

"I completed my studies in mechanography in Paris at the *Ecole Supérieure de Commerce.*"

As he made notes, the lieutenant's gaze shifted back and forth from my employment application to my *carte d'identité* to a small notebook in front of him in which he made notes. "I will now ask you some questions about mechanography, about the technical details of IBM-Dehomag as well as Bull and CEC keypunch and tabulation machines. I'll start with IBM-Dehomag."

I nodded.

"The internal operating properties common to those tabulators, would you please tell me about them, mademoiselle?"

The lieutenant didn't know how much I enjoyed talking about information processing and how to manage it. I relaxed for a moment and permitted myself a small inward smile. "IBM machines were standard in my training program. Also, I've had field experience using the Bull and CEC machines."

Lieutenant Lacroix smiled. "We use Bull and CEC tabulators in the Service. Most other European countries, including the Reich, rely on IBM-Dehomag machines."

"Yes, I know IBM's technology."

The lieutenant continued with questions about tabulator processing capacities, common malfunctions, and maximum and minimum rates of card flow. He took copious notes. "And, the most important elements of machine maintenance, mademoiselle?"

I outlined maintenance priorities.

"When processing malfunctions occur because of cards with dulled or incomplete keypunches, mademoiselle, how might you estimate repair costs?"

Like a theatre screen after a film ended, my thoughts went blank. I loved cost estimates—why a sudden blank? I shifted in my chair. I crossed then uncrossed my legs, dropped my pencil, slowly bent over and picked it up. "Lieutenant, could I have a glass of water?"

"*Mais oui.*" He rose and left the room.

I walked to the window and watched a crew unload a large crate containing an electronic tabulation machine from a truck. What it might cost if they dropped it?

I smiled and relaxed. The theatre screen again had images.

The lieutenant returned with a glass of water. I sipped the water and looked the lieutenant in the eye. "Component malfunctions and their costs are complex problems. I find it helpful to use a systems framework." I took a notebook from my shoulder bag, opened it, and began to diagram components of tabulation systems. "Here's how I would approach the problem. What I would do."

While talking, I put pencil to paper and outlined common malfunctions, staffing requirements for repairs, costs per hour, and the costs of repair parts. I diagrammed a model of calculations for operating and overhead repair costs. I turned my notes toward the lieutenant. He studied the interconnected lines, arrows, boxes, intermediate costs, and at the end of the final arrow a cost total.

I said, "This should take us to a near-complete estimate of costs. Though costs will vary with the severity of the problem. If we had more time, I would create probability distributions for cost estimates. A single-point cost estimate is always easiest to calculate."

I paused and looked for signs the lieutenant was following my logic. Good news: his eyes hadn't glazed over. "However, a single point estimate is rarely correct. I mean it's not the whole truth. Just a good start. But it needs to be placed in a distribution of possible costs."

The lieutenant sat back in his chair and studied my calculations. He again read my application form and reviewed his notes. "*Attendez, une minute, je reviens.*" He walked to the office across the hall.

A few minutes later he returned. His face beaming, the lieutenant extended his hand. "*Bienvenue au Service de Recrutement Militaire.*"

Lt. Lacroix's welcome brought me a moment of relief. Beyond the welcome, knowing that I had a job brought me my first feeling of security, however tenuous, since I left Aimée's apartment.

The lieutenant escorted me to the reception area. He said to the woman working there, "Please give Miriam forms for employment and payroll."

After I completed the forms, the reception clerk smiled and extended her hand. "*Bienvenue, je m'appelle Eve.*"

I shook her hand. "*Merci.* I am Miriam."

"We've made arrangements for you to stay at a nearby hotel, *Le Lieu.* It's affordable." She looked around, then whispered, "I'm not sure how to say that in Dutch." Eve laughed.

Say that in Dutch? And she laughed? I forced a smile. Eve's humorous reference to "Dutch" was like a bullet fired into the heart of my new sense of wellbeing. Eve knew of my Dutch origin. Who told her? Did others know? Did they also know I am Jewish?

My body tensed. As if a powerful circuit in a tabulator had been activated, my thoughts flooded with questions—each of them about my safety and security. In Paris, who had prepared my carte d'identité? Who had written 'Charles' on the employment application? My room at Le Lieu, had it been reserved for me prior to my arrival at the Recruitment Service? My interview with Lt. Lacroix, was it like a scene in a stage play, an exercise to establish authenticity? Beyond Charles and Ruth, how many people knew my true identity?

I had smiled when Eve laughed. But along with my newfound sense of security, only moments old, the smile had quickly melted away. Fear replaced my sense of security.

"Le Lieu is only two blocks away, Miriam, convenient to our offices." Her smile widened. "You can walk to work. No need to pay for a trolley or bus—these days no small matter."

"Thank you."

"And we've arranged for you to take your meals at a reduced rate in the hotel dining room."

"That's helpful. *Merci.*"

"We serve a light *déjeuner* here at mid-day. Of course, you can always choose to dine elsewhere. Please feel free to move from Le Lieu if you find more suitable accommodations.

"*Je vous remercie*, Eve."

Eve raised a hand. "I'm glad to help you get settled. In case you don't know, tomorrow, Sunday, we are closed." She smiled. "You'll have time to explore Lyon."

In bright afternoon sun, I walked along the crowded street to the hotel. My gaze flitted from face to face as pedestrians walked towards me. I remembered Papa's counsel: "Stare at one person and you may offend. Look at many and it's called people watching."

With each new face my earlier questions returned. Does that man know who I really am? What about that woman? If the police stop me, and ask for my carte d'identité, will it hold up under scrutiny? Will I?

At the front entrance of Le Lieu, I stepped aside for an elderly couple coming out. They carried battered suitcases. Even on this warm afternoon, they wore heavy black coats. He wore a wide-brimmed black hat, she a black head scarf.

The woman spoke in a sharp nasal voice. She waved an arm toward the lobby. "Well, *Le Lieu* has no rooms." She turned to me. "*Mademoiselle*, is there a hotel in Lyon with a vacancy?"

"I'm sorry, I don't know."

She glared at her husband. "You see? Did you hear what she said?"

The husband turned towards me.

"She'd know if there was a vacancy."

"No, madam, all I meant was . . ."

"No hotel in Lyon has a vacancy." She glared at her husband. "Do you understand? None."

The man replied in a soft voice, "My dear, the trains are still running. If necessary, we'll go to Clermont-Ferrand. Perhaps to Royat. We'll find something."

"And when we do, we stay. Hear me? We stay!"

"Yes, yes. Enough running." Their voices faded as they merged into the flow of pedestrians.

I smiled, relieved. The couple had asked no questions about my Belgian-flavored French. My smile disappeared as I wondered if a hotel room still remained for me.

I walked through the hotel's revolving glass door. Le Lieu's lobby, like the face of an elderly person, showed signs of wear and neglect. I inhaled the hotel's musty scent, one that mixed tobacco smoke, decaying carpets, and floor wax. Similar to La Petite Maison in Paris, the hotel's ornate gilded ceilings had grayed with accumulated grit. I surveyed the worn and faded fabric of the lobby's turn-of-the-century, overstuffed furniture. The once light beige paint on the walls had been darkened by years of tobacco smoke. I wondered about the hard times that must have been part of the lobby's history.

In contrast to the lobby's faded furnishings, the large brass chandelier in the center of the room's tall ceiling gleamed. Its six highly polished long arms extended outward, each with a dozen or more small pointed bulbs, like a crown on an elderly queen. The lights cast a soft warm glow. Le

Lieu bore its age with pride.

I threaded my way through the crowded lobby. Three large electric fans, each atop a tall polished metal stand, whirred at top speed: one beside the registration desk, two others near the front windows and door. They did little more than add a constant whine to the lobby's noisy conversations and stir humid musty air. I took shallow breaths.

I walked to the polished mahogany reception desk. On it a small brass sign: Registration. On the other side stood a desk clerk, a balding overweight man, perhaps fifty. He had long strands of black hair combed over the bald top of his head. The sleeves of his white shirt were rolled to his elbows. A gold clip held his necktie in place.

"I am Miriam Dupré." I stood with a firm formality. "I believe the *Service de Recrutement Militaire* made a reservation for me."

The desk clerk stooped and retrieved a reservation log from beneath the counter. A wide strand of hair fell across his face. He smoothed his hair, opened the log and slowly ran his index finger down a page with today's date at its top. "*Oui, Mademoiselle Dupré.*" His voice was deep and resonant. "*Bienvenue.*" He beamed a welcoming smile. "We are holding a room for you."

My shoulders relaxed. I leaned forward on the registration desk, pleased to have a room. Then I wondered when the hotel had first learned I was to arrive.

"*Madmoiselle* Dupré, I am Jacques." He raised a pudgy hand in a slight wave, nodded, and again passed his hand across the strands on top of his head. He placed a registration form on the desktop, rotated it toward me, and pointed to a line. "*S'il vous plaît,* sign here, *mademoiselle.*" His lips turned up stiffly in an obsequious smile. His teeth were stained. "I will need to see identification."

I signed the form and handed Jacques my carte d'identité. I took slow deep breaths. Would he accept my counterfeit card?

Jacques scribbled a number from the card on the registration log and then returned it.

From the corner of my eye, a quick movement prompted me to make a half-turn, left. On the edge of a group engaged in conversation, a short thin man in a tweed sport coat shook hands with an older portly gentleman in a gray suit. In a flash, the thin man's left hand slipped beneath the back of the portly man's suit coat. He removed the man's wallet from his hip pocket.

Surprised, I stared at the two men. The thief made a slight turn in my direction. Our gazes locked. My mouth fell open. But I uttered no sound.

The thief bore a strong resemblance to a familiar stranger I had seen often in Rotterdam coffee shops. In the time it took for me to consider the remote probability the pickpocket might be that man he nodded and gave me a half-smile. A smile of recognition? A smile of complicity?

I returned his nod and an uncertain half-smile. Maybe it was him.

The thief briefly resumed his conversation then walked toward the front door.

I carried my suitcase into the small self-service lift. I pressed the button for fourth floor, and then pushed the lever that closed the lift's gate. Crosshatched narrow bands of thin steel slammed shut.

At the bottom of the elevator shaft, the lift's motor clicked into gear then whined like a tired worker returning to his job. The car jerked briefly as its cable pulled taut. The car began its ascent gently rocking sideways.

Across the lobby the portly gentleman waved his arms. "*Aidez-moi!* Help—thief! *On m'a volé!* I've been robbed!"

Lugdunum

Fitful sleep. Nightmare images awakened me. Luftwaffe bombs, Rotterdam in flames, a cacophony of sirens and explosions. I squeezed my eyes tightly shut and clenched my fists.

I told myself to relax. Focus on the quiet of the hotel. I breathed at a measured tempo. "One, inhale. Two, exhale. Three, inhale . . ." The count continued. I relaxed my feet, calves, thighs, progressed to my upper body, and then lay still. Like coiled springs slowly released, my muscles unwound.

I strained to hear sounds of life, first from within the hotel, and then from the street below, rue Bellecordière. There was only the lonely quiet of the still-asleep hotel and the early morning silence of Lyon.

I remembered early morning in Rotterdam, the comforting sounds that rose from the street below our apartment: Merchants swept storefront sidewalks and chatted with one another as they arranged racks of garments, bins of vegetables and fruit. Not long afterward, I would hear the laughter of neighborhood children walking to school.

I wished I could will Lyon to awaken, that I could join in the comings and goings of ordinary people.

Moments later from rue Bellecordière came the squeaks of wagon wheels and the clatter of a horse's hooves on cobblestones. From the Rhône two blocks east came the blast of a freighter's horn. The grinding whirr-whirr-whirr of a truck engine's unsuccessful attempt to start.

Rattles and gasps, like a man grasping at, gasping for, life. Then came the engine's muffled roar.

I remained motionless, grateful for the sounds and relief from my nightmares. As my jumbled thoughts settled, my gaze traveled across the room, a washbasin in one corner and the curtained toilet in the other. I missed my home.

In a voice reminiscent of Mama, I said, "Stop pitying yourself, Miriam. Pity, pity. Is that what you want? We are at war. Hitler is after Jews. Give thanks you are safe, that you have a place to live and a job."

With a wan smile I reflected on my good fortune.

In the long hallway outside my room a male voice asked, "*Quelle heuere est-il?*" I turned to my alarm clock. Another male voice answered, "*Sept heures et demie,* half past seven."

My thoughts turned to shards of dreams. Not my bombing nightmare—fragments of dreams about life before the bombs. Mama's face, etched with small lines. Our Rotterdam apartment's rich colors, Mama's favorite chair. The oriental rugs Papa loved. Scents of Mama's Dutch pea soup.

I remembered Botersloot Straat and a visit from cousin Aimée. As we walked to Saturday Shabbat services Papa muttered, "*Grâce à l'insistance de ta Maman.*" He attended synagogue only when Mama insisted. His long legs set a fast pace. His face, as always in matters related to synagogue, was dark and brooding. "Sooner there, sooner done."

Ahead loomed the tall brick Bloompjes Synagogue, its cupola towered over Botersloot Straat, "Erected 1725," chiseled into a cornerstone. A neighbor walked in front of us. Margot pointed at his near-perpendicular ears. We girls giggled. Papa joined us. Mama hissed, "Shush."

An hour later, with a map as a guide, I walked at a fast pace along the Rhône, deep blue, wide and placid, then past Place Bellecour and Place des Jacobins. I stopped for a bowl of café crème and a croissant at a pâtisserie near the Hôtel de Ville. I ignored the young man who attempted to make eye contact with me.

I continued a short distance then entered and meandered through a network of Lyon's ancient narrow streets. I wound my way up a long hillside of apartment buildings, some from the nineteenth century, others built of stone, stucco, and timbers. They looked like they'd been constructed in a far earlier period, perhaps in the sixteenth century.

The buildings became less frequent and the hillside filled with trees and gardens. I walked along pathways through what appeared to be the ancient stubble of partial walls and foundation stones that had once supported buildings. I paused to read a sign. I stood on the location of Roman settlements that dated back over two-thousand years. Terraces of stone benches cascaded down a hillside to a wide flat arena. L'amphithéâtre des Trois Gaules, a marker said, The Amphitheater of the Three Gauls. At the time of Julius Caesar, Lugdunum, later renamed Lyon, had been the capital of Rome's three Gallic provinces.

My thoughts leapt to Professor Janik's literature course. "Yes, Miriam, yes, class, the first words of De Bello Gallico in Shakespeare's Julius Caesar will be on the examination." He slowly read the famous words. "'*All Gaul is divided into three parts, one of which the Belgae inhabit, the Aquitani another, those who in their own language are called Celts, the third.*'"

Near the amphitheater entrance, in the shade of a plane tree, a gray-haired priest stood with a small group of schoolchildren.

He nodded to me. "*Bonjour.*"

"*Bonjour, Père.*" I thought about the early Roman persecution of Christians and violent deaths in arenas. My heart beat faster. "*Ici,* here, *il y avait des gens,* were people, *les Chretiens,* Christians, I mean, were they . . . were they . . ."

The priest interrupted me. "If I understand your question, mademoiselle, yes. Around the year 160, in the reign of the Roman Emperor Marcus Aurelius, Christians died in this arena."

From deep in my imagination came loud roars, first from lions, then from the crowd in the amphitheater. Lions surged from beneath the grandstand, chased the Christians, caught them and sunk long sharp teeth into their flesh. Blood showered the arena. I closed my eyes to halt my internal horror film.

I reopened my eyes and said to the priest, "*Pourquoi?* Why?"

"*Le pouvoir des croyances, mademoiselle.* The power of beliefs. They lead some to kill. Others to defend. Some to sacrifice." He paused. "Many to die. Not unlike today." The priest turned to talk with the children. I began my walk down the long hillside toward the center of Lyon. In the distance were the two ancient rivers, nearest, on my right, the Saône, more distant, on my left, across Lyon, the Rhône. Against the steep hillsides along the Saône were the medieval buildings of the old city.

The priest's words intruded and echoed in my thoughts. "Beliefs. They lead some to kill. Others to defend. Some to sacrifice. Many to die." Then I thought about *Mein Kampf*. The destiny of the Reich. The Phoney War transformed and made real by the Reich's invasion of France, Belgium, and Holland. Rotterdam firebombed. Nazi propaganda, literature and films, about the menace of Jews. Images of life on the streets. "You, Jew, off the sidewalk!" Jews queued in long food lines.

The voices softened and then became silent. An icy presence gripped me as my thoughts drifted to my family. Their deaths. Fast and merciful? Or lingering . . . I didn't want to think about it.

Late that afternoon I returned to Le Lieu. In the lobby, people occupied all the chairs and couches. Other than an occasional whisper, they sat in silence. Some smoked cigarettes, a few sipped espresso. Behind the registration desk, Jacques stood motionless. Everyone stared at the polished maple cabinet and amber dial of the hotel's large floor model radio in the center of the lobby as if it was a new guest who had joined us.

As soon as I arrived an elderly hotel resident put his fingers to his lips and turned to me. "Shh. News of the war."

A news announcer, like a new guest in the hotel, spoke to everyone seated in the lobby. "To continue with our summary of recent events, the Dunkirk evacuation is nearly complete. Made possible after the Wehrmacht surprised Allied forces by a halt in its advance. At least three hundred thousand troops have been evacuated by boat to England. Paris will soon be declared an open city. The French government is expected to vacate Paris and relocate to Bordeaux."

Beside me, a young woman with dark curly hair and bright eyes whispered, "Evacuate in its pants is more accurate." I suppressed a laugh.

The news announcer continued. "The next voice you hear will be that of Prime Minister Winston Churchill, in a speech recorded earlier in the House of Commons." On the radio Churchill's resonant baritone voice boomed.

We shall go on to the end. We shall fight in France, we shall fight on the seas and oceans, we shall fight with growing confidence and growing strength in the air, we shall defend our island, whatever the cost may be. We shall fight on the beaches, we shall fight on the landing grounds, we shall fight in the fields and in the streets, we shall fight in the hills, we shall never surrender. And even if, which I do not for a moment believe, this Island or a large part of it were subjugated and starving, then our Empire beyond the seas, armed and guarded by the British Fleet, would carry on the struggle, until, in God's good time, the New World, with all its power and might, steps forth to the rescue and the liberation of the old.

Churchill's powerful speech mobilized me. Yes, we could fight back. Win! I turned away from the glum faces in the lobby. I entered the lift and pressed the button for the fourth floor. The lift's gate slammed shut. There was a sudden whir of the lift's basement motor and the car rose.

Then, as if an electrical circuit had been activated, the lobby came to life. A man turned off the radio. Animated conversations began. In my last look at the lobby, people sat upright. Some stood. Jacques patted his hair.

The War is not Going Well

During my first day of work at 10 rue des Archers, all day long I organized procedures, set up systems for personnel information, and managed files. By the end of the afternoon, I looked out the window at nearby buildings but didn't see them. Only later did I realize they were built of granite with inlaid marble and had dark windows. That day, whether inside or outside, I saw only paperwork. Page after page. And files, one stacked on top of another.

Earlier that afternoon Lt. Lacroix had stopped at my office to check on my progress. "A file may seem like, well, just a file. Paper and cardboard. But each file—"

I completed his sentence. "Each file represents a soldier, a life." Should I have kept my mouth shut?

The lieutenant raised his eyebrows in surprise. "Yes—that's right! We think alike." I returned his smile.

I relaxed and recalled training sessions at the Central Statistics Bureau in Holland. "I'm familiar with personnel records, lieutenant. I know that they represent lives, people."

My thoughts jumped to my hotel room in Paris. My conversation with Charles after he presented me with my carte d'identité. "You must create the character of Miriam Dupré. Beyond her address, who is she? What does she like? Where did she go to school? All this and more. Someday you may be asked."

At this moment, facing Lieutenant Lacroix, I wondered how well I had developed the character, the past experience of my alter ego, Miriam Dupré. I should expect more questions from the lieutenant, from people at the hotel. And questions from the Germans might come when least expected.

The lieutenant looked around the room. He waved one hand toward the file folders. When he spoke, his voice softened. "Yes, these are soldiers. Hundreds of thousands of them on active duty, many now in combat." His voice wavered. "Others killed in action."

My thoughts jumped to earlier that morning. Lt. Lacroix had called me to his office. After stepping into the room, I could walk forward only a couple of steps. Boxes were stacked everywhere. "You want to see me, Lieutenant?"

The lieutenant sat behind his desk making entries in a ledger. He looked up and gave a blank stare.

Then he nodded. His left hand smoothed his mustache.

"*Bonjour*, Miriam."

My "*Bonjour*, Lieutenant" was lost as he looked past me at someone in the hallway and nodded. "Yes, put those in the conference room."

I turned to see a soldier walking away, his arms filled with file folders.

"Sorry. There's so much going on." He lowered his head and closed his eyes for a moment, then looked up. "As you no doubt know, news from the front is not good. The war is, what can I say . . . is not going well." He stared at papers strewn across his desk. "I can't get my thoughts around it all—I mean, how the Germans bypassed the Maginot line. Our fortification against invasion. Decades in construction." He shook his head. "Bypassed."

"Yes, I've heard."

"I don't know what to expect. Yet we have to get ready. For something." The lieutenant stared at the ledger on his desk, then at me. "For the worst, the unthinkable." He paused. "It pains me to say that. But it's the truth, what we have to do." He stood and walked from behind his desk and stepped around boxes to stand beside me. "I need your help. Please, come with me."

The lieutenant led me down a long corridor that passed deep into the building. He unlocked a door. We entered a cavernous room filled with packing cases, some sealed, others opened. Next to the open cases were stacks of boxes, only a few of them open.

I pushed back the cardboard flaps of an open box. Inside were file folders. At a quick glance, I could see that each folder had a soldier's name. Some of the files had additional information below the name, such as antécédents médicaux, medical history.

"We now have two million men in uniform." He waved one arm toward crates of files. "Personnel records for many of them are in these crates and files. There are more records centers around the country. With soldiers' dates of service." His voice trailed off. Then, as if he'd removed a distraction, returned to full strength. "And training—I mean they contain records of the military training each soldier has received."

"I understand."

Lt. Lacroix continued as though I hadn't spoken. "As well as his principal military skills, and what else?" He answered his own question, spoke more to himself than to me. "A history of each soldier's past service."

"What do you want me to do?"

The lieutenant laughed. "Yes, that's important. First, you'll need to prepare an inventory. Log in everything that's here, crate by crate, box by box. Then for each box, list each soldier." He walked to a nearby shelf and removed a single sheet of paper from an open box. "Use this form to record the inventory. There are plenty more."

Lt. Lacroix sat on a small stack of boxes. "Keep in mind, many of these records represent men now in combat. Some will not return." He paused for a moment. "At least not alive." The lieutenant's face darkened. He spoke in a near-whisper. "Families will depend on us, our records, for death benefits, military pensions. Other men will return, wounded, some missing an arm or leg. Our records will connect them to financial support and medical services. Can you do this?"

I nodded yes. Like a fool, I had never stepped away from a challenge. Once I nearly drowned after a boy dared me to skate across a frozen pond.

"Will I have some help, some support?"

"Of course. I'll assign staff who'll work for you. Ten people are all I can spare right now. I'm pulling them from other assignments. Six women, clerks and tabulation specialists. Four men, military clerk typists and personnel specialists."

"Thank you, Lieutenant."

"I don't know how long you'll be able to keep them."

"Well, that's a start."

"If you need more people, I'll do the best I can. We're stretched tight. Everything is unstable. For now, ten will have to do. At least for a while."

"I understand."

The lieutenant closed his eyes for a moment. When he opened them he asked, "Did I mention, the war is not going well?"

An hour later, with no further guidance from the lieutenant, I met with my new staff, mostly middle-aged women. Using the army's records management forms, we began to inventory the storage room's contents. The day was warm and the room poorly ventilated. Opening each crate added more dust to the room's already dust-laden air. Soon many of us began to sneeze. My sneezes blew deposits of gray mucous into my handkerchief.

I placed a call to the building maintenance office. "Please, we need help with ventilation." Two hours later a maintenance crew arrived and pried open the room's steel and frosted-glass industrial windows. They brought in large floor fans, placed them around the room, and turned them on. Papers and files blew across the room.

"Point them towards the ceiling!"

Lt. Lacroix's words, "The war is not going well," reverberated in my thoughts. How were millions of French citizens dealing with this?

A Message from London
18 June 1940

Later that day, on my return to the hotel I passed a store's large plate glass windows. I glanced at the reflected image of a young woman walking—sweaty, dusty, and dirty. She walked at exactly my pace. Then came an embarrassing moment. That image was me.

I entered Le Lieu's nearly empty lobby, eager to bathe and change clothes. From behind the registration desk, Jacques waved. His deep voice boomed. "Mademoiselle Dupré, good news. The fighting is over—we will sign an armistice!" His face seemed to blossom.

Was Jacques's smile one of relief? Sad lament? Was it the smile of a Reich supporter? There were many of them in Lyon and throughout France.

I walked across the lobby to the registration desk. I said, "Jacques, have we surrendered?" My use of 'we' brought me up short. For the second time that day I wondered, had I adopted France as my home?

Jacques leaned across the desk. He spoke in a collaborative whisper. "Mademoiselle Dupré, less than an hour from now, at 1900 hours, there is to be an important broadcast. I will have the lobby radio turned on. Please join me. We will listen together."

At seven o'clock I joined many of the hotel's residents in the lobby. Beside me sat a young woman with curly black hair, about my age. She introduced herself as Simone. "I also work at 10 *rue des Archers.*"

"I remember." I laughed. "You were with me in the supervisors meeting. You said, 'The government evacuated in its pants.'"

With bubbling giggles, Simone leaned back in her chair. Then quiet and sober-faced, she leaned forward and feigned surprise. "*Moi?*"

Two men who I guessed were in their mid-seventies sat near the young woman and chatted. One of them, missing an arm, wore a WWI French army jacket, its sleeve pinned to the jacket's chest. In a thin voice he said, "I remember the 11th of November 1918, the German surrender."

The other elderly man said, "You mean our signing the armistice with Germany. Correct, M. Pleusiers?"

M. Pleusiers, tapped his cane on the floor, each tap an exclamatory mark of punctuation. "The tables [tap] were then turned [tap] the other way [tap]." He added further punctuation with slaps of his right foot on the hardwood floor.

A middle-aged bald man said, "'The war to end all wars,' we called it. I was in the trenches, the mud. One day I stepped on what looked like a rock. It turned to mush. A man's head."

A tall man, perhaps age eighty, joined the group. His sunken cheeks resembled those of a cadaver. He said, "I was there. At Compiègne. For the signing of the armistice. *Moi! André Bollé.*"

The men seated near him nodded. They murmured words I couldn't hear. Whatever they said prompted M. Bollé to sit rigidly erect.

M. Bollé continued. "I stood guard outside the railcar, the place of the armistice ceremony. Midway through the signing, Marshal Foch, chief of the French armed forces, walked down the railcar's steps. He walked past me." M. Bollé turned to me. "Foch was as close to me as I am to you, young lady. He spoke to me!"

M. Pleusiers tapped with his cane. "What did he say?"

"I will never forget his words." M. Bollé paused as if to remember. "'*Comment allez-vous, soldat?*' Those were his exact words, M. Pleusiers." M. Bollé scanned the faces of people in the lobby. "'How are you, soldier?' That's what he said to me." His face beamed with pride.

Ten minutes later Jacques announced, "It is nearly time. Please, no talking." He turned up the volume of the radio. Bursts of static overrode recorded music. At precisely at seven o'clock, the distinctive and resonant voice of the BBC announcer intoned, "This is BBC's Alvar Lidell. We now take you to a secret location near London. There General Charles de

Gaulle has formed a French government in exile, the Free French. The next voice you hear will be Charles de Gaulle." Goose bumps rose on my arms. Then de Gaulle's strident voice filled the room:

> The leaders who, for many years, have been at the head of the French armies have formed a government. This government, alleging the defeat of our armies, has made contact with the enemy in order to stop the fighting. It is true, we were, we are, overwhelmed by the mechanical, ground, and air forces of the enemy. Infinitely more than their number, it is the tanks, the aeroplanes, the tactics of the Germans, which are causing us to retreat. It was the tanks, the aeroplanes, the tactics of the Germans that surprised our leaders to the point of bringing them to where they are today.
>
> But has the last word been said? Must hope disappear? Is defeat final? No!
>
> Believe me, I who am speaking to you with full knowledge of the facts, and who tell you that nothing is lost for France. The same means that overcame us can bring us victory one day. For France is not alone! She is not alone! She is not alone! She has a vast Empire behind her. She can align with the British Empire that holds the sea and continues the fight. She can, like England, use without limit the immense industry of the United States.
>
> This war is not limited to the unfortunate territory of our country. This war is not over as a result of the Battle of France. This war is a worldwide war. All the mistakes, all the delays, all the suffering, do not alter the fact that there are, in the world, all the means necessary to crush our enemies one day. Vanquished today by mechanical force, in the future we will be able to overcome by a superior mechanical force. The fate of the world depends on it.
>
> I, General de Gaulle, currently in London, invite the officers and the French soldiers who are located in British territory or who might end up here, with their weapons or without their weapons, I invite the engineers and the specialized workers of the armament industries

who are located in British territory or who might end up here, to put themselves in contact with me.

Whatever happens, the flame of the French resistance must not be extinguished and will not be extinguished.

Static-ridden recorded music returned to the radio. For what seemed an hour-long minute, no one spoke.

M. Bollé broke the silence. "General de Gaulle does not accept the truce with Germany. Nor do I." He emphasized each word as he said, "We are the *Free French*."

I looked at the now familiar faces around the lobby. Who among them felt themselves a part of the Free French? Were some of them Nazi sympathizers? Who among them could I trust? Did any of them know the truth about my Jewish and Dutch background?

Jacques walked to a cabinet and returned with a silver tray with small champagne glasses. He paused before each person and nodded as they took a glass from the tray. He returned to the cabinet and removed a bottle of champagne, *1920 G.H. Mumm Brut Millésimé*. Jacques then moved around the lobby and filled each glass. Bubbles rose to their rims.

M. Bollé's eyes widened. In a strong voice, he said, "*Merci*, Jacques. I believe Marshal Foch would declare, '*1920 Mumm, c'est ce qui se boit de mieux!*'"

Jacques stood straight, like a soldier commanded to stand at attention. "*Mes amis*, my friends, *s'il vous plaît, levez-vous*, please stand."

Everyone rose.

Jacques raised his glass. "On this sad day, to General de Gaulle. To France!"

In a single voice, the group chanted, "To France!" M. Pleusiers waved his cane toward the ceiling.

At work the next morning, the mail brought me a note from Aimée. "I'm back on the job at the museum. Did you listen to the speech? De Gaulle brings hope. My museum work continues to go well."

I thought about the last time we talked, the "network" she mentioned. Aimée said Carmille was developing a similar project. I wondered what it was? Would I become involved in it?

Occupée et Libre
22 June 1940

Early on a cloudless summer morning, I left my room and entered the lift. Cables creaked until, with a jolt, the lift arrived at the lobby. The door, with its narrow bands of steel, swung open.

Jacques excitedly called from behind the registration desk. "A reminder, Mademoiselle!" Jacques face beamed with a bright smile.

"I know," I said. "Today we will formally sign the armistice!"

"*Oui!*"

The following day I overheard M. Bollé again tell the other elderly residents of the hotel his story about the signing of the WWI Armistice. This time he brought it up to date. "Yesterday at *Compiègne*, Hitler insulted us by mimicking Marshal Foch at the 1918 armistice ceremony. Halfway through it, he stood, an insult in itself, and then walked out, just as Foch did. Did I tell you Marshal Foch spoke to me?" The listeners nodded, yes. "I'm honored I was there for him—and thankful I was not there yesterday for an insult from that strutting little Austrian from Linz."

At the Military Recruitment Service, each morning Lieutenant Lacroix placed new editions of Lyon and Paris newspapers on a table near the mailboxes in the lobby. The stories spoke to citizens of France. After I read them, I felt even more like a refugee without a country, adrift and unsafe. People huddled together to share the newspapers. "What will the Germans do in Lyon? Will our lives change?" The questions hung in mid-air, unanswered.

Three days later, in the hotel lobby a stout man wearing gritty brown work clothes looked up from his newspaper and muttered to me, "Have you read today's news?"

I nodded. "Yes."

With hardly a pause he continued, "The Germans have divided us into zones. It's as though France has become two countries. *La Zone Occupée* and *La Zone Non-Occupée*. Occupied and Free Zones."

Simone walked out of the elevator and joined our group. Her dark eyes seemed to dance when she talked. Her never-ending arm and hand gestures punctuated every sentence, sometimes swooped to place glissando on a phrase. Her movements were like small birds flying around her petite body.

A man in a business suit, his face familiar, no doubt a resident of Le Lieu, looked up from his newspaper. In a raspy voice he said, "The Occupied Zone." He turned to me. "Have you looked at a map of that zone's territory? A wide swath across central and northern France. It includes the northern and western coasts. Sixty percent of our country. Under the direct control of Paris's new landlord, Adolph Hitler. Can you imagine that?"

"I saw a map in a newspaper."

M. Bollé, seated nearby, said, "Lyon and the remainder of France are in the non-occupied zone. Officials are calling it the Free Zone." His dark eyes flashed. "Free. Give thanks for that."

"Free Zone?" I asked. "Is it really free?"

M. Bollé said, "I'm fearful of what the Nazis call free."

Simone waved her arms. "Soldiers on every street corner?" She paused and looked around the group. "Two months ago, I escaped from Poland. At a prison camp in Poland the Germans put up a sign, *Arbeit Mach Frei*. Work makes you free." She hurled a sarcastic "Ha!" across the room. "Life is often the opposite of what the Nazis say."

I glanced around the lobby. A man in a dark well-pressed suit kept his eyes on Simone. Had he overheard her remarks? Was he German? A Gestapo officer?

The Demographic Service

M. Bollé greeted me over morning coffee in the hotel lobby. He sat down beside me. "We are four days from Bastille Day, yes? When all France celebrates freedom. What will the Germans permit?"

"We're in the Free Zone, M. Bollé. Why would anything change?"

"Yes, you might think that, but . . ." His voice drifted into silence. As if to dismiss me, he stood, gave me a look of doubt, and walked to the lift.

I walked to work in the unusually warm July air. By the time I entered 10 rue des Archers my blouse was damp with sweat. In the large steel-walled elevator, I pressed the button for the third floor. The elevator rose, silent except for the whirr of the shaft's gears and creaks of the car's cables. The industrial-sized doors opened onto a cavernous room. I thought about the tasks that awaited me: First, to set up an additional mechanography training workshop. Then to train and direct staff to accurately code, keypunch, and process thousands of data cards. Staff of the Military Recruitment Service commonly called them IBM cards.

Lt. Lacroix had told me our workshop would be similar to others already in operation, including one in Occupied Paris. "I'm glad we're not alone. I've never set up a workshop."

"I haven't either."

"I hope we can get help if we need it."

When I entered the room, the staff was already there. One man sat in a windowsill smoking. Most of them milled around the recently uncrated keypunch machines, tabulators, and processors. A few had begun to load boxes of punchcards onto shelves and cabinets rising halfway to the ceiling. I quickly called a meeting and began the work of getting organized.

Mid-morning Lt. Lacroix asked the supervisors to meet with him in the conference room. He sat at the head of the room's rectangular oak table. Twelve of us occupied chairs around the table. At least ten more stood behind us. Simone sat across the table from me.

"Please, your attention," Lt. Lacroix said. "It's warm in here, and I know you are busy. I will be brief." He then repeated what I assumed everyone had already read in the newspapers. "As you probably know, under the terms of the armistice, France is to be divided into two zones, *Occupée* and *Non-occupée*."

Simone looked at me and rolled her eyes. Her lips formed the words, "Yes, we know."

The lieutenant continued, "What you may not yet know, the National Assembly has voted to install the French government, well, the government of the *Zone Non-Occupée*, in the city of Vichy."

In a voice of disbelief, a supervisor said, "Vichy? It's only one hundred kilometers from Lyon."

Lt. Lacroix continued, "Yes, our neighbors in the Vichy government will administer laws and have legal authority for the *Zone Non-Occupée* portion of our country, including Lyon."

Simone and I acted as if the lieutenant's announcement was news. The day before at Le Lieu, M. Bollé had briefed us on designation of the nearby city of Vichy as seat of the Free Zone government.

Lt. Lacroix held a telegram. He looked around the room. His voice deepened and his speech slowed. "I have received this." He lowered his gaze to the cream-colored paper and gripped it as if it might attempt escape. "The National Assembly has voted to ratify a new government. *Maréchal* Philippe Pétain has been named Head of State."

He lifted his gaze toward the ceiling and then looked around the room. He made eye contact with each person. "I will be honored to serve under *Maréchal* Pétain." He again scanned the faces in the room. "I trust that you will, too."

People nodded.

"Thank you. That's all for now. Let's get back to work."

Along with Simone and me, supervisors seated at the table stood. The room buzzed with conversations. "Pétain! *Le Maréchal*!" A middle-aged man spoke over the hubbub of the room. "In the last war, I was at Verdun. Pétain turned defeat into victory! I said then, I say now, I will follow Pétain anywhere."

Simone's laugh bubbled across the room. She said, "With all due respect, when *Maréchal* Pétain was born Napoleon III was in power. Pétain is eighty-four years old. To follow him anywhere would not be difficult." Others laughed.

Lt. Lacroix looked up from his papers. "Oh, one more thing." Conversations stopped. Everyone turned to him.

"In the next few months, we expect our organization to be merged with SGF, *La Statistique générale de la France*. As some of you know, SGF is a smaller statistical and census bureau. When this occurs, we will be designated the *Service de la Démographie*, The Demographic Service. That's all for now. I'll keep you informed." Lt. Lacroix stood. Conversations resumed.

I walked a few steps toward the door. I stopped as it opened. A slight middle-aged man with thinning hair, wearing a rumpled grey suit, entered the room. From last year's seminar: Professor Carmille! His round, wire-rimmed eyeglasses, along with the books he carried, gave him the professorial look I remembered. His bright eyes scanned the room.

Lt. Lacroix braced to attention, his gaze riveted on the man in the doorway. "*Mon Général!*"

Everyone turned toward the man. He walked with a slight limp to the head of the table and stood next to Lt. Lacroix. He gave us a small smile and gently waved one hand in a greeting. "Please, be at ease, Lieutenant. I had hoped to be here earlier. Everyone, please excuse my tardiness.

"General Carmille, welcome."

"I have met a few of you. I am the director of the Military Recruitment Service. We will be working together."

Lt. Lacroix continued to stand at attention. "We just finished a meeting, sir."

Carmille smiled. "Thank you, Lieutenant. Please, stand at ease."

"Thank you, *Mon Général*." Lt. Lacroix then stood with his feet apart, his hands clasped behind him.

Carmille's gaze traveled around the room. He made eye contact with each person. He spoke slowly, his voice resonant. "As supervisors and managers, you are at the heart of our work. We have much to do in the coming months. Please invest time in a search for improvements in the processes and organization of our workflow. When you find possibilities for improvements, act on them. You needn't wait on my approval." He gave the group a businesslike, yet gentle, grin. "We are in this together. We will succeed together."

Lt. Lacroix said, "Thank you, sir."

"It's too warm to linger here. Please, go about your business. I wanted only to say hello and introduce myself."

That afternoon I knocked on the open door of Lt. Lacroix's small office. He looked up from his desk. "Yes?"

"Lieutenant, may I speak with you?"

"Of course. I have a few minutes." He pointed to the stack of papers before him. "These reports have to go out today." Then he nodded toward a chair surrounded by boxes on the other side of his desk. "Please, sit down."

"Thank you."

"What is this about, Miriam?"

"Our meeting this morning. Well, about M. Carmille."

"General Carmille."

"General?"

"I prefer to call him that. Before his appointment to head the Service, he was, still is, the Comptroller General of the French Army."

"Last year I attended his economics seminar at *École Libre des Sciences Politiques*. It was a large class. I doubt if he remembers me."

"You were one of his students?"

"Briefly. Just the seminar. A few weeks."

Lt. Lacroix leaned back in his chair. "Very impressive."

"Can you tell me more about him? I've read some of his papers and one of his books."

"I didn't know about the books."

"There are two. We used *La Méchanographie dans les administrations* in the seminar. We read some chapters in the other one, *Vues d'Economie Objective*. But the seminar was mostly about mechanography."

"You're well versed in his work."

"Not really. There's so much. His publications are like an iceberg. I know only what's visible, and not all of that. I know little about his background."

"I can share what I know, and that's not a lot." He tapped the folder on his desk and laughed. "I should say, I can share what I've read."

He opened a folder on his desk and scanned the first page. He read aloud. "Léon François René Carmille. Born in 1886 in Trémolat, in Dordogne. He grew up there. His parents were teachers. He was a bright and mathematically gifted student. He later studied at the *École Polytechnique*, X 06."

"X 06?"

"X refers to the crossed fronds in *Polytechnique's* crest. It is followed by the last two digits of the year of graduation. Most of France's distinguished engineers and many of our generals are graduates of *École Polytechnique*."

"I understand. M. Carmille graduated in 1906."

"Correct. He chose to serve in the French army's artillery."

The lieutenant turned to the folder's second page. He scanned it, running his index finger down the page, while he talked. "Carmille served as an artillery captain in WWI. He was wounded in combat and later awarded the *Légion d'honneur* and *Croix de Guerre*." The lieutenant looked away. Then the lieutenant seemed to speak more to himself than to me. "I knew something of his decorations and valor."

His eyes on the folder's papers, Lt. Lacroix continued to read. "After the war M. Carmille became part of the corps of *Contrôleurs des Armées*, consulted to government offices, and taught at the *École Libre des Sciences Politiques*. He also lectured at the Sorbonne on the history of mechanical computation."

I interrupted, "I have, well, I once had, printed copies of those lectures. Also, the lecture he gave to the banking technology congress— do you know about that one? 1937. I had a copy of that, too."

The lieutenant's eyes widened, and he sat up. "Yes, those lectures, they're mentioned here." He nodded towards the file he held and continued to scan its pages. "Carmille's book, *La Mécanographie dans les administrations*, was read by many government financial officials."

"I read it, too."

"In 1934 the Secretary General of the Ministry of War commissioned M. Carmille to assess the need for reform in the Military Recruitment Service."

"That's us, right?"

"Yes." The lieutenant continued to read. "Carmille presented five reports. It says here that he advocated comprehensive reform in the Recruitment and Mobilization Service Centers. Did you know about that?"

"I read a little about it."

"And, new to me, what about his proposal for a thirteen–digit identification number for each member of the armed services? The numbers would represent each soldier's age, gender, education and training, specialty skills, and so on."

"I knew he had proposed it." I could feel a rising excitement. With it, my voice rose. "If those numbers were in place, think of all we could do."

"You're way beyond me. What might we do?"

I spoke with enthusiasm. "Quantify current skills and capacities of divisions, battalions, different combinations of army units, their training needs, readiness for combat, their strengths. Deficiencies, too. I loved to tackle those kinds of problems. I saw in the methods and technology for doing all this the wave of the future. A lot of my fellow students at the School of Economics thought I was weird to care about such things. But the best professors and the dean agreed with me, urged me on."

"I'm afraid I wouldn't know where to begin."

In an eager voice, I said, "In our work here, we could convert our records to tabulator cards, all keypunched with information codes. Then process the cards, tabulate results, and generate statistical summaries pointing to priorities for action."

The lieutenant leaned back in his chair. "You sound like Gen. Carmille. You've thought a lot about this. You bring a lot of knowledge to the Service. I'm envious. My university studies were in the social sciences. Then I began to study law. Until the war."

"Only a temporary halt, I hope."

Lt. Lacroix shrugged. "Today I'm just a lieutenant on desk duty in a war we're losing." His voice trailed away. "I mean, a war we've already lost."

"It's too soon to know that. Things happen. There are many ways to fight."

His voice flat, Lt. Lacroix said, "We surrendered ten days ago." He looked at the papers on his desk. "I've got to get back to my reports." The lieutenant turned to the document on top of the stack of papers before him. "Oh yes, Gen. Carmille consulted with agencies of the government and represented the Minister of War on the Production Commission and Exchanges. He advocated the adoption of tabulator and punch-card technologies to modernize information processing for the entire government."

I blurted out, "He was way ahead of the French government, ahead of most European countries—with the possible exception of the Third Reich. He understood the power of mechanography. What it could do to bring speed and measurement into economic and financial systems."

"You know a lot more than you gave yourself credit for. I'm impressed. You know mechanography and its applications. You know Gen. Carmille's work."

I leaned forward. "I've studied it. In the world of government administration, what he has proposed is like going from horse-drawn carriages to piston engines."

"That's powerful."

"I've read that some people believe the Germans are making widespread use of the technology. Possibly managing supplies, armaments, personnel, food allocations." I sat back in my chair.

The lieutenant said, "If that's true, we'll have to run at twice the speed just to catch up."

I paused. "Should I refer to him as General Carmille? Monsieur Carmille?"

"Either way is all right. He prefers the simpler, civilian, 'monsieur.' But he told me 'general' is fine, if that's what I want to call him."

"Two of his books were texts in my studies at the university." I almost said, "In the Netherlands." Whoops! I added, "In Paris."

With no acknowledgement of my near slip of the tongue, the lieutenant continued. "I'll read you this final note about him. 'René Carmille was a member of various government commissions. His proposed financial reforms led to his appointment in 1932 as Comptroller General of the French Army.' And then, as you know, to his being named to head the Military Recruitment Service. That brings us full circle, back to where we started."

The lieutenant returned the document to its folder. "Now, I must get to work."

I felt my face redden as I stood. "I'm sorry to take so much of your time. Thank you for briefing me."

"His work means a lot to me, too. Perhaps we can find another time to talk. When we are not so busy."

"Yes, I would like that. Life at the hotel gets boring." I hesitated then said, "I know few people in Lyon."

I walked along the corridor to my workroom office. I reflected on Lt. Lacroix. He was handsome, not much older than me. Might we . . . then, as I entered my workroom, my thoughts migrated back to the mundane and everyday matters of the Service. Our cavernous space was crammed with tabulation and punchcard machines, file cabinets, shelves, typewriters, and desks—technology and materials that could transform government operations. The tasks facing me suddenly loomed large. For a moment I felt overwhelmed. I sat down at my desk and stared at the boxes, machines, and files surrounding me. If Gen. Carmille could tackle the financial and personnel management of the French government, then I could . . . could what? Well, by God, I could organize and manage the records stacked in front of me. And do it well!

Simone entered my office with an armload of files. "Miriam, where should these should be filed?"

I said, "René Carmille is here, Simone. We are working with him!" I spoke as if I hadn't heard her request.

Simone stared blankly at me. "What?"

I reached across my desk and picked up a stack of blank punchcards. "These cards will be punched. The holes in each column will represent coded numbers. And those will represent people, military capabilities, financial systems." I waved the cards toward the room's crates. "Carmille's management revolution—we're part of it!"

Simone gave me a blank stare and then a weak smile.

Simone's flat reaction notwithstanding, I felt a burst of enthusiasm, like a powerful wave that had risen from the bottom of the ocean. Then, as if the wave had crashed on a rocky shore, I remembered—France surrendered to Germany. We were under the control of the Reich. Rivulets of disappointment flowed down my imaginary seashore.

"A revolution in information processing?" Simone asked, her voice tentative. Then firmer, "Isn't it already going on elsewhere? You told me about your work with IBM machines in Holland. Central Statistics Bureau. Rumor among Lyon Jews I know is that the Dutch are using IBM equipment to identify and track Jewish families. You know about that? What about in Germany? The other Occupied countries? Will that happen here? Will we be part of it?"

I didn't answer her. Simone turned and walked away. Why hadn't I told her the truth about myself—a Jew, Dutch?

That night I lay awake. My imagination leaped out of control. Thoughts jumped from Simone's questions to roundups of Lyon Jews, to Luftwaffe bombs in Rotterdam, to my family, to buildings in flames. The once grand Boompjes Synagogue, had it become rubble strewn across its courtyard? Had Papa, Mama, and Margot become ashes? That special carrel of Lars's and mine, tucked away in a dark corner of the library's stacks, now rubble? My muscles tensed. My inner voice screamed, "Stop!" But nightmare images of bombs raining on Rotterdam continued. All the newspaper photos and stories of the bombs' destruction, news I wished I had never read, fueled the dark side of my imagination.

Did my family know death was dropping on them? Had they cried out as a bomb struck our building? Had they been trapped alive beneath the rubble. For a day? Longer? My heart raced.

Deaths. Faces of loved ones, now gone. My stomach tightened. Nausea welled up. I leaped from bed and ran for the toilet.

A Voice from the Past

Early on a warm July morning I waited in the lobby for Simone. We could walk to work together. She surprised me by coming through the hotel's large revolving front door. She hurried across the lobby to join me. Her hands waved toward the front door. "Have you been outside?"

"No."

"The Germans." Simone waved her arms. Her eyes widened. The golden-brown irises of her eyes seemed to shine. "Soldiers. Many of them. On the streets. They are like tourists."

"It's time to go to work. Let's go." I laughed. "We can look at the tourist soldiers."

"Sorry. I have things I must do first. I'll be a little late this morning."

On my walk to 10 rue des Archers, I looked up at the newly raised Vichy flags. The new flag was based on the French tricolor. Added were a baton with a circle of eight small gold stars beneath it in the center, white, band of the tricolor flag, red and blue bands on either side flanking it. I walked past a group of young German soldiers, their grey-green uniforms, field green the Germans called it, all neatly pressed. They entered a café, laughing and jostling one another. Simone was right. Except for the uniforms, they could be tourists.

In early August, Vichy flags flew from the tops of buildings, lampposts, and street signs. On walls and fences, posters of Maréchal Philippe Pétain in his French army uniform joined the flags. At the base of each poster,

Pétain's new motto for Vichy France: *Travail, Famille, Patrie.*

I muttered, "Work, Family, Homeland. Whatever happened to Liberty, Equality, Fraternity?" I liked the old motto. Those were principles I could respect, could stand for. Work, Family, Homeland did little for me.

During my early morning walks to work, German soldiers along the street sometimes stared at me. On occasion one of them might smile. Then in uncertain or mispronounced French greet me with a flirtatious, "*Bonjour.*"

When this happened, I felt my face redden. I just continued to walk, my eyes straight ahead.

One morning I looked at my reflection in a store's plate glass window. Then my brain played a trick on me. My thoughts returned to a time when I stared at my image and turned away from it. My thirteenth birthday. I had been the first in our family to awaken that morning. In the living room, I looked at my image in the mirror above the mantel. Why couldn't I be like other girls? My crossed eye—did it come from a flaw? A failure within me? A form of punishment from the Gods? Could I exercise the willpower to straighten it?

I stared hard at my mirror image. I summoned my mental energy and focused on that eye. An inner voice commanded, *Straighten!* I stared at my crossed eye until I lost focus and the mirror's image blurred. I glanced at the living room's clock. I had stared for ten minutes. I closed my eyes and bowed my head. Dear God, please take away my flaw. Another ten minutes of staring. *Straighten, damn you!*

My crossed eye defied my commands. I slumped. When I heard Margot get out of bed, I walked away, battle lost.

All was not lost. In my teen years, I excelled in academic studies as well as speed skating and judo. My body surprised me. I grew tall, thin, and shapely. Boys flirted with me. I learned to see myself as attractive. Well, more or less. But my view of myself, however lovely I wanted that image to be, was always moderated by my crossed eye. My flaw.

Over time, I came to accept that part of me. Still, I wondered, am I pretty? My uncertainties lingered. My crossed eye became the keystone in my foundation of self-doubt. During the next decade, those doubts lingered. But during my adolescent years my athletic prowess blossomed.

Coaches wanted to work with me. Boys wanted to be with me. My self-confidence, though shaky, strengthened.

On my early morning walks to 10 rue des Archers, I felt confident enough to return the flirtatious gazes of the Vichy French and German soldiers. Each time, with an inward smile I reminded myself, yes, I am worthy of their attention. Even with my flaw.

Sometimes, usually at night before I fell asleep, I dealt with my self-doubt by recalling Lars's kiss. I remembered what I had not told Aimée, had not told anyone—that I had spent the night in his apartment, in his bed. I recalled the sensations of his gentle touch. The thrill as he entered me—my first experience in making love.

In late August, on a morning walk to work I passed a young soldier. His face had become one of the familiar faces I passed each morning. When he gazed at me I smiled inwardly. With confidence and without an outward smile, I returned his look.

An unseen, somber, and familiar male voice ended my inner smile. *Miriam, they destroyed Rotterdam.*

I gasped—Papa? I looked around. I was well past the German soldier. There was no one near.

The voice continued. *The soldiers who stare at you, Miriam.*

I threw back my shoulders and quickened my pace. Yes?

They flirt with you, a young woman with a crossed eye. You enjoy the attention. The voice paused and then asked, *Tell me, do you think they know they are flirting with a Jew? A woman the Fuehrer would call not only subhuman, but also genetically flawed?*

I shook my head. Papa's private brand of humor?

As I approached 10 rue des Archers, a gust of wind sent swirls of dust along the street. Clouds parted. A bright sun sharpened my shadow. The windows of tall buildings reflected suddenly-arrived fluffy clouds and bright blue sky.

I glanced back at the soldiers. They had turned their attention to other young women.

Those soldiers are just boys, Miriam. Hear me, those boys and their brothers, their fathers and uncles destroyed Rotterdam. Killed your family, and your friends. Remember that. Remember who you are. Where you are. When the time comes, will you confront them?

Confront them? Why, Papa? They don't know me. Today I am the woman in my carte d'identité. Miriam Dupré, French. Not Miriam Meijer, Dutch Jew.

Are you? Who is this Miriam Dupré? Tell me about her. The voice paused. *One day, perhaps today, tomorrow, next month, you will be asked by someone to do that. Will you be ready? People unknown to you created Miriam Dupré. You must have lived her life. Fully. Talk about it, warts and all.*

The voice paused and then said, *For now, Miriam Dupré is out of harm's way. In the future, what will those unknown people ask of her—of you? And then, what is Miriam Dupré prepared to do?*

Wondering about Papa's questions, I opened the front door of 10 rue des Archers.

After the big door slammed shut behind me, I continued to reflect on Papa's question: *What is Miriam Dupré prepared to do?* Then came another question, *What will she not do?*

Autumn
October 1940

I walked across Le Lieu's lobby to the dining room. I imagined my start of the morning—the rich taste of coffee and a croissant. Or a freshly baked roll. That is, if the baker was able to get flour. Scarcities popped up ever more frequently. Usually when we least expected them. Simone said France now had to feed the German army. Recently, the hotel's breakfast rolls had been stale. At least two days old. In order to eat mine, I had to dunk it in coffee. My plans were to order a café crème. Then I wondered if the hotel had coffee, now rationed. Or crème. Along with butter meat, and eggs. If no coffee were served, I would, I told myself with reluctance then drink a cup of café national, the chicory substitute for coffee. If, if, if. Life seemed to have become a long series of ifs in a world of uncertainty. I remembered what Papa said after bad things happened, "It could be worse." Yes, it could.

Simone and I sat on the large couch in the lobby for a few minutes. She had heard rumors, but couldn't confirm, that her parents had been shipped to a prison camp, what some people now called a concentration camp. She said, "Am I next?" She wept.

I put my arms around her. "I worry, too." I debated whether to continue and then said, "I am a Dutch Jew."

"You are?"

"Some people in Lyon know my background. I fear word will reach the Gestapo. Then I don't know what might happen."

M. Bollé walked in and sat next to us in his favorite lounge chair. He smoked a cigarette. *"Bonjour, Miriam. Simone."*

"Bonjour, M. Bollé."

He called to Jacques, behind the registration desk. "Have you seen this?" He held up a newspaper. On the front page were photographs of Maréchal Pétain and Chancellor Hitler shaking hands.

Jacques's face tightened. *"Oui."* His brow creased. The corners of his mouth sagged in a frown. "Yesterday at *Montoire-sur-le-Loir.*"

M. Bollé tapped his index finger against the photo. "That meeting, what does it mean?"

Jacques shrugged. *"Maréchal* Pétain is a great man." Jacques's frown lines smoothed. In a confident voice, he added, "Pétain will do what is right."

"My sources tell me *Maréchal* Pétain now does Laval's bidding."

"Laval is only Prime Minister. Number two. I would never have appointed him." Then, in a voice less confident than a moment ago, Jacques said, "Remember, Pétain is our leader."

My thoughts lingered on my disclosure to Simone. I suddenly imagined a Gestapo agent brutally interrogating her. "Who are your Jewish friends?" My stomach contracted. My thoughts leaped to the security of my Jewish roots.

The High Holidays would soon arrive. Our family attended services at Boompjes Synagogue. Rosh Hasahanah, celebration of the Jewish New Year, and Yom Kippur, the day of atonement were, each year, periods in which we reconnected to our heritage. Boompjes was destroyed in the firestorm of last May. Would my heritage—would I—suffer the same fate? I tried to speak to Simone. Words shriveled in my throat.

Late that afternoon in my group's cavernous workspace, we opened crates and boxes, logged their contents. I sat at a large worktable covered with stacks of files. I inspected two files at a time and made entries on a master form. Each time I completed an entry, I moved those files to the top of a stack on the right side of my worktable. I then removed two files from the top of a stack on the table's left side, placed them before me and repeated the process. The files seemed never to end. I felt like King Sisyphus in Greek mythology, condemned to roll a boulder up a hill only to watch it roll back down. Then start over. For all eternity.

I was so focused on the files before me that I didn't hear the door open. I glanced up at Lt. Lacroix as he entered the room. Behind him was a tall man in a gray suit.

"*Bonjour*, Miriam."

I leaned back in my chair. "Ah, Lieutenant."

"I apologize for the interruption." Lt. Lacroix half-turned to the man behind him. "Miriam, say hello to a visitor, Charles Delmand. He is a reporter for *The Times of London*. I believe you and Charles have met. Charles, you remember Miriam Dupré."

I stood, mouth half open, eyes wide.

Charles smiled and extended his hand. "It's nice to see you again, Miriam."

I recovered my composure and replied, "*Merci*. My pleasure, M. Delmand."

The lieutenant said, "As you know, Miriam is trained in mechanography." He turned to me. "Charles is writing an article on our technology."

"Is that what brings you here?"

The lieutenant interrupted. "Miriam, you know the operations of our mechanography far better than me. Can you spend a little time with Charles? Introduce him to our work?"

Charles laughed. "I promise to be a diligent student."

"Tomorrow morning Charles will meet with Gen. Carmille. It would help if you could brief him on our work."

I pointed to the small stack of files on the left side of my worktable. "I need to log in these files. Then I'll be free."

"That's fine. In the meantime, I have a few more questions for Lt. Lacroix."

The two men walked toward the door. Charles glanced up at the clock. He turned to me. "It's nearly the end of the workday. Is there somewhere I could meet you for conversation and a glass of wine? I promise not to interfere with your plans for the evening."

"I have no plans for the evening. I'm staying at *Hôtel Le Lieu*, not far from here. *Rue Bellecordière*. Can we meet in the hotel lobby? In about an hour?"

"That works well. Though I should warn you," he said with a grin, "I had no lunch today. By then I'll be famished."

My thoughts leaped to our dinner in Paris, months ago. I remembered my hunger that night. With Le Lieu's shortage of food during the past week, I again felt that intensity of hunger—and a quick surge of anger. Many people talked of well-fed Vichy and Reich officials—no food shortages for them. I wanted to yell, "Charles, all over Lyon people are hungry! Can't you do something about it?" I took a deep breath and reminded myself that Charles had nothing to do with the food shortage.

"I would be pleased if you would join me for dinner. Can you do that?"

"*Oui. Avec plaisir.*"

Our dinner in Paris—the excitement I felt in Charles's presence. Perhaps Ruth had, too. She had acted as if she and Charles might have been intimate. Although, with Parisians I had learned, I could never be certain.

After work, I rushed to the hotel. I quickly bathed and put on a clean khaki skirt and red blouse. I arrived in the lobby as Charles entered the hotel.

We greeted each other with the French custom of cheek-to-cheek light kisses.

Charles held me at arms' length. His eyes scanned me, head to foot. "So good to see you."

Was there flirtation in his gaze? Or had that come from me? "Thank you. This is a nice surprise."

Charles extended his arm. I locked my arm through his. We walked out of the hotel.

This time one year ago, my family prayed in preparation for Rosh Hashanah. This year my prayers had simply been for survival. Tonight, I was walking arm-in-arm with an older man. The Rosh Hashanah I once knew seems like part of a distant past. One that belonged to another woman, a Miriam Meijer, not Miriam Dupré.

The dinner pyramid

The day had been warm, bright, and clear. In the evening's dusk, Charles and I strolled leisurely toward the Saône. Along the streets, tree leaves bore traces of yellow and red. We walked in silence across the wide expanse of Place Bellecour. Ahead of us, across the river, was Cathédrale St. Jean, its construction completed in the fifteenth century. Above the mountain behind it, the sunset glowed orange and pink. Vivid only moments earlier, the pastel colors softened and faded in the growing darkness. The air carried scents of the full, perhaps final, blooms of autumn flowers.

Near the Saône's pont Bonaparte, we turned right on quai des Celéstines.

After we'd walked a block further, Charles said, "I know a café, *Chez Claude*, nearby. Claude, the owner and chef, is very resourceful. He sometimes makes food purchases in the black market. He's very creative with whatever he can buy."

As we entered the café, Claude, a round man with long gray hair combed back from his wide ruddy face, nodded to me and greeted us warmly, "Charles, *mon ami!* Welcome. You have been away too long." He hugged Charles, and they, too, exchanged the customary bise.

During our walk Charles had told me he'd met Claude in Paris in the early 1930s. At the time, Claude managed a small bistro, one of Charles's favorites, in Montmartre. One winter evening seated at the bar alone,

Charles was the bistro's last patron. Claude joined him, poured them each a brandy. Claude talked of his wife, who had recently left him. He lamented, "Five years together. I gave and gave. Never enough! When I had nothing more to give, she is gone."

Charles said, "Twice I came close to marriage. I could never combine marriage with my work. So I remained alone." They drank brandy and shared stories of their lives until three o'clock in the morning.

"Claude, please meet my friend and colleague, Miriam Dupré. She works at 10 *rue des Archers*."

I extended my hand. Claude bowed and placed a light kiss on my fingertips. "Welcome, Mademoiselle."

"Is an outdoor table all right?" Charles asked.

"A perfect evening for it," I said.

Claude seated us at a table that overlooked the Saône. In the light of sunset, reflections of Cathédrale St. Jean sparkled on the river. On the distant side of the patio, two Nazi officers dined.

Charles studied the wine list. "We are in the heart of the superb vineyards." He smiled at me. "A glass of wine before dinner? Your favorite?"

"I would enjoy a glass of wine. But please, you choose. On my budget, I haven't learned to make Lyon wine choices." Charles laughed. Me too.

I liked the way Charles laughed. I recalled the year Aimée and I had studied biology. In our exchanges of letters, we had developed a truncated version of the Linnaean Zoological Nomenclature that classified laughter. We tested our system on family and friends. Had Aimée been present with Charles and me at Claude's bistro, she might have said, "Charles's laugh? Human, male, baritone, hearty." I imagined Charles's possible application of our system to a description of my laugh, "Human, female, alto, hearty."

A middle-aged waiter, his wide face creased with deep furrows of smile lines, came to their table.

Charles ordered a half-carafe of a local winery's chardonnay.

After the waiter left, there was a long silence. Then Charles said, "Your work at the Service? Is it going well?"

My gaze remained on the waiter. He stood at the café's bar placing a carafe on a tray. I nodded, yes.

My eyes on the waiter, in a subdued voice, I said, "The lieutenant

would know better than I. We're told major changes are about to happen."
My voice strengthened. "The Service will soon merge with SGF, the
statistical bureau."

"I heard about the merger. Rumor is the SGF people are not happy
about it."

I smiled. "That will be Gen. Carmille's problem."

"All those files in the room where you worked this afternoon, what
are they?"

"Personnel records of soldiers. I have a staff of ten. Soon it will grow
larger. We record and organize files. Thousands of them." My voice trailed
away. "Dull, but important, work. We are one workshop among many."

We again sat in silence. I continued to watch the waiter.

Charles leaned toward me. "You have an odd look on your face. Is
something wrong?"

"The waiter." I glanced at him and then at the Nazi officers. I spoke in
a whisper. "He keeps his eyes on the Germans. What's going on?"

"The anti-Semitic laws and regulations in Germany—they've begun to be
implemented in the Occupied Zone. Vichy's recent anti-Semitic regulations
and restrictions on Jews are following those of the Occupied Zone."

"Will the waiter have to wear a Jewish star?"

"Probably. For now, he doesn't have to."

I lowered my voice, "The Germans call Vichy France *la Zone Libre*,
The Free Zone. Is that an oxymoron?"

Charles smiled. He scanned nearby tables. He too lowered his voice.
"Your question about the waiter and the Jewish star? I believe what we're
seeing is only the forward edge of Vichy restrictions on Jews."

"Yesterday at the Service, a Vichy army officer who is Jewish, told me
he'd learned of his removal. Not just from his job." I was barely able to
control my voice. "From the army."

"You have a job at the Service. You're safe. That's what's important."

"Am I? You and I know the truth." I sat up straight. My face paled.
"You and some other people in your, what do you call it?" I whispered,
"The Underground?"

"You can call it that." In a near whisper, Charles said, "Or, the
Resistance."

I replied, "Whatever it's called, people, your colleagues, could leak information. Some of them may be double agents. Or collaborators. What if Vichy finds out my real name—learns I'm a Jew? Won't they come after me? What then?"

"What if, what if? We could chase shadows all evening. I know we can't ignore dangerous possibilities. But we can't succumb to fear."

"It's my life. I'd like to keep it."

"When I gave you your *carte d'identité* I said you would be protected with a new identity. School, family, friends, work history—all based in France, not Holland. You've prepared that, haven't you?"

I sat up, my back rigid. In a tense yet subdued voice, I said, "Here's a start. I attended schools in Paris. I excelled in mathematics and won a scholarship to *École Supérieure de Commerce de Paris*. My father was a carpenter. My mother died during my adolescence. Blood poisoning. I have no siblings." I looked at Charles for confirmation. "I know I must do more to round it out. But how am I doing?"

"You're doing well. Please, relax. You aren't hiding in the alleys of Paris or Lyon. You are in a good place. My associates and I secured your new identity. I arranged for your work at the Service. I can do other things. Keep in mind, you are not alone."

"I believe you. But I worry."

"I worry, too. Yet I know our best defense is to stay focused on the work we have in front of us."

"I know the work I do at the Service. What do we have before us?"

"You may have seen the newspaper photos. Hitler and Pétain."

"Yes. Did I miss something? Are there implications for me?"

The waiter arrived with our entrées. Crepes, a large omelet, and roasted peppers with goat cheese.

My eyes widened. "Those are huge!"

"I ordered *le grand* portions." Charles laughed. "I guessed you might be as hungry as I am. Let's enjoy our dinner."

After my first bite of omelet, I exclaimed, "Mmm . . . delicious! A rare treat. Dinners at Le Lieu are far less, well, less everything, and less nourishing. Eggs and meat have nearly disappeared." I had to restrain myself from wolfing down my omelet.

Charles ordered another carafe of chardonnay. We ate with gusto. Spurts of conversation centered on our entrées, the joys of good food and wine, and the growth of food shortages in Lyon.

The Nazi officers rose to leave. I watched them walk out of the bistro.

"The lieutenant asked me to brief you on mechanography. Do I need to do that?"

Charles grinned. "To ease my way into time with you, I convinced Lt. Lacroix I still had much to learn about the technology. Between us, I know enough about tabulators and mechanography to speak with René Carmille tomorrow. Thanks in part to you and our discussion in Rotterdam."

"I enjoyed our talk."

"I did too. Are you aware of the scope of mechanography inside the Reich?"

"Just a little. I've heard talk about the Jewish censuses. In Occupied Holland and in other countries."

"That's a good start. There's much more."

"How much more?"

"Let me begin with the larger picture. I find it helpful to think of the Reich as engaged in three wars. Or, I suppose we could say a single war on three fronts."

"Three? And they are?"

"First, on the military front the German government now fights a ground and air war against the Allies. Right now, most of it is in the air against Great Britain."

"While American freighters dodge German U-boats to supply the British. Right?"

"Right." Charles sipped his chardonnay. "The Reich also fights on a less visible second front—against enemies within Germany and the Occupied countries."

"The war against the Jews."

Charles refilled our wine glasses. "As you mentioned, the Reich has ordered a census, or registration, of Jews in each of the Occupied countries. Once those censuses have been completed, the technology of IBM's mechanography will equip the Reich to efficiently code, locate, and identify

Jews, the enemies within. It's already operating efficiently in Holland."

"Only the Jews?"

"Jews as well as groups that offend Hitler. Jehovah's Witnesses, gypsies, sexual deviants, and others the Nazis view as criminals. Once fully implemented, within France, Luxembourg, the Netherlands, Belgium, and other occupied countries, Austria, Czechoslovakia, Lithuania, and, oh yes, Poland and Croatia, as needed, IBM's mechanography will organize and print lists of these enemies—by street address, by city, and department or province or state. All that remains is for the Gestapo to use the lists to identify and round up Jews and other enemies of the Reich."

I swirled my wine and imagined roundups. I watched the wine flow around then down the inside of my wineglass. I thought of rumors I'd heard of arrests of old people and children who'd then been herded into railway boxcars, transported to prison camps.

Charles continued. "On both of these fronts, the Reich has achieved efficiencies of operations never thought possible. All this is powered by large numbers of Reich employees operating tabulation and keypunch machines, systems driven by the mechanography of IBM."

"Whether in Germany or Holland, France or elsewhere, the basic operations of the systems are the same. Right?"

"Yes. I believe, but can't confirm, that they may be part of many of the Reich's industrial applications, including armaments, and military supplies, civilian and military food allocations. And, oh yes, census records—the war against the Jews. In Berlin, the Nazi government is doing what you and your staff are doing, though on a much larger scale. At its core, information is coded and keypunched on 60- or 80-column cards. Machines read the cards. Programs are written to tabulate the data. Reports are printed. Just imagine, orders could then be placed for guns, butter, coffee—and Jews. All very efficient. And accurate, if the cards are correctly punched."

"At the Service, our machines soon will be ready to perform tabulation operations and then print summary information on men now in uniform."

Charles lit a Gauloise. "The beauty of mechanography is in its speed, efficiency, and accuracy." He spoke through the smoke drifting from his nostrils. "For example, consider the possible gains in efficiencies in, say, the supply and allocation of military munitions and armaments to field units. Labor shortages are rampant in every aspect of German life. Possible use of Dehomag—IBM—machines, eases the pressure for employing an army of clerks.

"On the second front," he continued, "once Jews and other undesirables are identified, then for some it's prison, for others, slave labor. For most, based on what we've already seen, execution. What Nazis call the Final Solution."

I shuddered. "I can't . . . my God . . ."

Charles then spoke like a classroom lecturer talking quietly to students. "On the military front, the war against the Allies is stalled. Göring and the Luftwaffe have been unable to subdue Britain. Even with U-boat attacks on British ships in the Atlantic, supplies and armaments continue to reach English shores. American supplies and replacements of lost shipments and freighters are ever larger. The American Navy is growing stronger."

Two Nazi officers arrived and seated themselves at an outdoor table.

I put my hand on Charles's arm and nodded toward the newly arrived officers.

His voice low, Charles said, "On the second front, against the enemy within, Hitler, Himmler, and Heidrich are riding a wave of victories."

"Ruth, in Paris," I said. "What she feared. It's coming true." I closed my eyes to accept the enormity what Charles had described. I took a deep breath and said a silent prayer for Ruth. I gulped my wine.

Charles refilled our glasses. "Yes, we're on the forward edge of the future Ruth feared." He looked toward the Saône. He raised his glass. "To Ruth. And to you, Miriam, to your safety and security."

I touched my glass to his.

Charles said, "I would like to help you paint a mental picture. About something I feel it's important for you to understand. About our work. *D'accord?*"

"*Oui.*"

"Please, close your eyes."

I closed my eyes.

"Imagine a tall pyramid with a large square base. Can you see it?"

"Yes."

"Imagine that the pyramid's sides reach upward, ever smaller, to its tip, called the pyramidion. Got the image?"

I nodded, yes.

Charles sipped his wine. "Now comes the tricky part. Imagine that you rotate, invert, the pyramid. In your mind, you turn it upside down. The pyramid's base then becomes its flat top. The top, or tip, the pyramidion, becomes the single point of contact with the ground. It supports the pyramid's mass and weight."

My eyes still closed, I said, "As if the pyramidion had become a fulcrum."

"You can think of it that way. Now think about this. In 1937 the Third Reich bestowed its most prestigious civilian honor, the German Eagle Award, on Thomas J. Watson, IBM's CEO. IBM, in Germany called Dehomag, the IBM subsidiary. IBM's technology is the pyramidion of the Third Reich's anti-Semitic efforts, possibly for important segments of the German economy."

I opened my eyes. "I didn't know about the German Eagle Award. IBM and mechanography—a German pyramidion. It's like Atlas bearing the heavens on his shoulders. IBM bears the Reich's attacks on Jews on its shoulders. Last year in the mechanography seminar, a student from Germany talked about the power of mechanography in his country."

My voice trailed away. I gazed across the bistro at the Gestapo officers. I turned toward Charles. "You said the war was on three fronts. What's the third?"

"The third front? The war against us."

"Us?"

"The Underground. The Resistance."

"Including me?"

"You are a card-carrying member."

"I am?" I took a large gulp of wine. "My *carte d'identité.*"

"Most of us have lost friends and family. We can honor them by working to slow, sometimes stop, the advances, the abuses of the Reich." He put his hand on mine.

"What are you telling me? Is there something I must do?"

"Only this—refine your Resistance identity. Practice. Talk about it. Become fluent. Minimize your risk. Beyond that, no one will require or force you to do anything."

"All you've said frightens me. But I'll help."

"Coffee?"

"Yes, please—Claude has coffee?"

Charles signaled the waiter for two coffees. "Claude is resourceful."

I asked, "Weren't we going to talk about Pétain's meeting with Hitler?" But my thoughts were on the warm touch of Charles's hand.

A Walk to Le Lieu

The waiter served us large cups of coffee, French style. I could not recall the last time I'd been served real honest-to-goodness coffee. I inhaled its rich aroma, took small sips, hoped to make it last.

"*Maréchal* Pétain's meeting with Hitler," Charles said. "I doubt if it would have taken place if Pierre Laval hadn't prodded him to do it. Laval hopes for the Germans to win the war. He wants France to be on the winning side." Charles smiled. "Victory means no reparation payments. Also, he's angry that Churchill, fearful that the Germans would use the captured French fleet to attack the British, ordered the fleet to be scuttled, sunk, at *Mers-el-Kébir*. Over twelve hundred men died. Most of France shares Laval's anger."

My upset over losses at Mers-el-Kébir was overcome by a wave of sleep. My eyelids drooped.

Charles continued, "The Allies hope that Pétain will become an ally and friend. In time, they believe, he will steer France toward the Allied cause. Even more, they hope that at some future date Pétain will orchestrate France's joining the Allies."

I rubbed my eyes. "It's late. What you're telling me is important . . . but I'm having trouble listening."

Charles continued, absorbed in his story. "In a few days, Pétain will speak to the nation. About the future of France."

I said, "Please, Charles, listen to me. I'd love to continue our talk. But the wine and food . . . I'm sleepy. Early in the morning, I'll get up and go to work."

"I'm sorry. I got absorbed in our discussion, in all I want to tell you. I lost track of time." Charles signaled the waiter for the check.

We said good night to Claude and then walked along Quai des Célestins.

I said, "The lights on the *Saône*. They're much dimmer than I remember."

"Everything is dimmer. Less light means less of a visible presence for bombers."

I looped my arm around Charles's arm. "The war changes everything. Even nighttime light." A few steps later Charles tucked his, and, my, arms close to his side.

We walked in silence. As we crossed Place Bellecour my awareness of the touch of Charles's arm was heightened. Did I want more than that?

On the other side of Place Bellecour we stopped. Charles turned to me and raised one hand to my shoulder. He placed his other hand on my waist. I leaned toward Charles and he gently pulled me next to him. We shared a kiss that lingered.

I hugged him as his lips touched the base of my neck. I whispered, "I've felt so alone. You've made me feel, well, that I'm not alone. That I'm desirable. But I'm not sure we should . . . I mean, with our work, what's before us . . ." I felt hesitant, yet attracted, pulled, to him.

"I know. Please, forgive me. You're a woman who excites me. I feel a magnetic attraction to you."

"And I feel that towards you, too. But I've had a long day. I'll face another one tomorrow. We'll see each other again."

"We will." He gave me a long hug.

I thought about, wondered at, Charles's transformation of the two of us into "we." The power of words. We resumed our walk, arm in arm, to Le Lieu. My thoughts drifted toward tomorrow and the mountain of work that would face me.

"I understand," Charles said. "My thoughts also keep going elsewhere—to tomorrow's meeting with René Carmille. He's an old friend and colleague. Our meeting will be about much more than mechanography."

The Path of Collaboration
31 October 1940

I sat in the lobby of Le Lieu with M. Bollé. Across the lobby sat a man in a dark suit. Jacques had called him Otto. Each of us read a morning newspaper. Jacques read a newspaper spread across the registration desk.

Otto had arrived at the hotel two days ago. As tall as Charles, but beefier and ruddy-faced. His eyes were heavy-lidded, as if he were bored or had been drinking. His eyes followed every comment made by anyone in the lobby. He spoke only to Jacques. His secretive demeanor frightened me.

The headline story in newspapers throughout France was yesterday's radio address by Maréchal Pétain. In silence, along with M. Bollé, Jacques, and tall secretive Otto, I read it.

Citizens of France, last Thursday I met the Chancellor of the German Reich. That meeting roused hopes and provoked concerns. I owe you some explanations regarding this. Such an interview was possible, four months after the defeat of our armed forces, only thanks to the dignity shown by the French in face of their trials, thanks to the huge effort of regeneration they have made, thanks also to the heroism of our sailors, the energy of our colonial leaders, and the loyalty of our indigenous populations. France has picked itself up. This first meeting between the victor and the vanquished signals the first recovery of our country.

Simone stepped off the elevator. "Miriam, ready to go to work?" M. Bollé and I said, "Shh. Reading Pétain's speech." Simone sat beside me and read the paper with us.

It is honorable, and in order to maintain French unity, unity that has lasted ten centuries, in the context of an activity helping to build the new European order, that I enter today upon the path of collaboration. Thus, in the near future the weight of our country's sufferings can be lessened, the fate of our prisoners improved, the burden of the costs of occupation mitigated. In this way the demarcation line could be relaxed and the administration and supplying of our Territory facilitated. This collaboration has to be sincere. It must exclude any thought of aggression. It must involve patient, trusting effort. Moreover, the armistice is not peace. France is bound by many obligations towards the conqueror. At least it remains a sovereign state. That sovereignty means it has to defend its soil, extinguish divergences of opinion, reduce dissidence in its colonies. This policy is mine. Ministers are responsible only to me. It is me alone that history will judge. Up to now I have spoken to you in the language of a father. Today I use the language of a leader. Follow me. Keep your trust in everlasting France.

Jacques watched M. Bollé and me, but not Otto, as we read. When we finished with the article and looked up, he raised his eyebrows and asked, "You have read *Le Maréchal*'s speech?"

We nodded.

"And in your opinion, he is doing the right thing?"

"*Le Maréchal* is searching for a path," M. Bollé said. "For survival. His and ours. Collaboration, he says, is such a path. Perhaps. It is too soon to know. I support him. But he, all of us, must exercise caution. When he says we are to 'extinguish divergences of opinion,' I disagree. We must remember France was not built on that. We speak. We argue. We fight—all these things have grown and matured France."

"And now, look where it has taken us," Jacques said.

M. Bollé returned to his newspaper.

I remained silent. So did Simone.

Jacques nodded at Otto, who returned the nod then looked at M. Bollé. Then Otto stared at me for a moment.

Pétain Visits Lyon
18 November 1940

On the morning of Pétain's visit to Lyon, hotel guests rose early. In Le Lieu's dining room, people occupied every table. The room buzzed with conversation.

"Pétain will be here, in Lyon."

"Yes, he is coming. But he has been here before."

"Pétain is an old friend of Lyon."

The rich and rare aroma of fresh coffee signaled the importance of the day. On many tables, reporters had pushed dishes aside to create space for press cameras.

Near the door to the kitchen on a long table were servings of juice, croissants, and an urn. I stared at the urn. Real coffee? I poured a cup. Yes! Fresh croissants? Yes!

M. Bollé sat at a large table of older men. The man seated next to him said, "*Le Maréchal* led us to victory at Verdun."

"He'll lead Vichy through our struggles," said another. "Create a new France."

"He's dedicating our new bridge over the *Rhône* this afternoon," M. Bollé said.

I waved to Simone who stood in the doorway. "Come. Enjoy real coffee. Croissants, too."

A short time later I walked to the registration desk. "I had forgotten the date," I said to Jacques.

Jacques threw his shoulders back. "Today, *Maréchal* Pétain honors us. Future generations will remember this day, mademoiselle."

On my walk to 10 rue des Archers, the Vichy tricolor flags flying from the front and the top, too, of every building surprised me.

In my mailbox was a note from Aimée. "That broadcast—no! What Pétain proposes is wrong. Boris hopes we can deflect, turn the direction. Starting from below the ground."

Aimée seemed to be even more enmeshed in the network she had often talked about. Behind her words I sensed darkness. I wondered again about a secret society within the Museée de l'Homme. An underground network? Didn't she realize her notes could be intercepted? Aimée and anyone connected to her might be at risk—including me. Even Gen. Carmille!

Mid-morning Lt. Lacroix called a special meeting of supervisors. Once everyone had assembled, he announced, "Many people are still delayed in coming to work. Crowds met *Maréchal* Pétain's train. Lined the streets to the *Hôtel de Ville*. Quite a morning. Quite a welcome."

Simone said, "Farmers and their horses and wagons brought traffic to a stand-still."

"This afternoon *Maréchal* Pétain will lay the cornerstone for the new bridge. Then he will address the people of Lyon. From the *Hôtel de Ville*." The lieutenant smiled. "Good news. You and your workteams will be excused from work this afternoon. Let's get as much done as we can this morning. That's all for now. Thanks."

I was the last supervisor to leave the room.

Lt. Lacroix called, "Miriam, could you stay for a moment?"

I waited for him to collect a few papers.

"There is a reception for *Maréchal* Pétain late this afternoon. *Hôtel de Ville*. I am invited. Would you like to join me?"

I felt a small burst of excitement. When I started work at the Service, the lieutenant and I had talked about getting together. It hadn't happened. Until now. But what to wear for such a special event as Pétain's reception? My excitement melted away. "I don't have the clothes for it."

"Please, it's wartime. People will come in work clothes. We can go to the bridge ceremony. Then the reception."

I thought for a moment. "*D'accord.* Why not?"

After the ceremonial dedication of the new bridge across the Rhône, Lt. Lacroix and I walked the short distance to the Hôtel de Ville, the center of Lyon's city government. The structure was completed in 1672, during the reign of Louis XIV. Both its architecture and interior design resembled the palace at Versailles.

Entering the central hall, I remembered my family's visit to the Dutch Royal Palace in Amsterdam. Papa had said, "In all of Europe, there is none to rival it."

The interior walls of the Hôtel de Ville were painted rich reds and blues, the ornate wood trim and wall panels in a contrasting cream. Crystal chandeliers and gold wall sconces lit the great room. Waiters in formal wear carried silver trays bearing fluted crystal glasses of champagne.

At the other end of the room, a small band played popular tunes. A singer, dressed in a suit, bow tie, topped with a white straw hat, sang in the style of Maurice Chevalier. In front of the band, a reception line inched its way toward Lyon officials and Maréchal Pétain. The gathering was a mixture of Lyon's workers, civic officials, Wehrmacht and Gestapo, as well as Vichy-French army officers. Some men were in tuxedos and ladies with them were in evening gowns. Others were dressed as if they'd hurried from work at a Lyon textile mill.

"Shall we?" Lt. Lacroix said.

"Wouldn't miss it."

We joined the long queue of the reception line. An hour later each of us shook Pétain's hand. Afterward I said to the lieutenant, "When he shook my hand his grip was firm and his hand soft. He seemed distracted. His eyes were on someone or something across the room."

"He was the same with me. Do you suppose at his age his mind wanders?"

"Or his thoughts carry heavy burdens." I looked across the room at a table of sandwiches and pastries. "I'm hungry. Are you?" Lt. Lacroix and I ate. Soon he finished but I continued to eat. Then I covertly slid two sandwiches and a few chocolate and coconut bonbons into my coat pockets.

After the reception we walked to Le Lieu. In the lobby, Lt. Lacroix extended his hand. "Thanks for joining me."

I shook his hand. Well, more like I held his hand. It wasn't a business handshake. "Good night, Lieutenant."

"Good night, Miriam. Please, call me Marcel."

"Good night, Marcel."

New Year's Eve 1940, Lyon

The last day of 1940 was cold and quiet. I had hoped Charles or Marcel, somebody, would invite me to a party. But no invitations arrived. Le Lieu's New Year's Eve celebration, held in the hotel lobby, attracted nine guests. Five were permanent residents: M. Bollé, me, Simone, and the Colbrides, and an elderly couple, heavy smokers. One of them always had a cigarette in hand or between their lips. Jacques had tuned the lobby radio to a Paris station playing popular music. Around the lobby hung Vichy France flags. Jacques called the flag Maréchal Pétain's contribution to Free France.

Below each of the flags hung a banner: "Happy New Year!" On the round oak table in the center of the lobby Jacques had placed a large crystal bowl filled with golden punch. Beside it were crystal glasses.

A half-hour before midnight Jacques descended to the cellar. He returned with four dusty bottles of wine and a magnum of champagne. He wiped the dust from the bottles and set the champagne beside the punchbowl. With a smile he twisted a corkscrew into each of the bottles. He placed crystal wine glasses on the table and poured vin rouge into some, vin blanc into others. He motioned toward the glasses and nodded to the guests. "Please."

Each guest picked up a glass of wine. After the first sip of his wine, M. Bollé said, "Jacques, *merci*. Wine from vintage years—a good omen for the year to come."

With a poignant smile, Jacques looked at his guests and spoke in a quiet voice. "My friends, enjoy. It may be a long time before we restock the wine cellar."

Moments before midnight, Jacques opened the champagne. He handed each guest a clean glass and then poured. Bubbles rose to the rim of each glass.

At midnight, the bells in the distant tower of Cathédrale Saint-Jean pealed an end to 1940 and signal the start of the New Year. Jacques had tuned the lobby radio to a BBC broadcast from a ballroom in London. At twelve midnight an orchestra played "Auld Lang Syne." In the London ballroom, people sang. I imagined a bandstand, an orchestra in white dinner jackets, and a large softly lit dance floor where well-dressed couples swayed while they hummed and sang the familiar and nostalgic song.

Jacques tapped his pen against one of the crystal wine glasses. Ping-ping-ping. Everyone turned to him. He lifted his glass. People followed his lead.

Speaking over the music, Jacques said, "My friends, a New Year's toast. To all of you, my heartfelt wishes for health and happiness. May we aid one another and our country—may we find peace and joy in the year to come!"

We raised our glasses. M. Bollé raised his glass and nodded to Jacques. "And to you, Jacques, to all of us assembled here, Happy New Year!"

After drinking their champagne, guests returned to their seats, sipped wine, and chatted. I looked around the room. This group, this configuration of people on New Year's Eve, would never happen again.

The radio broadcast returned to Paris and recordings of popular artists, Édith Piaf, Maurice Chevalier, and Josephine Baker.

I sipped my wine and listened. I relaxed into the comfort of the music and my overstuffed lobby chair. Memories of New Year's Eve one year ago flooded my thoughts—at home with my family, generous servings of Mama's favorite, sauerkraut soup with cheese, our apartment filled with rich aromas of the soup and freshly baked bread.

An elderly man sitting near me drifted into sleep. His wine glass slipped from his hand. The sharp sounds of shattering glass evoked images of exploding Luftwaffe bombs.

I sat up. Rotterdam burning. Fire roaring through my family's apartment. Lars, my family, gone. Charles—someday a lover? Stop the fantasy, Miriam. You are alone. Reach out to Marcel? Papa said to trust fate. I have. What has it gotten me? Nazis in the streets, in the hotel. How will this end? Will I find a way out?

On the radio, I recognized the plaintive voice of the American Negro singer and dancer, Josephine Baker. I had seen photographs of her— beautiful curves, large expressive eyes, sensuous lips. She had become a long-time resident of France and adopted the country as her home. She sang her signature song, *"J'ai deux amours,"* I have two loves, my country and Paris. Then Baker sang, *"Si j'étais blanche."* If I were white.

I relaxed and imagined Baker's voice as my own. It embraced and washed through me. I hummed as Baker sang, *"Je voudrais être blanche."* I would like to be white, for me what happiness, if my breasts and my hips change color.

Two verses later the song ended as Baker sang, "Tell me, sir, should I be white to please you better?"

I sang along with Josephine. Same melody but different lyrics. "Tell me sir, if my crossed eye were straightened, would I please you better? *Si je n'étais pas juive,* if I were not a Jew, would I please you better?"

1941 Begins

Early morning on New Year's Day Jacques posted an announcement on the glass doors of the dining room. *"Mes amies, the shortages created by the war now limit Le Lieu's menu. This I regret. Jacques."*

I took a fast walk along the Rhône. I enjoyed the exercise so much I ran most of my return to the hotel. Then, I joined Simone in the dining room. We ate a light breakfast—a breakfast in name only. Stale rolls and café national, a substitute for coffee made with chicory and ground acorns. After her first sip of the ersatz coffee, Simone recoiled. "Revolting."

We bundled ourselves in coats and scarves and began a walk around Lyon. After two blocks I said, "Hey, let's play a game. My cousin Aimée and I invented it. *J'espionne,* I spy. We used to play it in Paris."

"I love games. Tell me about it."

"In *j'espionne* we walked, each of us alone, for an hour around Aimée's neighborhood, the Marais District. We observed life on the streets.

"Our walks started and ended at the entrance to Aimée's family's apartment building on *rue du Temple*. I loved that old building—a Haussmann-designed stone building constructed in the nineteenth century renovation of Paris. The wrought-iron front gate was twelve feet wide and twice as high, built for horse-drawn carriages. Behind it, a cobblestone courtyard.

"At the end of an hour, Aimée and I would meet at a small café. We had a favorite window table with a long view of *rue du Temple*. Over coffee, we did what we called Tally the Score. We shared our observations during the walk. The strangest or most humorous observation won the game. The loser bought coffee and a croissant for the winner."

"Observations? What sorts of observations?"

"There were so many." I laughed. "Here's one. I observed an elderly couple having coffee in a sidewalk café. Each time, every time, the wife looked away, her husband picked his nose then inspected the fruit of his digging."

"Yuck."

"To me, that was funny. Was it more humorous than Aimée's sighting of a well-dressed lady at a trolley stop, perhaps hard of hearing. Aimée said, 'The lady seemed unaware that she was farting. So loudly that others turned to look at her.'"

Simone laughed. "I get it. Okay. I'm ready. Let's play."

I said, "Let's meet in the *Le Lieu* lobby in an hour."

Beneath a grey winter sky, Simone and I walked in opposite directions. The wind was brisk and cold.

An hour later I entered the lobby. Simone sat alone on a couch in the corner farthest from the registration desk.

I wiped my runny nose. I sat down beside her. "Maybe because it's winter. Or because of the war. My observations were noteworthy. But not funny."

Simone looked at me with an intense gaze. She said nothing.

Maybe I could get things started. "I have two observations, entries for our game. First, as I walked past a pharmacy, a teenager hopped on a bicycle and rode away. A man ran out the pharmacy door and yelled, '*Au voleur! Au voleur!* Stop, thief!' He chased the boy. The thief on the bicycle pumped hard. He soon disappeared."

Simone remained silent.

Why didn't Simone didn't say anything? She showed no reaction at all. Maybe I hadn't been clear about the game. The fun of the game is to report and talk about observations. "My second observation? In front of a grocery store, a woman secretly lifted a head of cabbage from a sidewalk display. She put it inside her coat. Walked away."

I looked more closely at Simone. Her face was ashen. One of her hands gripped the arm of the couch so tightly her knuckles were white. The other hand was a balled fist.

"Are you all right?"

Simone shook her head, no.

"Did something happen?"

Simone nodded, yes.

"What was it?"

"I don't know if I can tell you."

"Please, try."

"A German soldier on the street. Black uniform." Simone shuddered. "A skull on the collar."

"Gestapo," I said softly.

"He stopped a middle-aged man wearing soiled work clothes. Like he was returning from a factory job. Or hard labor. He wore an armband with a yellow star." Simone took a deep breath and paused. "The soldier asked the man to show him his papers. Then asked the man something else. I couldn't hear what he said. The man shook his head, no. He turned to walk away. The soldier stopped him. He again asked him something. The man shrugged. He reached inside his jacket. Brought out a pack of cigarettes. Gave the soldier one. The soldier put it between his lips."

"Where were you?"

"By then I'd ducked into a doorway, out of sight I hoped." Simone took a deep breath that became a gasp. "The soldier kept his hand extended. Palm up. The man gave him another cigarette. The soldier put it in his coat pocket. Kept the first cigarette between his lips. Stared at the man. He said, 'Feuer, Jude.'

"The man nodded. He took a pack of matches from his coat pocket. He lit the soldier's cigarette. The soldier jerked the matches away from the man. Then held out his hand—I think he wanted another cigarette. The man shrugged his shoulders, turned, and walked away.

"The soldier yelled, 'Halt!' The man kept walking. The soldier pulled his pistol. Pointed it at the man's back. He yelled, 'Jude—halt. Halt or I shoot!' The man walked on.

"With his free hand, the soldier steadied his pistol. Oh God. Then he fired! The man fell forward. Blood and brains all over the sidewalk. Dogs barked. The soldier holstered his pistol. He turned and walked away."

"What did you do?"

"Bit my fist till the soldier was out of sight. Then I ran. Through alleys. To the hotel." Simone burst into tears. She put her hands over her face. "I escaped from Warsaw," she sobbed. "My family's there. Trapped. The ghetto." She took a deep breath.

I felt light-headed. My thoughts jumbled one on top of another. A man killed on a Lyon street. My family killed in Rotterdam. Simone's family trapped, possibly killed, in Warsaw.

Simone said, "I recognized the soldier. One morning when we walked to work, he smiled at us. Flirted. Even worse, we smiled back at him." Simone closed her eyes and slumped. "The worker—his only offense? He was a Jew. Like me."

"You're not alone. I am also a Jew. And I am Dutch, not French." Simone's eyes widened then closed.

We sat in silence. I opened my shoulder bag. I lifted out the knife I'd taken from my attacker in Rotterdam. I gripped its bone handle. For the first time, I opened the knife's single large blade. On the blade's shiny surface there were fingerprints. Not mine—whose? My Rotterdam attacker's? I stared at the prints. Goose bumps prickled on my arms.

With my neck scarf I wiped the fingerprints from the blade.

The blade caught, reflected, a beam of light from the reading lamp at the end of the couch. I rotated the blade. It reflected the beam, like an ethereal presence, from wall to chair to ceiling. Like the soldier's pistol, the beam and the blade did the bidding of the hand that held it.

I stared at the blade. What might I ask of it? Today, nothing. Tomorrow?

I closed the knife and put it back in my bag. Then I held Simone's hand.

Simone gripped my hand tightly. She laid her head on my shoulder and sobbed.

Return to Work

The next morning I awakened to a cold room. I wrapped my blanket tight around me and thought about Lyon's frigid air. I wanted to prolong my last moments in bed. So warm. Outside, so cold. A wave of loneliness passed through me. With a burst of effort, I gave myself instructions: Up, Miriam, get up. Now think about work. Nothing else. Remember, the Demographic Service is safe. Your refuge.

At a November staff meeting, Lt. Lacroix had announced, "The armistice limits the French army to one hundred thousand soldiers. Under the armistice, the Mobilization Service is now prohibited."

Around the room there was a murmur of concern. One man said, "Will we lose our jobs?"

Lt. Lacroix continued, "We have administrative functions to perform. As most of you already know, we have become, officially, the Vichy Demographic Service." He smiled at the worried man, "You will not lose your jobs."

Simone interrupted. "Has our mission changed?"

"Now it is more complex. We have new responsibilities—as a French census and population records bureau, and an office of labor and economic statistics. We will continue to be the record keeper for the armed forces."

The new Demographic Service brought me a promotion and expanded supervisory responsibilities. With them came additional worries. So much needed to be done. My top priority was additional training for punch-card operators—the speed of their entry of data codes and keypunches was too slow.

The mobilization registry needed to be better managed. I took a deep breath and wondered how my group would do it. It didn't help when I remembered that the Demographic Service had operations in Paris, Puteaux, and Vincennes. They too needed to be better managed.

My expanded supervisory responsibilities, with more coding clerks and punch-card operators, brought a rush of pride. I wished I could tell Papa.

My thoughts, as if they had an independent life, jumped to my family, to prayers to mourn the deaths of friends in Rotterdam. I recalled how I valued the ritual of sitting Shiva—no longer possible. The first seven days after a death, my family's deaths, had passed. Even more, without the remains of my family, and without burials, there had been no sheloshim, thirty days of prayers. Something. I had to do something.

The candles in the hotel's dining room! I'll bet they're in the cupboard. If I lit one candle each night, I could beg, borrow, or steal enough of them for thirty days of mourning—my private sheloshim.

Looking up from my bed, I studied the ceiling's water stains. My imagination transformed the spread of brown globs into dark clouds of smoke hovering over Rotterdam. My warm breath collided with the room's cold air. Each exhale became a short-lived fog rising from my charred neighborhood's smoke and ashes.

Memories, each of them had powerful emotional charges: framed photos on our grand piano—Mama and Papa on their wedding day, Mama holding Margot and me as infants, Papa dressed in the dark suit he wore to teach in, Margot and me, 'the twins,' on our first day of school. Had all this been destroyed? An emptiness, a horrific void, nothing when once there had been something, possessed me. I pushed away.

"Up. To work," I commanded myself. "At least it's warm there." The sound of my voice, full and resonant, surprised me. It seemed more an unannounced visitor than a part of me.

I reached for my glasses on the bedside table. With an effort I placed my bare feet on the cold floor and stood. I inhaled sharply. The stale odor of the frigid room reminded me of pond ice in Holland.

I removed the heavy sweater I'd slept in, tossed it on the bed. A perfumed trail of Soirée de Paris mixed with my body's nighttime scent wafted behind the sweater. The aromas were soon overcome by the room's stale air.

I removed my t-shirt, shivered, and hurriedly splashed water on my face, my upturned breasts, and long arms. I lathered soap into a washcloth and washed my upper body, followed by a vigorous toweling. The towel's friction created a brief and welcome heat.

In the time it took for the room's gas burner to heat a small kettle of water, I put on two layers of underclothes, a tan blouse, and a thick black sweater.

I poured hot water into a mug containing yesterday's tealeaves.

Outside, the snowflakes shrank to tiny crystals. The wind returned, grew stronger, and soon drove a dense mixture of snow and ice against my window. Lyon's rooftops vanished into an undulating veil of white crystals.

I took two sips of my tea, frowned at the sour taste, and poured it out.

I looked into the discolored mirror above my washbasin and gazed at my high cheekbones, more common among Eastern Europeans than the Dutch. I combed my hair, now cut short, unlike its shoulder length in Rotterdam. There again in the mirror was my crossed eye. I thought of what a teacher had said about Margot and me on our first day of school. Like a jinxed coin, her words had stuck with me throughout my childhood: "The twins? Miriam is the one in glasses."

Papa used to stare at me for a moment and ask, "A green-eyed Jew?" Then he would turn to Mama and in a mock-serious voice, ask a second question. "Was it the postman?" He and Mama would laugh, joined by Margot and me long before we knew what the laughter was about.

Mama often kidded Papa about marriages of non-Jews into his side of the family. Her jests were always followed by an exaggerated accusatory look. After a pause she would deliver what Margot and I called Mama's punch line: "Your people didn't even go to Synagogue!" Papa, as if on cue, would stand and, with a flourish, bow. Margot and I would squeal with laughter.

A single gust of wind rattled the windowpanes. I peered across the now visible rooftops of Lyon. In the distance, the snow-covered foothills of the Alps—so different from the flat expanses of Holland. Another blast of wind rapped on the window.

The wind ceased. The air held a pregnant stillness. Then the Alps disappeared behind a gentle snowfall. Large snowflakes coated the surfaces of the city—roofs, streets, autos—as if they had been cast by a sculptor. Limbs of plane trees, like long white arms, reached toward the sky. In the sudden quiet, I thought about Mama, Papa, and Margot. Then Aimée. Would I lose her, too?

I put on my coat and took the lift to the lobby. In the dining room, I yearned for a croissant and coffee. Of necessity, I settled for a stale roll and a cup of faux moka.

I sipped faux moka until I was alone in the dining room. I walked briskly to the room's wide mahogany cabinet and swung open its two doors. On the second shelf lay a supply of white candles, each candle six centimeters long. I quickly grabbed a handful and thrust them into my coat pocket.

After departing the dining room, in the lobby I said a quick, "Good morning, Jacques." He looked up from his newspaper and nodded. I waved to Simone, who arrived to join me in our walk to work.

We walked out the door into a biting wind. We passed other people on their way to work, faces buried in neck scarves and upturned collars. The early morning sky was cold and black. A sliver of a crescent moon hung in an otherwise cloudless void punctuated by star-points of brilliant crystal. I inhaled the crisp air. I missed the familiar winter mornings of Rotterdam.

My thoughts centered on the Service and work. Pending changes and challenges in assignments: how to integrate hundreds of reassigned employees, train them, then expand operations in coding, keypunching, and tabulation.

Soon my thoughts drifted back to my evening with Charles. Since then, his occasional messages had reminded me of our connection. They prompted me to think about the battles to come on the second and third fronts of the war.

Two German soldiers walked past Simone and me. I remembered Simone's account of the worker shot dead. His death sentence—because he walked away from the command of a German soldier? My answer, "Yes," drove fear into my heart.

A New Mission

At noon I joined the supervisors for lunch in the conference room. I stood in line while the office manager, Eve, and two staff placed a large pot of hot broth, bread, plates, bowls, and utensils at one end of the large conference table. I remembered last summer's lunches: rich soups, cheeses, bitter greens and bacon, lightly cooked eggs all combined with vinaigrette into a salade lyonnaise, accompanied by golden crusts of freshly baked bread.

Simone, seated at the table, looked up. "A bowl of broth and a crust of two-day-old bread. Enjoy. Tomorrow we'll do a taste-test on three-day-old bread."

Around the table a few people snickered. They glanced at Eve, who winced at Simone's words. Others at the table gazed at their food or looked away.

Her voice soft, Eve said, "I do the best I can." Tears welled up in her eyes. Her face reddened. "I shop, I buy what's available. Available, that is, after the Occupation army takes whatever food it wants." She wiped her eyes. "Do you understand that? After the Occupation army shops. You can always go somewhere else for lunch."

Simone shrugged.

I said, "Sorry, Eve. We were trying to be humorous. You have a tough job in hard times. We appreciate you. What you contribute to us."

Eve smiled half-heartedly and nodded.

I served myself and sat next to Lt. Lacroix, across the table from Simone. "*Bonjour*, Lieutenant." After the Pétain reception Lt. Lacroix had invited me to call him Marcel. In the more than two months since then, we hadn't been alone. In public, I had been careful to refer to him as Lt. Lacroix or Lieutenant.

I listened to the flow of conversations around the table. They centered on mundane and safe topics that when—not if, when—reported by the Gestapo's spies would not trigger suspicions. The day before there had been a long discussion of the food shortage. Today we discussed keeping warm in the unseasonably cold weather. How to deal with the wind gusts that rattled apartment windows? Stuff rags around window frames. How much can anyone say about that? The conversations soon dwindled away.

Lt. Lacroix turned to me. "After lunch, could you meet with me?"

"Sure. In your office?"

"Yes. An hour from now."

I rapped lightly on Lt. Lacroix's half-open door. I peered in.

"Lieutenant?"

"Come in." Lt. Lacroix sat behind his desk. Sitting on the other side, his back to the door, Charles.

I felt a rush of excitement. My thoughts skipped to my dinner with Charles, the quiet beauty of the Saône that autumn evening, to our kiss. Since then he had sent an occasional "I hope you are well" message. I had often wished the evening and the kiss could've lingered. Or could have been renewed.

"Would you please close the door?" Lt. Lacroix's request brought me back to today, here, now. I disconnected from thoughts of the evening with Charles. Lt. Lacroix gestured toward the empty chair beside Charles.

I closed the door and sat down.

"Thanks. What Charles and I want to discuss with you is rather sensitive. Please keep it among the three of us."

I nodded affirmatively. My initial excitement about this meeting gave way to apprehension. My thoughts lead me to an imaginary room. Under the glare of bright lights, Gestapo officers questioned me, threatened torture. I shook my head and told myself to stop. I guided my thoughts back to Lt. Lacroix's office.

"Yesterday Charles met with Gen. Carmille. He has asked us, well, our section, to take on a special mission. Charles and I have just talked about it."

Charles's eyes were on the lieutenant. His lips pursed, then relaxed. He turned to me, lit a cigarette and inhaled. "Nice to see you, Miriam."

"Good to see you again . . . " After a brief pause I added, "Charles."

Lt. Lacroíx cast a quick look at me when I used Charles's first name and the familiar tu rather than vous. But he didn't ask about it.

Charles said, "I'll bring you up to date. M. Carmille has asked us to make a priority of a new and special program in the Demographic Service. Special." Charles's voice deepened as smoke rolled from his mouth and nostrils. "Lt. Albert Sassi will have overall responsibility. I believe you have met him."

I nodded. Yes, I had met Lt. Sassi. The staff at 10 rue des Archers viewed him as a bright and personable officer, a rising star. Two young women, key punch operators, talked often about his dark curly hair, sexy eyes, and stocky athletic body. Simone said he looked like a handsome rugby player.

"For this special program," Charles continued, "Lt. Sassi will manage the important functions Lt. Lacroix carries out for this department. Procure staff and supplies. Organize assignments. Clear the way so everyone can get their jobs done."

Lt. Lacroix said, "As part of the first stage of the project, you'll need to move, along with certain records, to a new work space on the fourth floor."

"What're we going to do?" Why did I have to ask? They could've just told me.

Charles slowly drew on his Gauloise and then stubbed it out in Lt Lacroix's ashtray. "What is it we're, hmmm, how to put it? Until a few months ago, the Demographic Service operated under its old name, the Military Recruitment Service. And under its old charter as principal record keeper for the French armed forces. Now, under the Vichy government, it has absorbed SGF, the French Statistical Service, and become the Demographic Service."

"Yes, I know."

"The basic functions of the Demographic Service remain about as before, including the things you and your people are doing, to prepare and organize soldiers' military records. Make sure our records are up to date."

I shifted in my chair. Why hadn't he answered my question?

Lt. Lacroix said, "The new mission will continue a portion of our former mobilization work."

"That's right," Charles added. "A portion. A special portion, extended in new ways." Charles took a deep breath. His dark eyes gazed at me. "We will ask, first, that your staff segregate records of soldiers with addresses in the south of France and Northern Algeria. Can you do that?"

I pushed back. "Will we be relieved of our current assignments?"

"Yes," Lt. Lacroix said.

"Then yes, we can do it. We'll have to sort through lots of still-unopened crates and boxes. Go through open files that are organized alphabetically, not geographically. Algeria and the south of France? Not all of France? Or the *Zone Libre?*"

Charles said, "That's correct."

"Keep in mind, we don't have a coded or automated retrieval process." As I spoke, I felt, with some irritation, that Charles and the lieutenant had withheld information from me.

Lt. Lacroix said, "We know."

I sat on the edge of my chair. "We'll need coding and keypunch machines. Tabulators as well as data cards. Lots of cards."

"No problem. We'll place additional orders."

"Place additional orders? Marcel, with all due respect, maybe we're kidding ourselves?"

"Kidding? What do you mean?"

"Week after week I have trouble getting enough data cards for our keypunch operators. Last week we completely ran out. Had to shut down, send people home. I waited two days for a delivery. When the shipment arrived, it didn't have nearly enough cards. There are other mechanography programs at 10 *rue des Archers*. The Service is consuming thousands of cards every day. With the new..." I felt my face redden. "We'll need an even larger supply."

Lt. Lacroix replied, "I understand. IBM cards are in demand. Here in the Occupied Zone, in Germany, Holland. In Czechoslovakia and Austria, too. Dehomag machines are engaged in operations everywhere."

"And those machines are hungry for cards," I said. "Something has to change."

"It's not a problem with a simple solution."

"Help me understand," Charles said. "Perhaps I can do something."

Lt. Lacroix turned to Charles. "We have a continuing shortage of blank keypunch cards. It's caused in part by difficulties suppliers face meeting quality standards for the cards. In order to be properly perforated by keystrokes, new cards have to meet narrow specifications. For example, after cards are keypunched the paper must have clean holes. Not fuzzy or ragged ones. Cards must retain their firmness yet be flexible. They must flow smoothly through tabulators. No jamming in humid weather. Or when the temperature spikes or drops."

I said, "Two weeks ago we received a large delivery of cards. When we used them, the cards warped. Jammed our machines. We had to throw them out."

"I remember," Lt. Lacroix replied. "A chemical analysis showed the cards lacked sufficient cellulose. I fired the supplier."

"Cellulose," I said. "I should've thought of that. Although firing a supplier doesn't solve the problem."

Charles interrupted. "I don't know much about the keypunch cards. But I know that cellulose is in demand. It's used in new synthetic fabrics, in thermoplastics, and in industrial machinery." His voice deepened. "And in explosives."

Lt. Lacroix said, "Wartime is all about explosives. Their production. Storage. Then use in combat."

"So the Demographic Service is in competition with the armed forces for supplies?"

Lt. Lacroix answered me. "I hadn't thought of it like that. Yes, I suppose we are."

Charles said, "Military tactics and battles have shaped every war. This war is driven by information, by mechanography. Mechanography is driven by Dehomag or Hollerith IBM machines and punchcards."

I said, "I can do little about our supply problem. If you give me a sufficient supply of useable cards, I'll do my best to meet our objectives." Then I added, "Whatever they are."

Charles and Lt. Lacroix were silent. They glanced at each other. A complicit silence?

I took a deep breath, try one more time, Miriam. My voice firm, I spoke in a measured cadence. "Please help me understand why we are having this meeting. What's the new special program? What is this all about?" I hoped I didn't sound like a whiney schoolgirl.

Charles said, "You're right to be annoyed. Lt. Lacroix and I are dancing around the truth."

I glared at Charles. "Let's end the dance."

Charles Looks Within

"I hope you'll forgive us," Lt. Lacroix said. "I'm uncertain about how to proceed. This is new territory for me. Charles, *s'il vous plaît,* will you brief Miriam?"

Charles inhaled his Gauloise. *"Mais oui, bien sûr."* He was silent for a moment. In lightning flashes of memories, Charles relived his first discussion with Miriam in Rotterdam. How he'd been struck by her intelligence and engagement, as well as her athleticism and beauty. The Paris evening with Miriam and Ruth. The calls he made to arrange her carte d'identité, travel, and assignment. Lyon—dinner at the outdoor café, the conversation, the Nazis seated across the café, and the warmth of Miriam's touch. The walk from the café to Le Lieu, her arm pressed against him. Their first kiss. Then as his lips rested in the soft curve of her neck, her musky scent. Miriam had awakened feelings Charles recognized as too long dormant. In the past he might have seen them as interference with his life and work. Suddenly, he welcomed them. With surprise and an effort, he forced his thoughts into the room, the conversation.

How much to tell her? Full disclosure would put her at risk. Can Miriam handle all she needs to know? Charles wanted to protect her. He reflected on his past interviews with potential agents, his assessment of their character and potential vulnerabilities. Could they, could Miriam, be trusted to hold secrets? To transmit information in confidence from sensitive positions in business and government? Charles felt some pride in his many successes, a few of them stellar—the placement of a senior aide in Chamberlain's office, a clerk in a Berlin command center who stole a copy of the German battle plan that bypassed the Maginot Line, even though it arrived a day too late.

Charles was only too aware of his mistakes. Not many, but when they happened people were hurt, or worse, executed. Last year one of his agents in Berlin, a government clerk, drank too much at a party and mentioned important friends in France. He also hinted at armaments information known only to insiders. The Gestapo arrested the clerk, interrogated and tortured him until he revealed his contacts. Then sent him to Auschwitz, and in all likelihood to his death. One of the clerk's French friends, also an agent, was found dead at the bottom of a Paris elevator shaft. Charles arranged for the clerk's network of agents to be conveyed in secret to a safe house in London.

In the two months since his dinner with Miriam, Charles had often planned to visit her. But each time he found himself engaged in an unexpected secret mission. An occasional note was often the best he could do. He reminded himself that his life of travel, combined with the secretive nature of intelligence work, afforded him little room for emotional connections. Falling in love? A luxury enjoyed by others. He counseled himself that his mistress in Paris, an enjoyable but emotionally shallow convenience, and other occasional liaisons for a night or two during travel, were sufficient love life for a senior intelligence official.

From the time he joined the French Secret Service, Charles reminded himself, he had accepted the reality of personal sacrifices. A love life and its corollaries, marriage and children, were among them. This fact of life was driven home by the intensity of intelligence demands after the rise of the Reich and the fall of France. His absence of emotional connections would have to do. Even as he said that to himself, Charles wondered if he might find a way to connect to a woman like Miriam. He immediately recognized the foolishness of that thought. He didn't mean a woman *like* Miriam. He meant *Miriam*.

Plausible denial

For over a minute Charles remained silent. Lt. Lacroix and I gazed at him.

The lieutenant broke our silence. He laughed. "*Bonjour,* Charles. *À quoi penses-tu?* What are you thinking?"

"Forgive me," Charles said. He gave a self-deprecating smile and shook his head sidewise. "I was distracted."

Charles's smile disappeared. His dark eyes locked on me. I didn't blink.

"If we continue this conversation, Miriam," Charles said, "you're going to learn very sensitive information. At some point in the future, it could put you in jeopardy. At the same time, what you learn, about the Service, about Vichy, will give you opportunities to advance the cause of liberty—recovery from all the Nazis have driven out of life in France. That is, if we continue. Take a minute to think about what I've said."

The three of us sat in silence. After a moment Charles said, "If you have reservations, Miriam, please tell us now."

I remained silent a moment further, as if to consider possible reservations. Charles's request required little thought. I reflected on how the Nazis had destroyed my life in Rotterdam and run roughshod across the continent. La Zone Libre, Vichy France, had become, at least for now, a safe enclave, as was the Demographic Service. At a minimum, I'd like to help protect it.

"Do I have reservations? Of course." I turned to Charles. "But they don't stand in my way. I want to continue to talk with the two of you. I want to help overcome the Nazis, what they're doing out there."

"I hoped you would."

Lt. Lacroix smiled.

I nodded. "Let's get on with it. Yes, I understand that what you'll tell me will be top secret."

Charles placed another Gauloise between his lips. I extended my hand. "May I?"

Surprised, Charles extended the blue pack toward me. I extracted one of the squat cigarettes, held it in my lips, and leaned toward Charles. He struck a match and lit my cigarette, then his.

I drew on the cigarette. I had smoked cigarettes only once before, in Paris with Aimée.

Charles raised his Gauloise as if making a toast. "Here's to the French smokes of the Great War."

I mirrored Charles's move. "And to Orwell, *Down and Out in Paris.*"

"*Down and Out in Paris and London,*" Charles said.

Charles's and my eyes met.

I smiled. "I know."

"Uh, Charles, weren't you going to give Miriam some background on her new assignment?"

Charles nodded, much like a professor acknowledging a student's classroom question.

"Okay. First I must ask, has she signed the Official Secrets Act?"

"She has," Lt. Lacroix said.

"Then I'll begin." Charles cleared his throat and turned to me. "Bear with me if I repeat some of what you already know. Please understand, there are limits on what I can tell you, at least for now."

"*D'accord.* I understand."

"The armistice of last June provided for the *Zone Libre* to establish a government, now based in Vichy, and for an army of one hundred thousand soldiers. Also to retain the French navy."

"French colonies, too," Lt. Lacroix added.

"Yes," Charles said. "And important for us, the Vichy government was permitted to maintain a limited form of the French intelligence services."

Lt. Lacroix cast the look of an insider at me, one that said we're in this together.

"Last August, Gen. Carmille met in Vichy with senior officers of the General Staff of the Army and *Maréchal* Pétain. He proposed three objectives for the Military Recruitment Service. The General Staff and Pétain agreed to support his objectives, provide the finances necessary to achieve them. However, there was one condition related to the third objective."

"I don't know the objectives. Will you tell me?"

"Yes. First, do you have any questions on what I've said?"

"No. Maybe later."

"The first two of Gen. Carmille's objectives were straightforward and in the view of Berlin compatible with the long-term interests of the Third

Reich. Berlin is unaware of the third objective.

"The first objective: Preserve the Military Recruitment Service. This has already happened, though now with a new name, the Demographic Service. The work and past programs of the organization have continued uninterrupted.

"The second objective: To evolve the Demographic Service into a civilian National Statistics Service, SNS. The SNS will provide census-based programs and a statistical foundation for government social policies. Gen. Carmille is passionate about this, and about ways of doing it better than in the past."

"Yes, I know."

"The Demographic Service has absorbed the old French Statistical Service, SGF. The Demographic Service's annual budget is 30 billion francs. The old SGF budget was 3 to 4 million francs. The new National Statistical Service, SNS, is well-positioned to achieve the second objective."

Miriam said, "Am I right, the first two objectives present no problems?"

"Yes."

"Objective three?"

Charles glanced behind him at the office's closed door and then looked at me. "This will bring me to the limit of what I can share with you today." He inhaled and then smoke drifted lazily from his nostrils. "Put simply, the third objective is to use mechanography to create a large base of mobilization information. One that could at some future date support the activation of the now demobilized French army. However, *Maréchal* Pétain stipulated that if actions related to objective three became known to the Nazis and led to Gen. Carmille's arrest, he and Vichy leadership would deny any prior knowledge. Gen. Carmille accepted this. In doing so, he put himself at risk."

I drew on my Gauloise and began to cough. I squeezed words through coughs. "If I participate in this third objective, do I put myself at risk?"

Charles's face softened. "Yes, a limited risk. We're skilled at building secrecy around what we do."

Lt. Lacroix said, "Large numbers of people working at 10 *rue des*

Archers will participate in objective three. To them it will be another data coding and cardpunch project. One that focuses on demobilized soldiers living within certain geographic boundaries."

I took a deeper draw on my cigarette. I exhaled and watched the smoke rise. "Why have you told me all this? You could've treated me as one of the others with an assignment to a routine project."

"Most people who work here are local Lyonnaise," Charles said. "They feel fortunate to have a job in uncertain times and to work in a safe place. Their daily work is routine, secure, and predictable—in a world that's unpredictable and anything but secure. Most of them want simply to earn a living and at the end of the day go home."

Miriam said, "Other than not being from Lyon, am I any different?"

"You are intelligent and very talented. You have unique and advanced specialized knowledge and valuable skills. You have demonstrated leadership. I believe you want to do more than most people to advance *liberté*."

"*Liberté*," I said, as if talking to myself. "*Oui*."

"Lt. Lacroix and I want you to join us. We will help you do that."

"Thank you." I smiled. "I'm honored."

Lt. Lacroix asked Charles, "Do you have any new information on the invasion? The location?"

"Still uncertain," Charles said. "Somewhere along the North African coast. French Morocco, Algeria."

"It's a long coastline. Even if we knew, it's best not to talk about it."

"Right. Starting now we need to build a base of information in order for us to connect with demobilized French soldiers. After the invasion our work could, I emphasize *could*, help speed demobilized soldiers to active duty. We may fail. But I'd like to give the Wehrmacht a grand French surprise."

"We can do it," Lt. Lacroix said. "My brother died in combat. For him, I'd like to create that surprise."

Charles turned to me. "Miriam and her people will compile records of military specialties and training. Once they've finished—"

In a firm voice, Lt. Lacroix interrupted. "We will give the Allies what they need."

Charles said to me, "There is some risk and more to tell you. We've covered enough for today. We can talk more at another time."

Lt. Lacroix stood and extended his hand to me. "We're glad you're here. And that you've joined us." I stood, followed by Charles. The three of us shook hands.

Charles took a few steps toward the door. He turned and flashed the two-fingered V, Churchill's signal for victory. Lt. Lacroix flashed the V to Charles.

What had I just done?

The next morning at the Demographic Service, Charles walked down the corridor to my group's workspace. He threaded his way through tall stacks of crates to my desk, tables on either side extending the work surface.

I looked up. "This is a nice surprise."

Charles smiled. "My apology for the interruption. I thought about our last conversation. There are a few more things I'd like to review with you."

"No apology needed. Do you want to talk now?"

"I have another meeting in a few minutes." Charles looked away, turned to me. His face at first suggested uncertainty about when we might talk. Then his face brightened. "What about later? Would you have dinner with me this evening?"

I gave him a wide smile. "Yes, I would enjoy that."

"I'm also staying at *Le Lieu*. Meet you in the lobby about eight thirty?"

Miriam and Charles

With encouragement from BBC's broadcaster Colonel Britton to "Splash the V from one end of Europe to another," each night throughout France the V appeared, painted on walls and streets. The following morning, Wehrmacht soldiers armed with black paint covered those symbols of hope. Train whistles blasted the Morse code V, dit-dit-dit-dah. Late at night in Paris, a man caught in the act of painting V on the wall of an alley was shot dead. On French radio stations, the Nazis quickly broadcast descriptions of the man's "foolish and disloyal" actions and its lethal consequences.

In the evening's darkness, Charles and I walked across Place Bellecour. Snow and wind swirled around the massive statue of Louis XIV and across the wide parade ground. On the base of the statue, in white paint, was a V, a mark of the growing Resistance. Our Resistance.

A strong breeze slapped our faces. Charles turned up his coat collar. I tucked my nose into my scarf.

Crossing the street near Place Bellecour I slipped on the ice. I grabbed Charles's hand. We continued to walk, hand in hand.

Ahead of us, across the river, rose La Cathédrale St. Jean. Even in the dimmed wartime streetlights, the cathedral's cream-colored stucco walls cast a warm glow. Before we reached the Saône's Pont de Bonaparte, we turned right and walked along Quai des Célestines.

I said, "We're not far from the café where we had dinner in October."

"Chez Claude. Is it all right with you to go there again?"

"Oui!"

With the arrival of winter, the outdoor tables at Chez Claude had been stacked along one end of the patio. A handmade sign, much like the one on the door of the hotel dining room, was taped to the front door. "*Mes amis*, I regret that rationing and food shortages limit our menu. Please accept my apologies." Claude's signature was scrawled below the note.

Claude's note reminded me that along with all of France, each day I was hungry while the German army consumed our food.

With a broad smile, Claude met us as soon as we entered the café. "Charles, *mon ami,* welcome!" He embraced Charles with a bise—his lips lightly touched each cheek. "And, mademoiselle, so nice to see you again." I extended my hand. Claude grasped it and gently placed a kiss on my fingertips. "I hope you are warm in the Lyon winter."

Claude seated us and then stood beside our table. "*Mes amies*, please permit me to select and prepare your entrées. Even with our limitations, I want you to have the best."

The waiter who had served us in October came to our table. I gazed at the six-pointed yellow star on heavy cloth pinned to the front of the waiter's white jacket. Will there come a time when I will have to wear that star?

I stared at the star until the waiter left to place our order. A different waiter, without a yellow star, served a table of men in dark suits. Gestapo officers?

Charles observed the path of my gaze. His face mellowed. Then the corners of his mouth drooped. "You should know that a few days ago colleagues told me that Ruth attempted to travel south by train. She intended to go to Cannes. At one stop a Gestapo officer challenged her *carte d'identitié*. He suspected the card was counterfeit. She was arrested."

I stiffened. "Will that happen to me?"

"I doubt it, though it's hard to know. Your card is better quality than Ruth's. It appears more authentic. Most likely Ruth'll be sent to a transit camp. Then to Dachau or Auschwitz. A colleague is attempting to track her movement. It's possible he'll be able to secure her release. Or as a last resort, her escape. Right now, I just don't know."

I toyed with my silverware. How many lives, friends, lost? Why?

The waiter returned and served us each a glass of chardonnay. A short time later he placed plates of steaming food before us. I inhaled the aroma of the rich wine sauce that covered sliced carrots and potatoes laced with, Claude later told me, shredded rabbit. I poised my fork over my entrée. "Forgive me, Charles, I must eat! The aroma is wonderful. And I'm famished."

Charles ate at a slower pace. He smiled as he watched me devour my entrée.

I leaned back and stared at my empty plate. I felt like a magician. Presented with a plate full of food, I made it disappear. "Claude is an amazing chef."

Charles laughed. "I'm not sure which I enjoyed most—my entrée or watching you eat."

"Yesterday I saw a mother with a young child. They sat on the street and begged for food. I had none to give."

"I'm sorry," Charles said. "We're trying to secure food to distribute to people in need. The Germans often intercept our efforts."

"To feed the troops, right?"

"Yes," Charles said, his face glum. He ordered two coffees. He lit two cigarettes and handed one to me.

We sat in silence, smoked, and sipped our coffee. Coffee. Real, rich coffee!

I said, "Today, about our conversation with Lt. Lacroix, is there more you can tell me?"

Charles's face tensed. "Yes, there's more. It's probably best to leave it in the realm of the unknown." Charles looked around the café. Many of the patrons had left. No table near them was occupied. His face relaxed.

"Sort of like looking at an equation that contain unknowns?"

"Yes, sort of."

I took a puff of my Gauloise. "I love to solve equations for unknowns. Let me see what I can do with this one." I slowly exhaled and watched the smoke rise. "I'll start with the conditions around the equation, the context. Preparation of the mobilization information base is a good place to start. We create files, punchcards, for demobilized soldiers living in southern France and Algeria."

"That's a sound beginning for the context. The unknowns?"

"The first unknown, storage. Once done, where will we store the files? The answer depends on how the files will be used. If the files are principally for such things as veterans' post-war pensions and medical care, benefits for widows and children, and so on, the main requirement for storage is a clean, dry, secure, and accessible facility. They could be stored here, or in Vichy, Rouen, Paris. Wherever."

"If the files are to be used in other ways?"

"Then the location for storage of the files becomes a major factor in the equation's solution."

"And this factor—I should say possible factor—location? How does it make the transition from unknown to known?"

"We have to find the driver behind the problem—the desired or hoped-for outcomes. I can define a driver by examining its functions related to those outcomes."

"And in this case? The functions of the card files for demobilized soldiers?"

"If the files will play a role in bringing former soldiers to active duty, then their storage should be centrally placed. First, near the soldiers' domiciles. Or, second, in proximity to the area where they'll report once mobilized."

"And then?"

"The location of the files must be kept secret. Except from the people who will use them. For example, if we hoped to mobilize former soldiers in North Africa, then it would make sense to store the files nearby, say in Algiers or Casablanca. Once done, we'll have another upside-down pyramid. At its inverted apex, the pyramidion, the card files. This new pyramid will serve the Allies."

Charles again looked around the café. Then he spoke slowly in a low voice, as if he chose his words with care. "We hope the United States will do more than supply Britain: declare war and join the Allies. That is yet to come. But within the coming year we believe there will be an Allied invasion of North Africa—as we discussed in Lt. Lacroix's office. But all this is still speculative."

"Of course." I felt special, privileged to be on the inside of plans to reshape the war. My thoughts leaped to the human costs likely to come with the invasion. Soldiers on both sides, and those in harm's way, civilians and children.

In a soft, firm voice, little more than a whisper, Charles said, "When the invasion happens, when, not if, we must have the information prepared, be ready to connect the military command with soldiers dispersed in civilian life. Bring them to active duty. Fast. Rapid mobilization— speed—will be essential. To do this well, we must prepare an accurate record of soldiers' military specialties, training, and branch of military service—infantry, armor, artillery, quartermaster, medics, and on and on. With this, we can speed the activation of specialized companies and regiments that are critical for military success."

I felt as though I had approached a solution to a problem posed by one of my professors. "The storage location? To complete my solution for our equation's one important unknown, I need to know a little more."

Charles grinned. "We'll need a storage location that simplifies and speeds our contact with demobilized soldiers." He paused and glanced around the café. "Along the north coast of Africa, Algeria, and the south of France."

"If that's the invasion zone, storage should be at its center."

"Even if I knew more, I couldn't tell you."

I reflected on the importance of speed when bringing armies to full strength. My staff and I would affect the conduct of the war, the success of the Allies. A current of excitement surged through me.

Charles signaled the waiter for two more cups of coffee. He again lit two cigarettes. He handed one to me. "Your analysis is sound." He beamed. "You have the makings of a good intelligence officer."

"Thank you."

In silence, we sipped our coffee.

"Share your thoughts?"

I hesitated and then replied, "I was thinking about our first conversation. In Rotterdam."

"I often think about that."

"You do?"

"Until then, I had met few people with your grasp of the new technology. And no one as lovely as you—or who held my interest as you did. As you do."

I felt my face become warm, probably redden. I toyed with my fork. "I also thought of our dinner here, nearly three months ago. Afterward, how I held your arm on our walk to the hotel."

"I liked that, your arm next to me. And I remembered the end of the evening. Our kiss."

"I did, too."

We again sat in silence. I was keenly aware of Charles's presence. I felt drawn to him. I felt a pulse deep inside me.

I took Charles's hand. "Isn't it time to return to the hotel?"

Charles paid the bill and we soon bid Claude au revoir.

Full Disclosure

In the dimly lit lobby of Le Lieu, Jacques waved to Charles and me as we walked to the elevator. Charles pressed the button for the fifth floor. "My room is on the fourth floor."

Charles laughed. "Ah, *mais mademoiselle*, the fifth floor is more comfortable." I laughed, too.

As soon as the elevator rose above the lobby, Charles turned to me. I slid my arms inside his coat and around him. We kissed until the lift stopped at the fifth floor. Our arms around each other, Charles guided me to his room.

Once inside, we again embraced and shared a long, slow kiss that lingered. Winter coats dropped to the floor, followed by my sweater. Charles shed his sport coat. I unbuttoned his shirt then he removed my bra. I pulled him against me. Our arms around each other, we took slow steps to the bed, toppled on to it, and kicked off our shoes. Charles removed my underwear. He put his lips to my breasts, then my legs. His hands stroked my body, and he gently massaged the soft V between my legs. I gasped. Then I unbuckled his trousers, ran my hands over his body. Soon he entered me. Our bodies began to move in a singular rhythm, our thrusts ever stronger.

Later, in the silent darkness we shared a Gauloise. I stroked Charles's chest. "Charles, do you trust me?"

"Of course."

"Have you ever been misled by a woman who wanted to know government secrets?"

"You mean taken to bed for ulterior motives?" He laughed.

"Yes. But I'm not asking as a joke."

He was quiet for a short time. "Yes, I have."

"Tell me about it."

"Paris, two years ago." He stopped, then asked, "Are you sure you want to know?"

"Yes."

"Long before I knew you, an attractive French woman, Ursula, a journalist she had said, sought me out after a meeting at the Louvre. After a brief discussion she said, 'Forgive my boldness. I would like to learn more about your work. Might we have dinner together?' Over dinner she seemed fascinated with my background, education, and my work as a museum consultant. I fabricated much of what I told her.

"During dinner her leg rested against mine. After dinner, hand in hand, we returned to her hotel room and made love. She soon fell asleep. I remained awake. I thought about her questions, her interest in my background. Something seemed off-center.

"Careful not to awaken her, I got up and tiptoed across the room to her purse. I opened it. Lipstick, makeup, tissue. A passport and a French driver's license. I discovered the purse had a small false bottom. I had opened others much like it. Soon it, too, was open. I found an *Abwehr*, German intelligence service, identity card with her picture. I replaced the card. As I returned to bed she awakened. Before making love a second time, we talked about the responses of senior French officials to the Austrian *Anschluss*. Having insisted on, and received, assurances of confidentiality from Ursula, I shared lies about military strategy discussions in the French high command. Later I gave myself high marks for creative story telling.

"That's it. Now, get some sleep. I have some papers I need to review tonight."

I rolled over and pulled the covers up to my neck.

I slept briefly. Charles's movements awakened me. I watched Charles open my purse. He examined its contents and tugged at the purse's bottom—it was real.

"What are you doing?" I yelled. I leaped out of bed. My left hand yanked the purse from Charles as my right hand slapped him hard.

"Damn you! Are you robbing me? Spying on me?" I pulled a blanket off the bed and with one hand held it around me. With my other hand I grabbed Charles's wrist and with powerful force twisted it.

"Ach!" Charles cried out in pain.

"Hand me your wallet. Your trousers and sports coat."

Charles did as I asked.

I relaxed my grip on his wrist then released it. Charles sat on the bed.

I rifled his passports and wallet. I found only francs and a few addresses.

Charles stared at me.

"Why are you staring?"

"I told you about my night two years ago with a charming woman who, I later discovered, was a German *Abwehr* agent. I had to confirm that the *Abwehr* hadn't created your Dutch and Jewish identity. Planted you here as an agent."

I glared angrily at him. "And?"

"My suspicions about you were unfounded. I was wrong. Please accept my apology."

"It's cold in here." I returned to bed and pulled the covers to my chin.

Charles got in bed beside me. We lay in silence. Charles attempted to put his arm around my shoulders. I rolled away.

We slept intermittently. At dawn Charles whispered, "Please, forgive me. I love what I know of the woman you've been, Miriam Meijer. I've fallen in love with the new woman you've become, Miriam Dupré.

"I feel betrayed."

An hour later we were dressed and in the hotel dining room.

Over faux coffee and stale croissants, Charles again said, "Please, forgive me."

"It's going to take time."

"May I ask, who is Miriam Meijer?"

"I am Miriam Dupré. But Miriam Meijer is at my core. She is my identity and truth."

"If I had gone to Rotterdam before the war and located you, who would I have found?"

"You would have found a diligent student excited about

mechanography, its application, its potential for the future. If you came
to our family's apartment in the late afternoon, you would have met Papa
returning from a day of teaching, having a glass of beer. Mama preparing
dinner, the apartment filled with rich aromas. My twin sister, Margot, at
the kitchen table reading a novel. Mama would've insisted you stay for
dinner. If you arrived after dinner, you would've found us in discussions and
arguments about European politics.

"And you, Charles? I'm aware of your dual working identities. Who
are you? Who is at your core?"

Charles took a deep breath. He spoke slowly. "My life has been
convoluted, the life of a secret agent. Aliases. False residences. I feel as
though I've lived lies for almost twenty years. It's become a way of life.
Perhaps I can change all that, I don't know." Charles paused. "At least with
you, I want to live and share the truth."

"Tell me the truth about Charles Delmand? Who is he?"

"I am Charles Delmand, a columnist for *the London Times*. And I
am Charles Secœur, a museum consultant who specializes in antiquities.
Charles Secœur will soon travel to Berlin to meet with Reichsmarschall
Hermann Göring."

I sat up. "You what? Why?"

"The Reichmarschall is worried about the authenticity of a Matisse
paining he recently acquired."

"Stolen from a Jewish home?"

"I don't know. Possibly. I think he purchased it from a collector. My
visit will be a rare opportunity to rub shoulders with a member of the
Reich's Supreme Command."

"Charles, the truth. Who are you?"

"The truth is not simple. I am both a *Times* columnist and an art
antiquities expert. I shift back and forth, from one identity to the other. It
depends on the needs of France, the *Deuxième Bureau*, and on my mission."

"Your description reminds me of a character in a puppet show."

Charles laughed. "You might say that."

"What about the voice of the puppets, the off-stage puppeteer? Who is he?"

"The puppeteer?" Charles paused. "I've never thought of myself in
quite that way."

"Well, give it a try."

"I was born in 1901. In 1923 I studied at the Paris *École Libre des Sciences Politiques*."

"*Sciences Po.*"

"Yes. From there I was recruited into what I believed was the French diplomatic corps. I learned my new employer was actually the *Deuxième Bureau*—the French Intelligence Service."

"Where did you grow up?"

"On a farm near the village of *Cauchy-à-la-Tour* in northern France."

"I would like to have known you as a boy on that farm. If I had come to *Cauchy-à-la-Tour*, how would I have found you? Should I have asked directions to the Delmand or Secœur farm?"

Charles was silent.

"Hello? Charles, where are you? What's going on?"

"Neither. You would have asked directions to neither of those farms."

"Well, Mr. Puppeteer, tell me how I would have found you?"

"I'm not sure I can do that. If I do, you will be the only person outside the French Intelligence Service who knows."

"If you don't, you'll keep part of yourself locked away from me. Separating us. Is that what you want? What's your commitment to me, Charles?"

Charles again fell silent. He lit a cigarette. Then he spoke slowly, as if carefully selecting each word. "To have found me back then? You would've gone to the village of *Cauchy-à-la-Tour* and asked for directions to the farm of my father, Oscar Pétain."

"Pétain?"

"I am Charles Pétain. A cousin of *Maréchal* Philippe Pétain. The *Maréchal* was born in *Cauchy-à-la-Tour* during the years when Napoleon III held power. When they were young, my late grandfather knew Philippe well. For generations, my family has been involved behind the scenes in high-level French politics."

Suddenly Charles seemed to relax. I sensed he felt relieved. At last, someone other than his colleagues, themselves living false identities in the foggy world of French Intelligence, knew the truth about him. He smiled—as if his disclosure improved his spirit. But it probably worried him, too. He was now vulnerable.

I smiled, as if buoyed by Charles's disclosure and trust. I interlocked the fingers of our hands and stretched. In a quiet voice, I said, "I don't have to be at work for an hour. Let's go back to my room."

Charles took my hand. "Yes, let's do that."

I felt something like an electric current zing from the center of my body to my fingertips.

As we stepped through the door into my room, I pulled Charles next to me. Our clothes fell away. I moved his hands over my body. "Touch me here." Then, "Now here." We made love in gentle, slow moves, sharing a new and intense passion.

Supply and Demand
March 1941

Overnight a blast of cold air put Lyon in a deep freeze. Even worse was the psychic blast that came from a note from Charles, delivered to me at the Demographic Service. "Miriam—bad news from Paris. In February, at *Musée de l'Homme* the Gestapo arrested nineteen people. Boris Vildé, Aimée's boss, and many others in the Polar Department. All charged with espionage. Aimée Connaix is not on the list of those arrested. Will let you know if I learn more. Love, C."

I said a prayer for Aimée.

In the coming weeks, once in a while I received a brief note from Charles and, as we had agreed, replied with notes equally brief. Our exchanges were worded to avoid identification of the sender and included words, references only he and I understood. Charles was ever the intelligence officer. I sent notes to Charles addressed to an office in the Louvre. Charles's notes to me usually arrived at the front desk of 10 rue des Archers. Occasionally they came to the hotel. I worried about Jacques reading Charles's notes, even though they were coded and had meaning only to the two of us.

My notes to Charles were full of questions. About my friend at the museum. About her safety. His replies were always guarded, sometimes hard to interpret, even for me. Their ambiguity protected both of us. But it prompted more questions from me. The cycle seemed endlessly convoluted.

The frigid days of the coldest winter in decades abated. I welcomed the arrival of bursts of warm winds that blew dust along Lyon's streets. The sunlight that fell on the new buds of tree limbs seemed like a resurrection of life. In window boxes and gardens, the colors of spring burst forth in new violets, primroses, and daffodils.

At 10 rue des Archers, over the more than two months since I received my new assignment, I had waded into my work. On my morning walks to work I tried to settle my jumbled emotions. I breathed deeply. I thought about Charles's report that Aimée's name was not on the arrest list. But was it possible she was using a nom de guerre? The network she talked about, was it part of the Resistance? If Aimée was arrested, could she implicate Carmille? And if she wasn't, then surly she was high on the Nazi's most wanted list.

That morning, my walk to work cleared my head. I arrived at 10 rue des Archers less disturbed than earlier. Demographic Service crews moved, unpacked, and organized files of demobilized French soldiers living in southern France and Algeria. New keypunch machines arrived and were installed, as were new tabulating and collating machines. My mechanography equipment and operators in my unit occupied much of the building's fourth floor.

After the initial weeks in which we unpacked and retrieved files, clerks began the paper-and-pencil coding of soldiers' information. A few weeks later I reported to Lt. Lacroix, "My staff has created a backlog of coded files large enough we can begin to keypunch." Soon operators' fingers pressed numbers on keyboards that created small rectangular holes transferring written alpha numeric codes to punch-cards.

Lt. Lacroix visited our office and called us together. He said, "You've done a terrific job in getting the processing underway." My people appreciated the recognition. At the same time, my growing apprehension about the work yet to come prompted me to make an appointment later that day with him.

When I arrived, he said, "You look upset. What's wrong?"

"Marcel, uh, Lieutenant, our coding and processing of the—special data." I stopped before using the words southern France or North Africa. Lt. Lacroix nodded.

"It's as if we're on a speeding train. A mile ahead, a boulder has rolled onto the track."

"You'll have to explain that."

"I'll run the numbers for you. We are to process information on at least three hundred thousand demobilized soldiers—perhaps as many as eight hundred thousand. The information for each soldier will require two, and in some cases three, cards. In addition, there will be cards required to operate programs for processing data and extracting information. No simple matter. Then there is the data tabulation."

Lt. Lacroix gave me a puzzled look. "Where are you going with this?"

"At a minimum we will have," I scribbled on a notepad and said as I wrote, "three hundred thousand soldiers multiplied by two cards per file, equals six hundred thousand cards." I paused and looked across the desk. "Then there are the cards that run the programs. One hundred thousand? Could be more, could be less."

"So, we're looking at, say, seven hundred thousand cards, minimum," Lt. Lacroix said. "I don't know what we have in stock. We can order additional cards from suppliers."

"I know what we have in stock—one hundred thousand cards. All dedicated to current programs at 10 *rue des Archers*. Our project here is one of many. Our warehouse has an uncommitted supply of twenty-five thousand punchcards. The flow of new cards to us is limited. My projections are the Demographic Service will consume its entire supply in a few weeks. I have requisitioned hundreds of thousands of cards. Suppliers say they're sorry but production of cards for use in Paris and Berlin has top priority. We'll have to wait. We're somewhere in back of the queue."

"Will we have to put a hold on operations, send people home?"

"That could happen. As things now stand, even if Gen. Carmille makes us a top priority within the Service, the available card supply will be less than what we need. Unless, of course, suppliers step up production."

I knew, Lt. Lacroix knew—the Allies will need the files for rapid mobilization of French forces in North Africa. Without the files? Stop, Miriam.

Lt. Lacroix leaned back in his chair. "For sure, that is a big boulder on the track."

"There may be a way around it."

Base Twelve

"A way around the card shortage?" Lt. Lacroix leaned over his desk toward me.

I opened my notebook, glanced at a page and looked up. "General Carmille has written about the advantages of using a base-twelve mathematical system to manage large quantities of information."

"That's a way around our card shortage problem? Am I missing something?"

I laughed. "Base twelve is a possible solution to our card shortage."

"Sorry, I'm not familiar with a base-twelve system."

"Most people aren't. But think about this." I leaned forward and put my forearms on Lt. Lacroix's desk. I extended my hands and spread my fingers. "We have ten of these." I wiggled my fingers. "As children, most of us first learned to count, to add and subtract, using our fingers. Toes, too."

"I was one of them."

"In school we learned to multiply and divide by 10. Easy. Move the decimal one place to the left or right. Base ten is our conventional approach to numbers. Familiar. Comfortable. But inefficient."

"Inefficient?" Lt. Lacroix grinned. "Seemed fast and easy. Worked well for me."

I smiled. "Stay with me. The fact that the number ten is divisible by two and five makes certain facts about calculations and divisibility easy to see. If the last digit of any number is even, the number is divisible by two.

If the last digit is zero or five, the number is divisible by five. There are two divisors in a base-ten system."

"I'm with you."

"It's different for base twelve. If the last digit of any number is even, the number is divisible by two. If the last digit of any number is divisible by three, that number is divisible by three. If the last digit is divisible by four, the number is divisible by four, and if the last digit of a number is divisible by six, the number is divisible by six." Eyes wide, I smiled. I felt like a teacher making a point to a class. "There are four divisors in a base-twelve system. Only two in base ten."

"That is an advantage? Are my eyes getting glassy?"

"The number ten is divisible only by two and five. That's it. Division by other numbers creates fractions. Not a huge problem. We're used to fractions. We've learned how to allow for fractional values. They're manageable. But in the coding and keypunching of mechanography they require extra processes, extra tabulation, and additional card space. That's inefficient."

"You want to get rid of fractions?"

"Imagine what might have happened if humans had been born with twelve fingers and toes. Instead of counting by tens, we would've counted by twelves."

Lieutenant Lacroix laughed. "Reminds me of something I'd find in an H. G. Wells novel. You're talking science fiction, Miriam. In our real world of everyday life, we work in tens, hundreds, thousands, and so on. What's your point?"

"Science fiction? I don't think so. In the real world, there are lots of base-twelve systems. Grocers order products in dozens and grosses. In apparel twelve dozen shirts equals a gross. Pharmacists and jewelers use a twelve-ounce pound. One foot on the Imperial ruler has twelve inches. In England minters divide shillings into twelve pence."

"We're in France."

I grinned. "Even for the French, there are twelve months in a year. The French day, like days everywhere else, is measured in two sets of twelve hours. In geometry a circle, whether measured in France or elsewhere, contains three hundred sixty degrees. Thirty sets of twelve degrees."

"I get your point. Go on."

"Unlike a base-ten system, with its two divisors, a base-twelve system supports more arithmetic operations. With its four divisors, a base-twelve system produces fewer fractions." I leaned forward and raised my voice, "Less space is required on cards and in card-based records. Data recorded in base twelve can be manipulated with far greater efficiency. When you're performing hundreds of thousands, even millions, of calculations, those efficiencies cut costs and reduce calculation time. They're valuable."

"I think I see where you're going with this. Please continue. Tell me how the use of base twelve affects your project?"

"Very simply, it would reduce the number of cards required. Speed our output."

Lt. Lacroix snapped, "And require us to retrain huge numbers of staff. I don't want to think about the cost."

"In his papers, lectures too, René Carmille talked about the advantages of using base-twelve systems in government statistical operations."

Lt. Lacroix looked more than surprised. Astonished. He mumbled, "I didn't know that," then began to organize the papers on his desk.

I sat back in my chair, closed my notebook.

"I'm scheduled to meet with General Carmille later today. Your project is on our agenda. I'll mention your base twelve suggestions. In the meantime, call our suppliers. Try to find a source for additional cards. Lots of them."

Mid-afternoon, Lt. Lacroix stopped by my work area. I was crosschecking codes on sheets of ledger paper spread across my desk. "Sorry to interrupt. I just met with General Carmille."

"Ah. Good discussion?"

"Yes."

We looked at each other expectantly.

I said, "Did you discuss our card supply problem?"

"I briefed him on it."

"You did?" The lieutenant had my full attention.

"I told him your suggestion to develop our data codes in a base-twelve system. He said, 'I understand the problem. Mlle. Dupré is right.

But making that change would require substantial staff training. We're working under tight timelines. I wish we had the time and resources to shift to base twelve.' Then he made a phone call to our largest and best supplier of cards. Afterward he said, 'Tell Mlle. Dupré she will have the cards she needs.'"

I felt a warm glow inside me. A smile lit my face.

"Gen. Carmille asked me to thank you."

"I appreciate your telling me."

"And he had a request."

"Yes?"

"General Carmille asked that you meet with him."

I sat up and looked Lt. Lacroix in the eye. My thoughts riveted on a one-word question. "When?"

"In ten minutes. Can you do that?"

The Discomfort of Truth

I stepped off the elevator at the fifth floor of 10 rue des Archers. I walked the long quiet corridor to the director's office. On the walls hung lithographs of nineteenth century sailing ships docked along the Saône and Rhône and the medieval streets of old Lyon.

I reflected on my base-twelve suggestions to Lt. Lacroix. Is that what Gen. Carmille wants to discuss? I understood base twelve well enough to suggest it to the Lieutenant. But Gen. Carmille once proposed base twelve for the entire French government. Did I understand base twelve well enough to talk about it with him and not make a fool of myself? I looked at my reflection in the glass of one of the lithographs—small and alone.

I paused at the open door of a large office. Inside, men in French army uniforms and women in civilian dress I'd seen around the building sat at desks. At a conference table, a group huddled over maps and charts.

I thought about base twelve. Then, with no forethought, I imagined I was a circus's trapeze artist in the upper reaches of a big-top tent. At the peak of an arc I released my grip from the trapeze bar. For a moment I suddenly hung motionless in mid-air. My stomach leaped to my throat. In that prolonged moment, my knowledge of base twelve flashed through my thoughts. Then I grasped the new bar that swung to me: a new base-twelve application. And then I swung to another bar. One application after another, I soared across the big-top.

I arrived at Gen. Carmille's offices. I walked into his reception room.

His door was open. I glanced into his office. He sat at his desk making notes—white shirt and bow tie, sleeves rolled up, suit coat on the back of his desk chair.

In a rush of self-doubt, I wondered if Gen. Carmille knew I was Dutch, not French, or that I was Jewish. If he found out, would he fire me? Ask me to resign? I stood immobile in his doorway, like a mannequin in a department store window.

"Ah, Mlle Dupré, welcome. Please, come in." He removed his glasses, rubbed his eyes, and put his glasses back on.

"I hope I'm not interrupting."

He glanced at me then at his wristwatch. "Not at all. I asked Lt. Lacroix if you might drop by." With a smile, he said, "Thank you for coming." He motioned toward one of the chairs on the other side of his desk. "Please, sit down."

I did, clasped my hands in my lap, and sat up straight.

"Lt. Lacroix told me of the punch-card shortage. He described your base twelve proposal. Very creative thinking on your part. I hope he told you that I talked with a card supplier."

"Yes, sir."

Another smile. "He also said you had read some of my papers."

"Yes, sir."

He stared at me for a moment. "I feel as though we've met. Have we?"

Mon dieu, perhaps he remembers me. I felt my face flush. "Uh, yes, sir. Autumn, 1939, *Ecole des Sciences Politiques*. I was in your mechanography seminar. You were an engaging teacher. I learned a lot."

"Thank you. Yes, now I remember. You sat near the front, toward the window. You had a friend also in the class." Does Carmille really not remember my friend? Does he know the danger he would be in if Aimée was caught? Should I tell him Aimée's name? Mention the Polar Department?

I laughed. "Yes, sir. That was Aimée."

"Ah, now I remember. She worked in the Polar Department. *Musée de l'Homme.*"

"Yes, sir."

"I talked with a man in that department, Boris Vildé, about uses of mechanography in development of the collection's records."

Was that all they talked about? Did he know about last month's museum arrests? Could I, should I, ask about Aimée's safety? Was his mention of Boris Vildé a test, a probe of how much I knew?

Lt. Jaouen rapped on the door and stepped inside. "Sir, a reminder, you have a meeting in twenty minutes."

Gen. Carmille nodded to him then turned to me. "Lt. Lacroix talked with me about your suggestions for base-twelve applications in our systems. You learned your base twelve lessons well. Now you've brought them to the Service."

"Thank you, sir."

"You are from Paris?"

I nodded.

"Other than our seminar together, where have you studied?"

Was this a test? I drew on my newly created identity, tried not miss a beat. *L'École Supérieure de Commerce de Paris.*"

"The French business schools provide excellent training. I hope you had an opportunity to study with Professor Anton Thibault."

Mon dieu, I've never heard of him. Could I finesse my reply? "Yes, sir. But I just attended a few lectures."

He leaned back in his chair. "Your success at the Service is living proof of our business school's excellence."

I felt my face flush. "Thank you."

"You also come recommended by Charles Delmand."

I wanted to add another thank you. My lips parted as if to speak. No words came. I hadn't expected him to mention Charles. I stared at Gen. Carmille and stammered, "Yes, I appreciate . . ."

"Charles is an old and trusted friend. Over the years I have benefited from his counsel. Do you know him well?"

"I believe so. We first met by accident in Paris, early in the war."

"Didn't you live there?"

I felt my face again redden. "Uh, yes, sir. But with the invasion, everything seemed to turn upside down. I tried to stay ahead of the Germans."

"You and a million other Parisians."

"Yes. Charles recommended that I come to Lyon. He said my training would fit well with the needs of the Military Recruitment Service."

Carmille raised one hand, a signal for me to stop. "Mlle Dupré, I won't ask more questions about how you connected with our organization. Or about Charles. I know that you and he are, shall we say, close friends." Had my face caught fire?

Gen. Carmille then spoke as if giving instruction to a student. "Let's treat our conversation thus far as a training exercise."

"Uh, yes, sir." Training exercise? Training in what?

"The last time I checked, my friend Anton Thibault was a professor of mathematics at the Sorbonne. Not a faculty member at *École Supérieure de Commerce de Paris*."

I slumped deep into my chair. If a door in the floor suddenly opened, I'd jump through it.

"Nazi interrogators are far more skilled than me. Hesitations. Inconsistencies. They listen for them. Pounce on them. Is there more you want to tell me?"

I took a deep breath, sat up straight. "Gen. Carmille, I don't know what Charles did or didn't share with you about me. Please forgive my nervousness."

"I understand."

"I have long admired your work. I'm honored to be here. To work for you."

"Thank you, Miriam."

I watched a pigeon walk along the windowsill and fly away. I wished I could fly with him. "I am prepared to tell you the story of my new life as a French citizen. The one Charles urged me to construct and rehearse. The story I would tell an investigator. Wehrmacht or Gestapo. As you have observed, I need to practice it. Or, as an alternative, I can tell you the truth. How would you prefer for me to proceed?"

"Let's leave your constructed story aside. I know some of the truth. About Rotterdam. About your studies at the School of Economics. The Luftwaffe bombing." Behind his round wire-rimmed glasses, his gaze softened. "I know you are Jewish, and about the loss of your family." He was silent for a moment. "Please accept my condolences."

I nodded and relaxed. "Thank you," I said, my voice little more than a whisper.

"Continue to rehearse the story you have constructed. One day you're likely to need it. I requested that we meet in order to get a sense of who you are, your presence."

"I hope you're not disappointed."

With a small laugh, he said, "To the contrary. I love your spunk. You're a brave young woman." Then returning to his teacher's voice, "You bring much to the Demographic Service."

"May I ask you something?"

"Of course."

"I know your work in mechanography, but little about you. Lt. Lacroix said you were born in Trémolat. He shared with me some of your army service record. Can you tell me more? Your personal story?"

"I'm not often asked that. I enjoy opportunities to reflect on my life, on our little town, though we later moved. The beauty of the Dordogne countryside. My parents were teachers. They found joy in learning, as if they were forever students."

I said, "My father was like that."

"They felt learning alone was not enough. Healthy teaching and learning were anchored in values."

I remembered Papa's words, "We, you and me, have to stand for something."

"My parents found joy in the achievements of their students, as well as my sisters and me. I learned to live by a simple maxim. We are all students. We are all teachers. A good life is filled with opportunities to teach and learn."

I said, "My father would've enjoyed a conversation with your parents. He and my mother taught my sister and me that we alone are responsible for the quality of our lives."

"Yes, I believe that, too. Even under trying conditions, there are opportunities to learn. To stand on your values. To build quality into lives."

"I think I read somewhere that Jules Claretie was a relative. Wasn't he a drama critic for *Le Figaro*?"

"Yes, as well as a newspaper correspondent during the Franco-Prussian War. He became director of the *Théâtre Français* and later was elected to the *Académie française,* alongside *Maréchal* Pétain."

It took me a moment to digest that—General Carmille's uncle and

Charles's grandfather knew Pétain. At least I had shaken Pétain's hand. "And you taught at the *École Libre des Sciences Politiques.*"

"Teaching helped me organize my thoughts, my approaches to accounting reform in government and the French Army."

"I read the paper you wrote for your conference, 'On Germanism.' The kind of reciprocity in teaching and learning we discussed was not part of the German worldview you presented in the paper."

He flashed a big grin. "You're right." Then the grin disappeared. "The German worldview is highly structured. I wrote of how it relies on the exercise of power. People are expected to have confidence in the knowledge and wisdom of those in authority."

"Even when they're wrong?"

"Yes, unfortunately. That worldview is at the heart of the Third Reich and Führer Hitler's approach to government. It is at the heart of issues that led us into this war. It transcends disputes over territory and economics."

"I first read the words, *Liberté, Égalité, Fraternité,* when I was in school. They became deeply lodged in me."

Carmille's eyebrows arched above his glasses. A warm expression crept over his face. "Lodged in me, too."

I smiled.

Carmille glanced at the wall clock behind me. "Please forgive me. I must soon leave. I have an appointment out of the office."

My face flushed. I stood. "I'm sorry. I've stayed longer than I should have. I've enjoyed our discussion."

"*Je vous en prie.* I've enjoyed talking with you." Carmille stood. "About base twelve, one thing further. I'm impressed that you saw its potential to improve efficiencies, reduce costs. Many months ago, I experimented with its use in card-punch and process operations."

"Were you successful?"

"Minimally. Systems and work habits are hard to change. I realized the substantial investment of francs and time that would be required to implement a change of this magnitude. We have the francs. But we have little time. I chose to stop the experiment. Until now, you're the only staff member that has seen the potential of base twelve. I'm pleased you're here, Miriam. I trust we'll find opportunities to continue our conversation. In the meantime, if you have a problem with your punchcard supply, please let me know. Just put a brief note in my downstairs mailbox."

"Thank you, sir. I will."

He walked me to the door and shook my hand. "Keep your project moving forward as fast as possible, it is important. The work you and your staff are doing means a great deal to the future of France."

I walked to the elevator. Gen. Carmille's parting words replayed themselves in my thoughts. "The work you and your staff are doing means a great deal to the future of France."

That night in bed, Carmille's words rolled through my thoughts like loose balls on the deck of a ship. I could not stop them. I did not sleep well.

The Jews of Vichy

Since receiving Charles's note a few days ago, I had looked forward to the weekend. "A picnic next Sunday—can we do that? I'll bring food and wine. You bring lovely you. C."

I thought about my standard ration card—1,160 calories a day, how inadequate. We starved so the German army could be nourished to oppress us. The cost of food on the black market had tripled in the past year. I had been hungry yesterday, and the day before. I would be hungry again tomorrow. Hunger had become my constant companion. A picnic? I laughed and spoke to an imaginary Charles. "For sure, if you can make it happen. Food, Charles, food!"

On Sunday morning I rose early. Beyond my window, a bright blue June sky signaled a good day to come. My thoughts leaped ahead to the afternoon. The shore of the Rhône. Relaxing on a blanket with Charles. Food! Well, sandwiches. A bottle of wine. I put on a comfortable, loose-fitting blouse and slacks. Picnic clothes. No sooner had I buttoned my blouse than I imagined Charles unbuttoning it.

Later, in the lobby of Le Lieu, I said good morning to Jacques and M. Bollé. Jacques stood behind the registration desk reading a newspaper. M. Bollé sat in his favorite wing-backed chair reading his newspaper. They looked up, faces grim. Each muttered a subdued *"Bonjour,"* then returned to their reading.

M. Bollé motioned for me to sit in the chair next to him. I sat down. He nodded toward his newspaper and turned so I could read along with him.

The headline: "Census of Jews Ordered by Vichy." The lead-in: "New law requires declaration of identity and possessions by all Jews. Sets new penalties."

Simone walked into the lobby, her curly hair bounced with each step. She greeted everyone with a bright, "*Bonjour*." I waved and motioned for Simone to join us. M. Bollé nodded to Simone and returned to his newspaper. Simone walked to us and looked over M. Bollé's shoulder. She joined me in reading his newspaper.

M. Bollé muttered, "*Mon Dieu*." He called across the lobby to Jacques. "A new census? What will they do with this one? They've already excluded Jews from the army. From businesses." He turned to me. "All the way down to the little guys, like my friend Jacob. A Jew. Dismissed from his job in fittings and alterations at Value Clothiers. Twenty-two years he worked there."

Jacques looked up. "And at the newspaper." He slapped one hand on the flattened newspaper. "All the Jews. Reporters, editors. Typesetters. People who ran the printing presses. All fired."

"Lawyers and doctors will be next," Simone said. "In Germany, it's already happened."

"I'm not surprised." I said.

"A means to an end." Simone replied. "Find the Jews. Put them out of work. Press them to leave the country. In Poland, my uncle had to sell everything to buy exit visas for himself and his family."

I put my hand on her arm. "Shhh." I looked around the lobby. A man familiar to me, close-cropped black hair, sat alone near the front entrance reading a newspaper. His eyebrows angled toward his nose, suggesting disapproval of whatever his gaze rested on. Most days he wore a dark suit. This Sunday, coatless, he wore a starched white shirt and necktie. I had never heard or seen him speak to anyone other than Jacques. Had he been listening to M. Bollé and Simone's comments about the Nazi census and the Jews? Her Jewish uncle? Did it matter? Then I remembered—these days everything matters.

Reading that news story, I remembered when I first learned of the new census. I sat in Lt. Lacroix's office. We were having our Friday review of the week. In the midst of a conversation about the supply of punchcards, there was a knock on the half-open door. Lt. Lacroix looked up. Before he could say, "Come in," Gen. Carmille entered. Lt. Lacroix and I stood.

"*Bonjour*, Lieutenant. Mlle Dupré. Please, sit."

"*Bonjour, mon Général,*" we said.

Carmille smiled. "Try as I might, I cannot get you, or others, to refer to me as *Monsieur* not *Général.*

Lt. Lacroix said, "Sorry, sir. *Monsieur. Général.*"

A half-second later I said, "Sorry, *Général.*"

We laughed. My face reddened.

Gen. Carmille took a seat next to me. His smile faded. He looked at Lt. Lacroix then at me. "The Vichy government. Do you know about their new census of the Jews?"

Lt. Lacroix said, "I had heard rumors it was soon to come."

"It upsets me," Carmille said. "Disturbing in two ways. First there are questions about whether such a census violates French law. Then there is the foolishness of their methods. How they are going about it."

"How they are . . . What are their methods?" I asked.

He glanced at me, then the lieutenant. "You are familiar with the Tulard System, yes?"

Lt. Lacroix nodded, yes.

"No, sir. What is the Tulard system?"

"André Tulard is a senior police official in Paris. He devised a method, now called the Tulard System, to be used for a census of members of the French Communist Party and for a census of Jews in Paris in order to organize a round up. Now Xavier Vallat is very interested in using such a system in a general census of the Jews including the non-occupied zone."

Carmille looked me in the eye then shook his head sidewise. "Tulard's method, his so-called system, stands as a monument to our inept French methods." His voice rose. "One more example of how our allegiance to old methods causes us to fall behind the rest of Europe."

I asked, "How does it work?"

"Mlle Dupré, Tulard's . . ." He paused. "*S'il vous plaît,* may I call you Miriam?"

My face flushed. "Yes, please do."

"Thank you, Miriam." Gen. Carmille walked to the open window and for a moment looked out. He turned to Lt. Lacroix and me. "The Tulard System uses a multipage form to record information on each person to be registered, counted, in the census. Each page is a different color. In their Tulard System training, clerks learn to write and record responses on the forms." He gave a brief laugh of disparagement. "Leaving aside the small point of accuracy, or lack of it, the most important element in Tulard training is to learn how to put pressure on a pencil."

"Pressure on a pencil?" I asked in a voice of disbelief.

"Impressions of what's written on the top page must pass through multiple pages of the form and its layers of carbon paper. This creates multiple copies of the top page's basic information. If the pressure is too light, then the later forms—"

I blurted out, "For want of a stirrup the horse was lost, for want of a horse the battle was lost."

Lt. Lacroix laughed. Carmille smiled and continued. "Once completed, the different-colored sheets are distributed to separate departments of government. The top, white, page stays in the police department. Then, and I'm not sure about this, the yellow page goes to the General Commission for Jewish Affairs, the GCJA. The pink copy to the Gestapo. Blue to the tax department." Carmille grinned. "Sometimes clerks mix up the distribution of colored pages. Distribution of pink and blue copies gets reversed. The yellow page is sent to the tax department, not the GCJA. Then it takes time and labor to sort things out. Lt. Lacroix, am I correct about the distribution of different colored pages?"

"Sir, I don't know."

"It doesn't matter. I think the two of you get my point." He looked at me. "The Tulard approach is a cumbersome and not-so-simple system with inherent problems."

I nodded.

"Now, a hypothetical problem. For you, Miriam. Imagine this. You are responsible for conducting the Jewish census in a large city, say, Marseille or Lyon. Each day hundreds of people register. Soon the total number of registrants reaches 1,000. Census registrations continue. The total rises to ten thousand. Then fifteen thousand. With more to come.

Assuming the Tulard system is used, each registration has multiple pages, each page goes to one of, say, five different places."

I cringed and thought of my family. Waves of disgust inundated, paralyzed, my thoughts. I sat back in my chair. One hand gripped the arm of the chair. My other hand waved, signaling Gen. Carmille to stop. I felt my face flush.

"Yes?" Carmille assessed the look on my face.

"Sir, I'm having trouble, uh, keeping up with you." I closed my eyes.

Without further thought I did something I had learned as a child. Papa had taught me. "To manage questions under pressure, out-of-control emotions? Transform them into quantifiable, manageable problems. Play for time while you focus, engage, quantify, and survive."

I said, "Uh, General, how many new staff will I be assigned to manage all this?"

"None."

My mouth gaped, my eyebrows arched.

For a moment Carmille stared at the ceiling. "Well, let's say you will be assigned five additional staff." His eyes came to rest on me. "That's no small number when, like right now, there's a shortage of skilled personnel."

I would play for time. I spoke as if I deliberated on each word. "In your hypothetical case, General, for the moment let's assume we have fifteen thousand registrations." Then I considered how to quantify the problem. "Each registration has five pages. That's seventy-five thousand pages. Those pages must be separated by color. Pages of different colors are sent to each of five different destinations. Am I correct, Lieutenant?"

"Yes."

"And the number of registrants continues to increase? Soon exceeding seventy-five thousand pages, right? And once the pages of the form are distributed to the departments, each department has to extract information." I looked at Lt. Lacroix.

"That's correct."

"How many days will we have to organize copies for the departments, complete the distribution, and extract information?"

"Speed will be essential. You'll have little time. Perhaps a few days."

I sat back in my chair, gazed at the lieutenant then at Gen. Carmille.

"Sir, my experience is that people, clerks and managers alike, want processing to be speedy, inexpensive, and high quality, that is, accurate. Put in a different way, they want information processing to be fast, cheap, and good."

"That's true," Carmille said with a smile.

"There's a hitch. Recipients must learn they can have only two of the three."

"Ah, yes," Carmille said, "processes can be fast and cheap, but they won't be good. That is, they won't produce accurate information."

I laughed, "Or they can be fast and good, but they won't be cheap, and so on."

Lt. Lacroix laughed.

Carmille's smile melted and his expression became serious. "We find humor in your hypothetical challenge, Miriam. Our colleague, Xavier Vallat, the Vichy Commissioner for Jewish Affairs, faces Col. Eichmann's demands. A real problem. My question to you is what, if anything, should we, should I, do?"

Before I could answer his question, the gravity of this no-longer-hypothetical exercise became apparent. I recognized the potential for its tragic impact on Jews. My disgust burst through the inner boundaries I had built to control it.

Then I believe I surprised Gen. Carmille, Lt. Lacroix, and for sure, myself. My voice rose as I said, "Please forgive me, General. For me your example is . . ." My mouth gaped, I stared in silence at Carmille. Then I said, "Sir, your hypothetical example is one thing. The census of the Jews about to take place is quite another. It makes me feel, how can I say it, angry, repulsed, ill . . . It triggers strong feelings." There was so much more wanted to say. People abused, their rights stripped away. Children and parents separated. And I wanted to know, Why? Why? Why?

"I understand."

I turned to Lt. Lacroix. "In case you don't know, Lieutenant, I am a Dutch Jew." I took a deep breath. I felt tears flow down my cheeks. "The hypothetical, perhaps real, numbers, of Jews counted in the census of the Jews. My relatives, perhaps? Pushed out of jobs? Homes? Herded like cattle to, to, where?"

Lt. Lacroix handed me a tissue. His voice soft, the lieutenant said, "Since you joined the Service, I've known about your background."

My body tensed. I wiped my eyes. "Mmm." I whispered, "Thank you."

I remembered the afternoon of my arrival at the Military Recruitment Service. Details rushed through my thoughts—my interview with Lt. Lacroix and my conversation with Eve, who told me that arrangements had been made for me to stay at a nearby hotel, Le Lieu. Eve gave me the English translation of Le Lieu, the place, and then said, "I'm not sure about the Dutch translation." I had wondered how Eve knew about my Dutch citizenship? So had Lt. Lacroix. Had his interview with me been a performance, like in a stage play? Gen. Carmille knew, too. There were people in Paris who prepared my carte d'identité. Who else knew? When so many people know the truth, what are the odds on a leak to the Nazis?

I struggled to control the turmoil inside me. I turned to Carmille. "Sir, I don't know if I can do this."

"You can, Miriam." Carmille leaned forward, his face close to mine. "There's always a way. We'll find it."

For a moment I was again in his mechanography seminar listening to him demonstrate how to solve a complex machine processing problem.

On Sunday morning Simone and I entered the hotel dining room for a mug of café national.

After her first sip, Simone pursed her lips and made a sour face. "Acorns and chickpeas." She took two more sips from her mug then pushed it aside. "On a more positive note, yesterday evening I went for a walk with William."

"Who's he?"

"Works in accounting at the Service. Tall guy, maybe thirty. Soft voice."

"I remember. Hey, he's nice looking. Where'd you go?"

"Other side of the Saône. First to *Cathédrale St. Jean.* He's Roman Catholic. Attends worship there. Then we walked around the old city."

"And you, a Jew?"

"Hail Mary! We had fun. What he doesn't know won't hurt him."

"Did you have dinner?"

"Not enough money for that. Just sandwiches with fancy names for cheese on thin bread." Simone's voice signaled excitement, "But we had a half-bottle of good wine. He took me into the *traboules*. Little passageways. Dark, winding. Between buildings. Through buildings. Like labyrinths."

I laughed. "If the Germans occupy Lyon, maybe we can hide there." Simone laughed, too. But I didn't hear her. My thoughts had skipped ahead to Charles's arrival—to our picnic, our day alone.

Picnic

On Sunday morning, I took a long fast walk across downtown to the Saône then continued along a shaded street parallel to the river. An hour later, exhilarated but winded, muscles aching, I sat in the hotel lobby. I held an open newspaper as if to read it. But my eyes were on the hotel's front entrance and my thoughts on Charles.

At noon, Charles walked through Le Lieu's revolving front door. He wore faded blue short-sleeve shirt and khaki trousers. He carried a wicker picnic basket. A large blanket was tucked under one arm.

"Charles!" I leaped from my chair and ran to him.

He dropped his blanket and greeted me with a kiss to each cheek and an energetic hug. "It's been too long."

I held him tight, enjoyed the sensation of his body pressed against me. I whispered, "Too long."

We rode a trolley north to Le parc des berges du Rhône, a quiet public park on the shore of the Rhône. As we entered the park, as if released from confinement I ran ahead and sprinted up a grassy hillside. I caught my breath and waved to Charles. "Up here."

In a shady and secluded spot that overlooked the Rhône, we reclined on Charles's blanket. From the picnic basket, Charles removed a bottle of Beaujolais and two small glasses. He handed one to me, poured wine into each glass, and then raised his. "To you, sweet lady."

"To us." We sipped our wine, sat in silence, and watched boat traffic on the Rhône.

I said, "Sometimes I imagine your travel. Wish I could go with you."

"I'd enjoy that. But the war makes simple things difficult."

"It's hard to know the truth about the war. Our news in Lyon is heavily edited, tilted to the Vichy and German points of view. Real, honest, news is rare. Most of the time, we have to settle for rumors. What's happening out there?"

"In northern Africa, the siege of Tobruk goes on and on. It's likely to continue through the summer. If the Allies can hold. Something is about to happen on the Eastern Front, but I can't talk about it."

I had learned to accept the limits of Charles's disclosures. I traced an imaginary F on Charles's hand and said, "Free French forces. I'm told they've joined the Allies in Syria." I traced another F. "Fighting against the Vichy French."

"We are a country at war with itself."

Sandwiches consumed, the bottle of wine near empty, we lay on our backs. We looked up at the underside of a canopy of branches and leaves, intermittently dozed, awakened, and dozed again. When Charles's finger traced a line down my arm, with my eyes still shut I turned toward him. His hand fell to my breast. I placed a hand over it, pressed it against me.

I whispered, "I wish we weren't in a public place."

Charles looked around. "We're alone. Out of view." He smiled. "What did you have in mind?"

I pulled the lower part of the blanket over our legs, then up to our waists. I rolled on to Charles. "This." I fumbled with his trousers, my slacks, and we made love.

After a shared nap, I awakened first. Careful not to disturb Charles, I pulled on my slacks, slipped out from under the blanket, and stood.

In a sleepy voice, Charles said, "Hey, sweet lady," his voice little more than a whisper. He sat up.

I poured the remainder of the wine into our glasses. I handed one to Charles then raised my glass in a toast. "To love."

"To love and to your touch."

We sat side by side on the blanket, shared the remaining sandwich, and two small chocolate bonbons. Our conversation reminded me of leaves on the Rhône, one topic drifted into another. Until I said, "Jacques told me that last month in Paris the Nazis arrested lots of Jews. Maybe over a thousand. Heard it on BBC, he said. There's been nothing in the Lyon newspapers. Is it true?"

Charles sat up and lit two Gauloises. He handed one to me as he exhaled a stream of smoke. "Jacques was nearly correct. His estimate was too low. In Paris, there was a roundup of Jews. I think it was the first in France. Over three thousand arrested."

"Three thousand?" I couldn't get my thoughts around such a large number. "Then what? I mean, what happened to them?"

"Sent to an internment camp. Pithiviers."

"What about the elderly? Children?"

"All of three thousand of them."

The wails of children paralyzed my thoughts. "Oh, God. What'll happen?"

"I don't, we don't, know." Charles inhaled his Gauloise. "When we find out, I doubt it'll be good news." He looked toward the river. Charles's gaze followed a tug boat that guided an empty barge downstream, a large swastika painted on the barge's hull. "And please, tell people at the hotel to be careful about when and where they listen to Jacques's radio. The Nazis take a dim view of radios, broadcasts, and people who listen."

"I'll tell them. Jacques is a free spirit. He seems to feel he's exempt from all the Nazi rules. And there is something I must ask you."

"Yes, Love, please do."

"Local newspapers have carried announcements about Vichy's plans for a census of the Jews. We talked about it at the Service." I summarized my conversation with Gen. Carmille and Lt. Lacroix. "Can you tell me more?"

"I don't know a lot. Only that it's coming. Hitler wants a solution to what he calls 'the Jewish problem.' Himmler is upset about this, too. He's putting pressure on Heidrich and Eichmann. The number of French Jews arrested to date is well below target."

"Below target?"

"The Nazis have quotas. What Carmille calls Germanic thinking—everything is organized, counted. Jews are no exceptions. They are to be rounded up, counted. Shipped."

"Like chairs, shoes, cattle," I said, my voice contemptuous. "Where will they be shipped?"

"I don't know. Probably to Pithiviers or Drancy. Remember the pyramidion? Systems are driving the numbers. Hitler puts pressure on Himmler, who leans hard on the Gestapo. Eichmann turns screws to increase the output of Jews. Make no mistake, they intend to rid Europe of Jews. If they can't be exported, they will be murdered."

"My God! A new census will do that?"

"One more step in the eradication process. For sure, Eichmann will coerce Commissioner Vallat, local police too, to produce Jews."

"Gen. Carmille said Vallat plans to use the Tulard System."

"Yes." Charles smiled, one that was more contemplative than humorous.

"That's a strange smile. What's it about?"

"The Tulard System." Charles shook his head. "So many problems. It may be Vallat's Achilles heel."

"Gen. Carmille spoke about it the same way. I think he's going to do something. I don't know what."

I stretched out on my stomach. Charles lay on his back and closed his eyes. We remained silent for a few minutes. Boats passed on the Rhône. Couples strolled along the riverbank.

I slowly traced a line up the inside of Charles's thigh, felt him harden. "I'm curious about what you've been doing. I've missed you." I squeezed him. "And this."

"And I've missed you." Charles put his hand over mine, closed his eyes, and turned toward me.

What had Charles been doing? What could he disclose to me? I had quietly accepted the imbalances in our relationship, with a large part of Charles's side veiled in secrecy. My side was veiled too, although my veil was less dense.

"To answer your question, the Charles Delmand part of me has been writing columns for *the Times*. Since March, his principal topic has been America's Lend-Lease Act. Delmand's columns have supported its passage, pointed to Lend-Lease's value. What it will mean to the war effort. Roosevelt has been an effective advocate for the Allies. He said, 'When your neighbor needs a plow, help him. Lend him yours.' Congress agreed and stipulated that Allied debts could be paid or exchanged for equipment and services at the end of the war. America will now supply the Allied armies and navies."

"A God-send."

"Once America re-tools, starts to crank out armaments and ships them across the Atlantic, the balance of the war will tilt. The only obstacles for the Allies will be submarine, U-boat, attacks."

"Plus the Russian front. Plus the small matter of the German Occupation of Europe."

Charles gave a sheepish smile. "Yes, there is that to consider."

"And Charles Secœur—what's he been up to?"

"Art consultation. Travel." Charles took a deep breath. "Berlin to Paris to Vienna to Budapest, then to Berlin and back around the circuit again." He paused. "With side trips to Linz. Secœur has been learning about art theft."

"A theft ring?"

Charles stared at me. Then from deep inside him came hoo-haas of belly laughs. His face reddened. He wiped his eyes. "Please forgive me. What I'm going to tell you is anything but funny." His face became sober. "Indeed, it's tragic. At the same time, what's happening is so absurd I'm stunned." He took my hand. "We are, you and me, witnessing the largest art theft in history. Its scale and size is unprecedented. Until now, outside of a few colleagues I've had no one to share it with."

"I'm eager to hear about it."

"The story is convoluted and far from over. I'm not sure where to start."

"In *Alice in Wonderland*, the king said, 'Begin at the beginning and go on til you come to the end, then stop.'"

The lines in Charles face softened. "Yes, I remember. Good advice." He paused. "At the beginning, Hitler was an art student with lofty aspirations."

"I think I've heard the story."

"Not this one, guaranteed. Have you seen any of his watercolors or paintings?"

"No."

"He was talented. In his paintings, he worked in the style of nineteenth century artists. His best work was architectural, pen-and-ink drawings and watercolor renderings of buildings. A critic recommended Hitler study architecture."

I smiled, one that was more mocking than humorous. "In a way, isn't that what he did? A self-taught social and political architect. So far, quite successful."

"I love the way you think." Charles sipped his wine. "Hitler became determined to transform and set new standards in the art world."

"Like he'd done with much of life in Germany. Now Europe."

"Exactly."

"Are you familiar with the Great German Art Exhibition, 1937?" Charles arched his eyebrows.

"No. I've heard of the Degenerate Art Exhibition."

Charles laughed. "Who hasn't? Both are important. They opened in Munich. 1937. The Great German Art Exhibition on June 18th at the House of German Art, a new museum Hitler built. The Degenerate Art Exhibition on June 19th at the Institute of Archeology in the Hofgarten. I, well, Charles Secœur, attended both events. The invitations arrived late spring, 1937."

Art in the Reich

In rich detail, Charles told the story of the events of May and June 1937.

The first week in May, three envelopes addressed to Charles, two of them linen and the third manila, had arrived at the Louvre. A clerk in Charles's office opened them. Each of the linen envelopes contained an invitation. She excitedly waved them at Charles. In a voice filled with awe, she said, "M. Secœur, look at this! Signed by, well, see for yourself." She handed the invitations, trimmed in gold leaf, to Charles. Each one had a personal salutation to Charles and bore the signature of Josef Goebbels, Reich Minister for Public Enlightenment and Propaganda.

The first invitation was to the opening of the Great German Art Exhibition, June 18, 1937, at the new House of German Art in Munich. It carried a handwritten note, "M. Secœur, a room has been reserved for you at the Hotel Kempinski Vier Jahreszeiten," and initialed, "JG." The second invitation was to the opening of the Degenerate Art Exhibition, June 19, 1937, at Munich's Institute of Archeology in the Hofgarten, a memorial park.

The manila envelope contained brief descriptions of the exhibits. From his contacts in the German art community, Charles had learned that fifteen thousand paintings had been submitted for the Great German Art Exhibition. After viewing the initial selection of paintings, Hitler launched into an angry tirade, charging that modern art and artists were incompetents, cheats, and madmen. He fired the Goebbels–appointed selection committee and appointed his personal photographer, Heinrich Hoffman, to choose the exhibit's paintings.

Hoffman's selections for the final collection, over nine hundred pieces from throughout Germany, included still life paintings, nudes, and landscapes, works depicted as pure and Aryan. They were chosen to represent Nazi ideals. "It's the art the Fuehrer loves," a German colleague of Charles had said. "He expects everyone to join him. Hitler is confident the exhibit will set enduring standards of art for Germany."

The Great German Art Exhibition's home, the recently built House of German Art, was a massive colonnaded neo-classical style museum designed by Paul Troost. The building was the Reich's first representative monumental structure. Charles recalled meeting Troost over cocktails at Berlin's Hotel Adlon in 1931. Troost was an early member of the Nazi party. His height, muscular body and bald, bullet-shaped head, along with his heavy iron-framed glasses, gave Troost an imposing presence that intimidated others. He died before the museum was completed.

Charles's conversations with colleagues at the Louvre confirmed that the choices and firing of the selection committee had injured Goebbels's political stature. Ever the astute marketer and propagandist, Goebbels scrambled to restore his political position in Hitler's inner circle. Hitler's associates, including Goebbels, remembered the surprise executions of the Nazi's Night of Long Knives only three years earlier. He knew no one was immune to Hitler's fatal whims. Goebbels proposed and secured Hitler's approval for a second exhibit, the Degenerate Art Exhibition. That exhibition would represent what Goebbels called "the era of decay."

Early on the evening of June 18 the Hotel Kempinski's concierge called Charles's room. "Sir, your car is here." The long black Mercedes sent by Goebbels delivered Charles to the House of German Art. Charles's limousine joined a queue of black sedans depositing guests in front of the marble columns of the building's main entrance. In the building's large adjoining foyer, Minister Goebbels, in a Nazi uniform, thin, his back rigid, stood in the receiving line and greeted each of the arriving guests. He turned his dark eyes toward Charles. His weasel-like face broke into a grin. "Herr Secœur, thank you for joining us." A quick handshake with a slight pressure to the left moved Charles down the line. Soon he entered the main reception hall. Charles joined a large crowd of guests, along with Nazi generals and Reich officials, and enjoyed hors d'oeuvres and champagne. Among the officials was Reichsmarschall Hermann Göring, the second most powerful man in Germany. Göring, his bulk even greater than the last time Charles had seen him, was resplendent in a tailored gold-trimmed white Luftwaffe uniform. Above his wide forehead, Göring's dark hair was slick against his head, as if glued in place. He directed a fixed vulpine smile at guests. Charles recalled rumors of Göring's morphine addiction.

On the other side of the reception hall, a cluster of admirers surrounded Leni Riefenstahl, the actress–dancer turned film producer. Her swept-back hair accented her high cheekbones and seductive eyes. She wore a two-piece suit that complimented her athletic body.

Hitler had seen Riefenstahl perform as a lone dancer in an art film. By all reports, he had been taken with her beauty. After he learned of Reifenstahl's talent as a film director, Hitler asked her to direct a documentary on the rise of the Third Reich. She repeatedly refused Hitler's insistent requests. But Reifenstahl finally agreed to do the film, *Triumph of the Will*. It was released in 1935 to rave reviews and worldwide recognition. The film played to packed theaters.

There was one exception to the rave reviews. Rumors among senior Nazis had it that Josef Goebbels attempted to stop the film's production. When that failed, he tried to prevent its distribution. It turns out Hitler had given Riefenstahl the assignment Goebbels had dreamed of. A year later Goebbels and Riefenstahl were friends and an affair had been rumored. On the night of the exhibit's opening, they moved around opposite sides of the room as if in a mirror image dance. Their separate paths prevented any contact over the course of the evening.

Goebbels worked the crowd, moving easily around the reception unhindered by his deformed right foot. A nod here, a handshake there, and subtle moves toward the room's most powerful men and attractive women. By midway through the evening, Charles noted, Goebbels had made direct contact with every lovely woman at the reception.

An hour after Charles's arrival, at the entrance to the reception hall there was a flurry of noise and movement at the entrance to the hall. An entourage of aides preceded Hitler into the reception. The Führer walked briskly to a lectern beneath a crystal chandelier at one end of the large rectangular room. There he stood, head bowed as in prayer, and waited for silence. After a final burst of laughter from Hermann Göring, a hush fell over the room.

After a brief welcome to his guests, Hitler paused. He scanned the room slowly and deliberately, from person to person, as if to assess each of them. "You understand now that it is not enough merely to provide this new museum, the House of German Art. The exhibit itself must also bring about a turning point. If I presume to make a judgment, speak my opinion, and act accordingly, I do this not just because of my outlook on German art, but I claim this right because of the contribution I myself have made to the restoration of German art. Our present state, which I and my comrades in the struggle have created, has alone provided German art with the conditions for a new, vigorous flowering."

Hitler began to speak faster. His words ran together. He gulped deep breaths when, as happened many times, the crowd burst into applause. At the first of these interruptions, Goebbels detached from the tall young woman, long blonde hair, thin lips, who then held his arm. At each successive interruption, Goebbels stepped sideways, taking steps so small as not to be noticed, around the perimeter of groups until he stood near Hitler.

His voice ever louder, face red, Hitler approached the speech's climax. Spittle formed in the corners of his mouth. His words seemed more spewed than pronounced. "This exhibition then is but a beginning. The beginning of the end of the stultification of German art and the end of the cultural destruction of our people. I have no doubt that from this mass of decent creators of art, several individuals will rise to the eternal star-covered heaven of immortal, God-favored artists of great ages!" His speech finished, Hitler slumped across the lectern.

His audience continued to applaud for a full minute. Hitler raised his crimson face, righted himself, and gasped to catch his breath. "Herr Führer, are you all right?" an aide asked. Hitler nodded. A second aide scooted a chair next to Hitler, who dropped into it, leaned back, and closed his eyes.

By then, Goebbels stood close to Hitler. He executed a quick step forward, raised his right arm in the Nazi salute. *"Seig Heil!"* As if on command, the audience, arms raised, in unison answered, *"Sieg Heil!"* Hitler rose from his chair, returned the salute, and then shook Goebbels's hand.

Goebbels beamed. He made his way through the crowd to rejoin his young woman friend. She, too, beamed. She extended her arms to Goebbels.

The following evening, the Mercedes again arrived at the Hotel Kepinski. With Charles in the back seat, the car passed through the gardens and ponds of the Hofgarten to the boxlike stucco buildings of the Institute of Archeology. Standing two and three abreast, people formed a queue that wound from the Institute's front entrance around the side of the building. The limousine stopped next to a sign beside the front entrance. The sign's letters, The Degenerate Art Exhibition, were off-center and appeared to have been done by an amateur sign-maker, no doubt deliberately. The sign's German word for art, *Kunst*, was contained within quotation marks. The sign suggested the exhibition was not serious art. Charles was certain it had been carefully designed and executed.

Uniformed attendants ushered Charles past the queue into the Institute. Inside, a large banner proclaimed, "Degenerate art—insults German feeling, or destroys or confuses natural form, or simply reveals an absence of adequate manual and artistic skill."

There was no reception line. Entering the Institute's modest reception hall, Charles was surprised by the density of the crowd. The room was unadorned and without the hors d'oeuvres and champagne of the previous night's exhibition. A modest Riesling was served in inexpensive wine glasses.

Joseph Goebbels, a dark-haired young woman on his arm, led a group of Nazi officers and Munich art critics from room to room. Crowds parted as Goebbels and his group came through. The Nazi officers accompanying Goebbels emulated his sneers, laughter, and derisive comments about the displayed works.

On one wall of an exhibit room that contained landscape paintings, "Nature as seen by sick minds," had been scrawled. In a room with paintings of rural people, graffiti proclaimed, "German farmers, a Yiddish view." In a room of religious art, "Revelation of the Jewish racial soul." Near paintings of female nudes: "An insult to German womanhood" and "The ideal— cretin and whore."

Charles stayed some distance from the Goebbels group. He stood in a small room, for a moment alone, and admired the paintings of so-called degenerate artists Marc Chagall and Paul Klee. The noise level in the hallway increased, and the Goebbels group entered the room. Goebbels pointed to the Chagall paintings and made comments drowned out by the din of side conversations. Goebbels, Charles noted, had a new escort. The woman on his arm earlier had been replaced. Josephine Baker, an American expatriate star of French stage and film, now accompanied him. She did not laugh at Goebbels's derisive comments.

Baker's presence at the event surprised Charles. A Negro, she hardly lived up to the Aryan ideal. Charles assumed she had been invited to the Degenerate Art Exhibit only, not the Great German Art Exhibition. He'd met Baker a year earlier at a cocktail party in Paris. Over a glass of champagne, on an impulse Charles invited her to have dinner. Her unexpected acceptance surprised him.

The evening was warm. They had walked to a nearby bistro and, although frequently interrupted by admirers who asked for Baker's autograph, enjoyed an informal dinner. Early in the meal she had said, "Please call me Josephine."

"I'm Charles."

The French transition from "*vous*" to "*tu*," formal to informal, was made. Personal conversation followed.

During dinner Charles asked, "Why do you stay in France, rather than return to New York?"

Her eyes sparkled. "Here I can do it all—sing and dance, perform with a freedom not allowed a Negro in America."

After dinner Charles walked Josephine to her hotel, George V. During dinner it had rained. The moist air carried the aroma of wet leaves. At the entrance to the hotel Charles extended his hand to say goodnight. She took his hand and pulled him to her in a warm embrace.

As the Goebbels group turned to the Klee paintings, Charles felt a hand touch, then hold, his arm. Josephine Baker stood beside him, her gaze fixed on Goebbels. Charles placed his hand on hers and whispered hello.

Her eyes still on Goebbels, Baker canted her head toward Charles. She whispered, "Why haven't you come to see me?" She kept her head turned toward Goebbels. "The south of France, the Dordogne countryside, is beautiful. Call me."

Charles recalled news photos of her medieval castle, Château des Milandes, in the south of France. He wanted to know more about both Josephine and the castle. When they parted after their dinner in Paris, she had said, "Call me."

"Yes, I will." Charles hadn't kept his promise. He imagined a conversation with her. "The demands of the *Deuxièime Bureau,* the German arms buildup . . . new agents." She would understand. He quickly recognized his thoughts as hollow rationalizations. Charles vowed to keep his promise. Someday.

The Great Art Theft

Charles stretched out in the park's soft grass. I lay beside him. He lit two cigarettes and handed me one.

Charles knew Josephine Baker! My thoughts leaped to memories of my intimacy with Charles. Then quickly took the shape of Charles and Josephine Baker in a darkened room. Their bodies close. They touched as lovers.

I drew on the cigarette. I imagined my inhaled smoke as a cleansing agent—to rid me of jealous thoughts about Josephine Baker. Yes, Charles knew her! But as an agent. Might there have been more he kept to himself? Stop, Miriam, don't walk into that quicksand.

Charles said, "Over the next two years, the Great German Art Exhibition attracted a respectable number of visitors—on average, three thousand two hundred each day. But the Degenerate Art Exhibition? Twenty thousand per day!"

I ended my thoughts about Josephine Baker and brought myself back to our conversation. "So much for Hitler's artistic standards."

Charles nodded his agreement. For a moment he looked away, as if in thought. "The exhibitions became watershed events, each with an impact opposite Hitler's intentions."

"They confirmed how out of touch Hitler's artistic standards were."

"Yes. He attempted to devalue the work of highly regarded artists. Klimt, Van Gogh, Cézanne, Picasso, Matisse. Many others."

I shook my head. "It's hard to understand. What's it all about?"

"Who understands anything about Hitler's interior life? I only know that the Degenerate Art Exhibition attempted to define the work of every artist in the exhibit as cheap and substandard. So-called evidence of the immorality of Jews and their sympathizers."

"Step right up, folks." I beckoned like a carnival pitchman and waved an arm toward imaginary paintings. "The art you always wanted, now at bargain basement prices."

Charles laughed. "You're joking, but that's close to what happened. The prices weren't bargain basement. But they were far below pre-war prices years for the work of those artists. At least in Germany. Goebbels saw a window of opportunity. He established the Commission for the Exploitation of Degenerate Art and appointed its five members. I'll be meeting with one of them soon, Hildebrand Gurlitt. The commission's job is to sell degenerate artwork abroad and then use the proceeds for charitable purposes."

"Charitable? You don't mean aid to widows and children—or do you?"

"Not at all."

"Let me guess," I said. "Charity begins at home?"

"Right. One of the first tasks of the commission was to acquire old masters. For the museum Hitler plans to build in Linz, Austria—to be the largest art museum in the world."

"A little gift for folks in his old hometown?"

Charles laughed. "Have you been told you're irreverent?"

I laughed with him.

Charles continued as before, "Not to be outdone, Göring launched his own charitable efforts to acquire fine art. Most of it confiscated from the homes of wealthy Jewish families—under the new laws, Jews were no longer permitted ownership. Göring placed the sculptures and paintings in Carinhall, the mansion on his estate in the Schorfheide forest, outside Berlin. Nazis who want to curry favor with Göring often present him with a Matisse, or Van Gogh, or some other degenerate artist."

"All stolen, of course."

"Correct. Since the middle of last year, Göring has added three valuable paintings a week to his personal collection. He's also made substantial purchases, including an expensive Vermeer, though I wonder about its authenticity."

"Like a child with free rein in a toy store." My voice trailed away.

"Goebbels, Göring, the commission—they've begun the greatest art theft in the history of the world."

I heard Charles's voice. I realized that since Josephine Baker was mentioned, Charles's words about Goebbels, Göring, and the commission had tumbled on top of each other. All I could think of was her beauty, her voice. The sad lament of her lyrics, "If I were white." How the song moved me, how I tried to make it my own. My heart raced. I couldn't stop my thoughts about Charles's friendship with her. Beautiful. Talented. World famous. Might I lose Charles?

Josephine Baker had invited Charles to visit her at Château des Milandes—it was as though she had suddenly joined Charles and me on the picnic. I had accepted Charles's long absences as a fact of wartime life. But I wondered if there was more to his conversations with Baker than he had shared with me.

I stared at Charles, my face long, unsmiling.

"You look troubled. What's wrong?"

"Your Josephine Baker. She's talented, famous, and rich. I've seen photos— she's beautiful." I became silent. Then I blurted words, faster and louder than I intended. "Are you, were you and she—?"

"Lovers?"

I lowered my eyes. "Yes," I whispered. "I didn't know how to ask."

"I am forty years old. Over the past twenty years I have had lovers. But I put my work in the *Deuxième Bureau* ahead of my private life. I formed no deep attachments."

He looked me in the eye. "Josephine Baker? If there had been no war, I don't know what might have happened. But war came. From time to time Josephine accepts assignments from the *Deuxième Bureau*. We became involved with each other—as colleagues, not lovers."

"She's an agent?"

"It's best to think of her as my friend. Yes, she is a *Deuxième Bureau* colleague. From time to time we talk. She works for, well, on behalf of, the Bureau. I would like to visit her castle in Dordogne." Charles took my hand. "I want the two of us to make that trip together."

I smiled and squeezed Charles's hand. "I'd like that."

An hour later we put scraps of food, utensils, and empty wine bottles in the picnic basket. Charles folded the blanket. Holding hands, we walked down the hill toward the river.

We walked over the crest of the hill. Just ahead of us, a man, coatless, hatless, wearing a white shirt, sat on a bench. He looked up at us and jumped to his feet. He jogged a few steps, and then at a pace just short of running, took long rapid strides toward the river.

"Charles, that man!" I pointed. "From the hotel?"

Charles stared at the ever more–distant man.

"How long has he been there? Was he watching when we, you know . . . Can we be arrested for that? Will he be at the hotel waiting to question me?"

Bouchon

N ear the park, we boarded a southbound trolley. I sat next to a window. Silent, I stared at people on the street.

"Miriam—are you with me?"

"I want to find that man, the one in the park. I'm certain he's staying at Le Lieu. Is he following us?" The trolley stopped. I watched a group of passengers get on board. At each stop, I continued to scan the faces of new riders.

Charles took my hand. "He's long gone. Whoever he is, his rapid departure says we caught him at something. Probably spying. Most likely on us." Charles grinned. "Now he has a problem. His job security depends on doing what he failed to do—remain unseen. He doesn't know what we might do."

"What if—?"

"Relax. I'll talk with colleagues at the *Deuxième Bureau*. They can help."

Near Pont Wilson we got off the trolley. Charles led me along the Rhône. After a short distance east on rue Childberg, we turned into a traboule that continued into a narrow alley.

"Where are you taking me?"

Charles laughed and took my hand. "Come on." Midway down the alley he ushered me through a weathered door beneath a single lightbulb that illuminated a small sign: Bouchon.

A tarnished brass chandelier lit four small empty tables and a bar with six stools. Two men in khaki work clothes sat at the bar. One of them turned and gave a nod of recognition to Charles. Charles nodded.

"You know everybody."

Charles laughed. "Not really. That's John, an old friend."

The bartender, a middle-aged man, rotund and bald, greeted Charles. "*Bienvenue*, M. Secœur." He waved toward the tables. "Please, sit anywhere."

Charles ordered a carafe of burgundy, a salade Lyonnaise, and the pork special. "Can we share?" I nodded. Charles walked to the counter and brought the carafe to our table. He poured the wine. The salad arrived, lettuce with bacon, croutons, mustard dressing, and two poached eggs, a basket of small croissants on the side. Then came a large plate of pork and pâté.

I starred at the servings. "At the hotel we're eating old turnips and stale bread. Sometimes there's no food at all. At night I dream of food. How, where, does he get all this?"

"Everything has its place." Charles laughed. "The challenge is to know where the places are."

Midway through dinner Charles said, "Tomorrow I'll be leaving for Paris."

"Remind me, what will you do there?"

"I'll meet Hildebrand Gurlitt, who is on the Commission for Exploitation of Degenerate Art. Goebbels appointed him, even though Gurlitt's grandmother was Jewish. Gurlitt's an interesting man. He was fired as director of an art museum in Zwickau and fired again as director of the Kunstverein in Hamburg. The museum boards said he pursued art that affronted healthy folk-feelings about Germany."

"Whatever those are. Goebbels must have felt a kinship with him."

"Well, Gurlitt landed on his feet." Charles toyed with his food. "He and the Commission continue to build major collections of art. They're getting rich on trades and sales commissions. I want to find out about the scope of their collection. Learn about their records. This war won't last forever. The Nazis will surrender, and records will be important in order to return stolen art to its rightful owners."

"If the owners are alive."

"Yes. I should've said return it to them or their families."

"Grand larceny—institutionalized, Charles, that's what it is. Do we have to sit back and watch it happen?"

"The Nazis have figured out how to pick the pockets of the art world."

"And flat-out rob Jews," I said.

"*Mein Kampf* tells them they're morally right. But any way you look at it, it's large-scale thievery."

I wiped away tears. "For Jews, abolish ownership. Take away jobs. Cancel passports. Sell exit visas to those who can afford them. Or, trade valuable art for visas."

"Those who can are leaving the country," Charles said. "Albert Einstein saw the future. He left when Hitler became chancellor. His property was confiscated. Soon there was a five-thousand-dollar bounty on his head. His name was put on a list of enemies of the German people not yet hanged. Sigmund Freud sold all that he had in order to buy exit visas and get his family from Vienna to London. He was only partially successful. He left four sisters behind. They were sent to the camps, probably murdered. Marc Chagall, Béla Bartok, and Arnold Schoenberg got out."

"Why didn't you leave?"

Charles laughed. "I'm French. The *Duxième Bureau* nurtures our hope for the future."

The two men at the bar rose to leave. One of them came to our table and shook hands with Charles. Charles said, "Miriam, I'd like you to meet my friend, John."

"*Enchanté*, Miriam."

I took John's hand. His French carried an American accent. "I regret that I must leave. Perhaps we'll have another opportunity to talk." He said goodbye to us and left.

I asked Charles, "Will I see you after your Paris trip?"

"After I meet with Gurlitt, I have two stops to make. First, Geneva. I need to learn about the practices of Swiss banks. Dehomag, IBM's German company, has developed systems to cross-reference bank account deposits and census data. I believe the Nazis use those systems to locate Jews and their wealth. Once located, they round up the Jews. Seize their wealth."

"They can do that? Is nothing safe?"

"They can. They are. Nothing is safe. Europe's banks with their IBM systems have become dark places."

"Nothing new about that, particularly in Germany."

"I know," Charles said. "Anything's possible."

"You said you had two stops to make. What's the second?"

"Berlin."

My stomach cramped.

Flames in the East
21 June 1941

L ate that Friday afternoon I entered the Le Lieu lobby. At the registration desk Jacques talked with a tall dark-haired man. White shirt and necktie, no coat. I recognized him! My picnic in the park with Charles—the man who had run away. My heart pounded.

Jacques glanced at me and immediately raised his index finger. His conversation with the man ended. The man walked away from the desk as I approached. When our paths intersected he nodded to me.

Jacques handed me a small envelope addressed, "To Miriam Dupré." The handwriting was Charles's, though scribbled as if written in a hurry. The envelope looked unusually wrinkled. Had it been opened by Jacques? Had he read other notes, learned about Aimée?

Across the top of the note, "M: <u>BURN THIS after reading</u>. Flames will rise in the East. Stay close to hotel. Love, C."

Saturday evening at 9 p.m. Simone and I joined Jacques and M. Bollé in Le Lieu's lobby. We listened to BBC news of the German invasion of the Soviet Union. In a recorded statement, Prime Minister Churchill said, "The blood-thirsty guttersnipe has invaded Soviet territory. The Russian people are defending their native soil. We are resolved to destroy Hitler and every vestige of the Nazi regime. From this, nothing will turn us— nothing." Listening to Churchill's rich baritone voice, I got goose bumps and my neck tingled. I loved his fearless rhetoric.

M. Bollé glanced at me. After a quick look around the room, he briefly raised his hand with Churchill's famous two-fingered V.

As I listened to more news coverage of the attack, I jotted on a notepad:

> German – Soviet pact. 2 years old? Wehrmacht = 134 div + 73 div in reserve = 3,000,000 troops + 650,000 from Finland and Romania. Eastern Front—<u>Baltic Sea north to Black Sea south.</u>

I stared at my notes. I thought back to a year earlier. The dirt and sweat in my attempts to return to Rotterdam. The cries of babies, mothers who desperately sought reassurances, old folks lost and disoriented. The acrid smoke of explosions. The stench of death. Everyone going somewhere, anywhere. People stumbled as they searched for shelter, for lost children.

Simone leaned over my shoulder, read the troop strength numbers I'd scribbled on my notepad. "The number of Wehrmacht troops going into combat—the Soviets aren't even close. The Wehrmacht's modus operandi—overwhelm the enemy with troops and force." Simone's face turned crimson. "I watched them march through Warsaw. Through all of Poland. I pray for the Russians. Resist. Delay. Fight, even in retreat." Her voice became louder. "Raise the German costs. Attack, attack, attack!"

Seated across the lobby, the man from the park looked up from his newspaper. He stared at Simone.

In the eyes of the Gestapo, would my notes incriminate me? On my walk to the lift I tore them up. I dropped the pieces of paper down the elevator shaft. As the lift rose to the fourth floor, I thought about my night with Charles. Only a week ago? Had he made it to Berlin? Was he safe?

Charles's last words to me, "You have a big job in front of you. The mobilization files for North Africa, they grow more important each day."

A New Census
24 June 1941

Mid morning, Lt. Lacroix rapped on the open door of my small office.

I peered over my desk's stacks of papers. "Marcel, *bonjour*. Please, come in."

"*Bonjour*, Miriam. Recall our conversation about M. Carmille's books? You mentioned you'd read them."

"I remember."

"An hour ago I met with Gen. Carmille. He asked me, asked us, to begin to outline options for new methods to record and organize French census records. He said we should include the development, well, possible development, of an identification number for each citizen. Didn't you tell me he had written about that?"

"Yes. The Americans have done it. People in their Social Security program have permanent identification numbers. Is that what he wants?"

"I'm not certain. First things first. Gen. Carmille wants us to organize the data from two censuses. The first one, in September 1940, ordered Jews in the Occupied Zone to register at police stations over the eighteen days to follow. It was carried out. Xavier Vallat, the General Commissioner for Jewish Questions managed it. We believe his people were overwhelmed by the data. You remember the Tulard files?"

I shook my head. "I remember."

"A second census is about to begin. Gen. Carmille calls it a survey of professional skills—from bricklayers to factory workers to mathematicians. Citizens born between 1881 and 1940."

I leaned back and stared at Lt. Lacroix. "1940—even young children? Every citizen?"

"Yes. All of them."

My thoughts buzzed like a tabulator. "At the hotel I've heard rumors about a new census."

"Himmler and Eichmann need to identify Jews for roundups. They're behind on quotas of Jews for shipment. The first census failed at that. The new, second census, begun just a week ago, contains one key item, Question 11, 'Are you Jewish?' Jews are to identify themselves. By name and address.

"The complexities of this census were not all present in the first one. A six-page catalogue on the new census was sent to police stations. There are multi-card files for each census registrant. Each card is to be marked with a letter to identify the type or class of the respondent. J means Jewish, NJ means non-Jewish or a person who has been investigated and cleared of Jewish family, N designates nationality and so on. A woman's maiden name requires a whole card. Without punch-cards this census will be virtually unmanageable."

"My God, if this weren't so serious it would be laughable."

"Yes, I know," Lt. Lacroix said. "German industry needs people. The second census will identify people, job skills, occupations, and so forth. For us, the value lies in use of the survey data when mobilization takes place."

"Will the second census be conducted on the whole population of France? That's millions, I mean, tens of millions of people. How many—do you realize how many cards, machines, and operators we'll need?"

"Not the whole population. The professional skills census will be restricted to the Non-Occupied Zone. It'll become part of the information kept on industrial workers. Maybe the Germans feel there are more untapped human resources for industry over here. Gen. Carmille wants us to carry out the survey here, I mean in the Free Zone. The files will be important steps towards readiness for mobilization. Chances for a mobilization are greater here than in the Occupied Zone."

"It'll be a massive project." My voice may have sounded as if I was already fatigued from the work to come.

"I just found out about it. Wish I could've given you a leg up. You know, a week or two advance notice." Lt. Lacroix laughed. "You would've had it all figured out by now."

"Sure thing, boss." I laughed. "No problem. We do ten people today, ten tomorrow. Day after day. The next thing you know we're at a million. Then two million."

The lieutenant's face became mock serious. "Oops, sorry, I left out Algeria."

"Any other countries?"

Lt. Lacroix ignored my question. "Can you help lead all that? Outline our options?"

"Of course. But please remember, my people are already facing heavy demands."

"I know. Right now, I'm most interested in you—your being on the new census project. Gen. Carmille has other staff that'll worry about machines and new staff as well as a card supply. I'll assign Claire Montrieux to help you manage your group's operations. Lighten your management load. At least a little. That should give you time to develop some ideas."

"That'll help."

"When Claire joins you, assign her some of your direct reports and most of the hands-on work you're doing. Then close your door and think about possible methods for the project. Later, when you have some recommendations, I'll connect you to senior people in the Service. Then we'll see what happens."

"What do you expect from me? I mean, what outcomes?"

"Keep in mind, here, central Lyon, and in a few other offices we want to build capacity. Increases in staff and our capacity for operations by the addition of processors and keypunch machines. New tabulators. Lots of them."

"I've seen lots of equipment unloaded from trucks," I said. "New people coming in the front door. The census you describe will require huge numbers of Dehomag and CEC machines. Tons of data cards. An army of technicians. In Germany they may be experienced in doing that.

But in France?"

"We have to do what has to be done to create massive new census records. I want you to guide us. Tell us how we can put it all together and speed everything up."

"I read a report issued by the head of the SGF, M. Sauvy. I found it hard to believe. The census and statistics people haven't yet completed work on the 1936 census. Sauvy accepts that as normal. Does Gen. Carmille?"

"I doubt it, even though he and Sauvy are old friends. The job Gen. Carmille has put in front of us is to bring census operations into the twentieth century. Gen. Carmille wants you to be a leader in that."

Early the following morning, Lt. Lacroix stepped inside my office, his face tense. "I'm on my way to a staff meeting. A couple of questions, *s'il vous plait*." He spoke more rapidly, as if his speech was produced under steam pressure. "What's the current status of the North African mobilization files—the demobilized soldiers? What can I tell Gen. Carmille?"

"Tell him we're nearly done with keypunching," I said, my speech racing to match the speed of Lt. Lacroix's. I paused, then in a steady, slow, cadence said, "A day or two more. Then we'll run reports and prepare the files for transport to Algiers. That will take a few days. Should have everything ready in a week, maybe less."

The phone on my desk rang. Lt. Lacroix nodded to me, as if to say please answer. "Miriam Dupré," I said, and then listened for a moment. "Yes, sir, I can do that. I'll tell Lt. Lacroix."

"That was Lt. Jaouen, calling from Gen. Carmille's office. He asked me to come with you to the meeting."

Charting a New Course

On the top floor of 10 rue des Archers, Lt. Lacroix and I stepped out of the elevator. We entered a long hallway. On either side of it were mahogany doors with polished brass fittings. The upper half of each door had a large pane of frosted glass with the name of a senior officer or department. On the corridor's right wall hung a Vichy flag, on the left, a portrait of Maréchal Pétain. At its far end was a partially open door with the words, "R. Carmille, *Directeur*." When we walked past it I glanced inside. Gen. Carmille was placing papers in a file cabinet. Lt. Lacroix and I entered the door beyond Gen. Carmille's office, the conference room.

Seated at a long wooden conference table were Lt. Jaouen, youthful and athletic, a few years older than Lt. Lacroix; Lt. Albert Sassi, who I had met; and a tall, lean French colonel, close-cropped gray hair, a brush moustache.

Lt. Lacroix and I sat down at the table.

In an unexpected high-speed flight, my thoughts detached from the room. I felt sweaty under my arms. What did the group, what did Gen. Carmille, expect of me? I swam in an out-of-control flood of images and emotions—the German invasion, bombs in Rotterdam, the deaths of my parents and sister, my being alone and stranded in railway stations, dirt and sweat, going to Paris, Ruth and Charles, the creation of Miriam Dupré. The flow of images slowed. Lyon. Le Lieu. The Demographic Service. Base twelve. Gen. Carmille. I closed, then opened my eyes, and put myself in the group, in the room, today.

I settled my thoughts with two questions. What I could contribute to this group? What could I contribute to the Service?

The colonel nodded to Lt. Lacroix. He turned and extended his hand to me. "*Mademoiselle*, I am Col. Edouard Duval."

I took his hand. "I am Miriam Dupré."

"*Enchanté.*"

Gen. Carmille entered the room carrying a stack of file folders. He sat at the head of the table. "*Bonjour.* I assume you have met one another. At my request, Miriam is joining our group. She has unusual and well-developed skills in mechanography, as well as superior mathematical and conceptual abilities."

He turned to me. "In this group, we operate under absolute confidentiality. Conversations do not leave this room. Do you understand and agree to that?"

I sat up, back straight. My eyes locked on his. "Yes, sir."

Carmille nodded. His left hand settled his glasses on the bridge of his nose. He gestured toward the people seated around the table. "Each of us has a unique connection to the Demographic Service. Together we share one mission—to win the war."

I remembered my early morning walk to work a year ago when I heard Papa's voice. "What will the people who created Miriam Dupré ask of her? What was she prepared to do? What will she not do?"

"A reminder," Carmille said, "in Lyon, life and work as well as safety and security are not what they once were. During our meetings, make no notes. When you communicate with each other or trusted outsiders, do it face to face whenever possible—even when inconvenient. Never by telephone or wire service. Phones and the telegraph are no longer secure. If you cannot communicate face to face, use a trusted messenger." He looked at Lt. Jaouen. "All of the Service's messengers must be trained to detect surveillance. They are to use the passageways between buildings, the traboules, more than the streets. At least for now, German soldiers do not know the passageways of medieval Lyon."

Carmille scanned the faces around the table. "Your experience and intelligence are the reasons I asked you to join this group." He grinned.

"Apply them."

He glanced at the stack of folders before him and opened the one on top. He scanned the first document in the folder.

"Before we begin, a word about our work. Last August, I met privately with the Vichy senior army command, and then with *Maréchal* Pétain and one of his aides. I discussed the importance of preparation for a clandestine mobilization. I told Pétain I planned to initiate such a project in the unoccupied zone."

I recalled Charles's telling me of the meeting. And now a first-hand account.

"The *Maréchal* said, 'I am aware of the project. Such mobilization preparations are illegal. I do not want to initiate them or bear the risk.' He paused, and then sent his aide to get us coffee. When the aide was gone he looked around as if to make sure he could not be overheard. 'You will have the necessary appropriations to do your project. If the Germans find out and stop you, I will declare ignorance of everything.'"

For a moment Carmille sat in silence. Then he said, "His initial comments reassured me—we will have the appropriations we need for the project." He paused. "Then his words, 'I am aware of the project,' unsettled me. Have we failed in our efforts to maintain secrecy?"

I cleared my throat. "Sir, might Vichy or the Gestapo have placed an agent among us?"

Col. Duval said, "That's always a possibility. I believe there is a more likely explanation. As the *Maréchal* is prone to do, might he play a double game with you? He may not have been aware of our project. But for his own reasons wanted you to believe otherwise."

Lt. Sassi said, "The Allies think that's his strategy with the Germans. Perhaps he's doing the same with us."

"Whatever the truth," Carmille said, "we have to move forward. Be alert. Secrecy must be our top priority."

Carmille paused and made eye contact with each person around the table. "I want to emphasize the *Maréchal's* words, 'If the Germans find out and stop you, I will declare ignorance of everything.' I believe you know what that means. Correct?"

Carmille raised his eyebrows and waited for what he just said to sink in, and then continued. "If anyone would like to leave the project, I will respect your decision. Now is the time to exit this room and the project." He again looked each of us in the eye.

Around the table we turned to each other in silence then returned our attention to Carmille. No one rose to leave.

Carmille smiled and nodded. "Very well. Let's begin."

He removed a folder from the stack in front of him and opened it. He took out a letter on Demographic Service letterhead. "On June 18, I sent this letter to Xavier Vallat, General Commissioner for Jewish Questions." Carmille's eyes traced the length of the letter. "I inquired about the new Jewish census required by the law of 2 June 1941—the census the GCJQ plans to conduct." He looked around the table. "I assume you are all familiar with the pending census."

Head nods answered his question.

His eyes on the letter, Carmille continued, "I reminded Commissioner Vallat that the Demographic Service has been given responsibility for all statistical operations for the population of France."

Col. Duval said, "I hope the Commissioner understood the full meaning of 'all statistical operations.' My experience with him is you cannot take anything for granted."

Carmille nodded affirmatively. "I informed Commissioner Vallat that the Demographic Service is to initiate, in the Non-Occupied Zone, the first census of professional activities. Occupational skills among all persons, ages fourteen to sixty-five. To quote my letter, 'Once completed, with our updates we will have, at any given moment, a general demographic profile of the nation.'"

Lt. Sassi leaned forward, "Essential for a clandestine mobilization."

I made eye contact with Lt. Lacroix and nodded.

"Related to that," Lt. Sassi added, "we will implement a program to assign a unique thirteen-digit number to every citizen."

I wondered if I would be responsible for quality control on the thirteen-digit project. My mind reeled as I did quick calculations on the size of the project. Thirteen digits for each person. Millions of people. Multiple punchcards per person. Quality? Errors? Even at a rate of less than a tenth of one-percent of all coded entries, there'll be thousands of incorrect keypunches. Thousands of incorrect entries and numbers.

Carmille nodded to Lt. Sassi, and then continued, "Three forces underscore the importance of our work. First, the new Vichy law, *Service de Travail Obligatoire* or STO. Wartime industries in Germany have a shortage of people with technical skills. Berlin expects the STO law to result in the import of more French workers to meet the Reich's critical manpower needs.

"Second, you are familiar with the priority the Reich and the GCJQ place on the identification of Jews. In our census we include the question, 'Are you Jewish?'"

I bolted upright in my chair. My voice intense, I said, "Sir, are we to be part of Jewish roundups?"

Carmille raised his right hand, a signal for me to wait, remain quiet. He looked at the letter to Vallat and read, "'This form,' meaning the Demographic Service's census form . . . then skipping a bit, 'will allow us to discover those Jews who have not yet made their declaration, so we can organize an inquiry as to,'" his voice slowed and intensified, "'the status of their belongings and their potential transfer.'"

His words reverberated in my thoughts, intensified my barely controlled anger. How could he do this? *The status of Jewish belongings and their potential transfer?* I remembered The Degenerate Art Exhibit, filled with art stolen from Jewish homes. In a voice louder than I intended, I said, "Potential transfer of belongings? Isn't that some kind of euphemism? Haven't the Nazis already taken everything they want from the Jews—from the poor and the wealthy alike? Furniture and homes. Gold jewelry—cheap as well as valuable."

The room was silent. All eyes were on me. I felt myself blush— and wished I could have turned off the heat beneath my face.

Gen. Carmille said, "Miriam, we know that senior Nazi officers are building personal wealth through the confiscation of Jewish businesses and personal assets. Gold, gems, valuable art. In my letter, I wrote, and I quote, 'An inquiry into the status of Jewish belongings and their potential transfer.' Please understand my words were deliberately and carefully chosen to appeal to their greed. In a heartbeat, Göring, Himmler, Heydrich, and Goebbels will see the implications for themselves of an efficient census and the creation of lists for roundups. Gestapo officers like

Eichmann will see an opportunity to curry favor."

There was silence around the table.

Col. Duval broke the silence. "The 14 May roundup of Jews in Paris, using lists yielded by the Tulard files, produced about three thousand five hundred Jews. *Deuxième Bureau* sources estimate that number was less than one-half the assigned quota, the expected total. They're not hitting their numbers. Yes, Berlin will renew pressure on Vallat to produce results, names and addresses of Jews, for additional roundups. For belongings—wealth—to be transferred, and bodies for factory labor. It's very clear that without slave labor by now the Reich would be bankrupt. Eichmann and Himmler are under great pressure. They are becoming impatient." Col. Duval leaned back in his chair. "The cumbersome files will continue to produce a huge volume of forms. They will soon become unmanageable." He flashed a wry smile then continued, "Yes, the production of lists may take a while."

Carmille nodded. "At the end of my letter I offer Commissioner Vallat our help in managing the GCJQ census data. We have the technology they need. I'm confident they'll turn to us for help. Perhaps not this week. Or this month. But turn they will."

I leaned forward. "Yes, sir! And when they do?"

Carmille gave me a parental half-smile and raised one hand. Then he said in a quiet voice, "And when they do, they will have to transfer all the census forms and data to us." He then spoke slowly, an emphasis on each word, "*We will own the census.* The creation of any and all lists of Jewish names and addresses will be under our control."

He paused, looked around the table, and then continued, "As Col. Duval has said, 'Production of the lists may take a while.' Yes, a long while." A smile lit Duval's face and, except for me, the faces of others seated around the table.

Gen. Carmille looked me in the eye. "Miriam, I know what the Nazis are doing is wrong. Morally wrong. But I, we, haven't the power to stop them throughout Europe. Not yet. But we can derail their abuses of Jews and more widespread abuses of French citizens. We can prevent roundups. Save lives. Perhaps thousands of lives. That's what I propose we do."

The room was silent.

"When I became director of the Mobilization Service, I didn't know about the Nazi census of the Jews. Now I do. Commissioner Vallat has placed an opportunity in front of us. *We will seize it.*"

I sat back in my chair, admonished myself, felt stupid. I should've seen Gen. Carmille's purpose. But I hadn't. His objective—to gain control of the census, prevent roundups—was clear. Was I the slowest person at the table, the slowest student in the class? Would Gen. Carmille ask me to leave the group?

Carmille ended the long silence. "In the conclusion of my letter," he continued, "I told Commissioner Vallat I would send an administrator to meet with him and explain how the Demographic Service is organized, how the Service works. And to describe the results made possible through use of mechanography. I suggested that our Service and his office could benefit from our joint efforts."

He looked around the table. "Are there any questions?"

Col. Duval asked, "The start of the project—do you know the estimated start date?" In the same breath, Duval answered his own question. "To know that we'll have to await GCJQ's failure to manage the data."

"Correct. Now, about the meeting with Vallat." Carmille looked at Lt. Sassi. "I would like you, Albert, to represent the Service and arrange to meet with him in Paris." He then looked at me. "Miriam, I would like you to accompany Lt. Sassi and provide him with technical support. Can you do that?"

Beaming, I glanced at Lt. Lacroix, as if to ask if he could spare me from our thirteen-digit project. He nodded affirmatively. I said to Gen. Carmille, "Yes, sir, I can."

As I thought about what would soon come, like a powerful ocean wave a feeling of euphoria arose within me and surged through my body, right out to my fingertips. Commissioner Vallat and the GCJQ will be overwhelmed by the data. The GCJQ will turn to the Demographic Service—ask if we can process the Jewish census data. I imagined the freight docks at 10 rue des Archers—the arrival of truckloads of completed census forms, mountains of forms. How would we convert thousands upon thousands of handwritten forms to keypunched cards? Is there enough manpower in all the Occupied countries to do the job? I knew we could figure it out. When we get the job done, then we'll delay the production of lists of Jews. Prevent roundups.

"Until we hear from Commissioner Vallat," Carmille said, "we will continue to plan for the Professional Manpower Census. And the clandestine mobilization." He added in a near-whisper, "And prepare to take over the census, prevent roundups of Jews."

A Discovery in Paris

At noon the following day Lt. Sassi and I traveled by train to Gare de Lyon in Paris. During the trip I thought about Aimée. Charles said he had learned she had returned to Paris. Had she avoided the Nazi roundups? Been arrested—or worse? Could I get in touch with her? My pulse quickened as I thought about an opportunity to see Aimée.

After we disembarked from the train, Lt. Sassi said, "I'd like to meet with Commissioner Vallat alone. Give me a couple of hours. Let's meet at the main entrance of *Hôtel de Ville*."

After Lt. Sassi hailed a taxi, I walked briskly to the Métro. I arrived at my stop in the Marais District. I jogged to Aimée's apartment building hoping to connect with her. I had so many questions. What had happened at Musée de l'Homme? Did she face possible arrest? Had she been in hiding? Where?

The building's large heavy doors that opened into the cobblestone central courtyard stood open. The elevator was not in service. The stairwell door was open. I raced up the stairs to the fourth floor. The walls of the stairwell were marred. Large chips of plaster littered the stairs.

The door to Aimée's apartment hung open. Only a single hinge held it in place. I called, "Aimée?" No answer. I immediately peered into the apartment—furniture was turned over, some of it smashed, and rugs were shredded.

I turned and walked to the apartment's front door. Paint had run down it. When I looked at the images painted on the door, my legs wobbled. Then lost their strength. I sat on the hallway floor. My heart pounded.

On the door was a large and crudely painted Nazi symbol for Jews—a black circle containing two triangles that overlapped to form a six-pointed star. The paint had dripped and run down the door. Within the circle the six-pointed star's background triangle was bright yellow—Jew. The foreground triangle was pink—homosexual.

Arms across my knees, I rested my forehead on them. I cried. With each sob, my body jerked. In what must've sounded like a child's voice I whimpered, "Aimée."

Images of childhood visits with Aimée came alive: my trips to Paris; Aimée's visits to Rotterdam; skating, dancing, running in the parks. Coffee shops.

Then I imagined what must've been a violent assault on her apartment, perhaps on Aimée, too. Gestapo rifle butts pounded on Aimée's front door. Nazi officers entered and attacked her, forcefully took her away.

From inside the apartment, I heard a scraping sound, maybe the movement of a wooden chair. Then footsteps, crunch, crunch, crunch on broken glass. I leaped up. "Aimée?"

A man in soiled khaki overalls and an oil-stained leather cap pushed open the kitchen's broken door. "*Mademoiselle*, may I be of help? I am Albert Graveau. Aimée and I work in the museum's Polar Department."

"I am Miriam Dupré. Where is Aimée?"

"That's my question also. Our boss, M. Vildé, instructed me to come here and locate some records Aimée had checked out. It looks like someone has broken in."

"And Aimée?"

"She is not here. I looked for something that might suggest where she has gone. I found nothing. If I learn news of Aimée, can I contact you?"

Without thinking I eagerly replied, "Yes, please do that. *Hotel Le Lieu* in Lyon. Miriam Dupré."

Graveau took a note pad and pencil from a pocket in his overalls. He wrote my name and Le Lieu, Lyon. "*Merci.* I hope to be in touch with you soon." He quickly departed. The sounds of his footsteps on the stairs diminished.

Then it hit me: Boris Vildé and museum resistants had been arrested—and Aimée disappeared—*months ago!*

To Berlin
21 June 1941

Charles arrived by taxi at Gare de Nord rail station. He checked his ticket, only a half-hour until his train would depart. When Charles exited his taxi, he was surprised by a queue that extended from the ticket windows through the rail station's main entrance and then a block down the street. He felt foolish that he hadn't allowed himself more time.

Once again, all of occupied Paris seemed in motion. The German army's sudden invasion of the Soviet Union had mobilized Parisians as well as resident German officers. Charles reminded himself that he'd had advance knowledge of the invasion from the Deuxième Bureau and should have acted on it. He might have avoided the queue. A man rushed into him, knocked him off balance.

Once inside Gare du Nord, Charles watched travelers elbow each other as they wedged themselves into coffee shops. Then they stood, three-deep, in front of counters. Customers waved their arms, yelled orders over the heads of people in front of them. Long lines extended from public toilets. Parents attempted to quiet noisy children. When a seat opened on a lobby bench, people shoved each other aside to get it. An elderly lady fell to the floor.

At a newspaper kiosk Charles scanned the front pages of Paris and Berlin newspapers. The headline stories were of the German invasion, immediate successes, and Soviet military responses. With the news services in Occupied countries under the tight surveillance of Goebbels's Ministry of Public Enlightenment and Propaganda, accounts of the invasion in one newspaper resembled those in another. The stories proclaimed the power of the Luftwaffe and the Wehrmacht and the soon-to-come defeat of the Soviet Union. Reich officials' reassurances to German citizens spilled into the French press. "Troops will be home for the Yuletide season."

Charles bought a newspaper and scanned the invasion's lead stories. His editorial instincts triggered the start of a mental outline of a Charles Delmand editorial for *The Times*: "A new chapter in European life has begun. . . . Just as life on the streets of Paris inched its way toward the ambience of the pre-occupation years, the Reich's sudden incursion into the Soviet Union has infused a new tension into every Parisian's, every European's, life—like an infectious epidemic that has spread across the continent."

Charles threaded his way through crowds that jammed the departure gates. With few minutes to spare, he boarded the first-class car on the express train to Berlin. He entered his mahogany-paneled compartment and slid his suitcase under the wide leather-upholstered seat. Charles opened his briefcase, removed papers and placed them on the table in the center of the compartment.

A conductor knocked on the window of the compartment door. Without Charles's acknowledgement, he entered followed by a uniformed Nazi officer. They gave Charles accusatory glares. Nothing personal, Charles thought, just the Reich's customary look of intimidation.

In turn each of the men scowled as they examined Charles's travel documents—his French passport, his reservation at Berlin's Hotel Adlon. Then they read his personal letter of invitation to visit the Ministry of Aviation signed by Reichsmarschall Herman Göring. Immediately the stern and suspicious expressions on the faces of Charles's official visitors became obsequious smiles. "Best wishes, Herr Secœur, for a good trip." They bumped into each other in their hasty departure.

Charles ordered coffee. He began to review the notes he had spread on the table. A few miles outside Paris the train jerked to an unscheduled stop. A conductor walked through the car. "All is well, all is well. The tracks are blocked by a disabled truck. Soon we will be on our way." After a perfunctory lift of his right arm he muttered, "Heil Hitler."

An hour later the train resumed its journey. Charles looked out his window. The train slowly passed a large old Mercedes moving van that was on fire—no doubt the truck that had blocked the tracks. It had been pushed into a shallow ditch alongside the tracks. Flames and black smoke poured from the cab and the cargo hold. All the vehicle's doors were open. Flames sputtered around wheel wells. Firemen aimed the nozzles of hoses toward the flames and plumes of smoke. Streams of water hissed into steam. The smoke's acrid odor of burnt oil and rubber seeped into the train. Passengers coughed, some in spasms.

Before the train arrived in Berlin there were two more unscheduled stops, each because of an unexpected blockage of the tracks. The first stop was caused by a large dump truck with two flat tires, its bed filled with sand and rocks, the second stop because of a missing rail. Railway cranes had to be called. Combined, the delays added almost three hours to the trip. It didn't take a Gestapo investigation to conclude that the track blockages were organized. The Resistance.

The train's scheduled late afternoon arrival time grew near. Yet hours of travel remained. Agitated passengers approached conductors with a repeated question, "What time will we arrive?"

"I will keep you informed. Please, we're doing the best we can."

Nazi officers paced the narrow corridors. Some made trips to the dining car, returned to their compartments, and then immediately walked again to the dining car. After a few moments they repeated the round-trip.

Charles walked to the first-class dining car, found a small open table. He ordered a foie gras sandwich and a glass of Riesling. Wehrmacht officers occupied most tables. A few of them had ordered dinner. Most declined food and instead drank cocktails. Conversations centered on Berlin dinner engagements the officers would miss and how best to placate angry wives and mistresses.

Light rain fell as the train entered Berlin's Anhalter Bahnhof station. In the station's domed lobby, the crowds of passengers had a higher density of military officers than at Gare du Nord. He walked through one of the station's tall arched portals.

Outside Charles took one look at the long taxi line and began to walk towards Potsdamer Platz. Ahead loomed the pillars and arches of the Brandenburg Gate. Well beyond it and out of sight was Charles's destination, the Hotel Adlon.

Charles walked along the old Ebertstrasse, renamed Hermann Göring Strasse. He waved to hail passing taxis. None stopped. Near Göring's official residence, a five-story, nineteenth-century, neo-gothic home, a battered old black Mercedes Benz limousine pulled alongside the curb and stopped. As if to defy the rain, the foldaway canvas roof had been lowered. Was the top of the ancient convertible too rotted to be of service? The sullen-faced driver motioned for Charles to get in, though, Charles thought, he easily could have turned and spoken to him.

"Hotel Adlon, please."

The driver's sullen expression became, first, a look of surprise, then a bright smile. "Yes, sir!" He strapped Charles's suitcase to the wide luggage rack across the rear of the car.

Charles sat on the backseat's damp leather upholstery, grateful to have transit to the hotel, however uncomfortable. Soon the Mercedes parked. "Here we are, sir, number seventy-seven *Unter den Linden*. Hotel Adlon Kempinski Berlin!" A uniformed attendant opened Charles's curbside door and held an umbrella over him.

Charles looked up at the seven-story brick and stone hotel. Arched palladium windows with dark green awnings framed the ground floor. Red flags bearing black swastikas flanked the main entrance. Beside it, a brass plaque dated 1905 had been placed beneath a bust of Lorenz Adlon. Charles read the words on the plaque. They commemorated the success of Adlon's appeal to Kaiser Wilhelm II: Berlin needed a luxury hotel equal to those of Paris and London.

Charles walked into the lobby. There were more swastika-bearing flags, a large portrait of Hitler, oriental rugs, and wall hangings in rich hues of blue, gold, and magenta. Polished brass chandeliers and wall sconces lit the room. The floors and pillars were of gray and black Italian marble.

From behind the wide mahogany front desk, a clerk welcomed Charles. "Heil Hitler." As soon as Charles identified himself, the clerk stood at attention, clicked his heels, and handed him an envelope with an embossed gold seal of Reichsmarschall Göring's office. Charles opened it. A typed message said, "Welcome to Berlin! A driver will await you in the lobby at ten o'clock tomorrow morning." At the end of the message, the handwritten initials, HG.

Charles glanced around the Adlon's crowded lobby. He turned to sign the guest register and said to the desk clerk, "So few military officers. I'm surprised."

"Yes, sir. Your observation is correct. The Nazi high command favors the Hotel Kaiserhof, a few blocks south. Near Herr Goebbels's Propaganda Ministry." The clerk gave Charles a weak smile, paused, and cast a downward glance. "We all serve the Reich as best we can." Another pause. He made eye contact with Charles. "I trust you will enjoy your stay with us. Are you interested in reservations for an evening in Berlin?" He added, eyebrows raised, "Or perhaps private entertainment in your room?"

"Thank you, no. I look forward to a shower and dry clothes. A hot meal and a good night's sleep."

"The Adlon will accommodate you. Heil Hitler."

The Ministry of Aviation

In the Hotel Adlon's lobby, Charles sipped a mid-morning coffee. At ten o'clock a Luftwaffe lieutenant, close-cropped blonde hair, blue eyes, athletic, stood before him. "Herr Secœur?"

Charles stood. "Yes."

The lieutenant clicked his heels and stood at attention. "I am Lieutenant Johann Rolfe." He and Charles shook hands.

The lieutenant joined Charles in the back seat of a black Daimler sedan. The car traveled the short distance to the Ministry of Aviation. The five-story stone-and-glass building had a functional modern design. The architecture of the new Reich—the Ministry's rectangular lines and flat roof—contrasted with the Wilhelmstrasse's ornate nineteenth century buildings. As the Daimler approached the Air Ministry's front gate Charles noted that behind the wrought-iron fence around the building's lawn stood the symbol of the Reich: a massive gold-leafed sculpture of an eagle. The eagle looked down on pedestrian and auto traffic—the Reich monitoring the movement of its citizens.

The sedan entered the front gate, then passed through the Ministry's landscaped grounds. It stopped beneath the roofed pillars of the portico. The driver opened Charles's door. Charles and the lieutenant entered the building's cavernous reception hall.

Officers filled the expanse of the room. A few stood in groups, sober-faced, engaged in conversations. Others walked quickly. Their heels tapped on the marble floor. The room echoed with footsteps and voices, occasional bursts of laughter. Charles glanced around the room. He nodded toward groups of officers and said to Lt. Rolfe, "Everyone seems so engaged. The Soviet invasion?"

"Yes, sir. We are working for victory."

"I appreciate Reichsmarschall Göring taking time to meet with me."

"Sir, art is the Reichsmarschall's great passion. Second only to military victories."

And wealth, Charles thought. Göring was amassing a personal fortune in his collection of stolen art. The two men stood in silence. Charles studied the seamless light marble lines that formed large imbedded rectangles in the floor's dark marble. The floor replicated the architectural theme of the building—squares and rectangles—brick and stone boxes of different sizes and shapes stacked and positioned at right angles to one another. The severity of the reception hall's angularity was softened by floor-to-ceiling drapes; their midsections tied back with cords created gentle curves in the deeply hued damask fabric on either side of the windows.

Charles said, "An impressive room."

"Yes, sir. As you may know, the Ministry of Aviation was designed by Albert Speer."

Charles recalled a 1939 reception at the Louvre. A friend said, "Charles, I'd like you to meet Albert Speer."

The men shook hands.

"Albert is the Reich's principal architect. He's here on an educational mission," Charles's friend said. He laughed. "Albert is here to study the use of curved lines." Speer joined Charles and his friend in good-natured laughter.

In silence, the lieutenant shifted from one foot to the other. "We are to wait here for the Reichsmarschall."

In a corridor leading to the Reception Hall, a buzz of voices and footsteps grew louder. A wedge of Nazi officers entered the hall. At the wedge's center walked Reichsmarschall Hermann Göring. Göring's girth and weight appeared almost the equivalent of the combined size of the junior officers on either side of him. Göring wore a bottle green uniform with a wide leather belt around his midsection. Above the rows of medals across his chest hung the Nazi Iron Cross, a swastika at its center. A gold-sheathed dagger dangled from the belt.

Charles recalled that the Nazi senior command, Himmler, Goebbels, and Göring, designed their own uniforms.

Göring extended his hand and flashed a wide grin. "Herr Secœur, welcome."

Charles shook his hand. "Reichsmarschall Göring, thank you for taking time to meet with me."

"Your work is important, Herr Secœur."

Charles thought about Göring's voice. Loud, although for a man his size it lacked resonance. Rather, his voice resembled vibrations of a thin sheet of polished brass.

"When the battles are over, and we are all long gone, art will remain. We are, you and me, Herr Secœur, agents of immortality."

"Immortality?" Charles stared at Göring.

"Agents of it, yes," Göring said, more to himself than to Charles. He flashed a wide smile. "Though we couldn't have done it without the artists." The Reichsmarschall bellowed a boisterous laugh and slapped Charles on the back.

Charles laughed. Lt. Rolfe joined him.

"Ah, lest I forget, Herr Secœur, I have decided that the Vermeer I purchased, well, traded for, is indeed authentic. We will have no need to review and discuss it."

Charles suspected otherwise. Göring's greed made him susceptible to art forgeries, to art hustlers.

Göring turned to Lt. Rolfe. "You will accompany Herr Secœur to Carinhall. I will travel in a separate car and meet you there. I have Reich business I must attend to."

Charles and Lt. Rolfe accompanied the Reichsmarschall, his chief assistant, and two aides out of the Ministry. Göring and his staff got in the rear compartment of a long black Mercedes limousine. The two aides sat in fold-down seats and faced Göring. Beside him sat his chief assistant. Charles and Lt. Rolfe entered the back seat of a smaller black Mercedes. From the front fenders of both cars waved the red flags of the Reich and the Ministry of Aviation.

Welcome to Carinhall

The Reichsmarschall's limousine sped through the streets of Berlin. Three car lengths behind it, the driver of Lt. Rolfe's car kept pace. At intersections Berlin police stopped traffic to allow unimpeded travel for the two flag-bearing limousines.

Lt. Rolfe turned to Charles. "Herr Secœur, do you know Carinhall?"

"Only that the estate contains a large and valuable art collection. Also, that it was named for Carin, the Reichsmarschall's first wife," Charles lied. He knew much more.

"Yes, sir."

"I would like to have known Carin," Charles lied again. He had met and talked with Carin at a Louvre reception. He compounded his second lie with a question implying further ignorance. "How did she die?"

"It was a rare blood disorder."

Charles debated whether to correct Lt. Rolfe. Carin had suffered from tuberculosis and died of a heart attack. Though Charles knew the answer to his next question, he asked, "Did she live on the estate?"

"Oh, no, sir. She died in 1931. Construction of Carinhall began in 1933. In 1935 the Reichsmarschall and his second wife, Emmy, celebrated their wedding at Carinhall."

"I'm told Emmy is a woman of great beauty. An actress, isn't she?"

"She was, yes, sir. We should all be so lucky."

Reliable sources at the Deuxième Bureau had told Charles that Hitler frowned upon Göring's marriage to Emmy Sonneman because she was an actress. He had an abiding distrust of the morals of professional stage and film stars. To close associates Hitler confided his hope that the relationship would bring stability to the volatile Göring, who still grieved. He worried that Emmy's softness would become like a cancer within Göring: "Make him less cold-blooded." Hitler eventually elected to tolerate Göring's choice of a wife.

"I wonder, and please forgive my question, do you suppose it has been difficult for Emmy to live at Carinhall in the shadow of the Reichmarhall's former wife, Carin."

"Perhaps. Though I'm told she spends most of her time at their home in Berlin." And then, like a classroom student who remembered something important, Lt. Rolfe beamed as he said, "The Reichsmarschall built a hunting lodge in East Prussia and named it Emmyhall, to honor her."

Near the front gate of the grounds of the Carinhall estate, the two cars slowed as they passed a large home with a peaked red-tiled roof. Lt. Rolfe pointed to it. "A comfortable accommodation for the estate's security." The Mercedes turned from the highway into the wooded grounds of the estate. The sedan first passed between two stone buildings, gatehouses for guards, and then along a winding road until it arrived at the Carinhall mansion. Behind it were garages and service buildings.

The main building, a stone structure, shaped like a three-sided rectangle or an E missing its middle arm, enclosed most of a long, oval-shaped drive. A steep tile roof further heightened Carinhall's three stories. The two wings of the home, the bottom and top of the E, attached to either end of a long main building. The central entrance extended from the body of Carinhall toward the driveway.

In the entrance's open door stood a woman in her thirties, light brown hair, shapely, eyes that seemed to invite more—gentle words, a light touch, perhaps a kiss—wearing a full-length maroon silk and brocade dress. Beside her stood a little girl, light brown hair, about age three. One of her hands clutched the woman's dress. When Reichsmarschall Göring stepped from his limousine, the little girl rushed to him and threw her arms around his legs.

Göring introduced Charles and Lt. Rolfe to his wife, Emmy. Charles detected the odor of alcohol on Göring's breath as he turned to the little girl. "And this is Edda."

Charles knelt in front of her. In German, he said, "I am pleased to meet you, Edda."

Edda looked up at her mother, and then at Charles. "And me . . . I . . . pleased to meet you, sir." Göring gave a hearty laugh and ruffled her hair.

"Come along, Edda." Emmy and Edda said goodbye to the Reichsmarschall and the guests, then departed.

Göring ushered Charles and Lt. Rolfe into a large entry hall, its walls filled with paintings. Sculptures, some large ones freestanding, others on pedestals, punctuated the entry hall's wide expanse. Charles felt as if he had entered a major exhibit at the Louvre, though this one was less artfully displayed. A man of medium height, balding, wearing a dark business suit, walked across the room and joined them. The Reichsmarschall smiled and shook his hand.

"Herr Secœur, may I present Herr Gurlitt, Hildebrand Gurlitt." Gurlitt and Charles shook hands. "Herr Gurlitt is performing a valuable service for the Reich. He is a distinguished member of the Commission for the Exploitation of Degenerate Art."

"I'm honored to meet you again, M. Gurlitt. We met in Paris many months ago."

Gurlitt smiled and nodded.

At the Deuxième Bureau Charles had been briefed on the work of Gurlitt and the Commission—seizing and selling masterpieces. Contemporary art, too. The best German works were shipped to Hitler and Göring. Some pieces went to German museums after Gurlitt secured a few for himself. Others were sold to collectors and museums. Funds were deposited in Swiss accounts.

Göring turned to Lt. Rolfe. "You and I will soon leave and attend to the business of the Reich. Herr Gurlitt will escort M. Secœur through Carinhall."

He turned to Charles. "Please understand, your tour will be limited to Carinhall's more or less public areas." Göring took Charles by the arm and nudged him toward an open door. "First, we will have schnapps to welcome you. Then I will leave you with Herr Gurlitt." Göring said to Lt. Rolfe, "Wait here. I will join you in a few minutes."

The three men entered a paneled room, its walls bearing rich tapestries, a few paintings, and bookshelves filled to capacity with leather-bound volumes. In front of the bookshelves was a well-stocked bar. On the floor were plush oriental rugs.

Walking to a mahogany table in the center of the room, Charles stumbled on the corner of a rug. He grabbed the table and steadied himself. A small vase on the table fell.

"My apologies, gentlemen."

Göring smiled and gave a wave of dismissal. Gurlitt frowned, righted the vase, and gave Charles a disapproving stare.

The Reichsmarschall walked to the bar. He returned with a bottle of schnapps and three small glasses. He filled a small glass for each of them. The Reichsmarschall stood beside the table and raised his glass. "To your visit, Herr Secœur."

Charles raised his glass and drank. Then he stood. "Thank you, Reichsmarschall Göring, for your kind hospitality. I am honored by your invitation to visit Carinhall, meet your lovely family, and M. Gurlitt. And for this opportunity to view your art collection. Perhaps the most famous in Europe."

Göring flashed a vulpine grin. "More schnapps, gentlemen?"

The Reichsmarschall filled, gulped, and refilled his glass of schnapps while Charles and M. Gurlitt continued to sip the first one each had been served. If Göring noticed he drank alone, he didn't acknowledge it.

In a loud voice Göring asked, "Do you realize the challenge the Reich faces, gentlemen? Need I discuss, over a hundred years ago, the French invasion of Russia?" After a pause, "Perhaps not."

Göring then continued with what he said he needn't do. "In June of 1812, Napoleon marched four hundred and forty thousand troops into Russia. He had grown old and fat. He'd made mistakes in Spain. Suffered defeats. But he remained confident. Deep in his bones, Napoleon believed in victory over Russia. That victory would give him the power to bring down England."

He looked at Charles and lowered his voice, as if to confide a secret. "Britain was then at war with America. Napoleon believed that once France defeated Russia, Britain would have to sue for peace or risk the collapse of the Empire." Göring poured himself another glass of schnapps.

"In Danzig, two million pairs of boots awaited to resupply Napoleon's troops. Eighteen thousand heavy draft horses transported siege guns and supplies. Ten thousand oxen pulled pontoon bridges." Another schnapps. "Napoleon arranged to feed and care for the thousands of horses and oxen. But, I'm told, he made one major error." Göring looked away for a moment and then stared at his visitors. "He approved a quartermaster's decision made without a full analysis. It had far-reaching consequences. You know about it?"

Charles and Gurlitt shook their heads, no.

Göring lowered his voice, as if again sharing a secret, "For the Russian winter, Napoleon's quartermaster bought a million greatcoats. At a surprisingly low price. Later he discovered the coats had tin, not brass, buttons. Tin is unlike brass. Brass can withstand extreme cold. But in the frigid Russian winter, the tin buttons failed. Soldiers could not secure their greatcoats."

Göring's face reddened. He glared at Gurlitt and Charles. "You understand? They could not keep warm!" His voice softened to a whisper. He shook his head sidewise, his jowls following a half-second behind the movement of his head. "The Russian winter—arctic temperatures—took its toll."

"You may know the rest of the story." Göring stared into his glass of schnapps. "In the spring of 1813, Napoleon returned to France with an army reduced from over four hundred thousand to ten thousand men." Another schnapps. He spoke as if deliberating his choice of each word. "The greatest defeat in military history."

Charles and M. Gurlitt sat in silence, their eyes riveted on the Reichsmarschall.

"German military planning is superior—as is our equipment. Our soldiers are well-trained. We are doing it right." Göring's voice became louder. He slurred his words. "By winter our men will be home. Victory will be ours!" He slammed his glass on the table and stood. "Herr Gurlitt, please escort Herr Secœur through the Carinhall collection." Göring formally bowed and with a slight sway nodded to Charles. He did an about face and walked from the room. His footsteps echoed in the entry hall, then ended with the slam of a door.

Gurlitt poured himself another glass of schnapps. "Another, M. Secœur?" Charles nodded, yes.

The men sipped their drinks. M. Gurlitt said, "The Reichsmarschall has known much success. A decorated flyer in WWI. A principal in the young Nazi party, close friend to Hitler. The developer and commander of the Luftwaffe. Now Hitler's second-in-command." Gurlitt sipped his drink. "In July of last year, Hitler appointed the Reichsmarschall to lead the air war against Britain. The Führer's goal, like Napoleon's, was to force a negotiated peace settlement and remove Britain from the war. Events didn't go as he hoped for. The Luftwaffe and Reichsmarschall Göring's air war degenerated into one of bombing factories, and then terror bombings of the civilian population, principally London. Operation Sea Lion, Hitler's plan to invade Britain, was postponed. Indefinitely."

Charles said, "And now the Reichsmarschall leads the Russian invasion. Operation Barbarossa." Charles sipped his schnapps.

"The largest armed invasion in the history of warfare. M. Secœur, you have witnessed a man who failed to bring Britain to its knees, angering Hitler—who now demands military victory. On the same battlefields where Napoleon failed."

Charles grimaced. He had seen Göring's alcohol consumption first-hand. What he hadn't seen, but had been told takes place daily, was Göring's use of morphine.

Gurlitt stood. He motioned to Charles. "Come. We have much to view."

Charles's thoughts remained on Göring, on his eyes—flat with unchanged expressions, tiny, undilated, pupils. The eyes of an addict. The eyes of a serpent.

The Loot of Carinhall

Charles walked into the reception hall alongside his host. Gurlitt fumbled with his suit coat pockets, found then removed a notebook from an inner pocket. He flipped through a few pages, paused to read, and returned the notebook to his coat. Gurlitt waved toward the reception room's walls laden with paintings. In a voice that resembled a guide at the Louvre, Gurlitt said, "Here we have selected paintings by Botticelli, Dürer, Van Gogh, Velázquez, Renoir, and Monet." He smiled. With pride in his voice, Gurlitt continued, "The Reichsmarschall's complete collection of these artists, stored elsewhere, is far more extensive. Though some are here. Out of public view, in Carinhall's private rooms."

Gurlitt again opened the notebook. Charles glanced at the entries, all handwritten in miniature handwritten script and neatly organized in a format that resembled an accounting ledger. Looking up from the notebook, Gurlitt said, "If there is an artist you're particularly interested in, please let me know and we'll find his work."

They walked from the reception hall into a wide corridor. Charles said, "This corridor alone could stock a gallery at the *Louvre*."

"Yes," Gurlitt said in a dismissive voice. He took Charles by the arm. "Come this way." From the corridor, he led Charles into large side rooms; some had tapestries, others had walls filled with paintings—rooms ablaze with color. Each room contained at least one sculpture.

In a room displaying the work of Chagall and Klee, Gurlitt said, "Last year Sumner Welles, from the American State Department, was here. He enjoyed this collection."

Floor by floor, corridor by corridor, room after room, Gurlitt escorted Charles through treasures of European art—Picasso, Metzinger, Gleizes, Mondrian, Grosz, Kandinsky, Nolde, Kirchner, many others.

"I attended the Degenerate Art Exhibit," Charles said. "As I recall, the work of some of these artists was exhibited there."

"Yes, the paintings by German artists." Gurlitt paused, his face reddened slightly. "Chancellor Hitler allows the Reichsmarschall, let us say, certain freedoms in his personal artistic choices. Please understand, it's not something we talk about."

"The size and breadth of Reichsmarschall Göring's collection—I'm amazed." Charles stood in silence for a moment. As if speaking more to himself than to Gurlitt, he said, "How did it happen? All this?"

"First, you must understand, M. Secœur, most of the Reichsmarschall's collection is not located at Carinhall. This is the tip of the iceberg. At other locations specially constructed buildings and vaults house the Reichsmarschall's collection, both above and below the ground. Selected caverns serve as storage facilities, many quite large, secure, with climate and temperature-controlled environments."

"One of them is Castle Rock?"

"Ah, you know about that?"

"I've heard rumors and know only a little. I've read that since the fourteenth century, cavernous vaults and passageways in the sandstone beneath Nuremberg Castle have been used for storage projects that required secrecy and discretion."

Gurlitt laughed. "Your facts are correct."

"I've been told the vaults contain works of art the Führer plans to place in the museum he will build at Linz. The vaults contain much of the Reichmarshall's collection."

Gurlitt gave a self-deprecating smile. "It's not something I am free to talk about."

"Leaving aside Castle Rock, how did all this . . . ?"

"Please permit me to interrupt. You are asking, how did the Reichsmarschall build such a collection. Yes?"

"Correct."

"There is no simple answer. First, remember that the Reichsmarschall is an active collector. He engages in purchases and exchanges or trades, as does any serious collector or museum. Including your *Louvre*, M. Secœur.

"This purchase, for example." Gurlitt pointed to a painting hung on the wall before them, its surface cracked with age. Charles had seen photographs of the painting but had never seen it first-hand. He didn't know it was at Carinhall.

"Painted by Vermeer, seventeenth century. Christ and the Disciples at Emmaus. Two disciples are breaking bread with the resurrected Jesus."

Charles studied the Vermeer piece, the love and concern expressed in the faces of Christ and the disciples. He tried to look away and failed, so powerful was the painting's visual magnetism. What might it have cost Göring to own this Vermeer? Charles attempted mental calculations of the possible cost of this or any other Vermeer. Charles remembered comments from colleagues at the Louvre that the masterpiece might be a reproduction—a fake.

Gurlitt said, "M. Secœur, just as the Reichmarshall did, you could've purchased this Vermeer for 1.61 million guilders. About seven million U.S. dollars."

Charles nodded. "I think not." He and Gurlitt laughed.

They walked across the room. Gurlitt continued, "Beyond purchases, there are exchanges, trades. The Reichsmarschall traded two works by Henri Matisse, *Still Life with Sleeping Woman* and *Pianist and Checker Players*, for this one." He pointed to the painting, *Reclining Nude with Cupid*. "By Jan Van Neck, a seventeenth century Dutch painter. Do you know his work?"

"I have only heard his name."

"I'm not surprised. Van Neck is little known outside certain circles. The Reichsmarschall is quite proud of the exchange that brought Van Neck into his collection."

Charles smiled. "Each of us has different tastes. I don't know if it's an exchange I would have made."

Gurlitt said, "The Reichmarschall's collection reflects his preference for the beauty of the female body. For paintings of nudes. It's helpful to remember that we all have different tastes."

The two men took Carinhall's central elevator to the next higher floor and entered its main corridor. "You asked about sources of the Reichmarschall's collection. Rarely does a week pass that the Reichsmarschall doesn't receive a gift of at least one valuable painting, sometimes two or three. Gifts from Reich officials and patrons of the arts."

"A collection this extensive—surely it's not all from gifts, trades, and purchases. Or is it?"

Gurlitt chuckled. "No, along with colleagues I'm honored to have played a small part in it."

"From your work on the Exhibition of Degenerate Art?"

"In the course of our work on the Exhibition, Reichmarschall Göring honored me with an appointment to the Commission for the Exploitation of Degenerate Art."

"Exploitation?"

"Yes. To manipulate to our advantage, through sales, what der Führer has called the Reich's artistic garbage. Then we use the revenue to develop the new national art museum Hitler will build at Linz. At first we weren't sure how to proceed. Our leader characterized the art as garbage. Who would buy it?"

"You found a way?"

Gurlitt smiled. "Yes. The sale of art is no different than other forms of commerce—one builds sales by creating demand. That's what we did. Perhaps you were in Berlin that day."

"No," Charles lied. 20 March 1939. He was there. "I read about it in the Paris newspapers."

The Commission had directed the police and Gestapo to pile degenerate art in the courtyard of the Berlin Fire Department. One thousand paintings and sculptures. Four thousand watercolors, drawings, and prints. Charles watched in disbelief as firemen put torches to the base of the massive heap of fine art. The work of Europe's artists discarded as trash by Nazis and transformed into flames and smoke.

Gurlitt gave a hearty laugh. "Our art-burning shocked the art world. Perhaps you, too, M. Secœur."

"I must admit, yes, it did." Even now, over two years later, memories of the burning made Charles's pulse rise, triggered the anger he felt when he learned of the burning—and created a desire in him to strike out. For the moment, Charles recognized his feelings for what they were—his father called them 'rage in a bottle.' He had vowed to himself, *Someday I will break this bottle.* Charles took deep breaths and in his thoughts repeated, *I will find a way.*

"From Switzerland came the Basel Museum's buyers, their pockets filled with tens of thousands of Swiss francs. Ready to purchase our so-called degenerate art. In a queue behind them, were other museums and collectors." Gurlitt smirked, "All of them ready to perform heroic acts: to purchase and rescue our art."

After walking through more rooms Charles felt as if he'd consumed a gourmet meal with too many courses. The two men took the lift to the first floor and returned to the reception hall. They entered the room where earlier they had sat with the Reichsmarschall. Gurlitt led them to the same table. He walked to the bar and returned with a bottle of schnapps. He uncorked it and filled two small glasses.

"There were other sources. One was very important to both Hitler and Göring."

Charles wondered, was it the ERR? If so, he wanted to hear it from Gurlitt. "May I ask, what was that source?"

"The 1940 Nazi government decrees declared Jews stateless. They lost all property rights. Jewish-owned art collections were officially deemed ownerless. Massive wealth waited to be claimed."

Charles sipped his drink, nodded that he understood.

"Hitler established the Reichsleiter Rosenberg Taskforce, Einsatzstab Reichsleiter Rosenberg, or ERR, within the Nazi party—named for Alfred Rosenberg, an intellectual force in the party. Rosenberg became chief of the ERR. In the occupied countries, the ERR became the official art procurement organization.

Charles lied, "I've heard of the ERR. But don't know much about its work."

"Hitler gave the ERR much power—to confiscate manuscripts and books from libraries, seize important art held by ecclesiastical authorities and Masonic lodges. To appropriate all the valuable cultural property that had belonged to Jews."

"Quite a scope."

"Correct. Thousands of art collections were seized from schools, museums, galleries. Homes and estates. Some of them, for example the Rothschild collection, were internationally famous. All of them became property of the Reich."

"In terms of quantity," Charles said, "the work of the ERR must've accounted for half, perhaps more than half, of the Reichsmarshall's collection. Am I correct?"

"Let me check." Gurlitt took out his small notebook and leafed through its pages.

"Hello." A woman's voice came from the doorway. The men turned to see Emmy and Edda Göring. Emmy wore a long pastel pink dress. Her hair fell loosely to her shoulders. Edda wore a light blue coat buttoned to the neck. "Gentlemen, I apologize. I must leave. Please allow me to say goodbye. I hope you will visit Carinhall again."

The men stood. Gurlitt and Charles bowed. "Frau Göring, Edda," the men said. Emmy extended her hand and walked toward them.

Charles extended his hand and stepped toward Emmy. His thigh struck the table. His table bump tipped over the long-stemmed glasses of schnapps. Charles lunged for the bottle of schnapps to stop it, too, from toppling over. But he knocked the uncorked bottle on its side. Charles then stumbled into Gurlitt. Schnapps ran across the table, splashed on Gurlitt's suit coat.

Gurlitt pushed Charles away.

"Oh, my goodness! Come, Edda." Emmy ran to the bar, Edda close behind her, and returned with two towels. She handed one to Gurlitt and with the other wiped the table.

"*Gnädige Frau*, Herr Gurlitt, please accept my apologies," Charles said.

Under his breath Gurlitt muttered to Charles, "Clumsy oaf."

Emmy said, "Herr Gurlitt, you have schnapps on your suit coat. Please let me take it for a moment."

"Oh, don't bother. I will . . ."

"I insist, Herr Gurlitt."

Charles helped Gurlitt remove his coat. He whispered, "I am so sorry, Herr Gurlitt. Please forgive me."

Charles handed Gurlitt's coat to Emmy, who said, "Come, Edda." Emmy took the coat and, trailed by Edda, walked out the door.

In silence, Gurlitt glared at Charles, sat down, and poured himself, not Charles, another glass of schnapps. He took a deep breath, gulped half the schnapps in the glass, and then sat back in his chair. He closed his eyes.

A few minutes later Emmy and Edda returned. Emmy handed Gurlitt his coat. "Schnapps removed, Herr Gurlitt. Your coat will soon be dry," she said with a bright smile. "And now Edda and I must leave for Berlin."

Gurlitt said, "Please accept my thanks for your kind hospitality."

Charles added, "And my thanks, as well as my apologies."

Emmy and Edda departed.

"Thank you for your hospitality, Herr Gurlitt."

A solemn-faced Gurlitt shook Charles's hand. "I have work to do." He turned and walked away, as if glad to be rid of Charles.

During the trip to Berlin, in the back seat of the Mercedes Charles reclined on the soft leather. He reflected on his day at Carinhall, on all he had learned. He thought about Göring's art collection and about Hermann Göring, the man. His excessive alcohol consumption and probable drug use. The air war with Britain, at best a stalemate, at worst, a battle lost. Now the invasion of the Soviet Union. Would the Reich's army and Göring's beloved Luftwaffe suffer the same defeat as Napoleon?

After he arrived at the Hotel Adlon, Charles hurried to his room. He packed his bag, checked out of the hotel, and was soon on the evening express train to Paris. An hour later, in the privacy of his first-class compartment, Charles ordered a double cognac. After it arrived, he locked the compartment door and pulled down the shade. He wrote a brief note to Miriam. "Lovely Lady, now returning to Paris. Hope to see you soon. C." He addressed the envelope, "Miriam Dupré, *Hôtel Le Lieu*, Lyon," put his note inside, and placed the envelope in his inner coat pocket.

Charles lit a Gauloise and sipped the cognac. He thought of Miriam's intelligence and sensuality, her affection, how much he cared for her, missed her. He reflected on the pain he felt in her absence. No wonder he'd stayed unattached all these years.

Charles thought ahead to his arrival at Paris's Gare du Nord station early in the morning. After he disembarked, he would walk through the main terminal to the unmarked door beneath the sign, Lost luggage claims office. Then down two long flights of stairs to an underground world where sounds of steam engines and rail cars passing overhead resembled the roars of animals trapped deep in the earth.

At the bottom of the stairs, he would open a heavy iron door and walk into a musty corridor lit by bare light bulbs. At the end of the corridor, he would enter the Deuxième Bureau's dispatch room. Hercule, a thin, balding, and bespectacled clerk with protruding ears, would peer across the counter and ask, even though Charles had been there a hundred times, "*Monsieur*, you are? Identification, please."

Once again, Charles would hand Hercule his passport. "Charles Secœur."

Hercule would straighten his glasses and then open a loose-leaf notebook. He would turn to a page, place the passport next to an entry, and then look up at Charles. After a nod of recognition, "How can I be of help to you?"

Charles would then remove the envelope from his coat and hand it to Hercule. "Please have this delivered to *Hôtel Le Lieu* in Lyon."

Then he would hail a taxi and go to the Deuxième Bureau. There would be much to report.

Charles looked out his compartment's window at the sunset and enjoyed the sun's rays of gold streaking across the vineyards. He remembered how much he had to do before he arrived in Paris. He lit a second Gauloise and sipped his cognac. Charles reached into his coat pocket. He smiled as he removed Herr Gurlitt's small leather notebook. He opened it and began to read.

The lists contained many well-known works of art. The scope of the Nazi theft of European art astounded him. He soon sat upright, body tense, pen in hand. He began a detailed outline of Göring's collection and the steps he would recommend to the Deuxième Bureau to recover the stolen art after the war.

As the train neared Paris, Charles put away his pen and notepad. In time, he thought. All things in their time. First, win the war, no small matter. But it will happen.

He reminded himself of his pledge to break his "bottle of rage," recover the stolen art. Return it to former owners—if they are alive. If not, to find the descendants of the original owners. Otherwise, arrange for trustworthy institutions to become the art's custodians, however temporary. *This is my pledge.*

The train entered Gare du Nord, slowed, hissed steam, and jerked to a stop at a passenger platform. Charles stepped off the train. Under his breath he repeated his pledge.

News from Paris
9 January 1942

"Good morning, Miriam," a sullen-faced Jacques offered. In the hotel dining room, I poured myself a mug of café national. I carried it into the lobby. M. Bollé handed me part of his newspaper.

At my first glimpse of the morning's headlines I spilled my café national. *"Musée de l'Homme Verdict: Guilty!"* The front-page story described the previous day's trial and verdict in a German court in Paris. Nineteen members of the Resistance network of the Musée de l'Homme were tried. All were found guilty.

Aimée—was she one of them? I threaded my way through the stories. With the press controlled by the Reich Minister of Propaganda, I shouldn't have been surprised at the stories' anti-Resistance rhetoric. Pro-Nazi propaganda that masqueraded as news. I diligently searched each story for the name, Aimée Connaix. I didn't find it. I reminded myself that Aimée could be using a nom de guerre.

Most of the accused were employees of the Musée de l'Homme. All of them were associated in some way with the museum. They were identified as members of the museum-based Resistance network, Réseau du Musée de l'Homme-Hauet-Vildé. Boris Vildé's name was prominent in the stories. Aimée had spoken of him. Vildé headed Aimée's Polar Department.

Charles said he had consulted with Vildé and his department. My heart skipped a beat. I re-read the newspaper stories. Might I have missed Charles's name? I hadn't heard from him for a while. Once again, I slowly scanned the stories. Charles wasn't mentioned. Aimée? I looked again. Not there. I breathed a little easier.

The newspaper stories reported that during the trial Judge Roskothen relied heavily on the testimony of one man: Albert Gaveau, a mechanic who worked directly for Vildé. Gaveau was a member of the Gestapo, a double agent. He sent detailed reports on the Resistance activities of Vildé and members of the Polar Department to the Gestapo. Gaveau did not appear in court. However, the newspaper said, Judge Roskothen placed much reliance on Gaveau's reports.

As I sopped up the spilled faux café I heard an inner bell of recognition. I remembered events during the day Lt. Sassi and I had traveled to Paris, my rush across the city to Aimée's apartment. The shock I felt when I saw her smashed front door and its sloppily painted accusatory swastikas. I sat in front of the door and wept.

A man in dirty coveralls had pushed open the apartment door. The man had politely introduced himself: Albert Gaveau! He said he worked with Aimée. "Our boss, M. Vildé, instructed me to come here and ask Aimée about some records she had checked out. She is not here. I looked around but found nothing. What a mess in there. If I learn news of Aimée, where can I contact you?"

"*Hôtel Le Lieu* in Lyon. Miriam Dupré."

Gaveau removed a note pad from a pocket in his overalls. He wrote my name and Hôtel Le Lieu, Lyon, in it.

Mon Dieu, how could I have been so naïve? I had handed Gaveau my name and address. In disgust with myself, I imagined I could've added, "Please arrest me." Gaveau said he hoped to be in touch soon. My stomach cramped. For a moment I couldn't breathe.

Gaveau had so easily pulled the information he needed from me. I reflected on that and tried not to feel foolish. I counseled myself that he had done the same to others, including Boris Vildé. But I became acutely aware that I had become another name on Gaveau's, and the Nazi's, list of possible enemies of the Reich.

Ten of the Musée de l'Homme defendants were found guilty of capital offenses. They received death sentences. Three defendants were sentenced to prison terms. Charges against six others were dismissed. No doubt Gaveau had a new list, one with my name on it.

I handed the newspaper to M. Bollé and plopped into the chair beside him. Tears ran down my cheeks. He placed his hand on mine.

Aimée's ransacked apartment, its door painted with the obscene anti-Semitic graffiti. I remembered the polite Albert Gaveau. How could someone, anyone, do what he had done? Pretend to be Vildé's trusted colleague, then file secret reports that led to Vildé's arrest for espionage. Lead an apparently normal life all the while secretly living another?

Then I thought of Miriam Dupré, the false Resistance-constructed identity for me, Miriam Meijer. Was I different, for better or for worse, than Albert Gaveau?

Would I, could I, do what Gaveau had done? I told myself no. But I wondered. If it was in the interest of what I believed to be a morally right cause, perhaps I would. Did Gaveau believe Hitler's cause was morally right?

A voice, Papa's voice, said, *Miriam, you are not Albert Gaveau. You haven't used false pretenses to betray people who trusted you, to support morally wrong actions. I pray you never will. But what will your protectors ask of you?*

Six weeks later newspapers reported that on February 23, at Mount Valerian, just west of Paris overlooking Bois de Boulogne, prisoners Jules Andrieu, Georges Ithier, Anatole Lewitsky, Léon Nordmann, René Sénéchal, Boris Vildé, and Pierre Walter were led before a firing squad and executed.

The death sentences of the women defendants were commuted. They were given prison terms and sent to concentration camps. Another kind of death sentence?

Still no news of Aimée.

But Turn They Will

In the SNS conference room, I sat at the large table with Gen. Carmille and his deputy, Lt. Raymond Jaouen. "Our project team will soon arrive," Jaouen said. Then we sat in silence.

Gen. Carmille gazed attentively at Lt. Jaouen, then at me. I looked him in the eye. A question that had nagged at me for a long time nudged its way into my thoughts. A question I never intended to ask. But suddenly there it was, a life of its own, leaping out of my mouth. "Gen. Carmille, SNS began as the Military Recruitment Service, then became the Demographic Service, and now it is the National Statistics Service." I paused to summon my courage. "Why the changes?"

Gen. Carmille walked across the room. He closed the door then returned to his seat. "Yes, I suppose it might seem contrived. Perhaps even a bit suspect, though I hope not to the Germans. I have told you about my meeting with *Maréchal* Pétain, about his secret funding and support of our work. But there's more. Much more.

"In August 1940, about six weeks after the country fell to the Germans, I met secretly with Gen. Maxime Weygand, Minister of War. We discussed what France would need in the future in order to rapidly mobilize the army. At that time, under the terms of the armistice, the army was being disassembled and decommissioned. Gen. Weygand and I discussed France's need for the technology, the systems, to mobilize rapidly. We discussed the importance of the development, in secret, of a mobilization capacity. The government bureau, *Statistisque Generale de la France*, had the capacity to manage only aggregate or pooled statistics on the French population. The job skills and competencies of individual citizens were not there. We needed those kinds of data, particularly as they related to military experience and military training among our citizens. And we needed the capacity to aggregate and manage large quantities of data on individuals. I knew this could be achieved, though it would have to be done under camouflage."

Lt. Jaouen said, "So the changes we've come through, including changes in the name of the Service, began?"

"Correct. We started with the Military Recruitment Service, already using mechanography to build large files of data on individual soldiers' retirement and health services. We added statistical capacities through expansion and a merger with the *Statistique Générale de la France*. We formed the Demographic Service. With further development and expansion of mechanography systems, the new Demographic Service evolved into the National Statistical Service with the capacity to mobilize former French soldiers. I gambled that the German passion for data and orderly statistical records would support these developments. That is, if their true nature were kept camouflaged. We successfully did that. The Germans approved. And now we have the opportunity to gain control of the Nazi census of the Jews."

The three of us were again silent. Gen. Carmille and Gen. Weygand— their thinking, their planning, had been years ahead of events.

My mouth fell open in surprise, perhaps in admiration, too. I often felt that way in Carmille's Paris seminar, wide-eyed, as he revealed the potential, the magic, of mechanography applied to government operations. This time the magic was about more than mechanography. It was about Gen. Carmille's vision of the future of France, his courage, and his willingness to put himself at risk. Camouflaged and working beneath the noses of the Germans, he made things happen.

Lt. Jaouen ended the silence. "Sir, I wonder, worry, can we do what has to be done? If we fail . . ." He looked away. "I don't want to think about it. We can't fail."

"We won't," Carmille replied, his voice firm. "We will delay, confuse, and further delay processing the Nazi census data and identification of French Jews. We'll complete the Mobilization Register. Strategically place it for the Allies to seize after the invasion of North Africa."

I asked, "Sir, a member of our team, Col. Edouard Duval. Can you tell me a little about him?"

"Yes. Have you met him, Lt. Jaouen?"

"Once, very briefly, in your office."

"Col. Edouard Duval is an old and trusted friend. He has had a long and distinguished career in the French army. Artillery. He's been my friend and colleague in the *Deuxieme Bureau*. We served together in the trenches in the Great War. My life was forever joined with Edouard's on a rainy morning. I glanced along the curved trench where we found ourselves. Edouard Duval, like me, then a lieutenant, stood just ahead of me. Above the trench, guns of the French artillery rose in the fog—ghost-like brass, iron, and steel sculptures. Ready to belch shells. Send death and dismemberment into German trenches. So, too, were the German guns, though they were aimed at us.

"Then came a whir, a whistle, and a second of dead air. My world turned fiery red. The blast flung me twenty yards through the air. I landed on top of the body of a soldier, his neck a bloody stub, his head gone. Blood gushed from my leg.

"Smoke and dirt filled the air. Duval crawled to me. He applied pressure to my wound and stemmed the flow of blood. *'Au secours! Aidez-moi! Medic! Medic!'* he screamed. He pulled a first aid kit from his knapsack and applied a tourniquet to my leg. 'Edouard, *merci*.' Heavy rain began to fall.

"'René, lay still,'" he instructed me. At a distance, I saw medical corpsmen in the trench. They carried a stretcher. Blood, mud, and the black grit of explosions darkened their once white uniforms. They slopped through the mud toward us.

'I can't move my leg.'

'You will—you're going to be all right, René. Medics are here. Léon François René Carmille, you're too strong to die. Not yet.' A medic inserted a hypodermic needle into my thigh. I sunk into a black whirlpool.

"In the trenches, I trusted Edouard Duval with my life. I will trust him with my life today. You can, too."

The Ferrets began to arrive. Lt. Lacroix entered the room, followed by Lieutenants Lacroix and Sassi, both of them brilliant, trustworthy, and experts in mechanography. A few minutes later our group's sixth member, Col. Duval, arrived. I reflected on what Gen. Carmille had just told us about him. He was the most experienced and senior member of the Ferrets.

The conference room door opened. A young man entered the room. His build and demeanor vaguely resembled Gen. Carmille. He took a seat at the end of the conference table. He and Gen. Carmille nodded to each other.

"Everyone, please say hello to my son, Robert. He will be responsible for keypunch and tabulation operations in our Verdun workshop. He'll also aid us, as needed, across workshops, on keypunching, staffing, and supervision. If you have questions on workshop operations, talk with Robert."

Gen. Carmille nodded to people around the table as he introduced each of us. "Lieutenants Jaouen, Lacroix, and Sassi, Miriam Dupré, and Col. Duval." Robert nodded to the group.

We welcomed Robert. "*Bienvenue,* welcome, *ravi de faire votre connaissance*, pleased to meet you"

Gen. Carmille continued, "As a practical matter Robert will spend much of his time as a troubleshooter in the seventeen regional offices. Here, Montpellier, Toulouse, Claremont-Ferrand and elsewhere. You have a list of locations. I'll follow up with procedures for secure ways of communicating with him. Robert, thank you for joining us."

Robert stood and left the room.

"Before we discuss routine projects, Edouard, would you brief us on what you've recently learned about the Reich's *Abhwehr.*"

"My underground sources report that Admiral Wilhelm Canaris, chief of the *Abhwehr,* indeed the entire German intelligence apparatus, has fallen into disfavor with Hitler. *Abhwehr* has consistently failed to give advance warnings of Allied troop movements. In addition, they have also underestimated the strength of Allied battalions. I like to believe that the *Deuxième Bureau* can take some credit for some of that." He beamed a wide smile.

Lt. Jaouan had said that Col. Duval had a specialized knowledge of

European intelligence operations. And that he had a reliable underground network of personal connections. I had just witnessed his value to our group.

We then discussed routine assignments and dates when projects were to be completed.

A week earlier, at an informal meeting of our group, Lt. Sassi had referred to us as the Ferrets. When the laughter ended, he said, "Hey, the name fits! Like ferrets, we're small and well-camouflaged. We work in the dark. We're sometimes thieves, lightning fast." The name stuck.

Carmille said, "We've come a long way since our first meeting a year ago. At that time, we wondered how to gain control of the Nazi census of French Jews. I shared with you my letter of 18 June of last year to Xavier Vallat, Vichy Commissioner-General for Jewish Questions. I offered our help in managing the GCJQ census data. I speculated that Vallat and the CGJQ eventually would have to turn to us. We had what they needed."

He looked at me. "You asked me, Miriam, 'And when they do?'"

"You reminded me, sir, 'We will own the census— all the names and addresses of French Jews. The creation of any and all census-based lists will be under our control.'"

Carmille said, "As I predicted, Vallat called. 'We face a massive backlog of completed census forms,' Vallat said. 'We don't have the staff to manage them. Can SNS help?'"

At that time, SNS had recently expanded and had sufficient staff to respond to Vallat's request. Carmille took a few moments to reflect on how, in late autumn of 1941, at his insistence and with Maréchal Pétain's approval, the Demographic Service had merged with the French Statistical Bureau to form the National Statistics Service, known as SNS. Henri Bunle, director of the Statistical Bureau and his old friend, had opposed the merger. Carmille prevailed.

"Yes, I told Vallat, SNS can help."

"But I will remind you, again," Carmille said, "whatever it takes, however we must do it, we will not be a party to roundups of the Jews of France." He sat straight, his gaze intensified.

"Yes, sir," I said. "How will we do that?"

Carmille's face darkened. "We will selectively penetrate and enter secret codes into the system. We will chop, block, and code information on Jews that is essential to the Nazis. Make it unusable. There's a term for it—to hack. Hacking."

"Hacking?"

"A word from the fourteenth century. It originally meant to slash or hack with a machete through dense foliage. That's what we'll do. But instead of hacking through a jungle of vegetation, we'll hack through a jungle of forms and information. We'll chop, block, and selectively clear it."

I smiled.

"Did I say something amusing?"

"No, sir. I remembered a story a professor told me."

"Can you share it with us?"

"In 1896, Italian Guglielmo Marconi patented the wireless telegraph. The established wired-telegraph industry did not take Marconi's invention lightly. In fact they were quite upset about the economic threat it posed to wired telegraphy. The Eastern Telegraph Company retained a frustrated wireless pioneer, Nevil Maskelyne, to protect the industry's interests.

"In 1903, at the Royal Academy of Sciences Marconi scheduled a public demonstration of his invention. From a distance of 300 km, Marconi prepared to transmit a wireless Morse code message to a receiver in London. A moment before Marconi's transmission began, this message was received in London—

'Rats, rats, rats
There was a young fellow of Italy,
Who diddled the public quite prettily . . .'"

Gen. Carmille chuckled. "Marconi had been hacked."

Around the table the Ferrets laughed. Col. Duval gave a loud belly-laugh. A moment later Gen. Carmille's smile disappeared.

Lt. Jaouen asked, "Is something wrong?"

Gen. Carmille glanced at the lieutenant and then made direct eye contact with me. "Am I correct? You have heard nothing from your friend—I believe she is also your cousin—Aimée?"

"That's correct, sir, why do you ask?"

"The road ahead of us bears much similarity to the road taken by the *Musée de l'Homme.*"

Lt. Jaouen said, "Please help us understand that."

Gen. Carmille walked to the window and in silence gazed out for a full minute. Then he returned to his seat. "Within the Polar Department, Boris Vildé and his colleagues organized a cell of the Resistance. The first, I believe. They engaged in actions the Nazis viewed as counter to the interests of the Reich. Treasonous. Actions so heinous the cell's principals were arrested. Ten of them were sentenced to death and executed."

"Yes, sir," I said. "But we're not, at least I don't think we are, doing anything like that."

"Not yet," he replied. "Two things you should consider. First, the Polar Department used mechanography to place secretly coded Resistance plans and actions on punchcards. Then they transmitted Resistance plans to other cells using the cards. Those cards could be read only by members of the Resistance. They were unreadable to anyone who did not have the codes, people outside selected members of the Resistance. Those cards contained sensitive information hidden from the Nazis. Aimée was the Polar Department's resident expert in mechanography. She was at the center of those actions.

"Second, in Paris, I attended a small secret meeting of the Marco Polo Network of the Resistance. Aimée was present. I outlined a way to hack our information systems and stop the identification and roundups of Jews in France. A way to prevent in France the efficient and successful roundups now underway in the Netherlands."

At his mention of the Netherlands my heart leaped out of control, began to pound like a drum. Was census information on my Jewish neighbors and families who lived through the Rotterdam firestorm—was it being coded on IBM cards? Then used to produce police and Gestapo lists for roundups?

"We have survived the arrest and execution of the *Musée de l'Homme* resistants. We will move forward with our plans to hack and stop roundups of Jews.

"But Aimée remains at large. She may know my—our—intent to hack the census of Jews. If caught, under the pain of a Gestapo interrogation she, perhaps like any of us, might reveal Resistance secrets. Aimée could bring down the walls of the Service."

We entered about two minutes of silence, though to me it seemed hours long.

Col. Duval said, "I will make certain that the *Deuxième Bureau* searches for Aimée. If she is found, she'll be protected."

There was another lengthy silence.

Lt. Jaouen said, "Sir, we are at war. We have the resources to fight. To stop the Nazis. To save the lives of Jews. We will hack our census data."

A Hard Truth
Autumn 1942

I watched the first trucks arrive and unload thousands of completed forms from the census of the Jews. I imagined similar deliveries to regional offices in Clermont-Ferrand and Limoges. Files that conveyed information about Jewish households—thousands of them—with each household recorded on multiple sheets of paper. The data on each sheet waited to be transformed from police files to SNS data cards. The Nazis and Vallat expected it would then be keypunched, organized into lists, and printed. From families to census forms to codes to keypunched cards to lists. I shivered as I thought about Eichmann's use of the lists. Could we, could I, prevent that?

Lt. Lacroix said, "Let's get started. We have lots of files to organize and process."

"How can we possibly process that mountain of raw data? There's not enough available labor in all of the Occupied countries to do it. Why the urgency?" Even as I said that, I wondered about the possibility of an initial step. How I might slow, even stop, creation of the codes and keypunched IBM cards.

Lt. Lacroix spoke to my unasked question. "The Vichy government has declared the importance of the files of the census of Jews. They're filled with critical information. They and the Reich want—need—that information. They want lists of Jews—Himmler and Heidrich's top priority. Remember Gen. Carmille's explicit instructions about data processing."

"Yes, I remember."

"You will need to unobtrusively work around your staff. Perhaps at night. Install Gen. Carmille's special program codes. Column eleven's information will be unusable to anyone who does not have the camouflage codes. Without those codes, lists of Jews cannot be printed."

I said, "We'll do what Gen. Carmille has instructed us to do: 'Hack the system, chop, block, delete, and selectively code census information on Jews.'"

"Correct."

Fear rushed through me—what if Gen. Carmille were to be replaced? Would I be asked, pressured, to keypunch and deliver that information— without the camouflage? Deliver the Jews to the Nazis? Could I create further delays? How much time would I have?

Soon after the first truckloads of census forms arrived, I met with Gen. Carmille. My voice trembled. "Sir, since January I've heard rumors about the Wannsee Conference and a shift of Nazi policy. In an extreme direction—to eradicate the Jews of Europe. It's chilling. Do you believe they can do that?" I gripped the arms of my chair so tightly my knuckles turned white.

Carmille said, "I'm told they . . . "

I interrupted, "Sir, in May and August of last year in Paris, the Nazis and local police rounded up over seven thousand Jews. This year, in July, over thirteen thousand, most of them foreign born, including four thousand children. All of them were locked in the Vélodrôme d'Hiver, a bicycle racing arena!"

Carmille walked around his desk and sat down beside me. "I understand what you're feeling. What's happening to the Jews troubles me, too. Deeply. But we have to keep our wits about us if we're to develop ways to combat the abuses."

"But, sir, no food. Little water. Few toilets. Jewish families forcibly removed from their homes. Taken first to *Vel d'Hiv.* Then herded—at gunpoint—into boxcars. Shipped to Drancy . . . then to . . ." I burst into tears. "To camps . . . murdered. My cousin Aimée . . . Was she one of them?"

Carmille put his hand on my arm. In a soft steady voice, he said, "I share your concerns about what is happening. But we have no way to learn about Aimée."

As anger surged through me, my face flushed. "Pierre Laval, you are acquainted with him, Gen. Carmille. Laval said, 'Vichy shed no tears over the fate of foreign Jews in France. Happy to get rid of them.'" I wiped away tears. "Admiral Darlan, former French prime minister, said the same thing. 'Stateless Jews who have invaded our country do not interest me. But good old French Jews are entitled to all the protection we can give them.' Well, Aimée is a good old French Jew. Is she protected? Where is she now?

"I'm one of those foreign Jews . . . disguised with a false name and passport. Are they going to murder me along with all the other Jews of Europe?"

"They may try. But you have some protection."

"I do? Who will protect me?"

"We will. SNS and the Resistance."

"Why doesn't that make me feel better?"

"There's no way I can remove your worry, Miriam. Remember, you have an opportunity to do something about the wrongs being committed. You can help others." He handed me a tissue.

I wiped my eyes. "Thanks, I have trouble remembering that." I took a couple of deep breaths. "Himmler and Eichmann. They'll lean hard on Vallat for lists of the Jews, right?"

"I assume so."

"When Vallat fails to produce, won't they turn to us? Demand the lists? If we produce them, aren't we then part of the process? Accomplices to mass murder?"

"They may turn to us. But we will not produce the lists. Please continue your present assignment. Stay on task. Column eleven's keypunches will obscure the truth. Confuse them. Remember, delay and denial are our weapons. If the Nazis question you, deny everything. Ask them, who is a Jew?

"Himmler and Eichmann think with German logic. They know that question has to be answered in order for them to achieve accuracy. Otherwise they'll feel uncertain. They'll worry that they may round up non-Jews. Eichmann is a champion of accuracy."

"Didn't the Nuremberg Laws address this question?"

"They did. The Wannsee Conference attempted to simplify the definition of a Jew, set in place a new policy to rid Europe of Jews. Before Wannsee, anyone with three or four Jewish grandparents was defined as a Jew, including people who converted from Judaism to other religions. Wannsee edicts removed those distinctions. The edicts have yet to fully permeate the ranks of the Gestapo."

I walked to a window, looked down at the street. "Sir, I read a census file on a Roman Catholic priest. He had converted from Judaism. Had two Jewish grandparents, married, and a third grandparent, widowed, who later married a Jew. According to the Nuremberg laws, was he Jewish? Further, what about exemptions under the Nuremberg laws? For example, Jewish soldiers who won combat decorations such as the Iron Cross? Did the Wannsee Conference eliminate all those considerations?"

"If we were to use the census to produce lists of Jews and we included that priest, or government employees, or everyday citizens with two, not three, Jewish grandparents—or Jewish soldiers who have distinguished themselves in combat—we would create problems for those people. And for officials. The Nuremberg laws, imperfect as they are, attempted to codify solutions to a loathsome problem."

I said, "Making those so-called racial determinations is not simple."

"The follow-up from Wannsee Conference is a lesson in how life doesn't always go according to plan. Even a German plan."

"So I am to continue playing the game—confuse and delay?"

"Yes." Carmille's expression softened. "This war, and our work, will someday end." Carmille spoke slowly. He emphasized each word. "Every day that we delay the lists, we delay possible roundups of Jews, their shipments, and deaths. We have to do what we can. We will do that. To buy time. Save lives."

Two Challenges
The Next Day

Immediately after the arrival of the first truckloads of census forms, Gen. Carmille asked Lt. Jaouen to call a meeting of our project group, the Ferrets.

Lt. Jaouen and I were the first to arrive at the conference room. A few minutes before meeting time Gen. Carmille arrived, accompanied by a French Army sergeant. Gen. Carmille sat at the head of the table, the sergeant beside him. Col. Duval arrived, expansive and smiling. He greeted his old friend warmly. A few minutes later Lieutenants Lacroix and Sassi arrived in the midst of an animated discussion. "Rommel is heading for El Alamein," Lacroix said.

"Second time around," Sassi added. "This time Rommel is short of petrol, tanks, and troops. The eastern front, Stalingrad, takes everything available. Rommel will not stand up to Montgomery."

When everyone was seated, Gen. Carmille nodded toward the enlisted man. "Most of you have met Sergeant Chalée, my driver." Chalée nodded to the group. "Before we start our meeting, please pass along to me the information packets I asked you to prepare." The three lieutenants passed uniform brown envelopes down the table. Gen. Carmille handed them to Sergeant Chalée.

I alternated looking down at my meeting notes and then at the sergeant. His face was familiar. From where? When? I recalled a memory recovery method Papa had taught me. Letters-to-words-to-discovery. My thoughts fired as rapidly as a machine gun. 'Think about what you want to know. Then quickly go through the alphabet. Start with the vowels. Then go to consonants. If any letter triggers a little excitement, follow it with another letter—a consonant after a vowel, a vowel after a consonant. Search for words beginning with those letters. Then say to yourself, 'I can't remember _____. At this point your mind may fill in the blank, fill in what's missing. A name, a place, a reference, and so on.'

I closed my eyes and applied Papa's method to the name of Gen. Carmille's driver. Where had I seen him? I soon imagined myself in the lobby of Le Lieu. A man stood at the front desk talking with Jacques. The man— Sgt. Chalée! Mon Dieu, is Sgt. Chalée one of us? One of them? I made a note: "Talk with Lt. Jaouen about Sgt. Chalée."

Carmille turned to Sergeant Chalée. "Please go to Vichy and deliver the packets to the office of the Commissioner for Jewish Affairs."

"Yes, sir." The sergeant collected the packets and left the room.

"Today, we have two immediate challenges," Carmille said to us. "The Nazi Census of Jews and the Mobilization Register." He gazed around the table. "Shall we begin?" Heads nodded. "Col. Duval, please bring us up to date on the Mobilization Register."

Duval opened a folder. His eyes scanned the top page and said, "The Register contains the names, addresses, and military identification of former soldiers and current reservists who reside in North Africa and southern France." He glanced around the table. "As Gen. Carmille knows, an Allied invasion of North Africa will take place in a few weeks. The rumored target date is 8 November." Duval paused, then spoke slowly, an emphasis on each word. "I should add, our discussion, all that we say here today, is top secret. To be discussed only with those who have top secret clearance and a need to know." Duval sent a rare scowl around the table.

"After a successful invasion, Allied forces will advance into Italy and the south of France. What Churchill calls the soft underbelly of Europe. Troops and mechanized divisions will move north."

Lt. Jaouen said, "Colonel, but for a few minor tasks, the Mobilization Register is ready. What are our next steps?"

"The Register's card files are to be delivered to Algiers. To the French Army's headquarters. The files are to be located in proximity to automated card readers, tabulators, and printers. That equipment is in place."

"Yes, sir."

"Can you have the cards and Register ready *prior to the invasion?*"

"Can we?" Lt. Jaouen glanced around the table. We nodded, yes. He turned to Duval. "Yes sir, we can do that."

Gen Carmille added, "During the invasion, Allied forces will seize the Register. Once they have the files, that information will speed the mobilization of French troops in Algeria and the south of France."

Duval stood and walked to a map of the coastline of North Africa pinned to the wall. He pointed to the coastline near Algiers. "A caution. Remember, the Free Zone and all French troops, facilities, and ships— including those in North Africa—are under the command of *Maréchal* Pétain and the Vichy government, as well as the German authorities." He returned to his seat. The room remained silent until Duval added, "And remember, loose lips sink ships." Around the table sober faces and head-nods gave way to a ripple of laughter.

Lt. Jaouen said, "No disrespect intended, Colonel. But we've heard that phrase so often, well . . ."

Duval laughed. "I understand."

I felt apprehensive. "Colonel, we'll complete our work on the Register. Have it ready for shipment to Algiers. But . . ." I wondered how to complete my sentence positively, not as a complaint.

"But?" Duval queried.

"Colonel, with respect, for I know this is wartime, I must ask a consideration. In setting dates and objectives for the Registry's shipment, please understand that my people, virtually all of them civilians, are stretched out. Beyond preparation of the Mobilization Register, management of the forms and data of the Jewish census has placed extensive demands on us. Add to that our management of covert codes and massive amounts of keypunching—all this strains our capacities. In order to do it all well, and prevent the lists of Jews, many of my people work double shifts. Every day."

Duval held my gaze. "Miriam, please know that I value what you and your people are doing. I'll take all you've just said into account. Do the best I can."

He then turned to Carmille. "Miriam raises an important problem. Shall we discuss the census of the Jews?"

"By all means."

His face pensive, Duval ran his fingers over his brush moustache. "I'm concerned about the recent removal of Vallat as Commissioner for Jewish Affairs—are there repercussions for us?"

Carmille replied, "Yes. The new Commissioner, Louis Darquier, known officially as Darquier de Pellepoix, is even more anti-Semitic than Xavier Vallat—if you can imagine that. Since taking office, Pellepoix has intensified pressures on local officials to round up Jews. Thanks in large part to the work of Miriam and her people, officials have had to rely on incomplete municipal records, not census data. Eichmann's targets for shipments of Jews have not been met."

I said, "Sir, our work on the Jewish census . . . We have a separate challenge. One we haven't discussed."

"And that is?"

"Secrecy—within our work groups, secrecy about covert code and keypunch operations." I made eye contact with each person at the table. "Our sabotage of the census. The few who know about it are sworn to secrecy."

Carmille glanced around the table. "There are two parts to this. First, at my direction, Miriam has instructed some of her staff to comb the census files for certain kinds of information. Then they are to produce diversionary reports for the Nazis. Those reports will address the complexities of the questions we have spoken about. For example, who is a Jew? Statistics on numbers of people who are first degree, second degree, or *Mischling* Jews?"

Lt. Jaouen said, "I'll have to ask for some clarification. First or second degree? *Mischling*?"

I replied, my voice matter-of-fact, as if I read a document, "Under the Nuremberg Laws of 1935, a Jew was any person with at least three Jewish grandparents. Or, if the person had only two Jewish grandparents, but was a member of a Jewish congregation, was married to a Jew, or was an offspring from a marriage to a Jew or an extramarital affair with a Jew, then that person was a Jew. A person who did not fit these categories but had two Jewish grandparents was classified as a *Mischling*, or mixed-blood, Jew of the first degree. With one Jewish grandparent, a *Mischling* of the second degree."

Lt. Jaouen leaned back in his chair. "That's a complex web."

Gen. Carmille said, "One that works to our advantage. Miriam and her people have set about to assess the Jewish ethnicity of tens of thousands of French citizens. A huge project. Add to that the complexity of Algerian Jews. You may recall that the Vichy government rescinded the Crémieux Decree, issued in 1870. It made full French citizens of all Algerian Jews. Negation of the decree didn't make it simple or easy to identify Algerian Jews."

Col. Duval said, "Am I right—when Himmler and Eichmann appear at our door and demand lists of Jews, we confront them with our work on the complexity of the problem?"

"That's correct," Gen. Carmille said. "It won't work for long. They'll react with anger and impatience. Wonder how we could be so misguided. By then we may have secured enough time for the Resistance to warn and possibly get large numbers of Jews away to the countryside.

"Then there's the truth of the cover-up. When Miriam's employees keypunch the cards for each household, they won't know column eleven's keypunched information is, for all practical purposes, unusable."

Col. Duval said, "To make sure we're all on the same page, the function of column eleven?"

Gen. Carmille replied, "Column eleven is designed to record in coded keypunches answers to the question, 'Are you Jewish?' When a machine operator presses keys to enter data on a punch card, everything will appear to be normal. As far as the operator knows, the keystrokes perforate column eleven as planned. But in fact, a master code will scramble column eleven's perforations. Questions related to religion cannot be answered. Certain operations cannot be performed." He paused and looked around the table.

"For example?" Col. Duval asked.

"For example—from keypunched census information on residents of a given neighborhood or community, it will be impossible to statistically answer the question, 'How many of the respondents are Jewish?' Further, and of greater importance, it will be impossible to answer the question, who is Jewish? Without an answer to that question, the names and addresses of Jews cannot be produced. That information is essential to Nazi roundups.

"We will not be able to define whether or not a respondent is a Jew. Should Eichmann or Himmler challenge us, our fallback position is the complexity of the definition of a Jew. Himmler won't accept that. But something is better than nothing." Gen. Carmille's eyes twinkled. "Remember, in the land of the blind, the one-eyed man is king. However flawed, our fallback position about the definition of a Jew is what we have to work with."

I leaned forward and rested my arms on the conference table. For a moment I lowered my head. Then I looked up at Carmille. "Sir, my people have processed and keypunched cards for thousands of households. Rest and sleep have become luxuries. They've had only a few hours each day to rest, restore energy. Those limited hours are being eroded by the time and energy required for the cover-up." What I didn't say was how fatigue and worry about the census dominated my thoughts, had become an obsession. Whether awake or asleep, the census and the Jews were always there.

Carmille looked around the table. "That's enough for today. Remember, the sabotage . . . it's a secret we must protect."

The Ferrets filed out of the conference room. I stopped Lt. Jaouen. "I'm worried about Sgt. Chalée. I've seen him at *Le Lieu* talking to people I don't trust."

"Sorry, Miriam. I must send some messages. Let's talk later."

ZNO—No Longer Free
15 November 1942

During my walk early Wednesday morning, I had to dodge a convoy of armored vehicles, tanks, and large trucks, their beds covered in canvas. They roared into the center of Lyon. From the trucks, German troops with rifles disembarked. They spread out through the city and set up checkpoints, which I avoided by walking in the alleys. Pedestrians, bicyclists, and drivers were required to produce identity papers. Armored vehicles joined trucks and continued into the countryside. Troops took possession of farms and set up armed observation posts. Later I learned that near the confluence of the Saône and Rhône rivers, the trucks delivered black-uniformed troops to the Hôtel Terminus, headquarters of Lyon's Gestapo.

Returning from SNS late in the afternoon, Simone and I entered Le Lieu. We joined M. Bollé and stood near the main entrance. Wehrmacht and Gestapo officers filled the lobby.

Her dark eyes suddenly large, watchful, Simone whispered, "What's going on?"

I shook my head. "I asked Lt. Lacroix. He didn't know."

M. Bollé said, "Rumor on the street is Hitler has ordered troops to occupy the *Zone Non-Occupée*."

Simone pointed across the lobby. "Look." Behind the registration desk the tall thin man in the dark suit who had become a permanent presence in the lobby worked alongside Jacques. "What's he doing?"

"He's the man who spied on Charles and me in the park. It looks like he's reviewing identity papers of hotel guests."

Simone paled and clutched my arm. "What if he checks . . ."

Jacques looked toward Simone and me. He made eye contact with Simone, smiled. He motioned for her to come to the front desk.

Her face apprehensive, Simone walked across the lobby. I remained beside M. Bollé.

When Simone stood at the registration desk, Jacques turned to the tall man. "This is the one I mentioned. She is called 'Simone.' I suggest you examine her *carte d'identité.*"

The man extended his hand. "Your identification, *mademoiselle?*"

Simone rummaged through her handbag. Her hand shaking, she handed him her carte d'identité.

He studied the card. "Hmm, there may be a problem with—"

Simone picked up the large inkwell on the registration desk. She flung it at the man. It hit him in the face. Black ink spewed over his face, into his eyes, dripped down his nose and cheeks. The ink transformed his face into a sinister mask. It spread a wide black stain on his white shirt.

Simone rushed across the lobby. She entered the revolving front door. There was a loud thud. Her head slammed into a heavy glass panel of the door. On the door's street side, the foot of a German soldier had abruptly stopped the door's rotation. The soldier held the door in place. Simone attempted to reverse her direction and run into the lobby. The door would not turn. Like a trapped animal, she screamed.

Pistols drawn, two uniformed Gestapo soldiers approached the door and Simone. One of them pointed his pistol at people in the lobby. The other pointed his pistol at Simone. At the peak of her next scream, the soldier holding the door released it. Simone fell into the lobby.

She stood up, put her hands on her hips, and glared at the nearest soldier. "You have no right . . ."

The soldier slammed the butt of his pistol into Simone's face. She collapsed. Blood flowed from a gash across her jaw. The soldier looked down at Simone.

"Jude pussy."

Transformation

The soldiers grasped Simone's arms, dragged her toward the front door. Stunned, in impotent silence M. Bollé and I watched.

Simone looked back at M. Bollé and me. Her voice weak, she pleaded, "Help me, please!"

I rushed to her and grabbed one of Simone's arms. I pulled her toward me. "You can't . . . "

A soldier pointed his pistol at my face. I wanted to hit him, yet I shook with fear, paralyzed. He pushed me away. M. Bollé guided me to a chair. He whispered, "Not now."

My chest heaved. I gripped the arms of the chair, my knuckles white.

The soldiers held Simone's arms behind her in a tight brace. They walked her out the front door to an olive-drab panel truck, opened the rear doors, and threw her into the cargo space. The truck's engine revved. The truck sped away.

In the lobby, silence spread like a thick fog rising on the Rhône. No one moved. Jacques approached M. Bollé and me. "I regret that Simone was less than truthful. Sometimes we need to relearn old lessons."

I glared at Jacques. My voice trembled as I asked, "How could you?" I slumped into my chair. M. Bollé took my hand.

Jacques pursed his lips. He gave me a perfunctory nod, as if to end any further discussion. He returned to the front desk. The German soldiers departed.

Across the lobby, fragments of conversations resumed. Soon the room buzzed with animated talk.

I imagined Simone in that truck, then in a jail cell until she was herded with other prisoners into a rail car. At the end of her trip—one of the camps. Auschwitz?

Numbness enveloped me. How many times would I experience this? Someday, would it be me in that truck? On that train?

M. Bollé sat beside me. He took my hand. We sat quietly. He pointed toward the lobby's front windows. "Look. Life in Lyon changes before our eyes." From the parapet around the roof of the building across the street, German soldiers unfurled two long rolls of bright red banners, each bearing a large black swastika. They rolled down the front of the building, framed the main entrance in red and black.

Eyebrows arched, M. Bollé waved one hand at the lobby. "And in here—notice anything different? What's missing?"

I wiped away tears. "I don't know. My brain has shut down."

"The Vichy flags. They're gone."

Red flags, some with eagles, others with swastikas, had replaced Vichy flags. The new flags had been hung above the registration desk and from lobby walls.

Through the front windows, I watched M. and Mme. Colbride, elderly residents of Le Lieu. They took final puffs on their cigarettes and carefully extinguished them. M. Colbride handed his cigarette butt to his wife who placed it, along with hers, in a small brown paper bag. They rushed through the entrance's revolving door as if late for an appointment. They stood beside M. Bollé and me.

"Have you seen?" Mme. Colbride asked in a loud voice. "We've just come from *Hôtel de Ville*." She pointed toward the lobby's large front windows. "Up and down the streets, we walked. All across Lyon. From doorways, lampposts." She pointed to the nearest swastika-bearing red flag. In a loud voice she said, "Everywhere—those flags!"

A Gestapo officer at the registration desk scowled at Mme. Colbride. A soldier standing nearby gave the couple sharp and disapproving glances.

M. Colbride placed his hand on his wife's arm. "Marking their territory, my dear."

The officer near the registration desk walked across the lobby to the Colbrides. He placed his face close to M. Colbride. "Marking territory? Do you imply we're dogs?"

M. Colbride's mouth gaped. "N-no, sir. I . . . I regret the misunderstanding."

"Your thoughtless remark, if repeated, will place you and your wife in jeopardy." He flashed a smile of condescension at the couple. "Once is forgivable." Again, the smile. "Twice is to face charges."

Mme. Colbride stepped forward. Her voice indignant, she asked, "Charges? For what offense? We are law abiding citizens of France." She stared at the officer. Mme. Colbride's lips parted as if to speak, but no words came out.

M. Colbride pulled his wife to his side. "Come, Rachel."

"Rachel?" The officer glared at the couple.

"Yes, Rachel." She raised herself to full height. "That is my name."

"Papers, please. Now!"

M. Colbride searched his inside coat pockets. Mme. Colbride opened her purse. A moment later, hands shaking, they handed identity papers to the officer.

The officer's gaze traveled from the documents to each of their faces and back to the documents. "Abraham and Rachel?" He tapped a finger on the papers.

The Colbrides paled as they nodded.

"Your badges—the star of the Jews. Why do you not have them on?"

Mme. Colbride's face reddened. "Because, because . . ."

M. Colbride stepped between his wife and the officer. "They are in our room. An error we regret. Please accept our apologies."

"Law abiding French citizens? You are in violation of the new laws." He gave a perfunctory smile. It ended like a quick gust of wind. "I now issue you a warning. If I see you again not wearing the yellow star, you will be arrested." He laughed dismissively. Then laughed again, as if he and the Colbrides shared an inside joke, and then spoke in a confidential voice. "You may soon be arrested anyway. Wearing the star may buy you some time. Consider my warning as a gift from a friendly hotel neighbor."

In the days that followed, along the streets of Lyon, beneath red flags German soldiers mingled with pedestrians and shoppers. The streets looked much as they did before the Occupation—almost normal. Almost.

Operation Torch

"Finally, positive war news," Col. Duval said. I stood alongside him and the other members of the Ferrets in the conference room. We had a lively discussion of recent war events as we awaited Gen. Carmille.

When Gen. Carmille entered the room. He gestured toward the table. "Everyone, please be seated."

Lt. Jaouen said, "Scurry, Ferrets." Edouard Duval's hearty laugh filled the room. We seated ourselves around the table.

Gen. Carmille grinned. "I'm pleased to see morale is improving," he said, with a lilt in his voice. "I've asked Col. Duval to brief us on Operation Torch."

Duval's face, along with the faces of people around the table, turned serious. He opened the folder before him.

"For quite some time, Stalin has been pressuring the Allies to start a new front in southern Europe—take the pressure off the Soviets."

"Victory at El Alemein boosted everybody's confidence," Lt. Sassi said.

"However," Duval continued, "the invasion of North Africa has been fraught with complications. I assume you are mindful of the fact that French forces in North Africa have been under the command of *Maréchal* Pétain and the Vichy government. As a reminder, don't overlook the fact that we are, too."

Carmille asked, "Edouard, the strength of French forces in North Africa?"

"Approximately sixty thousand troops. Most of them based in
Morocco. Plus a small naval fleet anchored at Casablanca."

"More than I thought."

Duval continued, "Eisenhower has been given command of Operation
Torch. He has set up headquarters at Gibraltar. In late October, he directed
American consul Robert Murphy to hold secret discussions with French
officers about cooperation during an Allied invasion. He sent Gen. Mark
Clark by submarine for further negotiations.

"Gen. George Patton commanded the Operation Torch invasion.
It commenced on 8 November. American and British forces landed in
Vichy-held French North Africa—Algiers, Oran, and Morocco. There was
strong resistance in Oran and Morocco. Not Algiers. In Algiers, the FFI,
French Forces of the Interior, de Gaulle's name for the Resistance, had
instigated a coup and arrested the Vichy commanders. This neutralized
French troops, mainly the French XIX Corps, prior to the invasion."

"The Mobilization Register. Has it been—do you know what's
happened?" I asked.

Duval's eyes smiled. "Seized by Allied forces yesterday. With
the Register in hand, our forces will mobilize former French troops.
Particularly those with needed technical skills."

Carmille said, "The Allied high command approached our Gen.
Giraud about taking command of French forces. Giraud said he lacked the
authority to do it. He said Admiral Darlan had that authority."

"An amazing man, our Admiral Darlan," Col. Duval said. "A highly
evolved political animal playing the ends against each other while in the
middle he thrives. He preceded Laval at the top of the Vichy government and
negotiated with the German High Command on reparations and provisions
for French political autonomy.

"And now we find him with the Allies, appointed by Gen. Eisenhower,
supported by Roosevelt and Churchill, and the Allied High Command, no
less, to take command of French forces in Algeria."

Duval paused and reviewed his notes. "Darlan was named 'High
Commissioner of North Africa.' Most vexing, I'm sure, to our friend Gen.
de Gaulle, who had to accept it."

Lt. Sassi asked, "The implications for continuation of combat?"

"Darlan ordered French forces to cooperate with the Allies. Combat stopped immediately."

Around the table, nods and murmurs of amazement.

Duval continued, "To close this chapter—I assume you've been outside 10 *rue des Archers* in the past few hours. There's a new German presence. Flags, troops, vehicles. When Hitler found out Darlan had joined the Allies he became angry—so angry he ordered German forces to occupy all of Vichy France. They have. Rapidly. The *Zone Libre*, the so-called Free Zone, is no longer *Non-Occupée*, no longer free."

I again felt the fear that had gripped me during my walk to work earlier that morning. Bright red flags with black swastikas—draped along walls, hung over doorways and windows, waved from flagpoles and lampposts. Everywhere, the markers of the dogs of the Third Reich.

Admiral Darlan
26 December 1942

Charles and I sat at a corner table at Chez Claude. On the bar stood a small Christmas tree with a few tarnished ornaments and a single strand of tinsel. A few festive red and green ribbons had been hung on the mirror behind the bar. At the only other occupied table, a young couple held hands and talked quietly.

"Charles, *Mademoiselle, bienvenue.*" Claude hugged each of us.

Moments later we sipped the house chardonnay. Charles took a rectangular brown envelope from his inner coat pocket. "I just received this packet from Paris." He opened it and withdrew two smaller envelopes.

Charles opened the first envelope, the dark brown standard issue of the Deuxième Bureau. He unfolded a sheet of paper and read its brief message. His face fell. In an intense whisper, he said, "Admiral Darlan has been assassinated."

I bolted upright in my chair. "What?"

"Two days ago, 24 December, Bonnier de la Chapelle, age twenty, entered Darlan's Algiers headquarters, the *Palais d'Eté.* Shot him dead. Local police reported de la Chapelle belonged to a royalist group that wanted to restore the Count of Paris to the French throne."

"That doesn't make sense. Even if true, it's no reason to murder a senior officer like Darlan."

"People have died for less," Charles said. "De la Chapelle was arrested hours after the assassination. He was tried and convicted yesterday."

"Don't you want to learn more? Can you talk with him?"

"He was executed by a firing squad this morning."

I gasped, "This morn—Why so fast?"

"Darlan jumped from a Reich supporter and Vichy commander to an Eisenhower-approved head of French forces in Northern Africa. To his credit he then stopped the combat between Vichy French forces and the Allies. Lots of powerful interests would've preferred that it continue. To complicate things further, some British and American secret service officers wanted to rid the Allies of Darlan. His ambition had gone awry."

"Why do you say that?

"He was smart and effective. But his focus always seemed to be on acquisition of power. He was very good at it. Though not so good at its use—too quick to advance himself and his brokered deals."

"Was de Gaulle behind Darlan's assassination?"

Charles shrugged. "Who knows?"

I pointed to the Deuxième Bureau envelope. "What's that note?"

"Oh, sorry. I missed it." Charles removed a small handwritten note from the large envelope and read it. "From my friend John, at the Allied O.S.S." Charles studied the note. "He asks, 'Was Harold MacMillan right about Darlan?'"

"Isn't MacMillan on Eisenhower's staff?"

"Yes, he's Churchill's representative. MacMillan's comment on Admiral Darlan, 'Once bought, he stays bought.'"

Charles then extracted a small sealed envelope from the Deuxième Bureau packet. From it he removed a folded white notecard, the letters JB embossed in gold on its front.

He read for a moment. "An invitation." Charles looked up and smiled. "From Josephine Baker."

My heart skipped a beat.

He studied the invitation. "She apologizes for the short notice. We're invited to a New Year's Eve party at her castle, *Château des Milandes*." He handed the invitation to me.

I felt an inner glow and sense of wonderment. "Is it possible . . . I mean, with the occupation, can we do it?"

Charles nodded. "I'll make a few calls. I believe we can."

Château des Milandes

On 31 December, Charles and I sat in the rear seat of the Mercedes limousine Josephine Baker sent to drive us from Lyon to Château des Milandes.

"Quite a car," I said. "First time I've ridden in such comfort. "

"The tip of a luxurious iceberg."

I linked my arm with Charles's, put my head on his shoulder. "*Château des Milandes*. I can't believe it." I examined the road map Charles handed me, traced our route across southern France to the château.

"A manor house so large most of us would call it a castle," Charles said.

On the map the château's location had been marked with a large 'X'— in the commune of Castelnaud-la-Chapelle in the Dordogne region in the south of France. I said, "Gen. Carmille was born in a village in that area." I gazed at the map and whispered, "I've never been to a château."

"We're in for quite a celebration." Charles said. "Built in 1489. It was the main house of the lords of Caumont until 1535."

"I wonder what it feels like to own a château."

"I'm told Josephine leases Milandes. Though I'm sure she could afford to buy it."

"Miss Baker leads quite a life."

"Josephine. She insists her friends call her Josephine."

Softly, as if testing the word, I repeated, "Josephine."

Our Mercedes arrived at the entrance to the estate. Our car joined the driveway's long line of limousines and crept toward the château.

The peaked and cantilevered slate roof of the stone castle towered five stories above the entrance. The upper floors had window turrets. The building resembled a castle from one of my childhood storybooks. Childhood memories—Margot and I nestled next to Papa as he read stories of princes and princesses, battles between medieval armies, fiery arrows bounced off castle roofs and walls.

In the foyer of the entrance hall, Josephine Baker, in a flowing red dress and a jeweled necklace, greeted us. Her black hair was curled in a short tight bob, with ringlets on either side of her forehead. She gave Charles a kiss and me a warm embrace.

"We have some time before dinner," Josephine said. "Could we go to my studio?"

I nodded. "Of course," Charles said.

Josephine guided us down a long, paneled corridor. Lights from wall sconces cast soft shadows on colorful oriental rugs. We came to heavy double doors at least three meters high. We entered a large room with shelves of recording equipment, music stands that held sheets of handwritten orchestral arrangements. Across the room were two grand pianos, each with music scores. An acoustic guitar laid on a piano bench, beside it an upright bass.

Josephine pulled three chairs together in the center of the room. For a moment she stared at me. She turned to Charles. "In the interests of security, I must ask, can I speak freely in front of Miriam?"

"Miriam is one of us. She has been since June of 1940."

Josephine smiled. "Good." She waved her right hand toward the music stands. "Look around. At first glance, you see music stands, musical compositions, and arrangements. Now, come with me."

From the music stand nearest us, Josephine picked up a musical arrangement of "Rhapsody in Blue." She led us across the room to a table and turned on its bare-bulb electric lamp. "Watch." She cautiously brought the first page of the musical score ever closer to top of the bulb.

Above the song title, words began to appear. At first blurred and dim, they soon could be easily read. "Exclusive. For the eyes of Admiral Darlan.

The remainder of the French fleet is to be scuttled."

I was astonished. With a smile, Charles gently closed my mouth.

Josephine said, "I carry musical scores with me to engagements. Once there, I exchange my scores with those of local musicians active in the Resistance. The musical scores have imbedded messages. When I leave I carry their scores and messages to Paris, Geneva, wherever." She laughed. "Sometimes, I pin secret notes to my undergarments. No German official has had the courage to inspect my intimate garments." She again laughed, this time loudly.

Josephine walked across the room. She returned with two musical arrangements from music stands. They were both from the Broadway hit show, *Shuffle Along.*

"I was only a dancer in the *Shuffle Along* chorus line." Her laughter bubbled. "But my facial expressions and offbeat antics gained me a lot of notoriety. And led me to," she waved one arm toward the expanse of the room, "all this."

Josephine autographed each of the arrangements with personal dedications to Charles and me. She handed us the signed arrangements. "These have messages for the *Deuxième Bureau,* Paris. If your car is stopped during your return to Paris, my personal notes to you should prevent suspicions and close examinations of the music. Worst case, if you feel the musical scores may be inspected, burn them or tear them up. Then let me know. *D'accord?"*

I started to object—I wanted to keep her signature, the autographed arrangement. Then I remembered this was about the war, not an autograph collection. I swallowed my objection.

Josephine pressed a button. A distant and brief electric hum followed. A balding man in a tuxedo entered the room. "This is Arturo. Like you and me, he is with the Resistance. He will show you to your suite. Please join us in the ballroom about eight o'clock. We will, even in wartime, enjoy a night of dancing, fellowship, good food, and local wines."

Arturo bowed to Charles and me. "This way, please."

As we left the room, Josephine gave me a warm hug. "You are lovely, my dear. I'm pleased you're with the *Bureau.* And with Charles—he's been alone far too long."

Josephine flashed her large brown eyes at Charles then looked at me and grinned warmly. "Who knows, Miriam, were you not here I might, hmm." She gazed at Charles. "What might we do, Charles?" The three of us laughed. Charles's face reddened.

"Now, please go with Arturo. I will see you later in the evening."

Officers of the Vichy-French army and a few Wehrmacht officers joined figures from the French entertainment world, including Charles Boyer, for the evening's lavish party. A Wehrmacht officer I had once seen in the Le Lieu lobby was there. Did I imagine it, or through the evening had he kept close surveillance on Charles and me?

Near midnight the room darkened. The band played Josephine Baker's signature song, "J'ai deux amours" . . . I have two loves, my country and Paris. The room's only light, a spotlight, shone on the small empty stage at the center of the ballroom. Then new spotlights pointed toward the ceiling and illuminated Josephine as she slowly descended a banana tree to the stage. She wore pearls, wrist cuffs, and a costume made of sixteen bananas. She wore nothing beneath the bananas—the costume she made famous in the 1926 Folies Bergère in Paris, La Revue Nègre.

All conversation in the room ceased as Josephine's voluptuous near-nude figure captured our attention. She sang as she suggestively danced to "J'ai deux amours." At the song's end, the spotlight was abruptly turned off. For a brief moment the ballroom was plunged into darkness.

When the ballroom lights came on the room burst into waves of applause, whistles, and cheers. Josephine was nowhere to be seen.

Late afternoon on New Year's Day, our Mercedes arrived at Le Lieu's front entrance.

Charles gave me a hug. "Happy New Year, love. I don't like to leave you, but I have *Deuxieme Bureau* business that can't wait."

"I don't want this to end."

"Nor do I. But for now it must."

I hugged Charles. "Thank you for a lovely trip. I've heard talk about once-in-a-lifetime experiences. Until now, I didn't appreciate that phrase." I gave Charles a long kiss. "I love you."

"I love you. A better year is coming, I promise."

Honor Your Heritage
6 May 1943

At the front of the auditorium, I entered through a door beside the dais. I waited on Gen. Carmille to join me. I surveyed the audience in the near-full auditorium. I glanced at the front rows filled with uniformed young men soon to receive their engineering diplomas and their commissions as military officers. Behind them sat families who beamed with pride.

A sign, Réservé, dangled from a white cord that marked the auditorium's last three rows. The cord was removed as the section filled with high-ranking representatives of the school and the French and German governments, including many army officers. But for two empty seats, the last row was a ribbon of black uniforms, officers of the Nazi Gestapo.

As the time for the École Polytechnique's graduation ceremony approached, a woman in a black business suit, hair tight against her head, and a lean-faced Gestapo lieutenant hurried through the auditorium's main entrance. They walked to the last row's two vacant seats. The woman carried a stenographer's notepad. Her round face with long jowls that drooped contrasted with the face of the lieutenant, lean, skin tight, jaw muscles that rhythmically tightened and loosened. Had the lieutenant's face been sculpted a viewer might have wondered if his protruding chin had been added as the sculptor's afterthought. The lieutenant's eyes scanned the audience like the rotation of beacon, one that would illuminate threats to the Reich. His face, tense yet so unexpressive he appeared bored, masked what I imagined to be a hair-trigger readiness to apprehend those disloyal to the Führer.

A ripple of movement spread through the auditorium as one, then two, and then many civilian and military faces turned to glance at the couple who'd just entered. Wehrmacht and Gestapo officers along with many civilians nodded and whispered, "Lt. Klaus Barbie."

After Barbie and the woman took their seats, a few rows ahead of them a stooped thin elderly man turned and stared at Barbie. Barbie stared back, long, hard, cold. The old man's face reddened. He turned away and then leaned over the shoulder of the man seated in the row ahead of him. In an audible whisper, he said, "The Butcher of Lyon."

Barbie's eyes darted from the old man then to a tall man in an overcoat who stood along the auditorium wall. He pointed a finger at the elderly man and jerked his thumb toward the rear entrance. In swift silence the man in the overcoat walked to the old man, put a hand over his mouth, and escorted him out of the auditorium.

Soon Gen. Carmille entered the auditorium. Ahead of him walked René Claudon, middle-aged, tall, brush moustache, an engineer specializing in bridges. He had become the second civilian to serve as director of the École Polytechnique since the school's militarization by Napoleon over a century earlier.

Gen. Carmille wore dark gray suit. I wore a dark blue dress.

I handed Carmille a file folder. "Your speech to the graduating class."

"*Merci.*"

I sat in a chair in the auditorium's front row. I had made a few editorial changes in Gen. Carmille's speech. I felt proud of the message he would soon deliver to the graduating class.

I remembered the ceremony when I received my certificate from Netherlands School of Economics. Most of all I recalled the embarrassment I felt when, as I walked across the stage to receive a special academic achievement award, Papa gave a loud whistle. Then, even worse, when the dean presented me with the award, Papa stood, whistled again, this time shrilly, and waved his clasped hands above his head.

Carmille joined Claudon on the dais. Once seated, he held the folder against his chest. His conservative suit and wire-rimmed eyeglasses gave him a professorial appearance, just right for the occasion.

Claudon rose from his seat and walked to the lectern. He smiled and addressed the audience. "On behalf of the school, we welcome graduating students and their families, our faculty, and guest officers. Our school's distinguished history dates to 1794, a product of the French Revolution and the Age of Enlightenment. Emperor Napoleon gifted the school its special military status and our motto, '*Pour la Patrie, Les Sciences et la Gloire.*'

"We are honored to have as our graduation speaker a senior French Army officer and distinguished graduate of the class of 1906, Gen. Léon François René Carmille. An artillery officer in the Great War, Carmille became a leader in the development of technology to strengthen government accounting, administration, and information management. His influential texts have been widely read. Gen. Carmille has served as comptroller general of the French Army and is regarded as an innovator in government administration. Today he serves as the director of the Vichy government's National Statistics Service."

I permitted myself an internal smile. The speaker failed to mention that since 1911 Carmille had been a member of the Deuxième Bureau, the French military intelligence service.

Claudon turned and nodded to Carmille, "*Je vous remercie . . .* Thank you for joining us on this special occasion."

Gen. Carmille stepped to the podium. He scanned the room then shook hands with Director Claudon. As he turned to the audience, for an instant the lens of his eyeglasses reflected the floodlights that lit the stage. It was as if a light beamed from each of his eyes. He placed his folder on the podium, opened it, and glanced at his notes.

The auditorium became silent. I looked around the room. All eyes were on Carmille. The stenographer beside Lt. Klaus Barbie held a pen above her notepad, poised to write, her upper body rigid.

Carmille's gaze moved slowly across the audience. "*Mes chers camarades,* members of the graduating class . . ." Students and their families leaned forward. Military officers sat as if at attention. As he began to speak, Carmille's voice was raspy and weak. As he delivered his address his voice gained power and resonance. It soon filled the room. He spoke of the contributions of French mathematicians and statisticians to France and to the world. He talked of the rich heritage they bequeathed to France and the students. From time to time Carmille glanced briefly at the seated Gestapo officers. As he reached the conclusion of his address, his voice firm and fully resonant, Carmille's gaze moved from face to face in the graduating class.

No force in the world can prevent you from remembering that you are the heirs of those who defended the soil of France, from those who were at the Pont de Bouvines with King Philip II Auguste to those who were on the Marne with Joffre. *Remember it!*

No force in the world can prevent you from remembering that you are the heirs of Cartesian thought, the mysticism and mathematics of Pascal, the clarity of the writers of the seventeenth century, and the work of scholars of the twentieth century, all this in France. *Remember it!*

No force in the world can prevent you from remembering the great numbers that are inscribed on the walls of your amphitheatres from Ampère, Fresnel and Arago, to Henri Poincaré. *Remember it!*

No force in the world can prevent you from reminding yourself that your elders have been great scientists, great engineers, and great soldiers, and all three at once. *Remember it!*

No force in the world can prevent you from knowing that your House has furnished such critical thinkers as Auguste Compte, Renouvier and le père Gatry—I cite only a few very different people to say that the freedom of thought has always existed on the Montagne Saint-Genevieve with rigor and tenacity. *Remember it!*

No force in the world can prevent you from knowing the role that your great elders have played in the constitution of the colonial Empire, from Admirals Rigaut de Genouilly and Courbet, from the Generals Faidherbe, Borgnis Desbordes, Archinard, Beaunier, Bailloud, and from the great Africans like Cavaignac, Bedaub, Lamoricière Bosquet, to the line of military engineers who have established ways of penetration of Africa and Asia, such as Germain and Joffre, Laussedat and Bernard. *Remember it!*

No force in the world can prevent you from knowing that the motto written in golden letters on the Pavilion, "For Fatherland,

Science and Glory," is the heavy legacy that constitutes the immense work of your elders and is for you a categorical imperative, which must guide your course of action. *Remember it!*

All this is inscribed in your soul, and no one can take any action on your soul, for your soul belongs only to God!

Gen. Carmille closed the folder containing his notes. My heart pounded with pride.

The graduating class burst into spirited and prolonged applause. A few members of the class stood, followed by others. Soon the entire class stood. Some cheered, as if they'd been released from bonds. Family, friends, and French officers joined them. Werhmacht officers remained seated and applauded lightly.

Members of the Gestapo sat motionless. Lt. Barbie's face flushed crimson. He gave Carmille a hard stare. Then Barbie stood. He walked quickly to the auditorium's main entrance, followed by the stenographer. She lagged behind his fast pace. Barbie banged the door open and exited.

Where are the Lists?
30 November 1943

In an ornate office at the luxurious Hôtel Meurice on Paris's rue de Rivoli, Reichsführer Heinrich Himmler, in an impeccable and freshly pressed field gray uniform, stared at Lt. Col. Adolph Eichmann seated on the other side of his desk. Over Himmler's left pocket, his Iron Cross medalllion sat above a single row of decorations. Beneath a receding hairline, Himmler's face, beady eyes, and rounded cheeks resembled a squirrel with a mouthful of nuts.

Eichmann, thin and tense, coatless, his khaki shirt sweat-darkened beneath his armpits, gazed intently at Himmler. He sat rigidly upright.

"Have you read this?" Himmler held up the editorial page of *The London Times.*

"No, sir."

"Then, please allow me," Himmler said with a mock smile. He read aloud.

War's progress?
By Charles Delmand

German military reports of the war's progress have been much like the weather in Occupied Paris—little sunshine, low-hanging dark clouds, and a cool wind blowing on all fronts. The invasion of the Soviet Union, once expected to lead to swift victory, has bogged down.

In Stalingrad, facing a Soviet counterattack, the German Sixth Army command received an order from Hitler: no retreat. But victory did not arrive. Casualties multiplied. In North Africa, following the Allies' successful invasion of Algeria and Morocco, Axis forces in Tunisia surrendered. At sea, after suffering heavy naval losses the German naval command ordered many U-boats to withdraw from the Atlantic.

The Times has learned that in January 1942, at a mansion in the Berlin suburb of Wannsee, a meeting of high-level German officials discussed the policy of the Final Solution of the Jewish Question and its implementation. The late SS General Reinhard Heydrich, chief of security of the Reich Security Main Office, chaired the meeting. Before his assassination, Heydrich had said the SS expected eleven million Jews to be eliminated—a euphemism for murdered—as part of the Reich's Final Solution. Across the Occupied countries of Europe, with one exception, the implementation of the Final Solution has moved forward country by country with murderous success. The one exception, France.

His face grim, Himmler said, "Though it pains me to say this, The Times is correct. Col. Eichmann, you know all too well, in France our quotas for arrests and shipments of the Jews of France have not been met." Himmler's voice rose. "We need lists—names and addresses of Jews. Arrests!"

"Yes, sir," Eichmann replied in a sullen voice.

Himmler leaned forward. As he spoke, jabs of an index finger punctuated the first and last words of each sentence. "We can't wait on the French police or Vichy authorities to hand us another Vel d'Hiv round up. Tell me, Col. Eichmann, why hasn't our census of French Jews produced the lists?"

"Vel d'Hiv produced over 13,000 Jews, Reichsführer."

"The French Police did the work of the Gestapo. Then you and the police had nowhere to put the captured Jews. A bicycle racing arena?" Himmler slammed his hand against the desk. "We need 13,000 Jews per week—or per day. Then shipment to the camps."

"Reichsführer, the census data is under the control of the National Statistics Service."

"Tell me, who controls the National Statistics Service?"

"The Vichy government. *Maréchal* Pétain."

Himmler waved a hand at Eichmann. "Since November of 1942 there has been a Vichy government in name only—Vichy and Pétain are impotent!" Himmler raised himself to his full height. "All France is occupied by the Reich."

Himmler glared at Eichmann. From beneath metal-rimmed glasses, Himmler's gaze penetrated, accused, and dominated Eichmann, as it did anyone receiving it. Since he joined the Nazi party in 1929, Himmler had developed the SS from a Nazi police force of fewer than three hundred members to a paramilitary organization that approached a million men. As Chief of German Police and Minister of the Interior responsible for German police and security forces, including the Gestapo, he had formed the Einsatzgruppen, the death squads of Nazi Germany. He planned and developed concentration—extermination—camps, the principal instrument of the Reich's Final Solution.

His voice thin, Eichmann said, "Sir, the census data is in the hands of the director of the National Statistics Service, Gen. René Carmille."

"And just who is he?"

"Comptroller General of the French Army," Eichmann said. He opened his briefcase, removed a file folder, and took a thin report from the folder. "This report tells the story. A few months ago, we learned that Carmille is an active member of the Marco Polo cell of the French Resistance. The cell's members are all senior French officials. You may recall, Reichsführer, we decided there was much to gain if we left Carmille in place, under surveillance. We placed two agents inside his organization. But we agreed to leave Gen. Carmille in place only short term." Eichmann tapped the report against his hand.

Himmler said, "Carmille's time has just about run out." He looked out a window. "And the lists? You can get them?"

Eichmann's face reddened. "My sources inside SNS report the census may have been sabotaged. It's possible the lists do not exist."

Himmler bolted up in his chair. He leaned across his desk. His cheeks reddened. "Sabotaged? Lists do not exist? The names of those responsible?"

"Sir, at present I do not have those names."

"The clock is ticking for Gen. Carmille. And, Col. Eichmann, for you as well. Produce results." A pigeon landed on the windowsill, walked across it, and pecked at the sill's surface. Himmler stared at the bird. "Are we like that pigeon, searching for crumbs? Who commands the Gestapo in Lyon?"

"Lt. Klaus Barbie."

"Tell Barbie we will not, *cannot*, tolerate this. You and Barbie are to take action. Produce results. Do what is necessary. Now!"

Eichmann stood and delivered a stern Heil Hitler salute.

In his office, Eichmann activated a secure phone line. "Get me Lt. Klaus Barbie, Gestapo headquarters in Lyon."

Eichmann tapped his fingers and stared at the phone.

Moments later, "Lt. Barbie speaking."

"This is Col. Eichmann."

"Yes, sir."

Eichmann's voice deepened. "The lists of French Jews—they have not been produced by Gen. Carmille and the National Statistical Service. Reichsführer Himmler is distressed. Lt. Barbie, we discussed this six months ago. Since then, no lists have appeared. Nothing has happened, Lt. Barbie. Nothing!"

Barbie whined, "If you remember, sir, I wanted to arrest Carmille then. You felt the Reich's interests were best served if we let him remain in place a few months longer."

Eichmann spoke in a resonant voice of command. "You, Lt. Barbie, develop a simple, effective plan. Then do what is necessary! Do not call me for approval. Go to the National Statistical Service. Get the lists from Carmille." Eichmann yelled into the phone, "I want the Jews of France. All of them!"

Une Faveur
20 January 1944

I rose a bit late, dressed, and rushed to the elevator. I hoped to find rolls, even stale ones, in the dining room. As I crossed the lobby my thoughts lingered on the keypunches and data cards. I had to make certain the programs and altered keypunches, among the thousands of cards processed, remained undetected by operators. And that the programs worked reliably, that the coded answers of respondents to column eleven's question, "Are you Jewish?" were consistently keypunched with the blocking code.

As I entered the dining room, from behind I felt a hand lightly grip my elbow. A voice whispered, *"Mademoiselle,* a moment please."

Startled, I flinched and turned. A thin middle-aged man in a rumpled brown suit faced me. His face was pale and deeply lined. I had seen him before. Where?

When the man's large eyes looked up at me, I remembered. The afternoon I checked into Le Lieu he'd been in the lobby—the pickpocket. I had watched him lift another man's wallet. That day our gazes had locked for an instant. I had turned away. My silence made it possible for him to exit the hotel and avoid arrest.

"Mademoiselle, you once did me a great courtesy, *une faveur.* Please permit me to return it."

"It's not necessary."

"Please, I will feel better if I do." He looked around the room. No one was near enough to hear our conversation. In a confidential voice, he said, "*Mademoiselle*, I know, as do others, that you work for Gen. Carmille. Be advised that the Nazis will tighten surveillance on him, on the Service, too. The Gestapo plans to act. Soon. General Carmille needs to protect himself. You do, too." The corners of the pickpocket's mouth drooped. His eyes widened. He spoke slowly, his voice intense, "I say again, Gen. Carmille cannot delay—he must protect himself. Now."

"How do you know this?"

"*Mademoiselle*, I live in places you will never know. Dark places. Where achievements are measured by harm, pain. I am not proud of it. But I am alive. Perhaps my words to you will offset a few of my wrongs." He walked a few steps toward the door. Then returned. "*Mademoiselle*, do you know a young woman, Aimée?"

"Aimée—yes!"

"She wants you to know she hides in Marseille. One step ahead of the Gestapo. But just one step."

"How can I contact her?"

"Perhaps we can talk on another day, *Mademoiselle*." After another furtive look around the lobby, the little man walked quickly to a side exit. He left the hotel and merged into a crowd of pedestrians.

I walked briskly to 10 rue des Archers. I rushed to the elevator and jogged down the corridor to Gen. Carmille's office. Only Lt. Jaouen was there.

"Gen. Carmille has gone to Vichy on business."

I described my brief conversation with the man in the hotel lobby. "His warning was clear. Urgent."

"I will tell Gen. Carmille when he returns."

That evening as I approached the front door of Le Lieu, a disheveled young woman in a soiled coat stepped in front of me. "You are Miriam?"

"Yes." I looked more closely at the young woman. She was emaciated. Her skin sagged, a chalky pale.

She glanced around and then put her face close to mine. "I have come from Simone—I escaped from Auschwitz. News of the horrors of the camp are known by few outside the gates. She wants you to know, begs you to tell others."

"Simone—is she all right?"

"No one there is all right." Her voice became an intense whisper, "Dirt, starvation, fleas, typhus. Death. Tell others. Tell them!"

A man in uniform approached Le Lieu's front door. The young woman turned and ran.

That night I awakened to memories of the young woman's voice. I imagined Simone dirty and ragged, fleas in her hair. Then ill. Then . . . I had to force myself to stop. I recited poems, song lyrics. Anything to take my thoughts away from Simone, to stop my images of her—dirty, flea bitten, clothes ragged. Stop, Miriam, stop!

I cried myself to sleep.

The Rotterdam Knife

In recent months, a sense of anticipation had risen throughout the underground in the occupied countries of Europe. Something dramatic would happen soon, resistants told one another. In my conversations with SNS colleagues, I wondered if rumors about a pending Allied invasion were true. Was there was anyone other than Charles I could trust with news of Simone and Auschwitz?

Memories of my conversation with the pickpocket nagged at me. I often recalled it word for word. But in spite of his warning, Gen. Carmille and all of us continued our work, our lives, as before.

I reminded Lt. Jaouen of the pickpocket's alert and mentioned the young woman's news of Simone and Auschwitz. "We need some kind of confirmation," Lt. Jaouen insisted. "In the meantime," he said, "we have important work to do. Let's stay focused on it."

Our quiet hacking of the census codes and keypunches continued to successfully block the identification of Jews. No lists were produced. I wanted to believe that the little man, the pickpocket, was wrong. And yet, his words continually intruded in my thoughts. Life in Lyon and the SNS continued as before. The news about Simone and Auschwitz kept me awake at night.

On the morning of 3 February, after I arrived at work, I told Lt. Lacroix I needed to run an errand. I didn't tell him I was going to chase a rumor that a nearby épicerie had coffee for sale! I put on a heavy coat, left 10 rue des Archers and walked across central Lyon. I thought about how Simone would've enjoyed a mug of fresh coffee. I wished she walked alongside me. For a moment I imagined her presence. Then I immediately felt an invasion of the pain of loss. Aimée, Simone. Mama, Papa, Margot. Who would be next?

I walked along the Rhône to the grocery store. I thought ahead to freshly brewed coffee. In my imagination, I inhaled its rich aroma, enjoyed its satisfying taste. When I arrived at the store I expected a queue. There was none. The coffee had been sold.

A half-hour later, my shoulders slumped in dejection, I approached 10 rue des Archers. Two dark green Panhard sedans passed me. They parked in front of the main entrance. Six men, three in black uniforms, three in dark suits and leather overcoats, stepped out of the sedans. I recognized one of the men in a leather overcoat, the tall, silent man from the hotel. He turned and for a moment glared at me.

The drivers of the sedans remained in their cars. I recognized one of them, from Gen. Carmille's office—his driver, Sgt. Chalée!

A Gestapo officer led the agents into 10 rue des Archers. I recognized him from pictures that had circulated inside SNS—Lt. Klaus Barbie.

At a safe distance, I followed the men into the building. After they disappeared into the elevator I ran across the SNS reception lobby. My hand trembled as I picked up the phone and called Gen. Carmille's office.

Lt. Jaouen answered. I yelled, "Barbie and Gestapo! In the building—elevator. Coming up. Director's office!"

A Gestapo agent in a dark suit, burly, with short black hair had remained behind. He jerked the phone from my hand. His face was pock-marked. His bulbous eyes resembled those of a frog. His breath stunk. He seized my right arm and twisted it behind my back.

"Who did you call?"

I said nothing.

The agent forced my arm higher. I cried out in pain.

"Who did you call?"

I remained silent.

The agent thrust my arm higher.

I gasped and yelled, "My office!"

"Do you lie?" After another wrench of my arm he released it and threw me against the wall. His face was within inches of mine.

"Your name?"

"Miriam Dupré."

He yelled, "Your home? School? Quick! Quick!"

"P-Paris."

"School?"

Suddenly I had to pee. Mon dieu, had a thousand rehearsals failed me? I squeezed my bladder and yelled, "*Ecole Supérieure de Commerce . . . de Paris!*"

"We go to your office. Your call—if they fail to confirm . . ." He jerked a pistol from the holster beneath his coat. An inch closer and the business end of the Luger would've poked out my right eye, the crossed one. Pull the trigger, that eye's no good anyway.

"Walk. Pray that someone confirms your call. Where do we go?"

"Fourth floor." I didn't wait for the elevator, still in use. I jogged to a stairwell and led the agent in a rapid climb, leaping two steps at a time, to the fourth floor. Twenty-one steps between floors. He became winded. I did not. We stood in front of the door to the large room where my staff and I worked. The agent pressed himself and his pistol against my back. He exhaled the stench of garlic and alcohol into my hair.

I reached for the doorknob, hoped and prayed for it to be locked. It was. I turned to the agent. "My key. I need my key."

He breathed deep rapid breaths. He kept the luger trained on me. "Find it."

I faced the door, my back to the agent. I slid one hand into my shoulder bag. Out of the agent's view, I hoped, I grasped the key and the bone-handled knife I had carried since I left Rotterdam—the one my attacker had used to threaten me. I brought my hand out of the bag. In the fingertips of my right hand I held the key. Tucked behind the key, in the palm of my hand and partially covered by the cuff of my loose-fitting winter coat, was the knife.

I dropped the key. It fell in front of the door.

I stood as if paralyzed. The agent and I stared at the key. "Pick it up," he commanded.

I slowly knelt. My right hand fumbled with the key. In quick moves, my left hand opened the knife's blade and I sprang to my feet. I whirled around. The blade slashed down, hard and fast, along the left side of the agent's unguarded face. He screamed.

The blade cut a deep gash. It began high on the left side of the agent's forehead, continued through his left eyebrow and eyeball, then alongside his nose and through his lips to the base of his jaw. The gash exposed his suddenly red teeth. Blood gushed over his mouth, down his neck.

The agent's left hand clutched at the gash. He tried to pinch together the long wound's floppy sides. He staggered backwards. His hand covered his left eye and part of the gash. He wiped blood from his right eye and stared at the section of eyeball held between his left thumb and forefinger. He moaned. A flood of blood in his eyes, he fired the pistol twice. The first bullet hit the doorframe. A second burrowed into the floor.

"Bitch—you blind me—I kill you!" He jerked the barrel of the luger toward me.

I leaped to his left an instant before he again fired. The bullet struck the wall behind me. A plume of plaster dust surrounded us. I lunged forward and plunged the knife's blade deep into his chest. I heard a muffled pop. With it came a sudden and short-lived jerk of his body. The agent collapsed like a large balloon suddenly punctured. His hand still clutched the pistol. Blood gurgled from his mouth. With his left eye gone and vision in the right one probably blurred by blood and shock, he fired a shot. It went into the ceiling. I kicked the weapon from the agent's hand. His body went limp. He lay motionless.

Doors along the corridor creaked open. In cautious movements, people peered out. The first of them might have seen me rush down the corridor and disappear into an exit stairwell. I ran down the stairs, two and three steps at a time, to the ground floor freight docks. Once out of the building I sprinted through Lyon's alleys to the nearby SNS offices at Place des Jacobins. Breathing hard, red-faced, I ran into the lobby.

The security guard, André, sat behind the reception desk. He looked up, startled. "Miriam—what is it? Are you okay?"

I yelled, "Code four. Call Charles. Tell him, the greenhouse."

"What?"

"No time." I screamed, "Code four. Charles. Greenhouse. Greenhouse!"

I ran into the street and returned to the alleys. Near Pont de Napoleon, I jumped on the rear of a flatbed delivery truck and crossed the Saône. In the old section of the city I jumped off the truck and ran into the traboules. I wound my way through a maze of narrow dark passageways. Deep in medieval Lyon, at Rue du Boeuf I exited the traboules. I soon arrived at familiar high hedges that surrounded a large garden. Inside the garden, I jogged to an old glass-paneled greenhouse, the rendezvous point Charles and I had selected many weeks ago. I pushed open its weathered door. Inside I inhaled the greenhouse's moist aroma, a mix of the perfume of flower blossoms and fertilizer.

I took a blanket from a shelf. Charles had put it there for an emergency. Hot and sweaty from my run, I began to cool down. I shivered and clutched the blanket around me. I sat in a pile of straw behind tall shelves filled with clay pots. I hoped André had sent code four. I prayed that it had reached Charles. I waited.

For the first time, I noticed the bloodstains on the front of my coat.

The Safe House

I struggled to keep my thoughts under control. I repeated to myself, my name is Miriam Meijer. I am twenty-seven years old. This morning I killed a man. A Gestapo officer. I stabbed him in self-defense—but it weighs heavily on me.

Killing a man is a powerful act. It caused me to wonder, who am I? Where am I? Where am I going?

I answered my questions. I am a Jew from Rotterdam. I can't go home—the Luftwaffe firebombed the city. My family died. Today, along with who knows how many thousands of Jews, my single purpose in life is to flee and hide from the Nazis.

I am known as Miriam Dupré, a name my friend Charles and the French Resistance gave me nearly four years ago. They also found me a job. I work for Gen. René Carmille, director of the National Statistical Service, called SNS, in Lyon. Well, I used to.

Flee, hide. Wait for Charles.

I gazed at the greenhouse door. My stomach cramped. I tightly clasped my bone-handled knife.

Minutes and hours ticked into an eternity. Then came the squeak of hinges as the old greenhouse's door opened. Charles entered. I rushed to him. We held each other tightly—the embrace of my life.

Charles took a step back. "Come, we have to hurry."

He escorted me through traboules, dark passages between and within lower levels of medieval buildings, constructed for silk workers hundreds of years ago. We came to the end of a traboule. Beyond its arched exit rose the round tower of a tall pastel blue stucco building.

"That's *Tour Bleu*," Charles said. The tower rose five stories above the entrance. We entered through a delivery door at the back of the building.

Soon we stood before a multipaned window in the fourth floor's wood-paneled living room. I gazed down into a walled and gated courtyard.

"Where are we?

Charles stood behind me, his arms around my waist.

"*Vieux Lyon*. A *Deuxième Bureau* safe house." He pointed toward the courtyard. "On the other side of that wall is *rue de Boeuf*, a cobblestone street built in the thirteenth century. *Tour Bleu* was constructed in the sixteenth century. The *traboules* connect *Tour Bleu* with many excellent escape routes through buildings and alleys." A moment later he added, "Oh, I forgot to mention, there are changes of clothing in the bedroom. In the armoire. I can supply more as needed."

I turned and faced Charles. "Clothing? I can't even think about it." I slumped into a chair. "I just killed a man." I reached into my shoulder bag. I held the bone-handled knife in my right hand. "With this." There were traces of blood on blade's hinge. My voice rose, tears streamed down my cheeks. "A man is dead. I did it, Charles. *I killed him.*"

Vivid images of events a few hours earlier streamed through my thoughts. The Gestapo agent's bloody face. The pop as my knife blade entered his heart. His body on the corridor floor, pistol in hand. Blood gurgled in his throat, flowed from his mouth. The pistol's final explosive report. I again felt my foot connect with the flesh and sinew of the agent's wrist. The weapon soared across the hallway, hit the wall, and fell to the floor. The gurgle ended. The agent's remaining eye closed.

I shook my head sideways to jar the images from my thoughts, but they remained. I muttered, "A dead man, Charles. I killed him."

Charles put his arms around me. In a soft voice, he said, "My love, please remember, we are at war. You defended yourself—did what you had to do. A man died. A wartime death. I'm proud of your courage."

I nodded. My voice weak and scratchy, I asked, "Where is Gen. Carmille? Did he escape?"

"The Gestapo arrested him. Took him to the *Hôtel Terminus*."

I wrapped my arms around Charles, buried my face in his shoulder. I began to sob. I held him ever tighter. Spasms wracked my body. I whispered, "What will they do to him?"

His voice firm, Charles said, "They will interrogate him. He's strong and experienced. Short of a decision to execute him, he'll survive. I doubt execution is an option. Most likely they'll transfer him to Montluc Prison."

"When they find out what I've . . ." I looked into Charles's eyes. "Tell me again—I did the right thing. Did what I had to do, right? *Tell me!*"

"You did what you had to do. You're a soldier in our Secret Army." He led me to a cushioned chair. "Please, sit. Try to relax. Is there anything I can get for you?"

"Coffee?"

"The *Deuxième Bureau* can provide clothing and food. We can shield you from the Nazis. But coffee?" He grinned. "That's more difficult."

Charles pressed a button on a side table. I heard the sound of a buzzer in a nearby room. A moment later a middle-aged woman in a dark blue skirt and sweater, matronly, long gray hair, entered the room.

"Miriam, this is Suzanne Hozet. She's a captain in the *Deuxième Bureau*. Captain Hozet is the officer in charge of the safe house. She makes certain security is tight, people are protected and fed, the bills paid. Other security officers on the premises are under her command. Suzanne runs the place and keeps our safe house safe."

Her grip firm, Suzanne shook my hand. She gazed at me for a moment and then gave me a warm hug. I imagined my mother's arms around me.

"You've been through a lot," she said. "You're safe here. We'll take good care of you. Let's go to the kitchen and have a light lunch. By the way, please call me Suzanne."

"Don't know if I can eat."

"That's okay. We can save it for later."

Charles, Suzanne, and I walked into the kitchen. The modern appliances retrofitted into the old room surprised me. At the kitchen counter a woman prepared soup and sandwiches. I inhaled the soup's rich aroma of garlic, onions, and peppers. My mouth watered.

Charles said, "The 1940 armistice called for the disbanding of the *Deuxième Bureau*. For all outward appearances, that's what happened." He paused and waved one arm. "But here we are—the French Intelligence Service and Suzanne. We run this secret hotel. For a select and specialized clientele. French spies, assassins, and counterfeiters, as well as highly placed double agents. On outsider might look at our guest list and say it's full of criminals. Others, after a look at the same list, would call it a list of the Heroes of France. I prefer the latter."

I smiled. My first smile since I set out to buy coffee this morning. "I'm traveling in good company."

Charles continued. "After the armistice, the intelligence service was organized under the name the *Centre d'information Gouvernemental*, headed by Admiral Darlan and Colonel Rivet. Both former colleagues of Gen. Carmille."

"I've heard him speak of Rivet. At SNS we've spoken of the late Admiral Darlan."

"Rivet and Carmille are old friends." To gain acceptance by the Reich, the *Deuxième Bureau* had to do little more than officially oppose communist and Resistance efforts. For the French Intelligence Service, to engage in duplicity against the German government was not difficult. We welcomed the opportunity. In the meantime, in London de Gaulle's Free French set up an independent intelligence service. De Gaulle must've felt they needed more secrecy than we could provide."

"What about me—secrecy about my being here?" Did my face telegraph my concern? "This *safe* house—is it *safe?*"

"You'll be fine. Suzanne is one of many Intelligence officers on and around the premises. The building is under tight and continuous *Deuxième Bureau* surveillance. Officers also keep watch from nearby buildings. All are armed. On the third floor of *Tour Bleu* is a secret communications center. We guard it closely. You have the best protection the *Bureau* and *Tour Bleu* can provide."

"Am I safe? You haven't answered my question!"

"No one can."

Hôtel Terminus
4 February 1944

The basement room was dark but for a bright light shining in Carmille's face. Carmille awakened to the sour metallic taste of blood, his blood. To damp trousers and the odor of urine, his urine. His arms and legs cramped beneath the ropes that tied him to a chair. His knee ached. He probed his teeth with his tongue. All there. Both incisors were chipped. He kept his eyes closed.

Klaus Barbie's voice, strident, accusatory—the last voice he'd heard before he passed out—was the first voice to penetrate Carmille's newly regained consciousness. Mixed with the voice was Barbie's sadistic cackle, a sound so familiar to Carmille during his interrogation. Like an echo in a cavern, the cackle continued inside Carmille's head.

Barbie's stern voice spoke to his subordinates. "Yes, he could use a washing."

Gallons of icy water drenched Carmille. His swollen left eye reflexively opened then snapped shut.

His face next to Carmille, Barbie leered at him. In a voice filled with sarcasm, Barbie said, "The traitor awakens!" Carmille breathed the backwater stench of Barbie's breath and body odor.

Carmille's right eye remained swollen shut. Behind it pulsed steady throbs of pain. When he attempted to open that eye, pain surged deep into its socket then throbbed across his face.

He tried to reconstruct events. Was it yesterday? Lt. Klaus Barbie and two, no, three armed agents had burst into his office, pistols pointed at him. Barbie leaned across his desk, pounded on it. "The lists of Jews. Eichmann wants them. I want them. Where are they?"

"I am Léon François René Carmille, Director of the National Statistics Service. We are responsible for the . . ."

"The Resistance agents, Frenay and de la Vigerie, when did you last talk with them?"

"I am Léon François René Carmille, Director of the National Statistics Service. I do not know those men. I have never talked with them."

"Where are they? We know you know. It is pointless to deny."

"I am Léon François René Carmille, Director of the National Statistics Service. Those men do not work for the service. I do not know them."

"When did you last talk with Jean Moulin?"

"I have never talked with him."

"What about Jean-Pierre Levy? And the communists, Villon and Brossolette?"

"Those men do not work here. I do not know them. I am Léon François René Carmille, Director of the National Statistics Service. We are responsible for . . . "

Barbie's hand jerked his pistol from its holster. He slammed the weapon's barrel against the side of Carmille's head. Carmille slumped over his desk. Barbie snapped handcuffs on Carmille's wrists and yanked him from his chair. Two Gestapo agents, their hands under Carmille's shoulders, dragged him from his office to the elevator, and then across the lobby to the street. They dumped Carmille on the rear seat of a Panhard. Doors slammed.

At a high speed, the car drove the short distance to the Hôtel Terminus. The agents took Carmille to a windowless room, damp, dimly lit. Carmille awakened roped to a chair. He breathed the odor of wet earth and decayed concrete. A basement? Subbasement?

The hours of interrogation produced no answers from Carmille. Barbie punctuated his questions with blows to Carmille's body and face. When Barbie slammed a truncheon against Carmille's left knee, Carmille again became unconscious.

Carmille awakened to Barbie's cackle. "Old war wound? Hurt? I can do more. Much more. Think about my questions. I want answers." He paused and then spoke slowly, as if underlining each word. "I want the lists of Jews. I will return."

Carmille heard footsteps behind him. They crossed the room. The slam of a door. Sitting far to Carmille's left, the room's lone sentry lit a cigarette.

Carmille's body ached. His agony brought memories of the Great War: a muddy trench, a mortar shell's explosion, fiery needles of shrapnel that pierced his left leg. One piece of shrapnel burned into tissue beneath his kneecap. Waves of pain permeated his body and his consciousness. Carmille remembered his resolve as he lay in that trench: *I can endure this*. He remembered Lt. Jaouen's report, a year ago, on Barbie's arrest and brutal, fatal, torture of Jean Moulin. Carmille asked himself, will an officer write a similar report on what happened here?

I can endure this.

Lt. Jaouen's Report

1 August 1943
To: Director René Carmille
From: Lt. Raymond Jaouen
Re: Confidential report, Jean Moulin

In London, 1942, Gen. Charles de Gaulle urged development of a unified Resistance command. To initiate this, on de Gaulle's orders Jean Moulin, lawyer, former sous-préfet in French governments and chief of France's 1930s Popular Front government's Air Ministry, was transported under the cover of darkness by plane from London to a drop zone in rural Provence. At 3:30 in the morning, during heavy rain and wind of a mistral storm, Moulin, along with two members of the Resistance, parachuted into the French countryside.

Moulin soon linked factions of the Resistance movement. His objective — to create a unified Resistance organization. He made additional trips to London to meet with de Gaulle. From Lyon and surrounding towns, Moulin recruited Resistance leaders and built the Secret Army.

On 13 March 1943, French police at the railway station at Bourg-en-Bresse, 40 miles north of Lyon, arrested a Secret Army courier carrying a dossier of documents. More arrests followed. The documents contained highly classified information, including battle plans, names, and code names of the Secret Army's hierarchy.

The courier was sent to the Hôtel Terminus. He was interrogated by Lt. Klaus Barbie. The courier confirmed much of the information in the purloined documents. These disclosures gave the Gestapo the names of key people in the Resistance, including members of the Marco Polo Network, and Resistance attack plans.

On 21 June 1943, at the home of Dr. Dugoujon in the Lyon suburb of Caluire-et-Cuire, Moulin met with Resistance leaders, one of whom, René Hardy, was late to arrive.

The Gestapo had followed Hardy to the meeting. They raided Dugoujon's home and arrested all those present, including Moulin. Some people alleged that Hardy had an affair with a female Gestapo spy who had alerted the Gestapo about the meeting. Others, more forgiving, said Hardy been careless about meeting security.

Moulin was held at Lyon's Montluc Prison. He was interrogated and tortured by Lt. Klaus Barbie. Barbie forced hot needles under Moulin's fingernails. He put Moulin's fingers in the hinges of a door then slammed it shut, breaking his fingers. Barbie beat Moulin with a whip. Handcuffs with screw-levers were placed on Moulin's wrists and then tightened. They cut into his flesh. His face yellow, eyes sunken, Moulin fell into a coma. He was propped up in a chaise lounge, his head covered in bandages.

A few days later, Moulin was transported to Gestapo headquarters in Paris. Moulin's injuries were so severe he could not be questioned. He was put on board a train bound for Germany. Moulin never regained consciousness. In route, he died in Metz on 8 July 1943.

Word of Moulin's betrayal and arrest, and then his torture and death, spread through the German command and the Resistance. "Death from injuries sustained in an attempt to commit suicide," was the Gestapo's official story.

The story had a ring of truth. In 1940, Moulin, as Préfet of Eure-et-Loir, had been arrested and imprisoned for his refusal to sign a German document that falsely blamed Senegalese French Army troops for civilian massacres. While in prison, Moulin slit his throat with a piece of broken glass—a failed suicide attempt guards said. Moulin covered the slit's deep scar with a scarf he later wore year-round.

Respectfully submitted,
Lt. Raymond Jaouen

Montluc Prison
5 February 1944

Two Panhard sedans stopped in front of Montluc Prison. The prison's two thick wooden doors, each five meters tall, swung open. Stone double walls surrounded the facility. Behind the walls, courtyards and flat-roofed three-story buildings. At the end of WWI, Montluc prison had been rapidly constructed. The government wanted it to be ready in the event of another outbreak of war. The prison opened in 1921. In part because of shoddy construction, the facility was rarely used. In 1932 Montluc Prison was declared unfit for habitation and closed. In 1939, following the outbreak of war, Montluc Prison, with a freshly painted interior, reopened.

Gestapo officers jumped out of the sedans. From the rear seat of the second sedan they pulled a semi-conscious René Carmille, his face bruised and bloodied, from the car to the street. Carmille stumbled as officers led him through the entrance to the interior courtyard. They continued into Montluc's main building, a warren of administrative offices and an infirmary. Three floors of prisoners' cells lined the sides of each floor's central corridor. From the first-floor corridor, activities in the second- and third-level corridors could be viewed through wide metal grates across the center of each corridor's ceiling, the grate in the floor of the corridor above it.

The officers took Carmille to a large high-ceilinged room. Above the room's entrance hung a permanent sign, Salle à manger, Dining room.

A new hand-painted sign, Infirmerie médicale, covered it. The former dining hall had become a twenty-bed medical infirmary.

A medical orderly in a once-white uniform stained with blood and dirt pointed to one of the infirmary's two empty beds. "Put him there."

Dumped on the bed, Carmille lost consciousness.

The new prisoner

In the infirmary, a young Gestapo officer, short-cropped blonde hair, ruddy face, athletic, his uniform freshly pressed, pulled a chair next to Carmille's bed. He held a clipboard and forms. He looked at the forms, then at Carmille and hesitated, as if uncertain how to question a French general.

Behind him stood Lt. Klaus Barbie. Barbie slammed his truncheon against the back of the officer's chair. "You are in control. You have a job to do. Do it!"

Addressing Carmille, the young officer said, "Sir, I need to complete entry forms for Montluc Prison."

Carmille nodded.

The officer spoke slowly. "Your date of birth?"

Over the next thirty minutes, through swollen lips Carmille mumbled replies to the officer's questions. His answers, combined with a Gestapo report attached to the clipboard, yielded sufficient information for the officer to complete the Montluc Prison admission forms.

> Léon François René Carmille
> Dossier 001669
> Fiche 001669
> 6-2-44

Verification of valuables: the prisoner has delivered the following at the time of entry.

> Money: FF 4,635
> Property: pocket watch

Fiche de Renseignements

> Born: 8-1-1886, at Tremolat, Dordogne
> Profession: Directeur de Statistiques

Domicile: Lyon – 27 rue des Remparts d'Ainay
Arrested: 3-2-44 in Lyon
Characteristics:
Light brown hair
Blue eyes
Nearsighted, glasses
Broken canine teeth
Facial cuts and bruises
Old wounds to left tibia and left knee
Health is deficient and precarious due to his age and physical condition
Immediate medical care is required

Motif: Belongs to a movement of the Resistance, the Marco Polo Network. Gen. Carmille was arrested in his office, National Statistics Service, 10 rue des Archers, Lyon. In his desk were two revolvers.

Transmission: A copy of Carmille's file will be sent to the Director General of the National Police, Central Service for French-German relations in the Libre Zone à Vichy.

Recommendation: With improvement of Carmille's health, conduct further questioning on Marco Polo and National Statistics Service's clandestine operations.

A Visitor

A month after René Carmille's arrest, interrogation, and incarceration at Montluc Prison, a guard rapped on Carmille's cell door. "You have a visitor." He unlocked and opened the door.

Unshaven, wearing a faded blue shirt, Carmille leaned on the cane in his left hand. A guard kept a tight and supportive grip on his right arm. Carmille limped to a small room off the prison's main corridor, a 'Visitors' sign above its door. He and the guard entered the room.

A Wehrmacht officer sat at the room's small table, a briefcase beside him. When Carmille and the guard entered, he stood. The officer, mid-40s, tall, narrow face, shaggy eyebrows, had black hair streaked with grey, a neat part on the left side. The tabs on the collar of his field gray German army uniform displayed the double braid of a major's rank. Above his coat's left breast pocket hung a medallion, the silver eagle of the Iron Cross First Class.

The major stood at attention and saluted Carmille. "General," he said, his voice a deep baritone.

The deep and rounded syllables of the major's voice, much like those of a professional singer, tapped into Carmille's memories. Carmille pulled his arm away from the guard and returned the salute. "You look vaguely familiar, major. Have we met?"

The officer smiled. "We met quite some time ago, sir. I am Franz Helmholtz."

Carmille's eyebrows arched. "Franz . . . "

Helmholtz smiled. "You may not remember me as well as I remember you, Gen. Carmille. I was a student in one of your courses— Mechanography in Government Administration.

"At the *Ecole Libre des Sciences Politiques*?"

"Yes, sir."

"When were you . . .?"

"1935."

His voice wistful, Carmille said, "Ah yes, I remember. You were older than most of the students. You did well in the course." He shrugged. "It seems a lifetime ago." He gazed at the officer as if sorting through a cabinet of memories. "Can we sit down? My legs are a bit weak."

"Please, sit. I learned that Lt. Barbie interrogated you. I'm sorry. The Gestapo's methods are unorthodox, often unnecessary."

The men sat on opposite sides of the table.

"May I ask, what brings you here this morning?" Carmille gave a brief laugh. "Aside from the Gestapo, I've had no visitors."

"Business, sir. To obtain information. Until recently I reported directly to Admiral Wilhelm Canaris."

"Chief of the Reich's intelligence service?"

After a moment's hesitation Major Helmholtz replied, "Yes sir, until recently."

"I've met Admiral Canaris. I'm familiar with the *Abwehr*."

"Three weeks ago, Hitler removed the Admiral as head of *Abwehr*— appointed him Chief of the Office of Commercial and Economic Warfare."

With a trace of a smile, Carmille said, "Impressive title."

"Yes." The major smiled, too. "I fear it's not a real job."

"The Führer made no secret of his dissatisfaction with the performance of the Admiral and *Abwehr*."

"The *Abwehr* was placed under the direction of Reichschfuhrer Himmler and the Reich Main Security Office."

"I'd heard rumors along those lines. But that's not why you're here, is it?"

"No, sir. Before I get to the purpose of my visit, I want to tell you how much I have admired your books and articles—applications of mechanography to government operations."

"Thank you."

"As you may know, that technology has been applied on a large scale in Germany. In government and in business. The Third Reich honored the president of IBM, Thomas Watson, with the nation's highest civilian award."

"I wish the French had been equally astute about use of the technology in finance, records, supplies management."

"Yes, it could have made a difference. For both our countries." Major Helmholtz held Carmille's gaze for a moment. "To return to the reasons for my visit today, sir, I've come to ask you about the National Statistics Service."

Carmille sat up straight, his face tight, expressionless. "Klaus Barbie and Gestapo agents interrogated me non-stop for two days and nights. No doubt there is a written record of my answers to their questions. I have nothing to add to what I've already said."

"Yes, sir, I understand." Major Helmholtz relaxed and said, "Might you recall the young woman who sat next to me in class? Brilliant student. Attractive in her own way. Helga."

Carmille relaxed also. "Helga? I remember her well—she scored at the top of the class on every exam. An alluring young woman with a razor-sharp mind."

"Preparing for your exams, Helga and I studied together. We began to go out to dinner. And to parties." A wide smile crossed Major Helmholtz's face. "She later became my wife." The major opened his briefcase and retrieved a small photo of a young woman holding a child. "That's Helga with our daughter, Katrina, when we lived in Berlin."

"A lovely photograph. I trust they are in good health."

The major's face fell. He slumped and leaned away from the table. "They died when an Allied bomb hit our apartment building."

Carmille sat back in his chair. His face expressed the weariness in his voice. "I'm sorry."

In a near whisper, Major Helmholtz said, "Thank you." He returned the photo to his briefcase and brought out a small notebook. "Getting on with our business for today, sir, may I ask you a few questions?" He paused. "I promise not to impose."

"Questions about?"

"I have been directed to talk with you and to confirm a few pieces of information. Quite frankly, I think the *Abwehr* already knows what I'll ask you about. But I've been ordered to ask." He gave a perfunctory smile. "So that's what I'll do. Please understand, if you would prefer not to answer a question, I'll respect that. This is not a Gestapo inquisition."

"Very well." Carmille nodded. "I'll attempt to confirm a few things for a former student—please, go ahead."

"Before we start, General, would you like a mug of coffee? I can have some brought in."

"Yes, please. Coffee would be nice."

Major Helmholtz spoke to a guard who soon left the room. He quickly returned with two mugs of coffee. Helmholtz removed a notebook from his briefcase, opened it, and studied the first two pages. The men sipped their coffee.

"General Carmille, the *Abwehr* believes that, with SNS's responsibilities for maintaining population records, your people could easily have accessed and used inside information on the French population."

"Accessed? Of course." Carmille laughed. "We created and maintained the files. They were used in many ways—to track population movement and demographics, income measurement, employment and unemployment by industrial sector, and so on. When you say, accessed and used inside information, do you mean for some nongovernmental or unauthorized purpose?"

"Yes, sir. For example, to select names and identities of deceased persons. And then transfer those names to secret files. Use them in the production of false, counterfeit, *cartes d'identité.*"

Carmille feigned surprise. Eyebrows arched, he said, "Major Helmholtz, such actions would be illegal."

Helmholtz smiled. "Yes, sir." The smile became a brief but hearty laugh. "However, the *Abwehr* senior command believes that SNS produced twenty thousand, perhaps more, *fausses cartes d'identité* for the Resistance."

"Anything's possible. SNS is a large organization, with over eight thousand employees in cities from Lyon to Paris. I often had a difficult time keeping track of everything. But could SNS employees create twenty thousand false identity cards without my knowing it? I think not."

Helmholtz wrote in his notebook. "Yes, sir. Let's put the identity cards question aside. I'd like to ask you about the Military Recruitment Service records."

"A very important area of inquiry, Major." Carmille's voice filled with enthusiasm. "Those records contained essential information about soldiers no longer on active duty—information needed for accurate and timely payments of military pensions and other compensation. For many of those soldiers and families, their only source of income in hard times."

"Yes, sir."

"Beyond pensions, the Military Recruitment Service authorized health services for veterans. Payment of France's debt of honor to soldiers who'd suffered wounds, including the loss of an arm or leg or as a result of combat wounds. Many of our veterans developed chronic health problems. A smaller number of them were under continuing treatment for heart and lung injuries suffered in the gas attacks of the Great War."

"Yes, sir. I understand. The *Abwehr* is concerned about a different issue."

"And that is?"

"The Military Recruitment Service had files on over eight hundred thousand former soldiers."

"Was it that many? Yes, we had files on a large number of soldiers."

"The files contained records of each former soldier's military training and skill proficiencies, including qualifications on specific weapons. If mobilization were to occur, those records would be essential for the rapid assignment of soldiers to specialty military units based on soldiers' prior training and weapons qualifications. This information would accelerate military mobilization."

"Again, you are correct."

"General Carmille, the Wehrmacht remains mystified at the speed of the mobilization of French army reserves immediately after the invasion of North Africa. What the Allies called Operation Torch. The *Abwehr* command believes SNS delivered at least one hundred thousand military reservists' files to Vichy French army offices in Algiers. Then during the invasion, those records were seized by the Allied command. They were used to speed the mobilization of French troops."

Carmille replied, "I've been told that some of the records were destroyed and others placed in a Jesuit monastery in the south of France. Perhaps records were sent to Algiers, I don't know. At risk of repeating myself, in an organization of thousands of employees, and in the midst of wartime, I should add, many kinds of records transmission would have been possible without my knowledge."

Major Helmholtz wrote in his notebook. Then he removed a file from his briefcase. "Finally, General Carmille, there is the important matter of the lists of French Jews. You offered Xavier Vallat, Commissioner General for Jewish Questions, the help of your organization in processing the census of French Jews. By then your organization had been reorganized from the Demographic Service into the National Statistics Service."

"Yes, that is correct."

"The lists of Jews were never produced. Although Reichsführer Himmler and Lt. Col. Eichmann insisted, without success, on the lists."

"Major, are you familiar with the 1935 Nuremberg laws?"

"Yes, sir."

"You, along with Reichsführer Himmler and Lt. Col. Eichmann, must appreciate the fact that at the time SNS was working on the census, we operated under those laws. In order to understand our productivity, or lack of it, you might find it helpful to again examine the Nuremberg laws and the imperfect implementation of the Wannsee Decree."

"Are you referring to the definition of a Jew?"

"Yes. You recall the Nuremberg laws, the legal importance of Jewish grandparents, and marriage to a Jew, right?"

"More or less, sir. I would need to study it more carefully."

"And the definition of a *Mischling*, or mixed-blood, Jew of the first degree or second degree?"

"Yes, sir." Major Helmholtz wrote in his notebook.

"Now, Major, apply those definitions, one at a time, to each of tens of thousands of census files for a determination of the respondent's membership in the so-called Jewish race." Carmille paused. "A complex challenge for data-entry and statistical clerks without advanced education, don't you think? The Wannsee Decree attempted to remove all that complexity—simplify the arrests of Jews, whoever they are. But the decree's implementation was slow and uneven."

Major Helmholtz sighed and closed his notebook. "I understand, Gen. Carmille." He smiled. "A complex challenge for any of us." For a moment he gazed at his former teacher. The major placed the notebook in his briefcase. "Thank you for seeing me and for the conversation. It was nice to see you again, sir."

"I hope you continue in good health, Major. May the war soon end."

"Thank you, sir. I wish the same for you. And for the war." Major Helmholtz held General Carmille's gaze for a moment. He began to speak, stopped, and then began again. "Sir, within Montluc Prison, is there anything I can do for you?"

"Thank you for your concern. I need nothing."

Later Carmille enjoyed a private laugh as he reflected on an imaginary answer to Major Helmholtz's question.

Major, the guards sometimes give us a shared razor for shaving—first to the prisoner in the cell nearest the guard's office. He shaves and passes the razor to the prisoner in the next cell. He shaves and passes it on to the next prisoner, and so on. My cell is located near the end of the cellblock. That location brings me the advantage of relative privacy. But each morning I am the last man on the razor. By then the razor is dull—prone to knick and cut.

I'm sorry, sir, Helmholtz might have said.

My request. Carmille looked down then imagined raising his gaze. What you can do for me, Major Helmholtz, is . . .

Yes, sir, what?

Can you arrange for me to be first on the razor?

Even as he enjoyed a moment of private humor, Carmille remembered his counsel to himself. After two days and nights at the hands of Klaus Barbie, he wanted no favors from any of his captors.

Life with Suzanne
Spring, 1943

I passed the mornings at Tour Bleu reading. I had long enjoyed Flaubert, also Suzanne's favorite novelist. We had long talks about Doctor and Madame Bovary, and the choices that faced nineteenth-century women who wished for independent lives. But the drama of Mme. Bovary's daily life paled when contrasted with the violent, often deadly, events of life in Lyon.

I felt thankful to have survived and escaped the clutches of the German Occupation. But tomorrow? Another story—more searches and seizures? Perhaps. Arrests of friends and colleagues at work? My arrest?

With questions like these during the day, I didn't look forward to nights—they were difficult. In the violent images of my dreams, the death of the Gestapo agent haunted me. I felt, night after night, the visceral pop of my knife blade entering his heart. Sometimes the dreams would then bring me Charles's voice, but more solemn, matter-of-fact. "Your knife blade ruptured his peritoneal cavity." Blood gushed from the agent's mouth. His eyes closed. Then opened. The agent stared at me and whispered, "*Mir-i-am.*" I always awakened, startled, alert.

Charles's occasional visits brightened my otherwise dark days at the safe house. Sometimes he stayed the night. The first time, we held each other close. We had so much to catch up on we talked well into the next morning: the war, life, death, and the future. "Do we have a future?" I asked as I finally drifted into a deep sleep.

The second night we held each other in a different way, hungry to consummate our passion. I hoped our lovemaking and my cries didn't awaken Suzanne. Later that night, my dreams contained fewer violent images than on earlier nights. But the images were still there. "Charles, how long will they remain? A year? Two? Forever?"

A member of the Resistance, M. de Parlé, often visited Tour Bleu to give reports to Suzanne. He was middle-aged, a small man, unshaven, his shirt soiled with grease. De Parlé, like most members of the Resistance, had chosen a nom de guerre, a war name and fictional identity. He claimed to be an auto mechanic. His real name and occupation? Who knew? My inquisitive nature made me curious about him, though a small inner voice advised against knowledge of his real identity. I noted his hands, not calloused, and fingernails, trimmed and clean. Even a slow-witted Gestapo agent could see he was no auto mechanic. If I had learned M. de Parlé's real name and I had then been taken prisoner, under torture might I have revealed it? Better not to know.

Early one evening, over a cup of tea, M. de Parlé said, "Tonight my mates and I will meet at the west end of *Pont de la Guillotiere*. At *dix heures*, ten o'clock." An impish grin on his face, he stood and said, "To quote Mr. Sherlock Holmes, 'The game is afoot.'"

De Parlé's quote of Mr. Holmes brought back memories of winter evenings in Rotterdam. Papa, with Margot and I snuggled on either side of him, would read Holmes mysteries aloud. Crimes committed, trails of evidence that pointed to perpetrators, then arrests. Stories that were intellectual challenges, only sometimes violent.

I thought about my work, the challenges facing me at SNS. At the top of my list: to hack the census data and block column eleven's information keypunched into the punchcards. Next on my list, our cover-up of SNS's failure to produce lists of the names and addresses of Jews. Then the production of thousands of counterfeit cartes d'identitiés, followed by the construction of a massive secret mobilization register to support the Allied invasion of North Africa, Operation Torch. All in a day's work. All illegal. People have been executed for lesser offenses.

Lt. Jaouen said, "Our *piratage,* our hacking of the information on Jews.

It's as if we thumbed our noses at the Nazi's final solution."

"If the Nazis learn about our work, we'll face prison sentences at Montluc. Or a train to Auschwitz."

"Or worse—a firing squad."

At least once a week M. de Parlé and other resistance operatives reported to Suzanne on their group's recent actions. Afterward she would go to the command center and transmit a report.

I was present during one of de Parlé's recent reports to Suzanne. "Last night," he said, "I was guarded by two French intelligence agents. I swam beneath the barges moored at the docks on the Rhône. We had learned the barges were filled with tanks of fuel for experimental German rockets. The fuel was volatile. Nearly two hundred soldiers guarded the barges. Many of them stood guard along nearby streets. Others were in patrol boats on the Rhône.

"In darkness, I swam downriver to the first barge. I attached the explosives. Below the water line. After I secured the explosives to the second barge I turned to swim to shore. Bright lights suddenly lit the barges and docks. Bullets whirred and splashed around me. I activated the detonators and dove deep. Above me, bullets pierced the water. I swam under water as much as possible until I got beyond the lights, toward the center of the Rhône. Distant voices yelled that they'd missed their target—me. I heard the motor of a patrol boat.

"On shore one of our men fired at the search lights. Knocked them out. A machine gunner opened fire on him. He may have been wounded or killed—I don't know.

"I swam downstream, crawled along the underside of a pier. A rat clawed his way down my back. Once on the street I put distance between the docks and me. Then I waited. Detonator, do your job! It did. Rocket fuel in the barges ignited and triggered a chain of explosions. Mother of Jesus, flames everywhere! Must've killed soldiers and crews. Maybe civilians, too. I haven't found out. I ignore the newspapers. The Germans censor every story."

I had heard the rumble of explosions along the Rhône. The night sky was orange for hours. Black smoke poured through the streets.

The following morning, in a study at Tour Bleu I drank a cup of tea. I sat alone and reflected on the destruction and deaths the previous evening. I stared at a photo hanging in the room. In it a group of children from about age four through adolescence, playful, full of smiles, sat on a hillside.

Suzanne walked into the study. She nodded toward the photo and said, "Those children lived at an orphanage in the village of Izieu. There were forty-four children, all Jewish. They were protected there. Until word reached the Gestapo. Klaus Barbie came to Izieu, arrested the children and the adults living with them. He held the children at Montluc Prison. Then shipped them along with the adults to Auschwitz, where they were murdered."

Earlier Suzanne had showed me a secret Deuxième Bureau report on concentration camps. In some camps, such as Birkenau, children, along with other newly arrived prisoners unable to do adult work, mainly elderly and disabled people, were required to undress and enter a so-called shower room. The Nazis told them this was so they would become clean before entering the camp. The room's doors were shut and sealed tight. Then lethal Zyklon B gas, deadly cyanide, not water, flowed from the ceiling's showerheads.

Suzanne said, "All that makes it possible for me to wage war on the Nazis—take lives without guilt. Still, killing, even killing a Nazi, is never easy." She sighed and dropped into the soft chair beside me. I grasped her hand. We sat in silence.

Was there, is there, a higher purpose to my survival? Except for Charles and Suzanne, so many people I have met in Paris and Lyon, as well as friends and family in Rotterdam, are either dead, arrested and shipped to a concentration camp, or presumed dead. Does God, if he exists, have a higher purpose for me? How will I know?

Is he the same God who loosed the Nazis on the world?

Spring to Summer, 1944

Above Lyon's streets, trees blossomed. In the walled garden of Tour Bleu, red tulips, magenta crocuses, and yellow daffodils bloomed. The ever-warmer days of late spring brought the bright blue skies of early summer.

Suzanne and Charles continued to receive reports of Allied bombing raids across France—10 April, Lille, 18-19 April, Rouen, 20-21 April,

Noisy-le-Sec and the La Chapelle port district of Paris, 19 and 23 April, Orléans. Thousands of French civilians died.

On the morning of 26 May, at *Tour Bleu* I stood at an open fifth floor window. I gazed at sandbags stacked along sidewalks in front of the buildings of Vieux Lyon. Some of the stacks were the height of a man, about 1.8 meters, others were two to three times that. At Cathèdrale St-Jean the sandbags rose like protective shields nearly halfway up its high walls.

From a distance came the drone of aircraft engines. They grew louder. Soon became a roar.

Silhouettes above us, and on the ground below us, winged shadows of Allied bombers, crossed Lyon. My emotions mixed joy at their arrival and fear of what they might do. As the shadows reached the distant side of the city, smaller cylindrical shadows dropped from them, like guppies giving birth. Explosions rocked buildings. In the distance fire leaped from one building, then one block, to another. Black smoke filled the streets, rolled across buildings. As if in a trance, I stared at the drama unfolding beyond my window. I recoiled as acrid smoke blew into my face.

Suzanne ran into the room, grabbed my arm, and pulled me to the floor. "Get down. Stay down! Follow me."

We crawled across the room to the hallway. Then we rushed down flights of stairs to the protection of Tour Bleu's deep basement. We sat on the basement floor, leaned against a wall. The walls vibrated as explosions blasted the city. Dust and plaster fell around us. I held Suzanne's hand tight. Would we be like my family, die in a bombing raid? But that morning, for us, within minutes it was over. On the other side of Lyon smoke rose above shattered buildings. Bodies lay in the rubble of the streets.

A day later Suzanne received reports on the Allied attack. Estimates of civilian deaths rose to more than seven hundred. Had I known any of them?

Lyon's ports and the factories of the dye and chemical industry had been hit hard. Bombs also hit Gestapo headquarters, recently moved from Hôtel Terminus to the École de Santé Militaire, near the center of the city.

Early the following morning, when I entered the kitchen Suzanne said, "I have news for you, sad news."

My pulse quickened. "Charles?" I braced myself. "Has something happened to him?"

She handed me a cup of tea. "Please, sit. No, not Charles. In the raid yesterday, two bombs fell on *Hôtel Le Lieu*. First reports say there are no survivors." She took my hand.

"No," I sobbed, "not again." The emotional jolts of the Rotterdam bombing returned—my unexpected losses. "Now my pals. André Bollé, M. Pleusiers. Good and decent men. The Lyon family I cobbled together."

Suzanne hugged me.

"I need time alone," I said to Suzanne. I walked downstairs to the courtyard and sat on a bench for two hours.

Evening newspapers reported that the same day as the Allied bombing of Lyon, the city of St. Etienne's staging yards and mining industry docks had suffered major bomb damage. One thousand civilian deaths were reported.

Later, alone with Suzanne, I said, "It seems so strange. One minute you have lunch. The next minute, a bomb explodes. Your home is gone, your family dead." Try as I might, I could not wrap my thoughts around the tragic daily news of Allied bombings. I forced myself to remember that Allied bombing raids, however tragic, were not deliberately aimed at civilians. Unlike the Luftwaffe attacks on London. I forced myself to recognize that Allied raids were conducted in the midst of Nazi atrocities against the Jews, the Reich's pursuit of the Final Solution. Perhaps the raids would help bring an end to the atrocities.

Her voice firm, devoid of emotion, Suzanne said, "A few days ago, the *Deuxième Bureau* received reports of the Allied bombing of a mountaintop monastery, Monte Cassino, in Italy—a Wehrmacht stronghold and key observation post. At least that's what the Allies believed. Over four hundred tons of Allied bombs were dropped on Monte Cassino. Leveled it. An inspection afterward found no German troops had been present." Suzanne took a deep breath. Her voice dropped to a near-whisper. "Over three hundred local women and children had taken refuge in the monastery. All of them died."

Compiègne—Camp de Royallieu
30 June 1944

No longer using a cane, René Carmille limped slightly as he walked across Montluc's courtyard to the open doors of the front entrance. A bright sun beamed on rue Jeanne Hachette and a queue of olive drab German troop trucks. The curtains of each canvas-covered truck bed had been roped open, like dark mouths that waited to be fed.

The morning's warm humid air hung heavy. Traces of the sweet scents of roses from nearby gardens mixed with the sweaty stench of prisoners' unwashed bodies. A guard directed Carmille to the front of long queue of prisoners that filed into the trucks. He climbed into the darkness of a truck bed. Men already seated on one of the slat benches scooted aside to make room for him.

A Gestapo guard mounted the truck-bed's lower step. He held up a small sheet of notepaper. Leaning in, he read loudly, "Love to Marie. Long live Free France!"

The guard stared at the seated men. He yelled, "Who wrote this?"

Silence.

The guard again shouted his question.

The prisoners remained silent.

The guard grabbed the shirt of the man seated nearest him and jerked him forward. The man toppled to the gravel road. His eyes on the seated prisoners, the guard put one foot on the fallen man's neck. "Very well. If the writer does not come forward . . ." The guard pulled his pistol from its holster and aimed it at the head of the prisoner beneath his foot. "This man will die."

In the darkness of the truck-bed's interior, a youthful voice said, "I wrote it."

The guard removed his foot from the neck of the man on the ground. He waved his pistol toward the seated prisoners. "You—the man who said that—out!"

A young, thin, and unshaven prisoner stumbled from the vehicle. The soldier slammed his pistol against the prisoner's head. He fell to the ground. The soldier kicked him in the stomach. Additional blows of the soldier's pistol to the young man's head lacerated his face and smashed his nose. Blood drenched his shirt.

After a final kick to the stomach, the soldier ordered, "Put him back in the truck." Two prisoners climbed down and lifted the unconscious prisoner into the truck.

The trucks departed Montluc. They soon passed from Lyon to a highway that took them north and west. An older prisoner seated next to Carmille, his right arm amputated at the elbow, asked, "Where do they take us?"

A prisoner seated on the bench opposite him replied, "The guards won't tell. I heard a driver say *Compiègne, Camp de Royallieu.*"

All France knew Compiègne's historic significance. Two major events in European and French history made Compiegne much more than a small city on the Oise River.

On 11 November 1918, in a rail car in the forests near Compiègne, Germany signed an armistice and surrendered to France's Maréchal Foch and the Allies.

After the 1940 fall of France, on Hitler's orders, the rail car was returned to the site of the 1918 German surrender.

On 22 June 1940, that car became the site of a second armistice, with France laying down weapons in a surrender to Germany.

Camp de Royallieu abutted the city of Compiègne. It had been built in 1914 as a training center for young recruits. In June 1941, Camp de Royallieu became a concentration camp under the authority of Reinhard

Heydrich's Security Service of the German Army. The Camp de Royallieu commander, an elegant Captain Doctor Illers, known for his peccary gloves and ivory cigarette holder, spent most of his time at his office in Paris. He relied on Sergeant Major Eric Jaeger to operate the camp. Jaeger, a small middle-aged man, had a heavy consumption of alcohol each day. He ran the camp as his personal dictatorship. Whenever Jaeger was seen by prisoners he was accompanied by his two enormous mastiffs. The dogs were rumored to have eaten fifteen prisoners alive. The rumors were true. The prisoners called Jaeger "Dog Man."

Late afternoon on 30 June, the convoy of troop-filled transports from Montluc arrived at Camp Royallieu. Along the column of parked trucks, guards yelled, "All prisoners, out of the trucks." Men shuffled out, a few in leg chains, others handcuffed.

As the truck beds emptied, the new arrivals viewed, on either side of the camp's large central courtyard, ten rectangular one-story wooden barracks, each designed to accommodate up to two hundred prisoners. Inside the barracks were straw-filled platforms, wooden bunks. At the distant end of the courtyard, barracks buildings contained the camp's administrative offices and a mess hall.

The guards assembled the prisoners in the central courtyard. Following the command, "Stand at attention," accompanied by his mastiffs, Sergeant Major Jaeger walked in front of the prisoners. He stared at them for a full minute. He then turned to a corporal. "Dismiss them."

As prisoners and guards walked to the barracks buildings, a guard yelled to nearby prisoners, "Take a good look—your next stop, Dachau."

A fellow guard asked him, "Hans, have you been to Dachau?"

"No."

"I have."

"What's it like?"

"It is larger and older than *Camp Royallieu*. More advanced."

"More advanced?"

"It has a crematorium."

The Last Train to Dachau
2 July to 5 July 1944

In the Compìegne rail yard, Camp Royallieu guards stood beside the twenty-boxcar train. Behind the steam engine, the tinder had been filled with coal. The train's whistle sounded as it prepared to leave.

Early on 2 July, the departure morning, the Gestapo placed a bale of hay and a large can of water in each of the train's boxcars. In the Camp Royallieu barracks, guards rousted the two thousand men who had arrived the previous day. The prisoners had come from all over the Occupied Zone. Guards divided the prisoners into twenty groups of one hundred men. Each group was herded into a railway boxcar.

The metal-sided boxcars, built to transport freight, had no windows. Most cars were flat-roofed. A few had arched ceilings that permitted a limited circulation of air. No matter the design, once the doors slid shut the interior air became still, heavy. When the train was in motion, the interior air circulated a little, but only a little. At each stop the air circulation ceased.

Soon after leaving Compiègne, the train made the first of many stops, some of them lasting for hours.

Guards grumbled, "Why does the train stop? We sit and wait . . . for what?"

Prisoners pounded on the doors. "Open! Open! Air!" The doors remained shut.

As temperatures climbed, prisoners reminded one another, "It's only a few hundred miles to Munich, to Dachau." But with more stops and long delays, the train seemed to meander, inches at a time. The heat in each boxcar became ever more oppressive.

Days were cloudless. Bright sun heated the metal boxcars. Water supplies were quickly consumed. Interior temperatures rose. Each car had only a large can for sewage. Crowding, the motion of the train, and jostling among prisoners soon upset the cans. Human waste poured over the floors. The sewage sealed floor cracks and eliminated trickles of fresh air. The stench of sweat and shit—intense and putrid—filled each boxcar's stagnant, hot air.

The absence of oxygen and lack of air circulation created oppressive conditions. Men gasped for air, for many of them each breath a struggle. Daily temperatures rose so high prisoners collapsed from heat strokes. Men died. In each boxcar, corpses quickly stacked up. The air, laden with the stench of volatile organic compounds from dead bodies, sickened many men. Vomit added intensity to the putrid odors.

Men pressed their noses into the narrow openings around doors to sniff trickles of outside air. Stronger men pushed them aside, inserted their noses.

As the heat of the day intensified, temperatures in the boxcars continued to rise. By the second day of no water, men drank their own urine. Many suffered attacks of dysentery. They voided themselves on the floor and on each other. Men died of dehydration.

Some men yelled, "Keep your clothes on, retain body fluids." Others yelled, "Take your clothes off, release body heat."

Prisoners struggled for breathable air—hot smelly air with ever-lower oxygen content. Men lost consciousness—heat strokes, lack of oxygen—and fell into the slime of the waste-covered floors. There they suffocated in waste as newly collapsed men fell on top of them. In mindless fits, men attacked fellow prisoners. One screamed, "I'll kill you," grabbed a prisoner and gouged his eyes out. Using fingernails and teeth, stronger men gashed the flesh of weaker men, pounded their heads into the floor's slop. One prisoner ripped off another's ear.

Lt. Raymond Jaouen gasped for breath. He lost consciousness and fell to the floor. Gen. Carmille reached out to break his fall, then attempted to put his arms around the lieutenant and lift him. His hands slipped. Carmille was knocked aside as more men passed out. They fell on Jaouen. Their bodies, slick with waste, were unmovable. In the rail car's hell, Lt. Jaouen suffocated.

Gen. Carmille sobbed in grief for his friend. Soon, nearly overcome by the heat, he entered a semi-conscious state. He thought of his long-passed childhood. He spoke to no one in particular, perhaps only to himself, as he muttered, "At Trémolat, on summer evenings . . . we sat in our yard. Talked and shared stories . . . the quiet patter of neighborhood families. All was well. Mama often read aloud. Her soft voice quieted us. Some evenings we would walk to a rock overlook and watch darkness fall across the valley." Carmille's never-ending monologue, filled with images and personal memories, represented idealized versions of his early years. His descriptions of memories gave him moments of respite far from the boxcar's heat, stench, and death.

The train arrived at Dachau Station. One guard said to another, "Six hundred and forty-three kilometers—four days for the trip. Before the war, it was a long one-day rail trip. What has happened?"

Boxcar doors slid open. Men, many of them naked, others barely clad, their bodies glistening with a slick brown paste, knelt or stood atop bodies next to the open doors. The stench from each boxcar flowed out. Guards backed away. Some retched.

From the open doorways, men peered out at Dachau Station. Their mouths hung open. Guttural noises had replaced words. A former clerk at SNS, a member of the Resistance, stood in a boxcar's open door. The skin of his face, browned with human waste, contrasted with the whites of his eyes.

Along the length of the train, soldiers pointed rifles at the boxcars. "Out! Now!"

Men wobbled as they came out of the rail cars' wide doors and attempted to climb down; many collapsed. With difficulty, others remained upright as they clutched rungs along the sides of boxcars, their knuckles white until soldiers pried their hands loose.

On the floor of each boxcar lay discarded cloth armbands and badges. Stitched on each armband or badge, triangles overlapped to form the six-pointed Star of David. The stars' triangles gave mute testimony to the identities and legal offenses of prisoners. Some badges had two yellow triangles—Jews. Others had triangles of two colors. A red inverted triangle that overlay a yellow triangle signaled a Jewish political prisoner. Professional criminals had two green triangles. When a green triangle overlay a yellow triangle, it signified a Jew who was a habitual criminal. Work-shy and asocial prisoners' badges had two black triangles, or stars. The badges of Jehovah's Witnesses had violet triangles. Pink triangles designated homosexuals. Overlapping yellow and pink triangles identified Jewish homosexuals. The badges, along with clothing stripped away in the heat, soaked in the muck on the boxcar floors. Many badges turned to a near-uniform brown—one badge the equivalent of another—like the prisoners, one the equivalent of another.

After the living exited the boxcars, crews wearing respirators began to remove corpses. They placed them on carts and wheeled them to an ever-larger pile of the dead. The stack of corpses spread across the grass of the rail yard. The stack rose to a height of two meters. It extended along the rails for one kilometer. Guards wheeled cadavers on carts from the stack to the camp's crematorium.

Two thousand one hundred and sixty-six prisoners had boarded the train in Compiègne. One thousand six hundred and thirty arrived alive at Dachau Station—over five hundred men, one-fourth of the prisoners, had died during the four-day trip. At some of the train's stops, the odors of death became so intense that many dead bodies were thrown out of the boxcars. Most corpses remained on the cars' floors.

It took four days to cremate the corpses.

Under armed guards, groups of prisoners walked along the unpaved road from Dachau Station to the concentration camp. One prisoner broke away from his group. On shaky legs he ran into a narrow alley. From behind, a guard pointed his rifle at the fleeing prisoner. "Stop!" Prisoners yelled, "No-o-o—stop!" The prisoner continued to run. As he neared the end of the alley a rifle bullet smashed his skull.

Along the street boys threw rocks at prisoners. *"Juden! Juden!"*

Townspeople walking along the streets turned away from the sights and odors of the semi-clad prisoners. A mother put her hands over the eyes of her young daughter. A matronly woman carried a clay pitcher of water into the street. Over the half-hearted protests of a sympathetic guard, she handed the pitcher to a prisoner. He gulped the water, the first slaking of his thirst since . . . how many hours, days? He passed the pitcher to the prisoner beside him. Another guard struck the pitcher with the butt of his rifle and shattered it. Wide-eyed, prisoners watched water pour on the ground.

As they entered Dachau, prisoners read the camp's motto, forged in iron and made part of the front gate: Arbeit Macht Frei, work makes you free. A few steps farther they walked beneath the symbol of the Reich, the eagle, wings outstretched, claws clutching a swastika. Rows of barracks buildings, a few with offices, and gravel-covered open space between buildings comprised most of the camp.

Early each morning, the barks of dogs and yells from the Kapo, prisoners assigned duties to assist guards, awakened prisoners. The Kapo were empowered to kill. After an assembly and roll-call, dead bodies were removed from the barracks. On average, each day fifteen bodies were sent to the crematorium. Over five thousand resident Dachau prisoners died annually, most of the deaths from flea-borne typhus, sometimes called camp fever or war fever. Although early in the twentieth century typhus had been virtually eliminated in developed countries, the disease returned in the density of population and filth common to concentration camps such as Dachau.

Above the camp loomed crematorium smokestacks. Bodies of prisoners turned to smoke and ash and rose into the atmosphere. The smokestacks became dead prisoners' airborne exit chutes.

The burning of the bodies of resident prisoners comprised only a small part of the Dachau cremations. Crematorium ovens operated at capacity. The high demand came from a combination of daily deaths among resident prisoners and the rapid execution of thousands of incoming prisoners who were judged unable to work—women, children, the elderly, and the disabled.

René Carmille arrived at Dachau dehydrated and stressed from the heat of the trip. He grieved the death of his friend, Lt. Jaouen. The pain of injuries inflicted in his Gestapo interrogation lingered. Dachau's unclean barracks and camp food lacking in nourishment further stressed his health.

An Order from Hitler's Supreme Headquarters

One evening in mid-August Suzanne rushed into the *Tour Bleu* kitchen. Charles and I had just sat down to dinner. She waved a sheet of paper and yelled, "Just received this—Hitler has ordered Gen. von Choltitz to destroy Paris! Charles, you have orders to get to Paris as soon as possible!"

Charles stood. "A race."

"A race?" I asked.

"A lethal race. Can we stop von Choltitz?" Charles's eyes signaled his next question before he asked it. "Will you come with me? It could be . . ."

"Dangerous? Let's go."

We walked toward the passenger gates in Lyon's crowded Gare de Lyon-Perrache station. Charles wore an open-collared shirt, slouch hat, and an old dirt-stained jacket, the scruffy clothes of a day laborer. I was dressed as a waitress. My hair had been cut short and dyed blonde. We carried SNS-created cartes d'identité. On a passenger platform we stood in the midst of a crowd. We boarded a second-class car on the eleven o'clock train to Paris.

Passengers jammed into our poorly ventilated car, its air laden with body odor. After the train's departure, we eventually dozed.

At two in the morning, the train arrived at the Paris's Gare du Nord. We disembarked and walked through the passenger area of the main terminal to a door beneath a sign, Lost Luggage Claims Office. Charles opened the steel door and we walked down two long flights of stairs. Far above us, the sounds of steam engines and rail cars produced muffled roars, like caged animals that wanted to free themselves.

We walked along a musty corridor lit by a string of dim and bare electric bulbs. At the end of the corridor, we entered the Deuxième Bureau's Gare du Nord dispatch room. Hercule, Charles noted, stayed unchanged. After many years of service, he remained as the room's principal officer and caretaker. He still peered intently across the counter through thick glasses. He wore faded black trousers, a khaki shirt, and a stained brown necktie. Hercule believed in the cleverness of the enemy and operated by what Charles and other agents called Hercule's rules: Play it safe. Confirm everything and everyone—there can be no mistaken identities.

Hercule again asked Charles the question he'd asked so many times over the years, "*Monsieur*, you are?" He gave Charles an expectant look. "Identification, please."

Charles handed Hercule his counterfeit carte d'identité.

Hercule straightened his glasses and opened a loose-leaf notebook. He turned pages, placed the carte next to an entry, and looked up at Charles. Hercule nodded.

"And you, *Mademoiselle?*"

I handed Hercule my false carte de identité.

Hercule turned a page in the notebook. He scanned the entries, placed my carte on the page, and then looked up.

Looking back and forth, Charles to me to Charles, Hercule asked, "How can I be of help to you?"

"I'm expecting a red packet," Charles said. "Has it arrived?" Charles had told me that in over twenty years of Deuxième Bureau service, he could count on the fingers of one hand the number of red—ultra secret—packets he had received.

Hercule shuffled to a nearby file cabinet. He returned with a small canvas bag, placed it on the counter, and handed Charles a pen and a form. "Sign here."

Charles signed. He opened the bag and removed a scuffed red leather packet.

Hercule nodded to a table and two chairs beneath a lamp in the corner of the empty room. "You'd best read over there, away from counter traffic."

Charles and I sat down at the table. For a moment Charles stared at the worn packet. Paris had fallen to the Germans in June 1940. Now, over four years later, we hoped the city would be turned over to its rightful owners. He opened the packet.

The Red Packet
Deuxième Bureau

23 August 1944
To: Charles Secœur

Action

1. No later than midnight 24 August, you are to proceed to the Seine's Pont d'Austerlitz.
2. On the left bank, at the entrance to the Jardin des Plantes, make contact with Captain Raymond Dronne. He commands a company of Spanish soldiers equipped with American tanks.
3. On the morning of 25 August accompany Capt. Dronne to the Hôtel Meurice. Capt. Dronne is to demand that Gen. von Choltitz surrender to Gen. Leclerc and the provisional government of France.

Background

Months ago, in a private meeting with General Dietrich von Choltitz, Führer Hitler assessed the general's willingness to carry out difficult orders. Von Choltitz had distinguished himself to Hitler when he ordered the destruction of the cities of Sevastopol and Rotterdam. He had liquidated large numbers of Russian Jews. Would he design a plan to level Paris — plant explosives citywide? Could Hitler trust von Choltitz to execute the plan and, when ordered to do so, destroy the city?

On 1 August 1944 Major General Von Choltitz was promoted to the rank of General der Infanterie. On 7 August he was appointed military governor of Paris.

Gen. von Choltitz has ordered explosives placed beneath the bridges across the Seine as well as at Tour Eiffel, and beneath the many monuments and buildings of Les Invalides, the Arc de Triomphe, the Opéra de Paris, the Eglise de la Madeleine, and more. On von Choltitz's command, the explosives will be detonated. The city's beauty will crumble.

Everything is prepared. Gen. von Choltitz awaits the command from Hitler. Troops await von Choltitz's order. Then they need only press the detonators' plungers.

On 23 August 1944 von Choltitz received this directive from Hitler's Supreme Headquarters:

1. The defense of the Paris bridgehead is of capital importance from both a military and political standpoint. Loss of the city would lead to the loss of the entire coastal plain north of the Seine and would deprive us of our rocket-launch sites for the long-distance war against England.

2. In all history, the loss of Paris has inevitably brought with it the loss of all France.

3. The Führer therefore categorically reaffirms his order: Paris must at all costs be defended by locking the city inside a strong position. He reminds the Commander in Chief of the West that reinforcements have been designated for this purpose.

4. In the city itself, the most energetic tactics, such as the razing of entire city blocks, the public execution of ringleaders, the forced evacuation of any quarter of the city that appears a menace, must be used to smash the first signs of revolt. This is the only way to prevent the spread of such movements.

5. The destruction of the city's Seine bridges will be prepared.

6. Paris must not fall into the hands of the enemy, or, if it does, he must find there only a field of ruins.

Gen. Leclerc is to have everything he needs to prevent von Choltitz's destruction of Paris. You are to support Captain Dronne and ensure Gen. Leclerc's success in accepting Gen. von Choltitz's surrender. Von Choltitz cannot, must not, succeed.

Charles handed the dispatch to me. I read until my eyes fell on a single sentence: Von Choltitz had distinguished himself to Hitler when he ordered the destruction of the cities of Sevastopol and Rotterdam.

Von Choltitz—his orders had led directly to the death of my family. I dropped the dispatch.

Enraged, I grieved for my family. I wept.

Is Paris Burning?

During the two days prior to the scheduled destruction of Paris, Swedish diplomat Raoul Nordling had private conversations at the Hôtel Meurice with Gen. Dietrich von Choltitz. He sought to persuade von Choltitz to disobey Hitler's direct orders to destroy Paris. "If Berlin is to lie in ruins," Hitler had said to aides, "so, too, will Paris."

In response to Nordling's repeated pleas to spare the City's beauty and the lives of Parisians, Gen. von Choltitz reminded Nordling, "I am a soldier. I obey orders."

The evening of 24 August, at dinner with trusted members of his staff, a wry smile on his face, Gen. von Choltitz said, "Ever since our enemies have refused to listen to and obey the Führer the war has gone badly."

Gen. von Choltitz's smile disappeared. His face sober and drawn, the general quietly confided to an aide, "Hitler may have gone insane."

Near midnight, units of Gen. Leclerc's 2nd French Armored Division and Capt. Dronne's mechanized infantry unit arrived at the Hôtel de Ville.

The early morning hour of Paris's destruction arrived. Expectant aides awaited the general's orders. But Gen. von Choltitz refused to issue the order to detonate explosives. The city and its landmarks remained intact.

An aide reported that Gen. von Choltitz received a call from the German High Command. "Sir, a moment please." Von Choltitz waited. Hitler, his voice loud and angry, screamed, "Is Paris burning?" Von Choltitz replaced the receiver.

A few hours later that morning, at the Hôtel Meurice Gen. Dietrich von Choltitz ate breakfast. He then peacefully surrendered to Gen. Leclerc. Gen. Charles de Gaulle became head of the Provisional Government of the French Republic. German troops, tanks, and mechanized units departed the city.

On 26 August, in the heart of Paris, Charles and I joined the victory parade down the Champs Élysées. Generals de Gaulle and Leclerc led the parade. Behind them marched thousands of soldiers and cheering, now liberated, Parisians.

We kept our eyes on Gen. de Gaulle, not far ahead of us. I worked hard to keep up with his long strides. I thought about de Gaulle as a man, restless and outspoken. As leader of the Free French, unwavering in pursuit of his goals. And as a symbol of hope—for the French and, though sometimes grudgingly, for Roosevelt and Churchill.

Charles and I stood tall. My heart pounded. Could life ever again be this exhilarating?

Charles Breaks the Bottle

That night, in the midst of thousands of rejoicing Parisians, Charles and I stumbled into an old friend and colleague of Charles's, his code name John. I remembered him from our dinner at the Lyon bouchon. Charles later confided that John was a senior agent in the American Office of Strategic Services, OSS. OSS's missions, like those of Charles's Deuxième Bureau, were clandestine.

Soon, arms linked, John, Charles, and I joined celebrations in the streets of Paris. We sang and danced with friends, strangers, and each other, moving from bistro to bistro and sharing the joy of victory. Throughout Paris, cellars of vintage wines emptied and were liberally consumed. Food that during the war had been hoarded and locked away, like prisoners until Bastille Day, was unlocked, opened, and enjoyed. Music and laughter cascaded along Parisian thoroughfares and from the narrow streets of Montmartre to the Place de la Concorde, from the Latin Quarter to the Opera House—Paris was transformed into a city breathing new life into itself.

Late in the evening I took Charles aside. "I love celebrating but it's become too much for me. I need to rest, to lie down." Walking to our hotel, I said, "I've never felt fatigue like this—it starts in the center of my body and runs to my fingertips. I'm sorry to take you away from celebrations. I want to go on . . . " I stopped and leaned into a doorway.

At our hotel, at a time when we might otherwise have had a light dinner, I had no appetite. During the night I slept fitfully. Shortly after daybreak, I made three trips to the bathroom. Each time I vomited. Charles called the Deuxième Bureau to request a physician. "During the celebration Miriam may have eaten some spoiled food."

The physician arrived. Charles excused himself and walked to his office at the Louvre. When he returned I had awakened. He said, "In the accumulated dust and papers on my desk, I found a fresh new envelope. In it was an order from the Deuxième Bureau to Charles Secœur. The bottom line of the order: 'You are to proceed to the Paris office of the Monuments, Fine Arts, and Archives program. Your new responsibilities will include the command of units retrieving all forms of art stolen by the Nazis.'"

I remembered Charles's description of his conversation with Hildegard Gurlitt during his visit to Göring's estate. "The sale of art is no different than other forms of commerce," Gurlitt had said, "one builds sales by creating demand. That's what we did."

Aghast, Charles had said, "Miriam, thousands of paintings, watercolors, drawings, and prints were piled up in the courtyard of the Louvre. Then they were torched. A giant Nazi bonfire. A cleansing of art, all the impurities burned out."

Even now, years later, memories of that burning caused Charles's pulse to rise, renewed his "rage in a bottle," and his vow to someday break that bottle.

The following morning, ready to go to the offices of the Civil Affairs and Military Government Sections of the Allied Armies, Charles paused at our front door. "Today, my love, I'm going after Hildebrand Gurlitt, Carinhall, the Rosenberg Taskforce, the Nazi's illicit collection of art. I will keep my vow."

I hoped Charles would release his rage, find peace.

At the offices of the Monuments, Fine Arts, and Archives program, the senior officer gave Charles a broad smile and extended his hand. "We have been expecting you, sir. Welcome."

Death and Life
28 August 1944

A few days later, when Charles returned to our Deuxième Bureau hotel I met him at the door. We embraced.

He said, "Your color is better. Do you feel as well as you look?"

I gave him what must've looked like an impish smile. "Until tomorrow morning."

"Tomorrow morning? What did the doctor tell you?"

"That I may be ill again."

"Again? Was it the bistro food? Damn! I should've been more careful."

I laughed. "No. Haven't you heard of morning sickness?"

Charles's eyes widened. His lips parted as if he might speak, but no words came.

"Charles, my love, I am two months pregnant—we're going to be parents."

My voice little more than a whisper, I said, "Charles, I have thought much about what I'm going to say." I paused and wiped away tears. "I will soon give birth. If the baby is a boy, I want us to name him René. D'accord?

Charles embraced me. "*Oui, mon amour,* René."

28 January 1945

On a cold winter morning five months later, Charles shared with me a secret message he had received from the Deuxième Bureau.

At Dachau, on 25 January 1945, France lost a champion of liberté, égalité, fraternité. General Léon François René Carmille died of typhus.

I burst into tears. Charles put his arms around me.

Restoration

One evening a few weeks later, Charles shared with me a draft of a Charles Delmand editorial he had just written for *The Times*. I read it with pride. His words would be read in London, Paris, and the capitols of Europe, perhaps even in Berlin. It began:

> *The war has not ended. But Paris is now free. Once again, we hope for the last time, Germany's military defeat is certain. Battles remain to be fought. Soldiers are yet to die. But the generals of Hitler's Supreme Headquarters know, the Allied High Command knows, the truth: the war is over. After twelve years, the so-called Thousand Year Reich has failed.*

There was a knock on our door. My heart raced. Despite Charles's words that the Thousand Year Reich had failed, the war wasn't over. Expecting the Gestapo, I reflexively grabbed the editorial from Charles, thrust it into a desk drawer, and slammed the drawer shut. I took a deep breath and opened the door.

"Aimée!"

For a moment we stood immobile and stared at each other. Aimée, as a dancer always thin, had lost weight. Worry lines etched her face. But she was alive! We embraced each other in long strong hugs. We wept.

I controlled my sobs long enough to ask, "Where . . . how have you survived?"

Between sobs, Aimée answered, "In Marseille. With a false *carte d'identité* prepared by SNS!"

Dachau, 30 April 1995
"Kennst du das Land wo die Zitronen blühen..." **Goethe**
"Do you know the country where the lemon-trees flourish..."

I am René Delmand, son of Miriam and Charles Delmand. On April 30, 1995, I accompanied my mother to the 50th anniversary of the liberation of Dachau concentration camp. She wished to honor Gen. René Carmille who, along with countless others, had died there. And to honor those who lived because of Gen. Carmille's courage.

Early that morning we met in Munich. At age seventy-eight, Mama, tall and lithe, her hair gray, still moved with the grace of an athlete. I greeted her with an energetic hug. She said, "You look so much like your father. The two of you could've passed for brothers."

We joined about thirty French Dachau survivors and their families on the Munich-to-Dachau bus. The day was rainy and cold. The bus was quiet, in part because of the advanced ages of the travelers and in part because of families' grief-laden memories of Dachau.

The driver turned on the radio. Lively music filled the bus. The contrast of the music with the solemnity of the trip jarred me. In German, I asked the driver to turn off the radio. *"Warum? Why?"*

I replied, *"Wohin fahren wir?"* Where are we going? He nodded and turned off the radio.

We stepped off the bus into the parking lot. Mama smiled as we entered a cacophony of European languages. "Our own Tower of Babel," she said.

At 8 o'clock, Christian services began in the chapels of the Protestant and the Orthodox faiths. Catholic services were held at the base of the altar of the great cross in the center of the camp. Many worshippers sat on outdoor stone benches around it.

In the rain, we sat as close to one another as our umbrellas permitted. Except for an old lady on a front bench, no umbrella, her head bare, who sat alone and motionless through the ceremony.

The Bishop of Munich said a traditional mass, as if this was an ordinary day. He conducted the service in German.

After the mass, we attended the Jewish ceremonies. Israeli national flags waved nearby making it easy to find the location. When a rabbi sang the Kaddish a capella, Mama wept. For me, Mahler's Kindertoten Lieder came to mind. Mama had once called it the most moving music she had ever heard. The rabbi's singing and Mama's tears touched me. After prayers in Hebrew, a man gave a pointedly worded speech on our obligation to provide Israel with the support needed to maintain the nation's strength and security.

During the Jewish ceremonies the rain stopped. Mama and I walked to the cremation ovens. In front of small buildings that housed the ovens, a brass band played traditional Bavarian songs. A children's choir dressed in lederhosen accompanied the band.

Leaving the ovens and the band, we strode to an adjoining lawn. Children played ball. Families sat in portable chairs around picnic baskets. Many women wore brightly colored shawls and skirts. Men wore dark trousers, white shirts, and vests. In the midst of the picnics, an old man in a striped pyjama jacket sat on a garden chair. Children surrounded him.

"Gypsies," Mama said. "This is their reunion of remembrance."

Across the lawn an elderly man walked arm in arm with his wife. His eyes were clear. He wore a striped pyjama jacket on which his prisoner number had been embroidered in red thread. Mama pointed to the number. "Sewn by his wife."

At the end of the morning, we sat beneath tents in Roll Call Square. Speaking more to herself than to me, Mama said, "Gen. Carmille stood here for the Dachau roll-calls." Tears rolled down her cheeks. During a long interval before a final ceremonial speech in German from a Bavarian minister, young people dressed in the striped pajamas of prisoners walked among us. They remain vivid in my memory. I recall nothing the minister said.

An American general gave a brief talk in English. He described the arrival of Allied troops at the gates of Dachau. Arbeit mach frei, 'Work will set you free,' the gates' wrought iron letters proclaimed. He described the troops' shock as they discovered the horrors of the camp, then he spoke of the horrors themselves.

We returned to the bus. On the fence near the camp's front gate hung a banner made of bed sheets. Handwritten on the sheets, in English, "We ask your forgiveness."

During the bus ride to Munich, and later at a mid-afternoon buffet, Mama said little. She had so much to remember—her family in Rotterdam, Charles, and Gen. Carmille, the thousands of Jews Gen. Carmille saved from Nazi roundups and murder. And their descendants, perhaps some of them present at Dachau on this anniversary of liberation.

Epilogue
Automation of the Holocaust: Success and A Failure

In the early days of the Occupation of Europe, the Reich ordered each country to conduct a population census, recording residents' names, addresses, and other identifying information, including religion. Census data were coded and keypunched on millions of small rectangular punchcards, commonly called Dehomag (the German IBM organization), or IBM or Hollerith cards. Tabulation machines, precursors to modern computers, then processed the census cards. The name mechanography was applied to these operations.

The holes punched into the coded columns on each of the cards identified key features of a person or family (number of members of a household, names, gender, ages, occupations, religion). Tabulations were completed and organized. Information was then extracted and printed. Reports generated from each census became foundations for important functions, such as civilian food rationing, tobacco allotments, assignments of people to jobs, and shipments of workers from occupied countries to German factories.

In the Reich and the Occupied countries, except for France, IBM/Dehomag machines processed and managed the cards and census data. In France, machines of the Bull and Compagnie Electro-Comptable (later an IBM subsidiary) companies were used.

Each census produced lists of Jews complete with their addresses. The lists were used for Nazi roundups of Jews.

Efficiencies of census operations in each country varied. In the
Netherlands, with its relatively homogenous population and history of
the government's use of punch-card systems and machine-based statistical
tools, Nazi appointee Jacobus L. Lentz directed an efficient census and
statistical service. To support the Dutch census, IBM's U.S. offices supplied
Holland with 132 million punchcards.

In the Netherlands there were short-lived outbreaks of violent
resistance to the Nazi occupation and the census/registration of Jews.
Lentz's operations produced an abundance of census data—and lists of
Jews. The Netherlands consistently met Berlin-issued quotas for shipments
of Jews.

The combination of census-generated information, and a sometimes
reluctant though nearly always compliant and civic-minded Dutch people,
made it possible for the Nazi authorities to identify and deport 107,000 of
the Netherlands' 140,000 Jews. 102,000 of them were murdered—a death
rate among the country's Jewish population of approximately 73%. By
Nazi standards, automation of the Holocaust was successful in Holland.

In contrast to the Netherlands, the French government's use of
automated information systems was fragmented, incomplete, and
ultimately failed. Unlike the Netherlands, France was home to an
ethnically diverse population of Jews, Christians, and Muslims from across
Europe, Asia, and Africa with different languages and customs. Since
1872 and the beginning of French census efforts, religion had been neither
identified nor recorded. Since the French Revolution, the country had
emphatically separated church and state. The inclusion of religion in the
new French census was, from its outset, controversial.

René Carmille, pioneer in the use of mechanized punchcard
information systems and then-director of the Vichy National Statistical
Service, wrote to the Commissioner General for Jewish Questions.
Vallat's organization had been overwhelmed by an unmanageable
volume of census data. Carmille said that he could unify the work of
their respective departments and combine all useful information on Jews,
the status of their belongings and potential transfer. He gained control of
the Nazi census of the Jews.

Having gained control of the census data, Carmille sabotaged, hacked, the data systems and prevented the creation of lists of Jews.

At the time of France's liberation in 1944, of an estimated 300,000 to 350,000 Jews in the Occupied and Free zones, about 85,000 had been deported to concentration camps. There, 82,000 of them were murdered—a death rate among France's Jewish population of approximately 25%. By Nazi standards, in France automation of the Holocaust had failed.

The dramatic difference between the rate of deportation and murder of France's Jews, 25%, and the Netherlands' Jews, 73%, occurred in part because of France's historically rigorous separation of church and state, making the identification of members of any French religious group difficult. But the principal factor in this difference was Carmille's clandestine sabotage of the system, actions that rendered keypunched cards unusable for the identification of Jews.

Because of Carmille, tens of thousands of Jews in France were never identified, rounded up, and sent to concentration camps. Their descendants, hundreds of thousands of Jews, live today.

In 1937, in recognition of IBM's contributions to the German government, the Third Reich awarded the coveted German Eagle Award to IBM's CEO, Thomas J. Watson. Three years passed before, in 1940, Watson consulted with senior diplomats in the U.S. Department of State and returned the award.

By then, like the monster in Mary Wollstonecraft Shelley's *Frankenstein, The Modern Prometheus*, IBM's support of the Holocaust had spread across Europe. During WWII IBM subsidiaries never ceased to supply the Reich with keypunch cards.

Just as the destructiveness of Frankenstein's monster did not end until the monster's death, IBM's support of the automation of the Holocaust did not end until the death of the Third Reich.

René Carmille

Léon François René Carmille was born on 8 January 1886 in Trémolat, Dordogne department, France.

His parents were teachers. A relative, Jules Claretie was a French writer and member of the French Academy, the preeminent French council for matters pertaining to the French language.

Carmille received his primary education at College de Bergerac and Lycée de Bordeaux. He then studied at the École Polytechnique. In 1909 he served as a gunner sergeant for one year in the 23rd Regiment of Toulouse. He became a lieutenant trainee at Fontainbleau and then was assigned to the 343rd Artillery Regiment in Angoulème.

In 1911 Carmille became a member of Le Deuxième Bureau, the French Intelligence Service.

In 1914 he married Madeleine, the daughter of a doctor at the Hôpital Militaire in Nice. Soon afterward Carmille was mobilized to the front lines of WWI and served in heavy artillery. He was promoted to captain, wounded twice, and awarded the Légion d'Honneur and the Croix de Guerre.

After the end of WWI, Carmille rose in rank and responsibilities in the French Army's division of financial control and administration. He represented the Ministry of War on statistical commissions and taught at École Libre des Sciences Politiques. During this period, he wrote influential texts on automated information management, mechanography, and economics. Carmille designed and advocated a system in which each French citizen would be assigned a permanent identification number. That system, similar to the Social Security Number system in the United States, was implemented. It continues to operate.

Following the armistice of 1940, Carmille was promoted to Comptroller General First Class and appointed director of the Vichy government's Military Recruitment Service, which became the Demographic Service and later was reorganized into the National Statistical Service (SNS). Carmille was successful in moving the processing and tabulation of the Nazi's census of French Jews from the Commission on Jewish Questions to the SNS.

Committed to a free and democratic France and appalled by the Nazi treatment of Jews, Carmille joined other senior officials in the Resistance's Marco Polo Network. At SNS Carmille secretly programmed keypunch machine operations to sabotage and render column eleven on the census punch cards useless to anyone without the secret code. Column eleven recorded essential Nazi census information (e.g., answers to the question, "Are you a Jew?"). Carmille became the world's first ethical hacker. His special programs prevented the transmission of census information needed by the Nazis to produce lists of names and addresses of French Jews. The absence of the lists thwarted Nazi roundups of Jews. Carmille saved the lives of tens of thousands of French Jews.

The Gestapo secretly placed agents in SNS. Following the discovery of Carmille's sabotage of the census and his Resistance activities in the Marco Polo Network, in February 1944 the Gestapo arrested Carmille. He was interrogated and tortured by Klaus Barbie, and then sent to Lyon's Montluc Prison. In the oppressive heat of mid-summer, Carmille was one of 2,000 men put on a train to Dachau. Over five hundred of the men died in route from the overpowering heat. Carmille lived. His deputy died on 'the death train.'

Carmille arrived at Dachau Concentration Camp exhausted. By year's end he had contracted typhus. On the 25 January 1945, René Carmille died. His remains lie among those of other prisoners who died at Dachau.

Carmille was awarded the Medal of the Resistance by decree, recognized as a member of the Marco Polo Resistance Network, and designated as 'Died for France.'

In the 1946 posthumous presentation of the Croix de Guerre avec palme to Comptroller General René Carmille, Prime Minister Georges Bidault remarked, ". . . under the guise of an economic and social mission created and organized by him, he prepared a plan for mobilizing the lifeblood of the nation. Suspected by the enemy, (Carmille) did not hesitate to continue his work, remaining at his post in defiance of dangers. Arrested in February 1944, he was deported in July to Dachau camp, where he died of exhaustion on 25 January 1945. A fine example of patriotism and self-sacrifice."

The Centre militaire de Traitement de l'Information de Paris at Fort Mont Valérien bears René Carmille's name. During the years prior to renovation and relocation, so too did classroom number 33 at the Institut d'edudes politiques de Paris, Paris Institute of Political Studies (324 Sciences Po), Paris, and a conference room in Ministère de la Defense.

To honor René Carmille's commitment to the French resistants regardless of political affiliation or religion, a major street in the city of La Seyne-sur-Mer, the place of a family property, then governed by a communist municipality, was named "General Carmille."

In 1946, the former Vichy government's Service National de Statistiques, National Statistical Service, founded by Carmille, became France's National Institute of Statistics and Economic Studies (INSEE). Today it is the only government department born during the Vichy regime that remains in operation. INSEE has over 5,000 employees.

The École militaire du corps technique et administrative (EMCTA), one of the four officer training schools of the Saint-Cyr Coëtquidan Military Academy, honored Gen. René Carmille's contributions to France by adopting his name for the 2008-2009 class.

Letter to Madeleine Carmille,
widow of René Carmille
Translated from the original French version

Lyon, 16 June 1945
10, rue Duquesne

Madame,

Though we have not met, please allow me to express my condolences at the disappearance of M. Carmille.

Yesterday at the mass in his memory, I thought of the day of his arrest. He had telephoned me the day before saying to come and see him. As I had a course to teach former officers in his department, I took the opportunity to visit him.

He had done me the honor of calling me to sit as professor of political economics to aide and support his Service and entrusted me with a course. I looked forward to those interviews where his insights were always based on history. We discussed economics and also what it could do to thwart the German grip.

He had previously presented me with an opportunity to go to England and I answered yes of course.

That morning around 10.30 am he told me he felt the net tightening around him but he had to stay until the end to be able to warn a few people in time. I admired the quiet courage with which he saw the worst, but remained devoted to his duty until the end.

He entrusted me, in particular, with the manuscript of a paper for the conference on sample surveys which he was to make a few days later before our Society for Political Economy, asking me to read it in his place if by chance the circumstances he foresaw prevented his reading.

He said to me: "I would like to be warned five minutes ahead to have time to leave . . . "

At a quarter past twelve the Gestapo arrived.

I read according to his desire, his paper at the meeting of the Society of Political Economy: it was undoubtedly his last work written in freedom.

He honored me with his confidence and benevolent friendship. I was able to appreciate it in the few interviews and conversations that we had and I understand in a small way the regrets and pain that you may have had from your loss.

I feel obliged to bring you the testimony of one of those who last approached him on the day of his arrest.

Please accept, Madame, my sincere condolences in respectful association with your grief.

signed   F. TREVOUX.

About the Author

Dwight Harshbarger is a West Virginia native, former psychologist, management consultant, corporate executive, and professor at West Virginia University. He is also the author of several historical fiction novels. In *Witness at Hawks Nest*, Dwight told the true story of Union Carbide's unsafe practices in the 1930 construction of Hawks Nest tunnel that caused the acute silicosis deaths of hundreds of workers—America's deadliest industrial disaster. *Witness at Hawks Nest* received the West Virginia Library Association's Book of the Year award. *Valley at Risk: Shelter in Place* tells the true story of Bayer CropScience's fatal explosion that threatened Charleston, West Virginia, with the same toxic chemicals that killed thousands at Bhopal. *In the Heart of the Hills,* Dwight captures choices and heartbreak during WWII in a small Appalachian community. *A Quiet Hero* is his fourth novel.